"Moonlight Enchantment is an enthralling tale of exotic Siam — a love story to treasure!"
—Rexanne Becnel, winner of *Romantic Times'* Reviewer's Choice Award for the Best Medieval Romance.

"You've missed me, too, haven't you?" he said in a husky voice as his hands stroked the contours of her back and hips.

"Yes," she said breathlessly, forgetting about her promises to herself not to relent, forgetting about everything except the way he made her entire being vibrate with excitement.

His eyes glowed in triumph. Then his mouth rained kisses on her face, her hair, her neck. His lips were whispery soft over her skin, and she arched against him, her hands clutching his muscular arms. That only increased the urgency of his movements. One hand cupped her breast, then caressed it. At her low moan of pleasure, his lips sought hers again with fierce insistence.

Just as he slipped his hands up under her jacket, however, a sound at the window made him abruptly stop kissing her. His face went rigid as he thrust her away and walked swiftly to the window where he stiffened in alarm.

"I think we've done enough for today," he said curtly. "I'll see you this evening at dinner."

D1559878

DEBORAH MARTIN

MOONLIGHT ENCHANTMENT

Book Margins, Inc.

A BMI Edition

Published by special arrangement with Dorchester Publishing
Co., Inc.

Printed in the United States of America.

FOREWORD

Your Gloria Diehl Book Club selections are chosen by an independent review board with members all across the United States. Board members are carefully chosen to represent all backgrounds, views, and reading interests. Any romance novel which bears the imprint *Gloria Diehl Book Club Selection* has been reviewed and recommended by the committee for its originality, reading interest, plot, and character development.

Chapter One

November 1892—Bangkok, Siam

Esme Montrose was floating in that state somewhere between waking and sleeping when a gentle, but persistent, call finally roused her.

"Essmay...Essmay..." the voices whispered outside her open window.

Recognizing the accent as Siamese, she sat up in the bed, then crept from under the mosquito net, and went to the window, grateful for the soft breeze blowing through it.

"Lamoon? Mai? Is that you? What is it?" she whispered. "You'll wake everyone."

"But, Essmay, if you not come quick, you miss lights," protested Lamoon, whose petite form Esme could clearly make out in the moonlight. Mai, a younger version of her sister, stood next to Lamoon. Beside them sat their *krathongs*, miniature hand-made boats no larger than the washbowl in Esme's room.

"Very beautiful lights," Mai chimed in. "You must see lights of Loy Krathong."

Esme sighed as she gazed down into the pleading eyes of her two friends. Always wanting to see the Siamese festival of lights, which occurred during the November full moon, she'd hoped to do so this year. Of course, Aunt Miriam had put a stop to that. As usual, she'd very firmly convinced Esme's father to forbid her to go.

"I told you I *can't* go," Esme said with real regret, leaning on the sill. "Didn't you get my note?"

They nodded, but persisted in their pleas. "You will like very much," they assured her. "Please come." Both girls gave her a petulant pout as they stared up at the window.

"You know what will happen if I go without permission. Last year when I sneaked out to attend King Chulalongkorn's birthday celebration, Father and Aunt Miriam forbade me to see the two of you for a month, among other things. Is that what you want?"

"They not find out—"

"No," Esme said, trying to force some firmness in her voice. "I mustn't go without Father's permission."

"Your father not be angry this time. You grown up now."

Esme suppressed a grin at the thought of trying to explain to her two Siamese friends why she wasn't considered "grown up" now. Mai and Lamoon already thought it scandalous that the eighteen-year-old Esme wasn't married and didn't have several children. No, she wasn't nearly as certain as they were that her father wouldn't be angry. But she didn't say that. Instead she took a different approach.

"There's also *Mem* Mil." The Siamese couldn't say Miriam very easily. "Millam" was the best they could manage, and over the last three years it had been shortened to "Mil."

"*Mem* Mil not find out," both Lamoon and Mai asserted, but Esme knew better. If an impropriety were involved, "*Mem* Mil" always found out. Aunt Miriam would then give Esme a caning and separate her from her friends again.

Esme looked down at the beautiful *krathongs* her friends had built, and wondered if it might be worth a caning to see hundreds of lighted boats set adrift on the river.

"I shouldn't go . . ." she repeated, this time more hesitantly, trying to remember the look on her father's face as he'd told her she couldn't go. But her curiosity was overwhelming.

The two Siamese girls took advantage of her reluctance. "We only go for a little while. You see. Very much fun and happy. See pretty lights and then come home, quick, quick."

Esme almost laughed at their wheedling. Because she was two years older than they, Lamoon and Mai believed she ought to have as much freedom as they did. The two of them were already married women with children, running their own households. Unlike her father and her aunt, they treated her like an adult, which always melted her resolve.

"Come now or we miss," they urged. "Come!"

Their pleas proved too much for her, coupled with her already fervent desire to go with them. "All right then, I will. But wait . . . I must dress first."

They giggled, but she ignored them. She knew that to them she was already overdressed, her em-

Deborah Martin

broidered batiste nightdress the height of foolishness in such heat and her day clothes even more so. Day or night, the two young girls wore only sarongs around their hips and legs with scarfs loosely draped around their breasts.

Esme moved about the room in the dim moonlight, groping for something to wear. But as she found her serviceable blue cotton dress, she hesitated. What if she were seen? She'd be recognized instantly as a foreigner.

Then she remembered the sarong and scarf Mai and Lamoon had given her. If she wore that, she'd blend in better, she thought, especially with the olive skin and black hair she had inherited from her French mother.

She hunted through her bureau for the outfit she'd hidden from Aunt Miriam's prying eyes and their tongue-wagging maid. Her strict aunt would be appalled to know that her niece, a respectable teacher in the school her father ran for the natives, kept a hand-sewn copy of the native dress tucked away under her prim-and-proper English clothing. Lamoon had made it for Esme out of shimmering royal-blue silk.

Once Esme found it, she hastened to don it. She tied the sarong about her waist in the intricate manner the girls had taught her. Then she wrapped the heavy scarf around her breasts, looping it over her shoulder and pinning it in place with a gold filigree pin her father had given her. Thank goodness Lamoon and Mai had made allowances for her modesty and had made her scarf wider than the ones they wore. It left one shoulder bare, however, making her hope that no one would see her slip out of the house.

"Hurry, Essmay!" they whispered again.

10

"I'm coming," she retorted, searching the room for a ribbon to tie back her full, straight ebony hair. "Oh, bother," she muttered as she realized there wasn't a ribbon in sight. She'd just have to suffer. At least the air would be cooler by the river. She slipped on the matching slippers Lamoon and Mai had given her. Then she climbed out of the window and dropped the few feet to the ground.

Quickly, the two sisters lifted their *krathongs* and moved through the jungle ahead of her, following worn paths that only they seemed able to see. As Esme followed, her heart pounded with anticipation. This would be even more exciting than the king's birthday celebration, she thought. She knew her excitement stemmed as much from the boldness of her actions as from the adventure itself, but she didn't care. She'd been cooped up in the house far too long.

Now more than ever she missed the freedom she'd had when her mother was alive. Thank goodness Aunt Miriam had never known the full extent of that freedom. She'd have been mortified. But Esme's parents had both flouted society by eloping together, so they'd had no qualms about raising their daughter unconventionally. Her father had allowed her to study anything she wished, even letting her learn Siamese from native tutors. Her mother, Renee, had seen nothing wrong with permitting Esme to play with the Siamese girls from the school. Lamoon and Mai had completed Esme's unusual education by telling her ancient Siamese folk tales and thrilling stories about the king and palace politics. But she'd wanted to see and do so much more.

And just when she'd become old enough to enjoy what she'd learned, her beautiful, vibrant mother

11

had taken her own life. At first Esme had been told that her mother had simply died. But from the day of her mother's death, Esme had realized something more was involved. Her father's mourning had been colored with an abrupt and uncharacteristic cynicism. Then after weeks of grieving, James Montrose had risen from his stunned sorrow and decided that he couldn't raise a young girl alone in Siam. Immediately, he'd written his spinster sister for help.

Miriam Montrose had wanted Esme to go to England, but James had been adamant about keeping his daughter with him. So Miriam had journeyed to Siam instead, bitter about leaving her pleasant life in England, but unwilling to disappoint her brother whose income she needed to survive. She'd brought with her rules and regulations that Esme was unaccustomed to, along with a thorough contempt for the Siamese "heathens" and for Esme's deceased mother.

Recently, in a fit of pique, her aunt had been the one to tell Esme that Renee Montrose had killed herself because of a lover. But Esme hadn't believed it, arguing with her aunt and then with her father that her mother couldn't have done such a thing. She would never have committed suicide nor taken a lover. Her mother hadn't loved anyone but her father. Then they'd shown her the note written in her mother's handwriting, but Esme had still insisted that something was terribly wrong.

Even now she believed it, and her staunch conviction irritated her aunt enormously. No doubt Aunt Miriam's displeasure with Esme's "obsession" concerning her mother's death was the reason Miriam had been especially strict lately.

Esme strode forward with determination. She

wasn't going to let her aunt's pettiness keep her from enjoying Loy Krathong. Esme desperately needed something to take her mind off her mother's suicide, and the festival might help do that.

So the three of them slid through the jungle, their way lit by the huge full moon staring benignly down on them. With pleasure, Esme breathed in the sultry night air. Banana leaves waved softly around her like large birds flapping their wings. Ahead of her, Mai stumbled over a coconut, and muttered soft curses in Siamese as she kicked it out of the way with her bare foot. Esme muffled her laughter, but watched the path more carefully as they moved along. A vine brushed her arm, while high above their heads she heard the sudden chattering of a family of monkeys whose reverie they'd disturbed. A strong scent of jasmine made Esme wrinkle her nose and then sniff the air. The jungle always seemed so alive at night. She rarely got to experience it firsthand, so she reveled in its sounds and smells.

Quickly, they reached the docks on the river. Others were already placing their *krathongs* in the water. Lamoon and Mai lit the candles on their boats, using someone else's candle, and then left Esme to launch their crafts. Esme watched in awe as hundreds of candlelit *krathongs*, piercing the darkness like millions of tiny lightning bugs, sailed smoothly past. Those that bumped against the shore were prodded back into the water by a friendly boy or girl.

Each boat was so well lit that Esme could even discern the craftsmanship. Most were woven of palm or banana leaves and painted in bright colors. Some were more elaborate bamboo constructions carrying small gifts for the goddess of the river—

tiny trinkets, small pieces of fruit, anything that the Siamese thought would appease the deity. The most fascinating vessel, she thought, was a giant, painted paper lantern mounted on a banana-leaf boat, with delicate silver ornaments hung from its sides. She gasped with pleasure as did the others when the king's *krathong* floated by, a splendid creation glittering with gold leaf, a jeweled cup nestled in its center spire.

The lights sparkled and glimmered as they danced over the water. Esme wondered to herself if this was the way fabulous London looked, bright and glittering. She'd often dreamed of going there, but she couldn't imagine anything that could compare to this floating cascade of candles.

Long after the last boat had passed and people had begun to leave, Esme stood silent, staring at the moon, which lent a sweet enchantment to the night. She didn't think she'd ever forget the beauty she'd just seen. Then a deep sadness engulfed her. She'd missed so many sights and experiences in this country where she'd been raised, and, although she'd grown up in Siam, she didn't really feel a part of it. But she didn't feel completely English, either.

Absorbed in her thoughts, she didn't notice that most of the crowd had dispersed until she looked up to find the three of them alone on the dock. The moonlit river so transfixed Mai and Lamoon that they jumped when she called to them. They hurried to her side. "Was it not beautiful?" and "Did you see mine?" they clamored as they accosted her gleefully.

She smiled. "Oh, yes, I liked it very much. But," she added with regret, "I must return home."

"Not to worry," Lamoon assured her. "We take

you back quick quick. We not break our promise."

Then Esme and the girls turned to find they were no longer alone. Two British sailors blocked their path, leaning upon each other. Their eyes narrowed speculatively as they spotted the three girls who froze in place.

"Lookee here, mate," one of the sailors said to his buddy. "I tol' ye these Siam girls be beautiful. And 'ow lucky we be that they be out for a stroll. Shall we join 'em?"

His partner assented loudly, releasing his companion to grab Mai roughly around the waist.

"Oh, stop, you wretched beast!" Esme called out unthinkingly in English, horrified at the way the man manhandled her friend.

In one swift movement the second sailor was beside Esme. "And 'ere's one who speaks English," he said as he grasped her upper arm roughly. "Mus' be Chinee by the look o' her light skin."

A choking fear gripped Esme, but she struggled to stay calm. "Let me go, please."

The sailor only laughed, then grasped both of her wrists with one meaty hand and pulled her up against him.

"Wha's wrong, little Chinee?" he rasped in her ear. "Don't a girl like you want some affection? We pay good, me and me mate,'specially if the service pleases us."

Her eyes widened as she realized what he meant. He planned to use her like—like one of those women in the brothels Lamoon had told her about! She struggled to escape his grip, frightened by the urgency in his voice. Just imagining what "services" he could exact from her against her will made her shudder uncontrollably. But he was stronger than his inebriated state indicated.

Deborah Martin

"I'm not a little 'Chinese!'" she told him desperately. "I'm English and a lady. You simply must let me and my friends go!"

"English?" the sailor said, his eyes raking her body. Then he let out a roaring laugh. "Ain't no English lady I ever seen who'd dress in one of these 'ere native dresses. You speak pretty fair English, I grant you, but I ain't fooled. You ain't no lady and I ain't no lord, so let's just 'ave some fun."

Then he slid his other hand under the thin piece of cloth covering her shoulder and pulled it down roughly. The material tore where it was pinned, baring her shoulder. She tried to twist away from him, but before she could, his face hovered close to hers, and she gasped at the sickening stench that overwhelmed her. The sailor kneaded her shoulder as he swayed against her.

"Let me go!" she demanded.

Then the sailor's clammy paw released her shoulder to grip her chin, and his mouth came down on hers. Revulsion gripped her. His moist lips pressed hard against her mouth, hurting her. But as his wet tongue thrust against her lips, she felt his hold on her wrist weaken. In fear and loathing, she jerked one hand free and clawed blindly at his face, wanting only to get away from the disgusting smell of his breath and the smothering assault of his lips.

Abruptly, he released her. "That she-cat scratched me!" he shouted to the other man who struggled to hold onto Mai and Lamoon.

In fury, he turned back to her. "I'll teach you, bitch, to claw your betters!" He raised one large hand in the air and, before Esme could escape, slapped her so hard she fell to her knees. "Before I get through w' you—" he began, but he stopped dead at the sound of another voice behind them.

16

"What's going on here?" said a man in the shadows, his tone steely, firm. His words hung like a menacing weapon in the still night air.

The two sailors stood dumbfounded for a moment, both seeming to recognize and fear the gentleman.

"It's nothing...nothing, guvnor," the sailor who'd struck her answered hesitantly. "Just tryin' to escort these young ladies 'ome."

"The ladies will be safer getting themselves home alone, Henley. I strongly encourage you to let them do so."

The gentleman moved further onto the dock. Though tears had flooded Esme's eyes at the shock of the sailor's slap, she could make out the outline of a very tall Englishman. He was dressed in evening wear which she'd only seen in magazines. The man's voice sounded calm, but he held his whole body rigid as if he fought to control some murderous urge. As he surveyed the scene before him, his eyes narrowed.

"Ah, guv', we was just 'avin' a bit o' fun," the sailor who still stood over Esme answered. "These native girls, they're the only women me and me friend 'ave seen in three months. And me mates say Siamese are the best—"

"I don't care what your mates tell you. I doubt Captain Lawson would either. There are whor... There are houses of pleasure for such sport. Now return to your ship. Don't force me to remove you physically."

The sailor paled at the mention of his captain. His fists tightened, and Esme wondered if he would put up a fight, but somewhere in his drunken mind fear of his captain and the implacable stranger must have overruled his anger and lust. After a moment of indecision, he turned away from Esme and walked over to his companion.

"Might as well be leavin'," he muttered to the second sailor as he passed him and went on into the jungle. "Ain't gonna 'ave no fun 'ere." His friend nodded quickly and followed him, clearly relieved to get away from their tall adversary.

As the two stumbled off, Mai and Lamoon, who'd stood transfixed during the entire exchange, hurried to Esme's side, exclaiming over her wounded cheek and ruined clothing.

"I'm sorry," the gentleman said to Esme, who still sat in a daze, one slender hand rubbing her cheek and the other clasping the torn remnants of her scarf to her breast. "I don't know if you understand English, but I wish I could tell you how very sorry I am that this happened."

Esme lifted her eyes to stare at him. His hair was chestnut brown and it seemed to glow in the soft moonlight. Now that he stood close, she could tell he was at least thirty years old. His voice, smooth and cordial, nonetheless had an edge of steel. He seemed completely at ease and in control of the situation. And a hardness in his eyes convinced Esme that he was accustomed to commanding men and making difficult decisions.

As Esme stared, incapable of speaking, the man scrutinized her with curiosity. Under his gaze, a slow blush rose up her neck and face. She lowered her head to escape his perusal. She wanted to thank him, but she dared not let him know she spoke English. She couldn't risk the possibility that he might find out who she was and tell her father or her aunt what had happened. If they learned of it, her aunt would make sure Esme was severely punished for going out with "savages" to witness a "pagan" celebration. Unfortunately, her father would just allow her aunt to do as she wished because he no longer seemed to know how to handle his daughter.

Watching her intently, the stranger offered his hand to help her up. She took it, keeping her face averted from his.

"Do you speak English?" he asked, and she pretended not to understand.

"We go now," Lamoon said, moving protectively to Esme's side.

"Wait!" he said, refusing to relinquish Esme's hand. "You must let me accompany you to your homes."

"We go now," Lamoon repeated, tugging at Esme.

"I insist on accompanying you," he said with forbidding firmness.

Esme's gaze shot to him in alarm. "No, you mustn't!" she blurted out. Then she continued more softly, "We can find our own way home."

His eyes narrowed. "You're English?" he asked incredulously.

"Well . . ." she muttered, not wanting to say more.

"Are you mad, girl, to be out here at this time of the night? Do you know what could have happened to you?"

"I know what *would* have happened if it hadn't been for you. Thank you for your assistance," she said earnestly, glad to be able to thank him. "We really must go now." She tried to leave, but his hand still gripped hers.

"I'll escort you back to wherever it is in this heathen town you come from. A girl your age shouldn't be out alone in Bangkok. Surely you realize that now." He continued to hold her hand in his as they stood there, making her conscious of the warmth spreading up her arm.

His reference to her age and the "heathen town" annoyed her a little, but the fact that he wanted to escort her home disturbed her far more.

"We'll be fine, I promise," she insisted, withdrawing her hand from his grasp. "It's really not as dangerous as it seems." She laughed shakily. "After all, we had no trouble in this 'heathen town' until your fellow Englishmen came along."

He gazed at her with frank surprise. Then his lips curved in a satirical grin. "That's quite true. We Englishmen seem to cause trouble wherever we go." His gray-blue eyes emphasized the sarcasm in his voice.

Esme colored again as she realized he'd taken her words as an insult to him as well. *How terrible of me,* she thought, *to say something like that after he has just rescued us.*

"No, of course not...I—I didn't mean to imply..." she stammered. "Please. I'm very grateful to you for what you've done. But I really can't allow you to trouble yourself any more by taking us home. We'll be quite safe, I assure you."

He caught the pleading note in her voice and smiled. "It's no bother—"

"Please let us go," she said, and this time her urgent tone was unmistakable.

"Of course." His voice seemed to tease. "By all means, go home. I certainly wasn't trying to impose." His tone softened. "But you might tell me your name, so that in a few days—"

Quickly, Esme cut him off. "That won't be necessary. You—you needn't bother yourself about us any further."

Then in rapid-fire Siamese, she told Mai and La-

20

moon it was time to go, secretly delighting in her benefactor's obvious surprise at her knowledge of the language.

Lamoon nodded before timidly approaching the gentleman. She bowed and *waied*, holding her hands together in the praying position the Siamese use in greeting. "Thank you so much, sir. You save us from bad men."

"I'm glad to be of service."

"You very kind," Lamoon murmured before taking her sister's arm and leading her back the way they'd come earlier.

Esme turned quickly to follow them, but the man restrained her with a firm hand.

"Can't you stay a few more moments?" he asked huskily. His fingers slid down her arm to grasp her hand. "I haven't talked to such an intriguing English girl in a long time."

Esme feared a repetition of what had happened with the sailors, but when she gazed up at him, she saw eyes she felt she could trust.

"I'm sorry," she said, with regret. "I—I really must go before my father . . ."

"Your father?" he said, one eyebrow lifting as he pounced on that one bit of information.

"I'm sorry. I have to leave," she said decisively.

"Then this is good-bye, I suppose." Before she could stop him, he raised her hand to brush it lightly with his lips.

Esme blushed. "Yes, good-bye." Startled by the strange tingle that shook her, she pulled free and fled into the jungle.

As she hurried through the night, trying to catch up with Lamoon and Mai, she found herself struggling with a mixture of emotions. When she thought of the two sailors, her whole body tensed in anger, but when she thought of the stranger who had confronted them, she felt strangely elated.

She couldn't precisely say he was kind. His eyes as he'd kissed her hand seemed to burn right through her in a disturbing way, far more disturbing than the clumsy caresses of the drunken sailor. But the stranger had helped her. She couldn't forget that, although there was no denying that he'd made her feel like an inexperienced child. Unconsciously, she walked more erectly. He'd called her an "English girl." Surely he could tell she was old enough to take care of herself. Then again, if he hadn't come along . . . She dismissed that thought from her mind with a shudder.

Mai waited for her on the path ahead. "Lamoon hurry on to make sure nobody in path. Poor Essmay. Bad man very mean to her." She embraced Esme with one arm as they continued to walk. "Lamoon and Mai very sorry that bad man hurt Essmay. We only want Essmay to see pretty lights."

"It's all right. Don't worry. I'll be fine."

"But what you tell *Mem* Mil?"

That was a good question, Esme thought. She would have to invent some story to explain the bruise that she was certain to have the next day. She tried to think of one, but she couldn't concentrate. She kept seeing the blue fire in their rescuer's eyes and his hair, shining richly in the moonlight. And his dress! Who dressed like that in Bangkok? It was simply too hot for such formal wear, yet he wore it as easily as if it were a second skin. Nor had he hesitated to confront those sailors.

But all this speculating would get her nowhere, Esme decided. She'd probably never even see him again.

* * *

As he boarded a ship at the docks in Bangkok, the Honorable Lord Ian Winthrop, British envoy to the court of King Chulalongkorn of Siam, wondered the same thing. He still wasn't completely convinced that his mind hadn't played tricks on him. An English girl dressed like a native? It was unthinkable. Surely she hadn't been English. She'd possessed the Siamese manner, and the delicate grace and slender figure which he admired in them. Her olive complexion also made her seem one of them. But her command of the English language had surpassed that of any Siamese he'd met in his two weeks in Siam. Despite her odd accent, she'd definitely sounded English.

Nor had her face looked Oriental in the least, with its blushing cheeks and wide, rounded eyes. Those expressive eyes! Dark and passionate, they reminded him of a tempestuous night sea. He fervently hoped she was English, because if she were, he might have another chance to glimpse those eyes.

But she didn't act English at all. He'd never met an English girl living outside England who felt the kinship with a country that this girl seemed to feel with Siam. Most certainly no expatriate would dress as a native. Ian shook his head as he entered his tiny shipboard cabin. He must see this intriguing puzzle solved, for it would prey on his mind until he got some answers.

"About time you got here, old boy," a voice muttered in front of him, startling him out of his thoughts.

"Godfrey! What are you doing here?" Ian exclaimed.

Godfrey Harmon, a military attaché assigned to the English minister resident in Bangkok, sat with

23

his ascot slightly askew, his flaming red hair no longer immaculately combed in place, and his frock coat slung over the nearest chair.

"Thought I'd see if you wanted to carouse in the city with me," he said a bit drunkenly, "like we did in the old days at Oxford."

"It appears to me you've already been carousing," Ian responded, removing his coat and tossing it carelessly on another chair. Then he began to loosen his ascot.

"Indeed I have." Godfrey stood a bit unsteadily. "But join me anyway. I'm sober enough to show you Bangkok at its wildest. After two years in this godforsaken country, I should at least have the chance to show off what I've learned."

"I've seen enough of Bangkok for one night, thank you. And I don't wish to reinforce the opinion everyone seems to have of me, that I'm a wicked rake."

"I should have warned you, I suppose. Everyone here is terribly conventional. All dashing young sons of earls are presumed guilty 'til proven innocent. Besides, you do travel with that fast crowd when you're in London."

Ian flashed his friend a wry smile. "And who might have told them that, I wonder?"

Godfrey affected a look of chagrin. "Why, old boy, just a bit of harmless gossip. Besides, it's true."

Ian laughed. "Just barely. I've been in London so little lately that I've seen less and less of the old crowd. Besides, our interests are no longer the same. And I certainly wouldn't consider myself a rake."

"Nor would I. But speculation always runs rampant in Bangkok. You have to admit, it makes for some amusing interludes. Like tonight." Godfrey gave a short bark of laughter. "Should have seen your face when that old harpie, Bingham, whisked her daughter away from you in the midst of a conversation. You were completely bewildered!''

Ian frowned. "I wish you hadn't paved my path with so much information about me that could be misconstrued."

"Don't worry, old chap," Godfrey said, starting toward the door. "You cut a dashing figure. The ladies will ignore the speculation and flock to you anyway."

Ian's eyes softened as he surveyed Godfrey's rakish pose that warred with his disheveled state. Then Ian chuckled in spite of himself. "At the moment I'm less interested in any of 'the ladies' I met tonight as I am in a slip of a girl I saw at the docks." His eyes narrowed assessingly as he reached out to halt his friend. "With your vast knowledge of local gossip, you might be just the one to tell me something about her. Do you know any British girls who speak fluent Siamese?"

"A few," Godfrey answered with a shrug. "How old is the said girl?"

"About fifteen, I'd imagine."

"And what does she look like?"

"Actually, she looked Siamese—black hair, dark eyes, slender build."

"Then what makes you think she's British?"

"Her English was flawless."

Godfrey snorted. "Doesn't mean a thing. Look at your secretary, Chan. His English is flawless, too."

"Yes, but his circumstances are unusual. He was educated in London. And among all the Orientals who go to London to study, I don't think you'd find a single girl. This one wore a native dress, but I'm sure she's English. Something about her ... her hair, her eyes ... something, I don't know, con-

Deborah Martin

vinced me she's English or at least part English."

Godfrey eyed Ian curiously. "You saw her at the docks, you say?"

Fleetingly, Ian wondered if he should tell Godfrey any of the particulars of his evening. Then his desire to find out about the girl overwhelmed his reticence. "Yes. Two Siamese women accompanied her."

Godfrey laughed. "Sounds like she was just a Siamese whore looking for a sailor. What did she do, accost you?"

Ian's lips tightened as he remembered the fright in her eyes as the sailor stood over her. "Not hardly. I assure you, she wasn't a whore."

Godfrey's comment irritated him. Ian had never been interested in casual whoremongering, nor had he had any desire to catch the diseases that ran rampant in Asian whorehouses. As for other women, Ian hadn't found one who could endure his extensive traveling in the East or who even interested him beyond the few weeks he stayed in one city. Except, of course, for Caroline. He smiled bitterly. There was always dear wild Lady Caroline....

He shook his head, knowing where such thoughts would lead.

Abruptly, he turned to Godfrey. "You know I wouldn't be interested in a whore. But I want to know who this girl is. She intrigues me. Let's just say I think her family ought to know about her nighttime forays."

Godfrey smiled. "Always the conscientious gentleman, eh, Ian?" He couldn't resist taunting Ian.

"Godfrey, you're an ass," Ian replied calmly, pouring himself some brandy from a flask on his desk.

"I know, I know," Godfrey replied, placing his hand on the door. "I won't stay where I'm not welcome. But I'll do some thinking on this girl of yours and see what I can discover. Right now, however, I'm heading for the nearest watering hole."

"Enjoy yourself," Ian said, toasting his friend as he disappeared through the door.

After Godfrey left, Ian carried the lamp to his desk. He'd discovered a great deal at the dinner he'd attended, and he wanted to jot down a few notes while the information was still fresh in his mind. But after only a few moments his mind began to wander again, back to the girl in the jungle.

This time other aspects of the incident occupied his mind. First of all, he'd certainly have to report Henley and his friend. His hands gripped the sides of the desk as he remembered the way Henley had struck the girl. She hadn't even cried out. She'd just sat there, stunned and terrified.

Unwillingly, he remembered other things, the silky look of her bare shoulder, the way the sarong clung to her hips when she moved away from him into the jungle. It had been a long time since he'd seen a woman like that, soft but resilient.

He shook his head, trying to free himself of the image. After all, she couldn't have been more than fifteen, hardly old enough to capture his interest. But his mind kept lingering on the expression on her face as she'd tried to avoid his questions. She wasn't a classic beauty. Her cheekbones were a trifle high, the full mouth slightly crooked. In the soft glow of moonlight, however, her hair shone like that of an enchanting moon goddess. A feisty moon goddess. The way her eyes had flashed at him as she'd insisted on seeing herself home alone reminded him of a tigress held at bay. No doubt she'd be difficult to manage.

He smiled at that. If her parents were indeed English, they must have a fine time keeping their daughter under control. Here she was, wandering through the jungle at night with a pair of Siamese girls probably no older than herself, dressed too indecently for any Englishwoman.

But, oh, she wore that dress well.

That settled it, he decided. He simply must find out who she was. After all, Bangkok's foreign community was small, and she'd stick out like a sore thumb if she were as wild as she appeared. Finding her surely wouldn't be too difficult.

But what would he do with her when he found her? *That* he didn't know.

Chapter Two

"Michaels, you must approach this entire occurrence with care," a young Chinese man told his companion in the curtained carriage. "Despite what your spies overheard the girl ask Henry Rushton, to do anything about her is far too risky."

William Michaels scowled bitterly. "More risky than what her questions to the minister resident about her mother's death might bring to light? Suppose her assertions that her mother couldn't have committed suicide cause others to investigate more thoroughly?"

"No one will believe her speculations. After all, it is not unusual for a girl to question such a tragedy."

"Perhaps," Michaels muttered, clearly unconvinced. "But I can't risk her prodding Rushton to action. She's intelligent and persistent. And one day she may remember the last day of her mother's life—when she accompanied Renee to the market-place."

"You should have been more careful. Giving those papers to the French attaché in a public place was unwise."

Michaels nodded grimly. "If I could undo it, I would. But at the time I saw little risk. The market was not one frequented by foreigners. I never dreamed someone I knew might be there. Worse yet, Renee came up close enough behind me to see the seal on the papers and to recognize them as the ones she'd seen me take from the Rushton's desk. I'm sure her daughter didn't realize what was going on. But someday she might remember seeing me that day. No, I think it best that I ensure the girl never says a word to anyone."

With worry etched in his face, Chan stared at the man who'd been his superior for years. "What about our work? Would you jeopardize it by killing her, too, like you killed her mother?"

"Of course not." Michaels waved his hand with impatience. "I'm not so stupid as to attract attention to myself. Besides, I'd be a fool to destroy such a flower. She's like her mother—intelligent, witty, beautiful . . ." Michaels stared blankly out the window, remembering.

Chan stiffened and drummed his fingers nervously on his knee. "You still lust for a dead woman who rejected you. Now you see in the daughter what you wanted in the mother. That worries me. It keeps you from thinking clearly. Do not allow your lusts to bring us both down."

Michaels's lips twisted in a cruel smile as he leaned forward to grip Chan's arm. "Keep in mind that you work for me. My 'lusts' are my concern." He released Chan's arm then and settled back against the seat. "But you needn't worry about your puny existence. I won't endanger either of us."

"So there will be no more murders, no more fake suicides?" Chan asked, his face showing that Michaels's statement only somewhat mollified him. When there was no answer, he plunged on. "It is bad enough that I have to engineer them for my part of the business. If you do so also . . . No one must assume any connection between us. Fortunately, you made her mother's suicide convincing enough that Montrose was not suspicious about his wife's death. But if his daughter dies, too, he is certain to wonder about it. Then who knows what he could discover? If *he* asks questions of the minister resident, his close friend, we are in greater trouble than with his daughter asking Rushton questions."

"Trust me." Michaels sneered. "I don't need to kill her to keep her quiet. I've thought about it. I could marry her. Once she's my wife, I can make certain she never speaks of these things to Rushton or anyone else. I'd have her under my control."

Chan relaxed some. "That would work," he murmured, his brow pursed in thought.

They traveled along silently for a few minutes before Chan suddenly leaned forward with an uneasy look on his face. "Marrying her is an excellent idea. But it is harder for Europeans to arrange a marriage than it is for my race. Are you certain her father will allow the marriage? His wife might have told him years ago about your pursuit of her. That certainly will not prejudice him in your favor."

Michaels smiled. "Ah, but I don't think that's a problem. So far Montrose hasn't intimated to anyone that he knew of my desire for his wife. If he knew, he would have confronted me about it." The

31

smile faded and his mouth tightened. "She probably dismissed my entire proposal as too inconsequential even to mention. It's a pity she chose to reject me. If she'd been my lover, I could easily have deceived her when she saw me taking those papers."

"I have always wondered why she did not immediately tell Rushton what she had witnessed."

Michaels's suddenly soft expression lent his face a pensive quality that warred with the crimes he spoke of. "She would have, I think, if I hadn't seen her in the doorway and taken her off guard by kissing her. My overture so upset her that she left the dinner immediately."

Chan looked grim. "Good fortune was yours that night."

"Yes, but it didn't last. Not only did she see me in the marketplace the next day, but she knew the attaché well enough to know I shouldn't be handing him British consular papers. At least my killing her, once I decided to do it, went smoothly. After all, I couldn't have done anything if her husband had been in town. With him gone, it became an easy matter to confront her that night while everyone else in the house slept."

"You had to kill her, I agree. But are you sure you were careful, that you didn't leave anything that might have triggered the daughter's suspicions?"

"Of course. I covered all my tracks. Before I forced Renee to drink the poison, I made her write that note saying she killed herself for the love of another man. I threatened to kill her daughter if she didn't write it. She knew how serious I was. She didn't even attempt to hide that she knew all, for our eyes had met at the market and I'd seen in them her knowledge of the truth. So I made her fear for her daughter. Stupid woman! As if I could have risked two murders! But she didn't know that. She did what I said. I was so careful. But I wasn't careful enough."

Chan cast him a sharp glance. "What do you mean?"

"She insisted before I killed her that she'd left a note relating all she'd seen in a place I'd never find."

Chan sat forward in his seat, an expression of alarm on his face. "You never told me that!"

"At the time I thought she was lying to save herself. But what if she wasn't? Just because nothing has surfaced yet doesn't mean it won't later."

"Now her daughter is asking the minister resident questions and there could be an investigation—" Chan said in a horrified whisper.

"No, I can't take the chance," Michaels cut in. "If I marry the girl, I can silence her once and for all."

"True," Chan agreed, but he continued to look uneasy. "But can you convince Montrose to accept your suit?"

A grin crossed the merchant's face. "I've had to work on that. I proposed twice and he turned me down. But the aunt is on my side, for she wants the money I'll give her if the girl marries me. And I've found a way to convince the girl's father that his daughter really must be married—and only to me."

The carriage had at last stopped at the deserted street where Michaels had requested he be let off. As he reached for the door handle, his companion clasped his arm and scowled.

"Wait!" he told the old man. "What do you intend to do?"

Michaels smirked. "Shakespeare once wrote, 'Reputation is an idle and most false imposition,

oft got without merit and lost without deserving.'
I plan to prove how right the great bard was. How
long do you think her father will resist my suit if
someone should intimate she's had an affair with
a married man?"

"How could you begin such a rumor without having it traced back to you?" Chan asked curiously.

"That's easy enough. Plenty of reckless gamblers
are indebted to me in this city. I'll find someone
appropriate. By the time of Rushton's ball next
week, the girl's name will be thoroughly ruined in
Bangkok. I'll see to that!"

Then chuckling to himself, Michaels left the carriage.

Miriam fretted as she watched Esme slide into
the brilliant amethyst ballgown. "Why the somber
face? You'd think your first ball would excite you
more. It may be the only one you ever attend in this
dreadful country."

"I am excited, Aunt Miriam," Esme assured her
aunt, although she was far more nervous about the
ball than she wanted her aunt to know. "I just don't
know if I'll fit in, if I'll behave properly. What do I
know about balls?"

"I suppose you'd rather go to one of your native
friends' celebrations or some pagan festival," Miriam said with a sneer.

Esme frowned. Her aunt still hadn't forgiven her
for asking to go to Loy Krathong. She'd also been
very suspicious about Esme's bruised cheek the
next morning. Esme had claimed to have fallen in
the night on her way to the kitchen for a drink, but
Miriam had been reluctant to believe her. Fortunately, her aunt had absolutely no proof of what
had really happened.

"Are you listening to me, Esme?" Miriam called her back sharply to the present.

"Yes, ma'am."

"This is the proper place for a girl of your breeding to be seen, not in some schoolhouse with native women. I've told your father for some time that you really must be settled. You can't go on associating with uncivilized women and running wild. It's time you found a husband, and this ball is perfect for that."

Esme groaned, and her aunt's lips pursed in a thin line.

"I'll have none of your sighs, girl. All the local merchants—including that delightful William Michaels—will be at this event. Government advisors and soldiers and a few other eligible men will be there as well..."

Esme's aunt continued in that vein, but Esme didn't pay attention. She turned her back to her aunt and grimaced. Clearly, she was to be put on display like a painting at auction. And for Mr. Michaels of all people! She shuddered as she thought of the bald merchant who'd courted her recently, flashing her unsettling glances when he thought she wasn't looking. At least her father didn't share her aunt's desire to accept the merchant's proposals. Still, the evening ahead would be tedious if Miriam insisted that Esme dance often with the merchant.

But even as Esme worried about the ball, her eyes were drawn to her image in the mirror. She had to admit her gown was the most gorgeous creation she'd ever seen. It made her look like one of the women in *Harper's*. She pirouetted slowly before the mirror, admiring the delicate lines. Fortunately, the bustles her mother had always been encumbered with were now out of fashion, so that only her new silk camisole, drawers, and taffeta petticoats lay under the gored satin skirt that swished around her ankles. The bodice fit her well, showing to advantage her slender waist and firm breasts. Although she felt a little uncomfortable with the low neckline—none of her day dresses were so revealing—she was pleased with the way she looked.

Flashing her aunt a quick smile, she said, "Thank you so much for having the dress made for me. It's lovely. I know it was frightfully expensive and I do appreciate it."

Her aunt snorted. "I can't leave this wretched city until I see you properly married, so I have to take steps to show you off. This ball gives me the perfect opportunity to dress you so you'll be appreciated by the right man."

Esme tried to ignore the cold motives her aunt expressed, but it cut her to the heart that Miriam never did anything out of affection for her. Sometimes Esme wondered if Miriam had an ounce of feeling in her at all.

Her aunt launched into another lecture. "Enjoy yourself tonight, but remember your place. You're only a teacher's daughter, and you should be careful with people above your station. Not that they would bother with you. But the upper classes tend to be, well, a bit wicked. The men take advantage of young girls whom they have no intention of marrying. So remember to carry yourself modestly. And if the British envoy should notice you, be polite but reserved. I know the ball's in his honor, but as an earl's son, he's certain to be decadent."

Miriam's words reminded Esme of the real reason she dreaded the ball. The stranger might be there. Only a week had passed since Loy Krathong. If he was still in Bangkok, a man of his station would certainly be invited. What if he recognized her? Would he tell Aunt Miriam? Fearfully, she gazed at her cheek in the mirror to see if any traces of her bruise remained. It seemed to be gone but....

"Stop frowning so, Esme," Miriam said, bringing her out of her reverie. "You'll never find a husband wearing that glum expression."

"I don't wish to marry," Esme said in a low voice, staring once again in the mirror at her young face and troubled black eyes that looked mournfully back at her.

"You say these wicked things just to spite me, I know," her aunt told her furiously. "You must marry. Your father wishes it. I wish it. Otherwise, you'll be a spinster schoolteacher in this horrible city all your life, and I'll never return to England where people are civilized. Besides, your precious mother would have wished it as well." She sniffed. "Not that it matters what she would have thought. I didn't approve of James's marriage to that ... that Frenchwoman. No doubt with a firmer, more appropriate mother, you would have learned to curb your wild impulses."

Esme turned to face Miriam with her eyes flashing. "My mother was a saint, the best mother anyone could have had," she said fiercely. "I won't have you speak of her like that!"

Miriam drew herself up, her face beginning to flame. "You won't have me ..." she sputtered. "*You* won't have me ... Let me tell you something, miss. I don't plan to act as nursemaid to a rebellious chit all my life. I want to return to civilization. I'll see that you're married and out of this house as soon as possible, if I must marry you to the oldest, ugliest eligible bachelor in the city! Mr. Michaels has asked

Deborah Martin

for your hand twice already, but James refused him because *you* don't like him. If you don't watch your step, you'll find yourself married to him yet. So you'd best remember on which side your bread is buttered or you will regret it!"

Esme hesitated for a moment, shocked at the venom in her aunt's voice. Then, her voice filled with all the pride she could muster, she replied, "I don't care how you threaten me. I won't have you speak of Mother that way. Besides, if Father knew of your plans, you'd have no money to live on and you know it."

Miriam blanched but swiftly recovered. "I'll admit it's a trifle inconvenient that our father left my inheritance under my brother's care. But I know how to handle James. He's always felt guilty that he wasn't firmer with you in the past, particularly since your mother set a bad example by—"

She broke off at the mutinous look that suddenly crossed Esme's face. "Well, never mind that. One slip from you will be all the proof he needs that you require a husband, and you'll be out of this house in an instant. Keep that in mind."

With that, Miriam turned on her heels and left the room, leaving Esme so shaken she had to sit down.

"I will not cry . . . I will not cry . . ." Esme repeated slowly to herself, determined not to give her aunt the satisfaction of seeing her upset. Then again it would serve Aunt Miriam right, she thought peevishly, if she showed up with a tear-streaked face and destroyed all of her aunt's matchmaking plans.

She took a moment to compose herself. No, she wouldn't let Aunt Miriam ruin this night for her. She'd enjoy herself and show them all that she could be entirely proper when she wanted to be.

She gazed a moment longer at her sad face in the mirror and then deliberately twisted her down-turned lips into a smile. She wouldn't be cowed, she vowed. Then she straightened her shoulders and left her bedroom to face the world.

An hour later, Esme stared up at the Rushtons' house with a mixture of eagerness and trepidation. She scarcely noticed the oppressive heat so wrapped up was she in her conflicting emotions. As she followed her aunt up the broad stone stairs, she forced herself to relax. After all, she reminded herself, she was among friends here. The minister resident, Henry Rushton, was her father's dearest friend. His wife, Blythe, had also been very close to Esme's mother, and Esme had visited the Rushton house often, both with her father and by herself.

How ironic, thought Esme, as they entered the foyer. If Blythe had known how Esme dreaded what she might find at the ball, Blythe would never have sent the invitation.

But before Esme could worry anymore, Blythe met her and Miriam at the far end of the foyer. "Esme, my dear, you look absolutely stunning. I'm so glad you could come," Blythe said, her lovely face the picture of affection.

Miriam, however, received a less cordial greeting, for Blythe disliked Miriam's treatment of Esme.

"Where's your father?" Blythe asked Esme, pointedly ignoring the older woman.

"He didn't feel well. I wanted to stay home with him, but he said there was no need."

Her aunt sniffed indignantly. "Of course not. James is just shirking his responsibilities as usual." She turned to Blythe. "I insisted that Esme come.

Someone must look out for her, and I felt she needed to move in society for a change."

"Yes, of course," Blythe answered, though she shot a sympathetic glance at Esme who was glaring at Miriam. "You've come to the right place for that, my dear," she told Esme.

Blythe then led them into the large parlor, chatting to Esme about the latest dresses the recent ship from England had brought. Esme listened attentively, relieved to have her mind occupied by more pleasant thoughts. As Blythe talked, Esme relaxed and began to gaze about her. People stood pleasantly conversing in small groups around the room, which was filled with warm light. Esme's eyes widened at the sparkle and rich colors of the women's gowns. Her dress compared poorly to the lush brocades worn by the merchants' wives, but she didn't care. She was simply happy to be where people were carefree, where lectures were not the order of the day. Like a starving woman, she greedily drank in the glittering sight.

Suddenly, she realized that several people were staring at her oddly. Bewildered, she glanced at Blythe, but the older woman hadn't seemed to notice. Two officers she barely knew cast knowing leers in her direction, and she shivered. What on earth was happening? Had she worn her dress incorrectly? Was it too immodest in cut? One glance around the room told her that her dress was more modest by far than many of those in the room.

Then everything else was forgotten as her eyes locked with the questioning gray-blue gaze of a stranger. No, not a stranger. The man now staring boldly at her would have been difficult to forget, and she certainly hadn't. He had that same wavy brown hair setting off the deep tan that no doubt came from spending months at sea. His powerful shoulders and hands exuded authority. The harsh planes of his rugged face contrasted sharply with the soft curls that surrounded it, but she knew most women would consider him handsome. Yet his eyes were what she most remembered. Now they held her mesmerized, their steely depths hinting that she too had been recognized. As if to confirm it, the man's lips relaxed in a knowing smile, and ever so slightly, he bowed toward her.

Quickly, she turned back to Blythe and her aunt. She could feel the color creeping over her face. Desperate to avoid the man's gaze, she fanned herself with the delicate palm-leaf creation her aunt had given her as respite from the heat. But nothing cooled the uncomfortable warmth spreading through her body.

She sensed rather than saw him come toward them.

"I see Lord Winthrop has spotted you, dear," Blythe whispered affectionately in Esme's ear. "The gossips say he's a notorious rake, but I don't believe it for a minute. He's been the picture of propriety all evening." She smiled wickedly. "More's the pity. But I simply must introduce him to you. I know he'd find you fascinating."

"Please, Blythe—" Esme began, but the gentleman had already reached them. Riveted to the spot, she watched in horror as Blythe moved to greet him.

"Why, Lord Winthrop, I hoped you might come our way. There's someone I wish you to meet." While Blythe played the perfect hostess, Esme awaited her doom in silence.

She wanted to run. Her mind shouted *No!* as the gentleman's eyes sought hers again, but she knew she was trapped. Gathering what little inner strength remained, Esme raised her eyes to his, this time careful to make her expression impassive.

As Blythe introduced them, with Miriam looking on in surprise, Lord Winthrop's scrutinizing eyes never left Esme's face. As if from a distance, Esme heard Blythe say that he was the new envoy from Britain, and her heart sank. Now she was really in trouble. He was no doubt one of those men who lived by the strictest rules of society. He would feel it his duty to report her escapade to her father.

"Miss Montrose's mother was Lady Laplante of the Paris Laplantes, you know," Esme heard Blythe saying. "She left it all to marry James Montrose, a schoolteacher, and to come out here to Siam. Isn't that just so romantic?"

"Dear Blythe," Miriam cut in, flashing what she evidently thought was a winning smile at the envoy. "I'm certain his lordship doesn't want to hear about my niece's parents."

"I take it then that you're not Miss Montrose's mother?" Ian asked in thinly veiled amusement.

"Indeed not. I'm James's sister, and I'm most thoroughly English. I act as my niece's chaperone now."

"Then perhaps you'd permit me to steal her away for the next dance," he stated as the strains of a waltz filled the room.

"We would both consider it an honor, wouldn't we, dear?" she said as her eyes dared Esme to defy her.

Esme was thoroughly terrified. She didn't want to dance with him. The only way she could escape being detected was if she didn't go near him. But she couldn't risk angering her aunt by refusing his lordship's invitation. Blythe was looking at her curiously already, clearly wondering why she hesitated at all.

"Yes," Esme said civilly. "I'd be delighted."

Miriam's eyes glinted with pleasure as the envoy escorted Esme away. For once, Blythe and Miriam seemed to agree. So much for her aunt's admonitions that she should be polite and reserved around the envoy. Aunt Miriam had clearly decided that Lord Winthrop was as eligible as anyone. Esme nearly groaned aloud in frustration. How would she make it through an entire dance without giving something away? But perhaps she was just worrying herself needlessly. Maybe he hadn't remembered a thing.

Yet how could he have forgotten? She certainly hadn't. The slight pressure of his firm hand against her back already sent tingles radiating through her body. No, she certainly hadn't forgotten that evening.

"You're very quiet," he murmured close to her ear as they crossed the parlor. "I promise I won't bite."

"Forgive me, my lord," she said with forced calm. "I don't often meet a man of such distinguished credentials."

"Then we're even. I don't often meet such an intriguing woman at provincial balls."

She laughed nervously. "We've just met. How do you know I'm intriguing? I might be the dullest girl in the room."

"I have an instinct about these things," he said smoothly.

By this time, they'd reached the ballroom. Firmly, he clasped her hand in his while his other arm embraced her waist in a tight grip. Though his smile was polite, she felt trapped. She couldn't de-

43

cide if he'd recognized her. Surely he would have said something by now if he had.

She avoided his gaze as much as possible, trying not to search his face for signs that he recognized her. Desperately, she cast about for something to say to take his mind off her.

"I'm curious, my lord," she said with sudden inspiration. "Why were you sent here? Have the French and English finally worked out their differences? Will there be a treaty?"

He stared at her in surprise. "You see what I mean? You're already proving to be intriguing. So few women your age are interested in politics. How old are you anyway?"

"Eighteen," she said with eyes lowered.

"I'd have guessed you were younger," he remarked.

She remembered the way he'd spoken to her at the docks, and her heart pounded. She knew she didn't look particularly young tonight, but she had looked young that night on the docks.

"Only eighteen and already knowledgeable about politics," he murmured.

"Well, my father—" She stopped abruptly as she remembered that she'd mentioned her father the night of the festival.

"Yes?" His gray-blue eyes gleamed in open amusement.

"He thinks it's important for both men and women to know about such things," she continued, her chin jutting up at him stubbornly as she realized she was acting like a guilty urchin.

"Your father sounds like a wise man. I suppose he's taught you a great deal."

Lord Winthrop seemed so genuinely interested that for a moment she let down her guard. "Oh, yes. He insisted that I learn everything—history, mathematics, languages—everything."

"What languages do you speak?" Lord Winthrop queried.

"French, some German—"

"Siamese?" he asked with such adroitness that she'd nodded before she even realized where the conversation had headed.

The smile on her face faded abruptly as a glint of triumph lit his eyes. "Not very well, of course," she added, a sudden queasiness assailing her. "The Siamese, I mean."

"Ah, but it's unusual anyway to find an English-woman who speaks such a difficult language," he said with a hint of a smile. "I'm sure you're much more proficient than you let on."

"Really I'm not," she protested weakly.

"You know, Miss Montrose, if your father has given you as much education in Siamese history and culture as he has in the Siamese language, you could possibly answer a question that has weighed quite heavily on my mind of late."

"I could certainly try," she said bravely, trying to ignore the heavy sarcasm that laced his words as his arm tightened around her waist.

"You see, I witnessed an interesting Siamese festival a week ago on the docks. I heard that it is called Loy Krathong. Do you happen to know what the Siamese were celebrating?"

She had to fight the sudden impulse to pull away from him. Surely he'd guessed who she was, she thought with a sinking heart. But why hadn't he just come right out and asked her?

"I'm not sure," she hedged, glancing up into eyes that were suddenly an icy blue.

"Really?" His lips curved in a mocking grin. "And

45

I suppose you'll claim you've never seen the festival yourself."

A sigh of defeat escaped her lips. So he did know. She felt curiously relieved to have it out in the open at last. "Yes, of course I've seen the festival," she said, tilting her face up to him in open defiance.

He smiled, triumph showing in every line of his face. "It was you on the docks, wasn't it?" he asked with calm assurance.

"Yes," she responded, silently cursing him for his keen eye.

"What were you doing there?" he persisted.

"I went to see the festival, just as you did, I gather."

"Your father and that iron-maiden chaperone of yours allowed such a thing?"

Esme's face clouded over. Now he would know she'd sneaked out without permission. Of course he would tell. She felt a sudden surge of anger at him. What right had he to question her in this manner? He was as bad as Aunt Miriam, demanding to know all about her life, wanting to control it. How dare he?

She stiffened in his arms and lifted her head proudly. "That is no concern of yours, my lord." Her black eyes met his cool blue ones mutinously.

She thought he'd be angry, but instead his eyes almost imperceptibly softened and his mouth curled in a knowing smile.

"Slipped out of the house, did you?" he taunted.

"I was invited!"

"Oh, of course you were. By those two Siamese girls, I suppose. But I hardly think your family sanctioned the expedition or you wouldn't have worn that native costume."

She was silent, concentrating her gaze on his gray silk ascot.

"An extremely provocative native costume, I might add."

Her gaze flew to his in alarm. "Please," she said softly. "You shouldn't say such things."

"You're an odd one to talk about propriety," he remarked, his eyes lingering with boldness on her lips.

"Mrs. Rushton was clearly mistaken and the gossips were right," she said firmly. "You're a terrible . . ." She stopped as she realized she shouldn't call him a rake to his face.

"Yes?" he asked with quiet amusement.

"You're not the kind of man I wish to be seen with," she said weakly. "I shouldn't continue to dance with you."

Unperturbed, he clasped her unwilling body more closely and continued to dance, half carrying her around the room.

"Oh, yes, you should," he said, a hint of a calculating smile crossing his face. "That is, unless you want me to tell your friendly chaperone about the incident on the docks."

"You can't!" she cried, her face showing her mortification. "Surely you aren't that cruel!"

"But, my dear, I can and really should. For your own sake. No young attractive woman should be allowed to act as recklessly as you did the other night."

Numbly, she let him lead her around the room. She'd known this would happen. Oh, why did she always have to be found out? "I don't suppose I could convince you not to say anything," she said, her eyes downcast.

"On the contrary," he said enigmatically, his fin-

Deborah Martin

gers tightening around her hand. "You might be able to persuade me."

In her aggravation, she hadn't noticed that they were moving steadily closer to the open wooden doors that led into the back parlor. Before she could stop him, she found herself waltzed through the room and out onto the gallery. To her complete alarm, she was completely alone with him under the moonlit sky.

"What are you doing? Why have you brought me out here?" she asked, alarmed by the way his gaze traveled arrogantly over her body. They'd stopped dancing, but he continued to rest his hands on her waist, holding her far closer than was proper. It was cooler outside than it had been in the stuffy ballroom, but she still felt overwhelmingly warm.

"I've a proposal to make, my dear, one I'm sure you'll agree to readily. I won't say a word to your family if you'll grant me one small favor." He lifted his hand to brush a delicately curled tendril of hair from her cheek. She flinched.

"What do you want?" she asked in a small voice, afraid of his answer but curious to know what she could possibly give him.

"It wouldn't be a difficult request for you to grant. A shade improper perhaps, but that shouldn't deter you, considering the reckless life you lead."

Her eyes began to glisten with unshed tears. "I'm not as bad as you think," she protested, trying to back away.

"I don't know whether to believe you or not," he said, his eyes narrowing as he gripped her waist more firmly. Leisurely, he allowed his eyes to travel down to where a bead of perspiration gleamed between her gently heaving breasts.

"What do you want?" she asked again in a breathless whisper, frightened by his closeness and the way his eyes devoured her.

"Only this," he murmured before lowering his head to hers and capturing her trembling mouth with his firm one. At first she froze, shocked at his action and the insistence with which his lips moved over hers. Then she pushed at his broad shoulders and twisted her mouth away.

"You mustn't!" she cried out, remembering the only other time a man had placed his lips on hers.

"Why mustn't I?" he murmured huskily. "Don't tell me you've never been kissed before."

"I have . . . but not . . . not—"

"Not by a man who knew what he was doing perhaps?" he asked, his hand gripping her chin and raising her head so that his smoldering eyes stared into hers. "I suppose your escapades would be limited to boys or old men out here."

Her eyes flamed at his accusations. "Oh, no, my lord," she retorted, infuriated by the contemptuous implication of his words. "My experience is limited, I'm afraid, to drunk sailors. And I'm quickly discovering they're not much worse than men of your class."

"I can't believe Henley was the first to kiss such a sweet mouth." His low murmur both thrilled and frightened her.

Then his lips took hers again, but this time more insistently, coaxing her lips to soften against her will. She struggled to escape the iron-like firmness of his arm, but to no avail. She found herself going limp, her knees weakening beneath her as his mouth played over hers with sensuous thoroughness. He released her chin, and his hand slid down to caress her slender throat. But when his tongue pressed against her mouth, seeking entrance, she

49

struck out wildly, suddenly terrified by the intimacy of his kiss.

Her fear must have reached his inflamed senses, for he pulled back reluctantly to stare at her, his smoky eyes showing his surprise.

Unbidden, tears filled her eyes. "You can't! You mustn't!" she whispered, her hands weakly beating against his chest. "You don't know what you're doing!"

He released her and stared at the teary-eyed girl in front of him. "That wretched sailor really was the first, wasn't he?" he asked, his voice suddenly gentle.

"I *told* you that!" she said, tears slipping down her cheeks. "I told you!"

"Yes, you did," he answered, a trace of remorse in his voice as he gathered her into his arms once again. "I'm sorry I didn't listen. Shh, shh, it's all right now. I won't hurt you."

Trembling, she leaned against his chest, too upset to resist letting him hold and comfort her as she wept softly. He searched for his handkerchief, and, finding it at last, offered it to her. She wiped her eyes and blew her nose in a most unladylike manner.

"How was I to believe you could be so naive?" he told her. "What was I supposed to think after last week? Young well-bred ladies don't go sporting at night scantily clad."

She knew he was partly right, and she blushed to think that her actions had made him believe she was a wanton woman. At the same time, she felt he'd assumed far too much.

She sniffed. "Do you make a habit of believing the worst about everyone? Next you'll tell me you assumed I was a lady of the evening because I was accosted by sailors."

He grinned. "I assumed nothing. Actually, at the time I thought you were an innocent girl who'd gotten herself into trouble by being unwise. Then tonight, when I found out you were older... I should have trusted my first instinct."

"I just wanted to see the lights, that's all," she burst out, somehow comforted by his admission. "Aunt Miriam is so insufferable, and Father seems to believe she knows what's best for me. I couldn't bear it another minute, don't you see? I had to see some beauty for a change. I had to see the lights, and they wouldn't let me go."

He stood listening patiently, his arms crossed over his chest, letting her spill out her anguish to him.

"And if you tell them..." She stopped. Why was she telling him all this? Why should he care? He had more important worries in his life than her petty concerns. She looked out at the grounds of the consulate as she hesitated. Jasmine scented the air with a cloying sweetness.

"Yes? Go on. What will happen if I tell them?"

"That will be the end."

"Oh?" He raised his eyebrows skeptically.

"Aunt Miriam says if I make one more mistake she'll force me to marry some merchant. If she does, my life will be over."

"I hardly think the consequences would be as bad as you say," he remarked drily.

"I'm sorry," she said as she stiffened, his condescension wounding her pride. "I shouldn't have mentioned it. Do as you wish. Tell them if you feel you must." She turned to leave the gallery.

But his hand grasped her upper arm, preventing

Deborah Martin

her from moving. "Don't worry. I won't breathe a word. I must admit, however, that your aunt's concern for your behavior is well placed. But the least I can do to make up for my 'misjudging' your character is to keep silent."

"Thank you," she murmured, uncertain whether to trust him.

He stared at her for a moment then his hands slid once more around her slim waist. "I'd prefer another kind of thank you," he said gruffly.

She gazed into his smoky blue eyes and hesitated. She knew exactly what he wanted. Well, he'd agreed to remain silent. Raising herself on her tiptoes, she brushed his forehead with a kiss.

"That won't do," he rasped before lowering his lips to hers. Yet this time his kiss wasn't harshly insistent but gentle, almost persuasive. Unaware she did so, Esme curved against him and slid her arms around his neck to clasp him more closely.

At the touch of her hands at his nape, he abruptly released her, a ragged breath escaping his lips. "I've had you out here far too long, little one. We'd best return to the ballroom before your reputation is permanently besmirched. Better yet, go on alone and I'll find another doorway to enter through. No one need know we've been out here all this time alone together."

She looked at him quizzically, but his face was an impassive mask.

"Go on," he said roughly. "Go back to your safe little world before I change my mind."

Without another word, Esme slipped back into the house.

Chapter Three

When Esme entered the ballroom, she realized she still held Lord Winthrop's handkerchief tightly in her hand. She hesitated for a moment. Should she go back to return it? No, that would be inviting trouble. Besides, she needed time to compose herself before she saw her aunt again.

Quickly, she circled the ballroom until she reached a small dressing room. When she slipped inside and found the room empty, relief flooded through her. She went to the mirror and gazed at her reflection, surprised to see that except for her reddened eyes and nose, her face had changed little. After his kiss, she'd somehow expected her face to be transformed into a woman's. But the face of a girl still stared back at her.

She splashed some cold water from the washbowl onto her face. Then, uncertain what to do with Lord Winthrop's handkerchief, she tucked it into her bodice out of sight. She'd deal with it later. Carefully, she straightened her dress, smoothed her hair, and started out of the room.

She'd scarcely reached the door, however, when it opened to admit her aunt.

"Where have you been?" Miriam's sharp eyes took in every detail of Esme's appearance.

"I . . . I felt a little ill, so I came in here to wash my face," Esme stammered, trying not to sound guilty.

Miriam's gaze turned suspicious. "I shouldn't have allowed you to dance with the envoy. After you left, I heard the most awful things about him."

"You needn't have worried," Esme broke in. "Nothing happened."

"Thank heavens for that." With one more appraisal of Esme's appearance, she appeared to accept her niece's answer. "Come along then. Mr. Michaels is waiting for his dance."

"Yes, ma'am." As she followed Miriam out, Esme shivered to think how close she'd come to being discovered. Her aunt would have been enraged if she knew that Esme and Lord Winthrop had been alone on the gallery. But the crisis was over, she told herself, and she was safe.

Ian watched with mixed feelings as Esme danced in the arms of yet another fawning merchant. It offended his aesthetic sense to see her delicate waist pawed by lecherous hands. But she endured it with patience, only blossoming in the arms of the few young officers she was paired with. He envied those officers, for his few short moments with her hadn't satisfied his curiosity about her. Nor had it dimmed the instant attraction he'd felt.

He turned to Godfrey who was talking animatedly to another consular official, George Walker.

"You see that girl, the one in the purple gown?" Ian asked when they paused in their conversation. He nodded his head discreetly toward Esme and her partner. "What can you tell me about her?"

Godfrey laughed and exchanged smirks with the other official. "Funny you should ask, old boy. George and I were just talking about her. She's the daughter of one of the teachers here, a good friend of our host. I've only met her a few times, but with so few foreigners around here and so much idle time to gossip, one doesn't need to know a person to *know* a person, if you take my meaning."

"And what is it you 'know' about her?" Ian asked with impatience.

"A week ago she had a reputation for being an innocuous enough young thing, though a bit too eager to run about with the natives. But I just heard the juiciest bit of gossip about her."

"Some that you invented, no doubt," Ian retorted irritably.

"No, no," George cut in. "This came straight from the horse's mouth."

Godfrey leaned toward Ian in a conspiratorial manner. "I can hardly believe it's true, for her air is quite virginal, don't you think? But I have it on the best authority that she's old Henry Rushton's latest mistress."

For a moment, Ian felt as if someone had punched him in the stomach. Then he reminded himself how innocently she'd behaved on the gallery. Surely that hadn't been an act, he told himself.

"I just danced with the girl, and I have trouble believing she's that experienced," Ian said, though he couldn't stop his eyes from wandering to where she stood smiling at a young captain.

"It's just like you to say that. You're such a gentleman you take women at face value. Of course, in
this case your reluctance to believe ill of someone
is understandable. To be honest, she shocked us all.
I mean her father's so terribly protective of her that
she only began attending social events recently,
when she was so old he could no longer keep her
at home. We'd all assumed she was quite the innocent."

"She's no innocent, according to Rushton's secretary, Lawrence," George added. "Lawrence told
me himself about the affair."

"Would Lawrence have any reason to lie?" Ian
asked, a part of him still shocked into disbelief.

"He'd be a fool to lie about something like that,"
George insisted. "Actually, he was horrified when
he let it slip."

Ian had met Lawrence, who hadn't struck Ian as
the type of man to lie about a girl's reputation. And
why lie about his own superior and risk his position? His eyes hardened as he realized Lawrence
probably told the truth.

Godfrey continued, "We've all known for years
that Henry's quite the ladies man when Blythe's
not around. But to seduce his best friend's daughter! Why, the man's a devil! Still, it's easy to see
how it happened. The girl's here all the time with
Blythe. Such a shame, though. She could have made
a very good marriage if news of the affair hadn't
leaked out. Poor girl."

Poor girl, indeed! thought Ian. God, she was a perfect actress. Better than Caroline had ever been, and
that was saying a great deal.

An image of Caroline as she'd looked the first time
he'd met her came unbidden to his mind. Racing
across his father's estate on her magnificent mare,

she'd been the picture of loveliness. He should have realized then that her carefree abandon was only part of the thorough wildness that governed her.

But her wildness had attracted him. His first years in the foreign service had forced him to be always restrained, always tactful, so that her flouting of even the most important social conventions had been like a breath of fresh air to him. His illusions had ended the day he'd found her, his betrothed, taking her pleasure in the barn with a groom. Only then had he realized that social conventions weren't the only ones she flouted. She lacked regard for any rules—social, moral, or ethical.

Bitterly, he thought of the pain she'd caused him, the humiliation. She'd wanted to marry him anyway, of course. The whole incident had meant little to her. But that had been the end for him. As abruptly as he'd fallen in love, he had fallen out of love. Looking back, he realized he probably hadn't really loved her at all. He'd simply been enamored of the freedom she seemed to represent. He should have made her his mistress instead of offering for her. Perhaps if he'd done that, the pain of her betrayal wouldn't have been so keen.

Now, once again, he found himself attracted to a young wild thing, a supposed innocent. And again, the innocence proved to be just a charade. He frowned as he realized how Esme had tricked him. He could still see her sobbing when he'd tried to kiss her. She'd seemed sincere enough, but that just proved how adept a deceiver she was. No doubt she'd thought that if he knew her true character, he'd tell her father and aunt about her sneaking out of the house.

He ought to, he thought, just to punish her for

making a fool out of him. But that would involve him in a situation he was better off staying out of. For if she continued with Rushton, she was bound to get pregnant and the less Ian's name was associated with hers, the better. Her father might decide that he'd enjoy having a noble for a son-in-law. No, he had no desire to be caught in a marriage trap again. If he were wise, he'd give Esme Montrose a wide berth until he left for Chiengmai.

For the rest of the evening he tried to dismiss her from his mind. But her face continued to haunt him as he danced with a particularly simpering young woman. Instead of the blue eyes flirting gaily up at him, he saw midnight ones flashing. Carefully curled fair locks became shining black tresses that shimmered around their owner's shoulders in the moonlight.

By the time he left the ball much later, he was no closer to erasing thoughts of Esme Montrose from his mind than he had been hours before.

"How was the ball, dear?" James Montrose asked the next morning at breakfast, giving Esme one of his rare smiles.

"It was lovely, Father," she answered, trying to force some enthusiasm into her voice.

At the ball her aunt had matched her up with so many fools and old men that she hoped she would never see another ball gown or dance another waltz in her life. The evening had gone from bad to worse as one man after another had treated her with a blatant disrespect that she'd found confusing. One of the officers had gone so far as to ask Esme for an assignation later on. When she'd attempted to shame him into an apology, he'd seemed surprised. She couldn't imagine why the men of the community had suddenly been so crude in their advances. But their behavior had driven her to insist that Miriam bring her home early.

"Esme's popularity was astounding," Miriam was saying. "Even the British envoy requested a dance with her."

"I'm not surprised," James responded. "Last night she looked the very image of her mother. I almost regretted not going." He flashed his daughter an affectionate grin.

Esme thrust her bad memories of the ball aside, basking in her father's light mood.

Miriam noticed the two happy faces and snorted. "You two can sit around and engage in this sentimental nonsense, but I'm going to see about this evening's dinner," she remarked, rising abruptly to her feet. "I might even pay Harriet a visit."

Esme almost choked on her fruit at the thought of her aunt taking charge of dinner. Despite Miriam's busybody nature, she wasn't adept at handling the domestic side of their lives. She couldn't deal with the Siamese servants (except for the one maid who obeyed her every command) or with the strange requirements of living in a foreign country. Esme had helped her mother run the household for years, so she'd taken over its running after her mother's death, continuing to do so even after her aunt had come.

No, Esme thought as she watched her aunt leave the room, far more likely her aunt was going to share the latest gossip with her friend next door, Harriet Bingham, who somehow managed to ferret out the nastiest truths about everyone in the foreign community.

James observed his daughter as she struggled to repress her irritation. "I know Miriam can be tiresome," he told her. "But be patient with her. She means well and only wants the best for you."

Esme struggled to refrain from telling him just how far her aunt would go to make Esme behave. But she knew it was neither the time nor the place to enlighten her father, even if he would believe her. She wanted to enjoy her father's rare good mood.

"Now what's this about dancing with the envoy?" he asked brightly, reaching for more fruit. "Was he a handsome young devil or another old stuffed shirt like that last envoy?"

Esme stared down at her plate, trying to control the blush creeping over her face.

He scrutinized her closely. "I take it he was a handsome young devil." James lifted one brow in speculation. "No matter. From what Rushton's told me, I don't imagine he'll be in Bangkok much longer. He'll be off to Chiengmai soon."

Esme tried to keep the disappointment from showing in her expression. For some absurd reason, it saddened her to think Lord Winthrop would be leaving the city. "What will he do in Chiengmai?" she asked in a politely dispassionate tone.

"Convince Prince Mataya not to send an army against the French, we hope. The Siamese are understandably upset by the way the French have been surreptitiously moving into that territory. We don't want them there either, of course, but force on the part of the Siamese will just give the French the excuse to declare war on Siam. That wouldn't suit British interests at all."

"Why not?"

"Because if the French win, they'll want to add Siam to their empire. They don't seem satisfied with just Cambodia and Annam. If they annex

Siam, we'd be directly across the border from them since Burma, our own colony, borders Siam on the west. Despite Burma, however, we wouldn't want them to take Siam. Our trading interests here are extensive."

"Will there be war?" she asked fearfully.

Her father looked pensive. "I hope it doesn't come to that. You and I would be in a pickle then, wouldn't we? We'd likely have to leave, and I can't countenance that. But I think war's unlikely. Rushton says the British want to make north Siam an independent buffer zone between the British empire and the French. The Siamese would prefer that the British simply defend Siam militarily from the French, of course, but we absolutely refuse to do that. In the meantime, until an agreement can be reached, we don't want the Siamese to provoke the French needlessly."

She leaned forward with curiosity on her face. "Why isn't Mr. Rushton handling this then? Why Lord Winthrop?"

"Lord Winthrop, is it now?" James asked, for the first time in a long time seeming to see his daughter as more than just a child. His face clouded over for a moment.

"We did dance together once, Father," she said gently.

"Ah, yes. Well, Lord Winthrop has a great deal of experience dealing with the French in other parts of Asia. I suppose the powers-that-be thought him best suited to dealing with the French here as well."

"But that's absurd! Why, he doesn't speak Siamese and he knows nothing about the country! At least Mr. Rushton speaks the language."

"Such fervor over politics!" James exclaimed, his eyes narrowing. "Is it just the politics that has you

61

so bothered? Or is it Lord Winthrop whom you find not to your liking?"

She avoided his gaze. "He's rather arrogant, that's all."

"I take it he didn't approve of your casual approach to life."

Esme winced as her father came perilously close to the truth.

"I've never seen a man get such a reaction from you. I'll have to meet the man who can turn my generally uninterested daughter into a spitting virago," James said with a mixture of amusement and distress in his voice.

"You wouldn't like him," she answered, terrified that he might indeed try to talk to Lord Winthrop. "He's just a snobbish aristocrat who tries to tell everyone what to do." She knew that wasn't quite the truth, but she had to prejudice her father against Lord Winthrop. If they ever did talk ... She shuddered to think what her father would say about her escapade.

"Your mother was an aristocrat, too, child." Her father's eyes, so recently merry, now saddened once again. After that reminder, he lapsed into his usual melancholy silence, staring out the window at the overgrown jungle beside their house.

Esme cursed herself for making her father think of Renee. She too missed her mother, she wanted to tell him. Though she knew the reasons for it, his obsessive grief disturbed her. In his few periods of normalcy when he was his old self, she thought he was coming out of his sadness. But he always plunged back into his morass of sorrow, leaving her feeling utterly and terribly alone.

"A gentleman is here to see you, sir," the maid announced, entering the room and pulling both

Esme and her father from their thoughts.

As her father left the table with a frown still imprinted on his face, she wondered who their visitor was. She started to rise, but a familiar voice coming from the drawing room made her freeze.

"Mr. James Montrose, I assume?"

The deep masculine voice struck a chord within her. *What is Lord Winthrop doing here?* she thought in terror. Had he decided to tell her father about her escapade after all? Stealthily, she crept to the doorway, intent on hearing every word that passed between her father and the envoy.

"I'm sorry to disturb you, sir," the voice continued, "and I know we haven't been introduced, but Henry Rushton told me where to find you and assured me you could help me. I'm Ian Winthrop, the new envoy. Rushton said you might know where I could find an interpreter for hire."

Esme felt only partially relieved. Whatever Lord Winthrop's professed reasons were for seeking out her father, she wouldn't feel completely safe until he was gone.

"I'd be more than willing to help you," James answered. "I've heard a bit about you from my daughter."

"Your daughter?"

"She says you danced together last night."

Esme's cheeks burned. Why did her father have to repeat her words? Now Lord Winthrop would assume she'd been mooning over him. Arrogant monster! She wished she could wipe the smug look off his face, which she knew he must be wearing.

"I remember Miss Montrose. She said you were ill. Are you recovered?" Lord Winthrop's voice was polite, but she detected a bit of amusement in it.

"I confess that my illness was not of a physical

63

nature. I detest balls. Haven't been to one since my wife used to force me to accompany her."

Esme heard Lord Winthrop chuckle. "My sympathies are with you in that. They can be dreadfully boring."

"I'm glad you understand," James replied good-naturedly.

She fumed. Lord Winthrop had certainly found the way to soften her father. So much for her attempts to prejudice her father against the envoy.

"I hope you didn't find last night's ball too dull," her father continued.

"Not at all. Actually, your daughter made it very entertaining."

Esme nearly groaned aloud. Why did Lord Winthrop have to say that? No doubt it was a prelude to telling her father all.

"Did she?" her father asked. She could tell from his tone that Lord Winthrop's statement didn't sit well with him. "You know, she took a bit of a dislike to you. I hope you didn't give her a reason to do so."

The note of challenge in her father's voice was unmistakable. Esme held her breath, waiting for Lord Winthrop's answer.

"I think, sir," he said, a hint of an edge to his voice, "that your daughter doesn't like those who point out her faults. I simply remarked that she seemed a bit ... unrestrained, if you know what I mean. It was a rather high-handed thing to say, I'll admit, but I didn't intend to upset her."

This time it was James who chuckled, but Esme could tell he was also perturbed. "I'm afraid Esme's mother and I gave her too much freedom. Then her mother died when Esme was fifteen. Esme has grown up 'unrestrained,' as you say. But she's my only comfort."

"I'm sure she is, sir. I didn't mean to insult her."

Esme's hands balled into fists. No, he hadn't meant to insult her when he'd kissed her so brazenly! No, he was of course the perfect gentleman! What would her father say if he knew exactly what Lord Winthrop had done on the gallery the night before? The man was infuriating, and she sincerely hoped lightning struck him for the lies he was telling now!

But the memory of his kiss lingered, burning her lips once again with its fiery boldness. She tried to wipe the sensation away with her hand, but she couldn't forget the hardness of his lips on hers and the melting warmth that had spread through her body.

"Would you like something to drink, Lord Winthrop?" she heard her father ask. "Some tea perhaps?"

"I'd appreciate it indeed. This hot weather has me parched."

"Esme! Esme, are you still in there?" James called, and Esme jumped. She nearly tripped, trying to return to her place at the table on the other side of the room.

Shakily, she answered, "Yes, Father?"

"Be a dear and bring us some tea. I don't know where your aunt has gotten to."

"Certainly, Father," she called back as she headed for the kitchen. Her aunt was nowhere in sight. *Probably still at Mrs. Bingham's*, Esme thought in disgust.

When at last Esme entered the drawing room, the two men were discussing Siam as if they'd known each other all their lives. Without a word, she

Deborah Martin

placed the tray on the table in front of them, uncomfortably aware that Lord Winthrop's eyes surveyed her from head to foot. Instantly, she felt self-conscious, and her throat tightened as he continued to watch her. She was abruptly aware of how hot and sticky the air was. She forced herself to resist the urge to smooth her skirt and brush the damp strands of hair away from her face.

"Sit down a moment, child," her father requested.

"But I really should see about dinner," she protested, keeping her back to the man whose eyes bore into her.

"Surely you can stay a few minutes, Miss Montrose," Lord Winthrop put in smoothly. "Your father's been advising me on how to choose an interpreter. I'd be interested to know if you have any suggestions as well."

Esme knew she was being baited, but she wouldn't let him have the satisfaction of seeing her turn tail and run.

"Why, Lord Winthrop," she said coolly, turning to settle herself on the settee beside her father. "I can hardly imagine what advice I could give that would be of value to you."

She raised her eyes to meet his, not knowing what she'd find there. His intense gray-blue eyes danced with amusement, and a slow smile passed over the hard planes of his face.

"But you know so much about the country and its people. Your discussion of Loy Krathong last night was quite illuminating."

Her father glanced sharply at her, and she struggled to control the impulse to rage at the man across from her. How could he? With great difficulty, she maintained her composure.

"I've learned a great deal about Siam from Father's students and my Siamese friends," she replied, "but such secondhand information could hardly be of use to you. Father has seen more of the country than I have."

She waited for Lord Winthrop to laugh. He would tell her father everything and her life would be over. She forced herself to look at his implacable features, her eyes defying him, daring him to expose her. They stared at each other for a long moment. His face mirrored his amazement at her audacity and then his admiration.

When at last he answered, however, his voice showed no feeling at all. "I'd still like to know your opinion, Miss Montrose. Based on your secondhand knowledge, of course," he emphasized. "You see, your father told me I should choose an Englishman who speaks Siamese to accompany me, but I wonder if a Siamese who speaks English might not be better."

"I tried to tell his lordship," James broke in, "that Siamese who speak English fluently enough to deal with delicate discussions are as rare as hen's teeth around here."

"I'm afraid Father's right, my lord. Such an interpreter would be difficult to find."

"So you too think I should choose an Englishman?"

"A Siamese would be the better choice, of course, but you may not have such a choice."

"Is there no one who would qualify?" he asked her.

"You might try the Jesuit orphanage," James answered. "All of their boys speak fairly good English and some read and write it. A few might be old enough to suit your purpose."

Deborah Martin

"No one else? I was told many of the Siamese noblemen's sons have been taught in England."

"That's true," her father agreed. "Unfortunately, most have government posts and would think it beneath them to serve as an interpreter to a foreigner."

"Then I shall try the orphanage as you suggest."

At that moment, Miriam entered the room. "James, I've just been to Harriet's and you'll never believe—" She stopped abruptly when she saw Lord Winthrop.

"Good morning, Miss Montrose. Your brother has been giving me advice about an interpreter," he said smoothly.

Esme couldn't believe the obviously calculating look her aunt shot Lord Winthrop or the thin smile that touched her lips.

"Lord Winthrop," Miriam replied, her eyes narrowing. "So good of you to pay us a visit." Abruptly, she turned to her niece. "Esme, don't you think you should leave the two gentlemen to discuss these matters alone?"

Esme swallowed her pride and began to rise, but her father's hand stopped her.

"I asked her to stay, Miriam. We've been having a very informative chat."

Miriam's lips tightened but she said nothing in reply.

"It doesn't matter," Lord Winthrop interjected. "I've finished my business here and really must be going."

"Then my daughter will see you out, your lordship. She can point you in the direction of the orphanage." James looked quickly at his sister, but her face was expressionless, although she darted a quick glance from Esme to Lord Winthrop.

Esme told herself that she had no desire to be alone with Lord Winthrop again, but the thrill that suddenly gripped her was undeniable. As she led the way to the door, she felt his presence behind her and wondered what was in his mind. Was he thinking of exposing her? No, if he hadn't done so by now, he probably wouldn't. But she couldn't believe he'd come only to get information about an interpreter.

Once out on the porch, she began to direct him to the orphanage, but he stopped her. Placing his hand at her elbow, he turned her around to face him.

"Have you been telling tales about me to your father?" he asked, his hand leaving her elbow to trail gently down her arm.

"No worse than the ones you've been telling," she protested, her lips tight as she faced his cool scrutiny.

"That's hardly fair, my dear. After all, I could have told your father a great deal more. I don't need to invent anything to shock him."

"You—you won't say anything then?"

"Of course not. I gave you my word, didn't I?"

"Then why did you come here? I hardly believe it was to find an interpreter."

Her sarcastic tone prompted him to laugh mockingly. "You're right about that. I've been asking myself the same question. I told myself that I'd just snatch another little glimpse..." A wicked grin flashed over his face. "And perhaps make you nervous, which I seem to have succeeded at."

"You're a wretched man!" she cried out. "And I don't have to stand here and endure your taunts. What if I am 'unrestrained?' Though I think it's hardly fair for you to make such a judgment when

Deborah Martin

you scarcely know me—but what if I am? All I did was go out with my friends to the docks. Why is it your concern? Why can't you just leave me alone?"

His lips hardened. "You can dispense with the act with me. I've already said I won't say a word to your father. About that or any of your other indiscretions."

"I—I don't know what you mean," she said, confused.

His grim smile chilled her. "Let's not fence anymore with words. There are better ways the time could be spent."

His hand now clasped hers. He lowered his gaze to her slender hand as his thumb rubbed ever-widening circles in her delicate palm. She too looked down and realized that her fingers were trembling. She snatched her hand away. His eyes like blue steel rose to her face to pierce her composure, mesmerizing her. She tried to will herself to look away from his gaze, smoky with passion, but she felt trapped in its depths.

"It's really a shame I must leave Bangkok in a few days," he continued, his eyes never leaving her face. "If I had more time, I'd try to convince you to show me as much affection as you do your other admirers. Who knows? Once you came to know me better, you might stop asking me to leave you alone. As it is, I'll have to wait until I return."

Before she could retort that she had no other admirers and certainly didn't wish him as one, he lifted her hand in his once again to press a kiss into the sensitive palm.

"*Au revoir, ma petite*," he said before walking away, leaving her to stare blindly after him and to wonder how she'd entangled herself with such a man.

Chapter Four

Esme stared after Lord Winthrop in worried silence. Then, as she started to enter the house, she nearly collided with Miriam, who was hurrying out the door. Miriam turned aside for a moment to flash Esme a warning glance as she passed by.

"May I have a word with your lordship?" Miriam called to Lord Winthrop in a voice that demanded obedience.

He paused, an expression of contempt briefly crossing his face. Then he nodded, and Miriam accompanied him down the road. Esme watched them, unable to hear the exchange, but troubled nonetheless. What could her aunt possibly be telling him? Esme doubted it was something pleasant; she only hoped it didn't provoke him too much.

Too flustered by the morning's events to remain there, she wandered around the house to the outdoors kitchen. She hoped to lose herself in work.

She desperately needed to take her mind off Lord Winthrop.

She helped the maid shred carrots for the Siamese salad her father so liked, but her mind wandered back to the envoy. She told herself he unnerved her only because he was so devastatingly handsome. No one in Bangkok, she felt certain, could match his long, perfectly formed limbs and powerful shoulders. And those eyes! Each time he turned them on her, a thrill of both fear and fascination gripped her. They seemed to see into her very thoughts, but she knew his perceptiveness was deceiving. His behavior toward her had shown he had no idea what she was really like. Sometimes, she realized, it was as if he saw someone else in her place and tried to make her fit that other image.

Ah, well, Esme decided, it did no good to think about him. He was a puzzle. He hadn't revealed her secret yet, although she couldn't help but wonder what he and her aunt were discussing at that very moment. Perhaps she would have been better off telling her father everything in the first place.

With the salad finished and nothing else to do, she reentered the house and walked past her father's study. He startled her from her thoughts, calling to her as he saw her flit past the doorway.

"Come here, dear, I want to speak to you for a moment."

She sighed. Her father was certain to ask her more about Lord Winthrop, and she just didn't know what to tell him.

"Sit down, Esme," he said as she entered the room.

Dutifully, she sat in the chair he beckoned to.

"Lord Winthrop seems enamored of you. You gave me the impression you didn't get along at all."

He paused for her answer, his kindly brown eyes watching her closely.

"As I recall," she replied, "I told you I didn't like him. I've no idea what he feels about me, but I imagine it's a slight emotion. He is, after all, far above my station."

"You shouldn't talk that way," he said tenderly. "Your mother was born a lady even if I'm a mere teacher."

"Oh, Father," she said, rising to put her arms around his waist, "it's you who shouldn't speak that way. You're every bit as good as he is or better. You know I don't care about titles and fortunes."

Gently, James held her to him, brushing her hair away from her face as he'd done so many times when she was a child.

"Sometimes, Esme," he said hesitantly, "I think Miriam was right. I should have let you go to England. You could have learned to be a proper lady. You might have had a good husband, one to match your beauty and intelligence. Here you're hardly ever seen by anyone who would be good for you."

"You're good for me," she whispered.

"No, dear. The truth is I'm very bad for you. Your mother and I both let you do as you wished, because we truly believed it was best. But I was wrong, as your aunt's so fond of pointing out. I'm afraid for you, child. His lordship told me you were a bit un-restrained and I know he's right. Someday you'll go too far. Then I'll have to send you to England and get you away from this wild place."

"I wouldn't want to leave you," she said softly.

He ruffled her hair. "I must admit, dear, I'd have difficulty sending you away. You're my little trea-sure. I want to do the right things for you, but some-times I just don't know how."

Deborah Martin

Esme's eyes filled with tears as she tightened her arms around her father's waist. Guilt overwhelmed her. Here she was trying to hide from her father what she'd done when he really only wanted the best for her. She should tell him what had happened. Surely he would understand. She should confess all, but she was so afraid that Aunt Miriam would convince her father to make her marry once she heard the story.

Yet she hated deceiving her father. Perhaps if she made him realize how she regretted disobeying him, he'd forgive her. She had to try. She couldn't bear to go on keeping her secret.

"Father," she began, "I really must tell you something—"

She broke off as Miriam entered the room, clutching a bundle in her arms. With vengeance in her eyes, Miriam came to stand before Esme and her father.

"Your daughter's really done it this time, James. She's gone too far," her aunt announced with a twisted smile.

"What are you talking about?" James asked, suddenly defensive.

"I'm talking about her affair with a married man," Miriam said coldly.

"What?" Esme replied, her face mirroring her shock. Her father's gasp beside her made her furious with her aunt for making such an awful accusation. He clutched her to him as he glared at his sister.

"Who's told you this ghastly lie?" he demanded.

Miriam shrank a little as she saw his fury, but she persisted. "I heard about it from Harriett. Her husband wouldn't reveal the man's name, but she says the story's all over town, so it won't be long before I find that out, too."

To Esme's relief and her aunt's consternation, her father threw back his head and laughed. "The old gossip must have been crazy when she bought that tale. You can't tell me you believed her." Then he sobered. "But we mustn't allow her to spread such a lie about Esme. You'll have to tell her she's mistaken."

"You may not believe that," Miriam said stiffly, "after I tell you everything else."

"Everything else?" James asked, his glance turning to Esme who looked from her aunt to her father in confusion.

"First, allow me to ask Esme a question or two."

"Miriam, I really don't see the point—"

"Be quiet and listen. Then you'll see what a hellion you raised."

Miriam's tone persuaded Esme's father to remain silent.

Miriam fixed Esme with a cold stare. "You deny that you've been having an illicit love affair with a married man?"

"Of course I deny it," Esme said, giving her aunt a look of withering contempt. "What a ridiculous assertion!"

"Then let's consider another assertion. Tell me, do you also deny this is yours?" Miriam undid the bundle she'd been clasping to her chest, and pulled out a piece of blue silk.

Esme blanched as she recognized her sarong and scarf. She'd stuffed them hurriedly in the bottom of one of her drawers, and had forgotten to hide them in a safer place. A wave of nausea hit her as she realized that her aunt intended to use her escapade to lend credence to the other rumor.

"Are you going to pretend," her aunt continued, "that you don't own these . . . these pieces of inde-

Deborah Martin

cent clothing? Because if you are, you might explain why you were on the docks a week ago last night."

Esme's heart sank as she realized her aunt knew everything. She glanced at her father for help, but his face was impassive as he awaited her answer.

"The clothes are mine," she whispered. How had her aunt found out? Had her two Siamese friends spilled the truth? She couldn't believe Lamoon and Mai would betray her like that, they'd known what would happen if her aunt ever learned the truth. The more obvious choice was Lord Winthrop, who'd just been speaking to her aunt. "Who—who told you about the docks?" she asked tremulously.

Her father released his hold on her abruptly.

"I'm the one asking the questions here, young lady," Miriam retorted. "I've heard a great deal about your little escapade, so don't try to create some story to cover for yourself—like the one you gave me about that bruise. You went to see that heathen gathering without the permission of either myself or your father. Two sailors accosted you, and Lord Winthrop came gallantly to the rescue. Have I left anything out so far?"

"No," Esme said faintly.

"Lord Winthrop insisted that nothing happened on the dock. As if I could believe that! I remember that bruise. And I certainly don't trust him either, alone at night with a barely clad young girl. Even if I believed that the story of the married man isn't true, I'd have to wonder if you have any virtue left after those sailors and a notorious rake like Lord Winthrop finished with you."

Both Esme and her father gasped in shock.

Her aunt continued, ignoring their reaction, "No wonder Lord Winthrop was so eager to dance with you last night. I should have known when I couldn't find you that you'd disappeared into some quiet room with him for another lewd dalliance. You wicked, wicked girl!''

"Did he tell you all that?'' Esme retorted, her black eyes flashing with rage. "Do you honestly believe I'd do such a thing. That I'd let him . . . let him have his way with me?''

"Of that I'm not completely certain, to be honest. I searched your room after I spoke with him. That's when I found that wretched costume and something even worse—this handkerchief that was near your ball gown. And that's all the proof I needed.'' She held high the offending piece of linen and then handed it to Esme's father. "I might add that the handkerchief bears initials that match Lord Winthrop's. With that and your meeting on the docks, I can well imagine what happened during your long absence from the ballroom. It's enough to make a decent woman ill.''

"That's enough!'' James said sharply. "Don't you think you're jumping to conclusions a bit?''

"I don't know, James. What do you think? She disappeared into the ballroom with Lord Winthrop, but when I entered it a few moments later, I couldn't find her anywhere. Then after a long absence, I found her in the dressing room, acting very nervous. Shortly afterward, Lord Winthrop emerged from the back parlor. I wondered what was going on, but didn't think too much of it. Until I found his handkerchief with her ball gown, that is.''

"But surely you aren't suggesting that Lord Winthrop compromised Esme?'' James demanded sternly, surprising his daughter with his hard tone.

"I don't know what to think. But the fact remains that she was out at night in this—this thing . . .''

77

Deborah Martin

She waved the dress wildly. "And she was taken for a common whore by sailors. Such behavior makes me wonder if Harriett's 'gossip' was accurate after all."

"I can hardly believe this." Her father slumped into a chair and buried his face in his hands.

"Father, I haven't had an affair with a married man!" Esme protested. "The whole thing's absurd."

"But the other is true," he muttered, running his hands through his hair.

"She's exaggerating everything—"

"You did sneak out and go to Loy Krathong."

"Yes, but—" she began.

"You admit that, because you can't deny it," he said, lifting his head. His eyes glittered with pain. "Your aunt has evidence strong enough to convict you."

"Father! I wouldn't lie to you! Nothing happened between Lord Winthrop and me! And I certainly haven't...haven't been involved with a married man!"

Her father shook his head sadly. "I don't know what to believe anymore. Even if Harriett has somehow gotten wind of an exaggerated tale, the fact that you sneaked out of the house and disobeyed me makes me wonder what else you've been doing behind my back. You did lie to me. You told me you couldn't stand Lord Winthrop when all the time you were slipping away to rendezvous with him in private. You sat in this drawing room, pretending to be little more than a stranger to him when all the time..."

"Father," Esme said desperately, "I wasn't lying. I don't like the man, and I certainly would never have met him secretly. Lord Winthrop and I have done nothing wrong together. You must believe me! I admit I went to Loy Krathong, but Lord Winthrop

78

stopped the sailors from hurting me and then we three came home. I wasn't alone, you know. Lamoon and Mai were with me the entire time. They'll vouch for my innocence."

"I'm sure they would!" Miriam spat out. "And I suppose you expect us to believe two heathen girls who'd do anything for you. They wouldn't think twice about lying."

Esme ignored her aunt. "Father, *nothing happened*. Surely you know me well enough to know I wouldn't discard my virtue so easily."

"And last night?" he asked.

"We were alone for a few minutes," she answered, raising her eyes to meet his steadfastly.

"You see!" Miriam nearly screamed in outrage.

"But nothing happened," Esme continued. "I asked him not to tell anyone about seeing me last week. He agreed. I . . . I cried some, I'm afraid, so he offered me his handkerchief which I forgot to return. That was it. We parted ways."

"And nothing passed between you other than that?" James persisted, his eyes narrowing.

Esme couldn't stop the blush that rose to her face.

"I think I have my answer," her father replied.

"Father!" she cried, moving to kneel beside him. "It's not what you think! I would never disgrace you that way. Please, Father, ask him. He'll tell you what happened. He's an honest man."

"And why should he tell me the truth?" James asked, his lips forming a thin line. "If indeed he took my daughter's virtue, would he admit it when she will not? He knows I have no proof, and you won't accuse him, so why should he reveal himself?"

"Because he's innocent," she told him, clasping his knee with her hands, her eyes now flooding with

79

tears. "We're both innocent." She turned her head to glare up at her aunt. "It's only that woman with her evil mind who makes it seem otherwise. Can't you see she wants you to believe a lie?"

Miriam began to retort, but James's raised hand stopped her. His eyes looked at Esme with pity, making her despair. "Poor child," he said, reaching down as if to stroke her hair and then jerking his hand back without touching her. "You're so much like your mother. So beautiful. I can almost understand your being involved with a man like Lord Winthrop."

"You must believe me, Father! I'm not involved with anyone! No one! It's all lies!" Tears streamed down her face, unchecked.

Her father watched her silently, his face showing how torn he was by the sight of her crying. "It's not all lies, child. You said so yourself. So how can I know what is true and what isn't? Your aunt has been right all along, I'm afraid. She said I was wrong not to be stricter with you. She warned me that if I weren't careful, you'd end up as faithless as your mother. But I suppose I never quite believed your mother was faithless. I kept thinking there'd been some mistake."

Esme's expression turned defiant. "There *was*! I know it, Father. Mother was never faithless. She loved you!" Esme cried fiercely, wiping her tears away with the back of her hand.

Miriam snorted. "So we're back to that, are we?

James flashed Miriam a warning glance, then turned back to Esme. "Listen to me, Esme. Much as you don't want to believe it, your mother deceived us all."

"I'll never believe it! I was with her that day and she didn't seem sad or depressed or anything."

"Your mother was very good at hiding her feelings if she thought they would upset you, dear. I couldn't believe it myself at first, but the letter was most definitely in her handwriting and she died with the bottle of poison in her hand."

"Someone must have killed her," Esme insisted. It was the only explanation she'd been able to give for her mother's strange death.

Her father gave a bitter laugh. "I almost wish that were the case. But think about it. Who would kill your mother? And why? No, she committed suicide, and all for the love of some man whose name I don't even know. She was faithless, and I didn't even realize it. That's the worst part of it all."

"She wasn't untrue to you. I'm sure of it," Esme insisted. "And I'm not untrue to you either. I would never betray you. I love you!"

"Yes, I think you do. But don't you see? You've already begun being deceitful. Worse yet, you've been indiscriminate with your favors—just like your mother was. It's happening all over again. I couldn't save your mother, but I can save you from destroying your life. You're still my daughter. I must ensure that you take responsibility for your actions. Otherwise, who knows what outrageous transgression will be next?"

"What will you do?" Esme asked, her voice barely a whisper. Her father's face had now stiffened into an unreadable mask, and, for the first time in her life, she feared him.

"There's only one solution," Miriam said, seizing the moment. "We must find her a suitable husband."

"Oh, no," Esme said in defeat. She should have known it would come to this.

"I don't suppose the envoy would marry her,"

81

Deborah Martin

James said wearily. "She's far beneath him in station, in spite of Renee's family heritage. And he doesn't strike me as the sort to marry against his will just to save a girl's reputation."

"This is insane," Esme muttered. "No one outside this room knows what happened that night except Lord Winthrop, Lamoon, and Mai."

"It's not that night I'm worried about!" her aunt responded. "It's the other story that's on the lips of everyone in the foreign community."

"Then who will marry her, Miriam?" her father asked.

"Mr. Michaels will. I'm sure of it. He's asked for her hand twice before. And I don't think he cares much about Esme's reputation since he danced with her repeatedly last night, even though everyone must have already been talking about her affair." Miriam looked grimly at her niece. "He'll marry her all right."

"But you can't make me marry him!" Esme cried.

Her father looked at her, tenderness warring with some other elusive emotion. "Isn't there another way, Miriam? Can't you just take her back to England? That's what you've always wanted, isn't it? You can put her forth properly there, and no one will ever know what's gone on here."

"That sort of thing has a tendency to follow one," Miriam replied, crossing her arms across her chest.

Clearly, she was no longer willing even to be saddled with her niece in England. With a mixture of anger and pain, Esme realized her aunt was determined to get her married.

"True," her father said hesitantly.

"You've said yourself she needs a firm hand to teach her not to make her mother's mistakes. Michaels will give her that."

82

"But Michaels... I don't really like the man," James replied. "And I—I just don't know if I can give her to a man so much older than she."

"He's not that much older. He's only in his forties." As Esme's father continued to look uncertain, Miriam changed tactics. "You should also consider that she might have a child. Would you want the child to have no father?" she asked maliciously.

Esme's eyes lit up in fury. She knew what went on in the bedroom. Lamoon and Mai had told her everything. It horrified her that her aunt could think she'd done anything like that.

"There's no child," Esme cried. "If you give me to that—that wretched merchant, I assure you he'll be the only one to give me a child, if he's even capable of doing so." Being around her Siamese friends had made her incredibly blunt about men's sexual prowess, although she knew less about what happened between a man and a woman than she let on to Lamoon and Mai.

But her bluntness only shocked her father. "I can't believe my own daughter would speak this way!" he said, visibly upset. "Miriam's right. You've been left to run wild far too long. Mr. Michaels is perfectly respectable. He won't take you and then toss you away like...others would."

"What about love, Father?" Esme asked, her eyes pleading with him. "Doesn't it matter?"

"I suppose you think you love this married man—"

"There is no married man!" she sobbed out.

"Or Lord Winthrop—"

"Never!" Esme said.

Her father gazed at her. "Well, perhaps not them. But you hope to love someone. I assure you, dear, you'll be better off with someone you don't love who

83

will indulge your every whim, than with someone you love who doesn't love you."

"Can't it ever be mutual?"

"No," he said harshly. "It never works that way."

His obvious reference to her mother pained her. But his willingness to give her to a man she didn't love hurt her even more. "Please, Father, I don't wish to marry Mr. Michaels." She buried her face in his lap as sobs wracked her slender frame.

"But you'll marry him anyway," he said emotionlessly, not touching her.

Her father's coldness chilled her. She drew into herself, willing the tears to stop and her breathing to become even. Guardedly, she lifted her head, but her eyes avoided her father's, afraid of what she might see.

Instead she rose from the floor to look straight into Miriam's face. "You've wanted this all along, haven't you? You want to be rid of me, so you can go back to England and still keep your precious inheritance."

Miriam looked shocked. "You see, James?" her aunt retorted, returning Esme's stare with one just as bold. "Your daughter's become a very wicked girl. She shames the family and then accuses perfectly innocent people of malice." She sniffed loudly. "Are you going to sit there and allow her to say these things to me or will you take some action for a change?"

"That's enough, both of you!" James said sharply, rising from his chair to stand between them. "Esme, you're confined to your room until I come to some decision in this matter. Miriam, I think it would be wise if you leave us both alone until we've had a chance to think over the possibilities."

Miriam drew herself up proudly and stalked from

the room. Esme remained. She laid her hand on her father's arm.

"I really am sorry, Father," she said, her lower lip trembling in spite of her attempts at control. "I never meant to hurt you by going to Loy Krathong. It was a foolish act. But I promise it won't be repeated."

"You kept it hidden, Esme. That's what disturbs me. It makes me fear that the rumor about this married man and your aunt's accusation about his lordship are true."

"Father! I'd never do such a thing. Never!"

He looked at her pleadingly. "Esme, don't break my heart more by lying. Tell me the truth about this married man. Who is it? What is his name? If you'd give me some sign that you regret what you've done, I could find it in my heart to forgive you."

"You must forgive me without hearing a name," she said in despair, "because I can't give you one when there's not one to give. I can't regret what I haven't done. You'll have to accept that someone is spreading this vicious lie about me!"

"And who would do such a thing? Can you tell me that?"

That was the problem. She had no idea why someone would seek to destroy her reputation. "No," she choked out.

"People don't create horrible rumors without a reason, Esme," he said wearily. "Stories like that are only spread when they contain a grain of truth. I'm sorry, dear," he continued tenderly as she turned her face away from him. "Even if the story is exaggerated, it is certainly based on something you've done, and I can't let you continue to run loose in Bangkok. This Loy Krathong thing, for

85

example. It's bound to be bandied about the city in no time by Lamoon and Mai—"

"They wouldn't—"

"And that will just give people more reason to believe you're anything but a proper lady."

For the first time in her life, Esme felt some of her anger directed toward her own father. Bitterly, she said, "Isn't it a little late to make me into a proper lady, Father? All those years you thought it fine that I lived as I wished. Now suddenly my actions have become crucial. Is that really fair?"

James blanched as he recognized the truth of his daughter's statements, but he refused to yield. "No, it's not fair. But that doesn't change the fact that something must be done. I may have come to accept my responsibilities later than I should have, but now that I see them, I must behave as a responsible father. This may sound odd, but I must do so for your mother's sake. She wouldn't want you to repeat the same mistakes she made."

Esme looked at his stony face and realized that this time her father wasn't going to change his mind. With despair in her step, she left.

She wasn't there to see the solitary tear that escaped from her father's eye.

Ian stood on the ship's deck, staring out over Bangkok. He hadn't had much luck at the orphanage. Anyone talented enough to be an interpreter was away on another job, so he was back where he'd started. He could use the consulate's interpreter until he left the city, but the consulate was reluctant to provide him with one after that. Thanks to some mix-up in communications, they'd assumed Chan was Siamese and hadn't bothered to make arrangements for an interpreter. There was an interpreter at the consulate in Chiengmai, but that didn't help him during the trip.

Too bad he couldn't hire Esme Montrose, he thought, and then laughed at the image of her trying to get Siamese crewmen to pay attention to her. *Such a spirited little thing,* he thought. *She'd certainly liven up the long trip.*

But even if she weren't a woman and a completely unrealistic choice for interpreter, she wouldn't go with him now. Not after the conversation he'd had with her aunt that afternoon at the Montrose house. The woman had heard about the episode on the docks from Harriet Bingham. Undoubtedly, Esme's Siamese friends had been too talkative, and the story had filtered into the foreign community.

Unfortunately, Esme's aunt had learned of his involvement and had reached the worst conclusions possible. When she'd first confronted him, he'd felt an uncharacteristic desire to protect Esme by denying everything, but he'd rapidly realized that would be unwise. He'd had to admit to the parts that were true so he could set her straight on the parts that weren't.

She hadn't believed a word he'd said. She'd even accused him of being Esme's lover, for she'd gotten wind of the rumor about her niece and another man. She'd then insinuated that Ian must have been the one to ruin her niece.

But Ian had pointed out that he'd been in town little more than a week, hardly enough time to engage in a torrid love affair, particularly since he'd been busy with his duties the entire time. He wasn't about to tell the woman the man's true identity, but he could tell that Esme's aunt wished to corner him into marrying her niece. He didn't want that for certain.

Still, he hated being forced to tell her aunt the events of that night. But the more he thought about it, the more he knew he'd had no choice. What else could he have done? To deny it ever happened was out of the question, so he'd settled for making it sound as innocuous as possible. Of course, Esme would never believe that her friends had spilled the truth and not him.

Why did it matter so much to him anyway what she thought of him? She was just another promiscuous young miss who'd discovered the pleasures of lovemaking long before she should have. He'd recognized her wild streak the first moment he'd seen her. It should have put him off, he knew, because she was so much like Caroline. But for some reason it hadn't. It still didn't. Damn, if she didn't stick in his mind. His imagination played games with him, showing him visions of what that curtain of black hair would look like spread on a pillow. Her dark eyes haunted him. When she was angry, they flashed, and when she was aroused, as she'd been last night, they glowed like black pearls.

A pity he wouldn't get to experience his imaginings any time soon. But he must put her behind him. He needed his mind free of encumbrances if he were to do his job in Chiengmai. Then when he returned to Bangkok, he could take the time to get to know Miss Montrose. Ah, yes, he'd like that very much. She resisted him now, but even that resistance wasn't very strong. She'd have three months or so to lose her antipathy. Before long she would admit she was as eager to have him as he was to have her.

But what if her aunt and her father did force her to marry before he returned? He doubted they'd be successful, for as Godfrey said, no one would have her now. But what if someone wanted her after all, perhaps one of those merchants at the ball? The thought made him stiffen. He hated thinking of her married to any of those men.

Why couldn't he put her out of his mind? He wanted to do something—to return to her house and find out what they intended for her. But he knew the wisest course was to stay away and keep his name out of the affair as much as possible.

"Lord Winthrop?"

Ian turned to find Chan, his recently appointed secretary, standing behind him, flanked by two Siamese men and Somkit, the consulate interpreter.

"Yes, what is it?"

"I've brought the boat pilots. You may wish to talk to them. They say the trip will take six weeks."

Ian groaned. "Six weeks! I was told three! You know the consulate promised I'd be there in a month. I didn't even plan to leave until next week."

Chan relayed this bit of information to the interpreter who passed it on to the men.

The older Siamese man consulted with the younger one. They discussed furiously, waving their arms and gesturing at the sky from time to time. Then they spoke at length to the interpreter.

"They say if you have the houseboats pulled by steam launches," the interpreter told Ian, "they can perhaps be there in a month. This is the best time of year to travel. The rains have left the canals high, but not too high. But steam launches are expensive."

Ian ran his fingers through his hair wearily. "Tell them we'll use the launches. We'll pay them whatever it takes to get us there in a month."

The interpreter relayed the message. The men

smiled broadly and *waied* to Ian. Then they spoke
again to the interpreter.

"They will get you there in a month, they say,"
the interpreter told Ian.

"Sir, may I speak with you privately?" Chan
asked.

"Certainly," Ian answered, leading him down the
ship's deck away from the other men.

"Sir, remember this is the Orient. Like most Orientals, the Siamese will say anything to placate you
and will consider it good business to do so."

"I know. They believe in being amiable, in pleas-
ing at all costs. If they sense you want something,
they'll tell you they can get it for you even when
they can't."

"So what if these men cannot get to Chiengmai
on time?"

"We have little choice," Ian replied, glancing
warily back at the two men. "By all accounts, these
two are the most skilled in the business. We'll just
have to hope they can get us there reasonably soon.
The French are moving quickly, and Prince Mataya
is reportedly very anxious."

"Yes, you said that the expeditionary force they
moved into Mong Sai last week worries him."

"Damn the consulate!" Ian muttered. "They've
really made a mess of it. I could have been here
sooner had I known it was necessary. We'll just have
to do our best to leave Bangkok earlier than we'd
planned."

"We still don't have an interpreter."

"I know. If I must, I'll force the consulate to lend
us Somkit. Rushton won't like that one bit. He
claims he can't spare the man. If I give him no
choice, though, he'll have to. But we've still a few
days to find our own interpreter, since we can't get

our party together in less than three days."

"Then shall I tell them to be ready to leave in three days?"

Ian's brows drew together as he frowned. "Yes, I suppose you must. But say we won't pay them unless they transport us there in a month. That should give them sufficient incentive. And tell them I don't need a boat for myself. That might help. The fewer boats we have to move, the better."

As Chan walked back to the Siamese men, Ian watched him leave. He wished he'd never let Lord Rosebery convince him to lead this thorny expedition. So much was at stake. Aside from the talks at Chiengmai, there was his other more delicate and equally important mission of finding the spy who was passing information to the French. But at present the French and the nervous Siamese occupied his full attention.

With the French pushing steadily westward, the Siamese were worried. Siam had never been colonized by any European country, and they didn't wish to relinquish their independence now. Britain insisted that the Siamese were exaggerating the problem, but Ian wasn't so sure. From all reports, France now had its eye on northern land that bordered British Burma. Ian hoped to get more accurate reports from the Siamese in Chiengmai. Reports that reached Bangkok had been contradictory since the whole thing began. The Chiengmai consul had been ill for some time and couldn't handle his diplomatic duties, and Rushton had had more pressing duties in Bangkok, so the job had been given to Ian.

It was a sticky job at best. If the French really were moving into territory they'd promised England they had no interest in, then Siam would at last have graphic proof that, for all its blustering, England wasn't going to protect it by taking on a major power.

There could be war. No question about it, Ian decided as he turned toward his cabin. He must reach Chiengmai as soon as possible, or people like Esme and her father might find themselves in deep trouble. Siam might not be a European colony, but if pressed by the West, it could react in the volatile way so many rebellious natives of English colonies had in the past. Anyone with a white skin could be in danger.

Suddenly he remembered what Esme had said a week ago. "After all, we had no trouble in this heathen town until your fellow Englishmen came along." In a flash he saw her as she looked that night, her hair caught by the wind, shimmering in the moonlight, while she held the blue silk tightly against her heaving breasts. Pray God her words weren't prophetic. Pray God that between the French and the English there wasn't enough trouble in Bangkok to mar that beautiful face.

With that sobering thought, he entered his cabin.

Chapter Five

Esme stood in her room, staring out the window at the mysterious jungle as she had so many times since the day before. If only she could escape into it. Just disappear. But where could she go? What could she do? Siam might be her home, but it wasn't always kind to foreigners. Despite King Chulalongkorn's efforts to westernize the country, the Siamese regarded all white people with suspicion. And as for her friends... Lamoon and Mai loved her, but their husbands would never allow them to support her. No, a foreign woman couldn't survive alone in Bangkok.

Besides, her family would find her. After all, how many young English girls lived in Bangkok? Every one of them was known. She wouldn't stay hidden for long.

Esme heard the door open behind her and her eyes filled with tears. The time had come.

"Mr. Michaels is here," her father said behind her in an aloof voice. "He's heard the rumors, but has renewed his suit anyway. He wants to see you."

Esme knew without asking that her aunt's claim that Lord Winthrop had also compromised her had now become part of the gossip mill, and had more than likely been spread by their own servants. So instead of one rumor there were now two rumors circulating about her.

"I suppose you wish me to tell him I'll marry him," she said without turning around. She couldn't face her father yet.

"That isn't necessary. He knows you'll be a reluctant bride, but he also knows, as do I, that you'll come to care for him in time."

"That's not the same thing as love, is it?" Esme turned away from the window to meet her father's gaze squarely.

He stiffened, a flash of pain crossing his face. "You don't want love. Love can destroy. Look at your mother. When she met me, she gave up everything for what she foolishly thought was love. When that proved false, she fruitlessly followed another dream of love that led her to end her life. At least with Michaels, you'll be spared her pain. What's more, you'll live comfortably, even richly. That will do you more good than some fickle emotion."

"I know you don't believe that, Father. Nor do I. I am like Mother, for I must love the man I marry, and my affection can't be bought. She relinquished her inheritance for you. I know I'd have done the same in her place."

He flinched at her words. Then his gaze grew stern. "But you're not in her place. You admitted you love no one in particular. If you had another suitor, I'd consider him. But under the circumstances . . ." He hesitated, as if reminding himself of his decision, then went on more firmly, "William Michaels will be good to you. In a few years you'll thank me for choosing so well."

Esme squared her shoulders and lifted her chin with determination. "For this, I'll never thank you, Father. Never."

"We'll see," was all her father said, his tone of finality making it clear that the discussion was over. Then he gestured toward the door.

She preceded him from the room, her face a mask of indifference but her heart bitterly rebelling.

When they entered the drawing room, William Michaels was standing by a portrait of Esme's mother, staring at it with a mixed expression of pleasure and hatred that puzzled Esme. Her father didn't seem to notice, however, for he greeted the man cordially as soon as they entered the room.

Then their attention shifted to her. She held her head straighter, knowing that her father wouldn't want her to disgrace him by any show of rebelliousness. But she couldn't help feeling like a sacrificial virgin, for Mr. Michaels appraised her as if she were a piece of merchandise to be bargained for.

She returned his appraisal with a critical one of her own. So this man was to be her husband, was he? She tried to tell herself he wasn't an ogre. When they'd danced together at the ball, he'd attempted to amuse her with stories of his travels, some of which had even interested her. But none of that had changed the involuntary shiver that passed through her whenever he came near her. She couldn't put her finger on what she found so distasteful in him. Granted, he was older than she, at least as old as her father. And he was nearly bald. But those things didn't bother her so much as the bold light in his eyes whenever he looked at her and a certain cruelty about his mouth.

After surveying her, he turned to her father with a kindly smile painted on his face. "May I take Esme for a walk? I think we should discuss some matters privately."

Her father's gaze turned to Esme, and he nodded. "Yes, but don't go too far. Not at least until things are . . . are more definite."

"Of course. You're completely right." Turning to Esme, Michaels offered her his arm. "My dear, will you accompany me?"

"If I must," she couldn't resist saying, but immediately regretted it when her father flushed. "I mean, if you please." Lowering her eyes, she took his hand, but inwardly her mind raced. She had to find a way out of this ludicrous situation. She must! Perhaps Mr. Michaels didn't know the full story. Her father hadn't said which rumors the man had heard. Perhaps if he knew everything, he wouldn't want to marry her.

Thus, as soon as they left the house, words tumbled from her mouth. "Mr. Michaels, has Father told you why he's suddenly so willing to accept your suit?"

The merchant smiled almost imperceptibly, as if he knew why she asked the question. "I'm afraid, my dear, your father didn't have to tell me. The stories concerning your . . . ah . . . infidelities have circulated freely about Bangkok."

She blushed. "And you still wish to marry me, even though I've supposedly been compromised by at least two men?" she asked bluntly. She was mortified to discuss such things with a man she scarcely knew, but she must frighten him off, she told herself.

He smiled again and patted her hand. "It doesn't really matter. I'd marry you no matter what people said."

Now that odd intensity was back in his eyes, making Esme wonder why he pursued her so tenaciously.

"What do you mean? Why do you wish to marry me?"

"You're young, beautiful, intelligent. What other reasons do I need?"

"But my aunt told me you could marry anyone you wish because you're wealthy." She didn't add that her aunt had urged Esme before to accept Mr. Michaels's proposals and avail herself of that wealth.

"I don't wish to marry anyone else."

His voice had a hard edge to it that she hadn't noticed before.

"Why not? There must be other beautiful girls who'd marry you for your wealth. Girls who aren't . . . so compromised."

"Possibly there are. But I only want you."

Frustrated, she jerked her hand away from his arm. "But I don't want you! Can't you see? I don't wish to marry you! If I'm forced to marry you, I'll be unhappy and make your life miserable. You can't want that, can you?"

Throughout this outburst, Mr. Michaels stood watching her, a bitter smile pasted on his face. "You look very much like your mother, do you know that?" he said quietly as he observed her with interest. "You have her beauty, but you don't have her cool grace."

His sudden comment stunned her. She'd known her mother knew Mr. Michaels, but now she wondered what their relationship had been. "How close were you to Mother?" she asked with a curiosity she couldn't hide.

At her question, he eyed her warily. "Your mother and I were friends," he said, his eyes narrowing. "But that has nothing to do with us."

Esme feared it had far more to do with her than Mr. Michaels would say. A terrible thought suddenly occurred to her. Could Mr. Michaels have been the man her mother's note said she'd killed herself over? Esme stole a quick glance at Mr. Michaels, who'd placed her hand on his fleshy arm once again. No, she couldn't believe her mother would have preferred the balding merchant to her handsome father.

"You'll be happy with me, you know," Mr. Michaels continued as he led her down the heavily rutted road to the side of the river. His voice was almost menacing, belying the comfort he intended with his words. "You'll have servants at your command and a house by the sea as well as one here in the city. With me, you'll see the world. What more could a young woman want?"

Emboldened by her fear of his strange manner, she asked frankly, "Do you love me, Mr. Michaels?"

Her question seemed to startle him, for he stopped abruptly in the path. "I want you to be my wife. That's enough."

She recoiled from his firm statement. "You want to marry me, but you hardly know me. I could be as deceitful as my aunt seems to think. I could take a lover or anything—"

Mr. Michaels jerked her around to face him, the soft pudginess of his face distorted into a mask of ugliness. "You'll *not* take a lover, I assure you! Once you're mine, I won't have you belonging to anyone else. Do you hear?" He began to shake her, leaving

Esme dumbstruck that her father could have so misjudged him. This was no longer a man who wished to have a younger wife for his companion. This was a man obsessed.

"You've no choice," he continued. "Once we're married, you'll stay with me. And I'll make you desire me, you'll see." His voice was hoarse as he whispered the words, drawing her close enough that she could smell his cloyingly scented breath. He gripped her arms so tightly that she feared he'd bruise them.

The shock showing plainly on Esme's face seemed to bring him to his senses. Instantly, he thrust her away from him, wheeling around to gaze over the river that flowed peacefully past the city. For a few moments, he was silent. Esme became more nervous as the silence continued, broken only by the faint cries of occasional Siamese merchants hawking their wares on the water.

"I'm sorry, dear," he said finally, once more the considerate gentleman. "You see, I care for you a great deal. Sometimes I get carried away by the thought that you'll soon be mine."

She didn't answer, but for some reason she didn't believe his explanation.

"We'll get on very well together," he went on. "I know we shall."

By this time she was shaking her head mindlessly. "I can't marry you," she whispered. "I don't care what Father says. I can't marry you."

"Why not?" he asked, pinning her with his stare.

How could she tell him the real reason? That she didn't love him? It would matter even less to him than it did to her father. "I just don't wish to marry you," she said feebly.

The assessing gaze he fixed on her made her trem-

Deborah Martin

ble. "But you will," he murmured with a grim smile, gripping her arm to lead her back to the house.

She tried to wrench away from him, but for a merchant used to spending his days in an office he was surprisingly strong. So she attempted reasoning with him.

"You won't be happy with a woman who doesn't want you. Eventually you'll regret marrying me," she said, her heart beating madly with her need to convince him.

"I think not," he replied, and she could find no trace of kindness in his voice. "But don't worry. I'll treat you like a queen. Soon you'll forget that you didn't want to marry me."

Esme fell silent as she realized that Mr. Michaels had his mind set and didn't intend to change it. But she knew she couldn't marry him. She wasn't even certain she could stand to be with him for more than a few minutes. He frightened her. If she were forced to marry him, she'd do something drastic.

As they walked toward the house, Mr. Michaels was once again the picture of gentlemanly courtesy. But Esme no longer cared. Nor did she notice the jungle noises and calls of the exotic birds that so delighted her. When they reached the house, Esme couldn't look her father in the eye or even speak to him. Absorbed in her own despair, she left the casual conversation to Mr. Michaels. She stood there woodenly, scarcely able to answer any questions put to her.

With the realization that her father intended to marry her to Mr. Michaels, she found she no longer knew what to say to him. Her father mistook her silence for obstinance, so after Mr. Michaels left, he ordered her to her room. But she was glad to be

100

alone with her thoughts. She only wished they weren't so disconcerting.

That night she tossed and turned in bed, trying to get to sleep but unable to forget her conversation with Mr. Michaels. How could she marry a man she detested, a man she feared would abuse her? It was unthinkable!

Yet she was trapped, for her father wouldn't listen to her. She sobbed into her pillow, wondering how she could convince him to release her from this insane marriage. At last she fell asleep to troubled dreams in which Mr. Michaels and her father hounded her through town crying, "Whore! Whore!"

She woke up at dawn in a cold sweat. Pushing the mosquito net from the side of her bed, she sat on the edge and massaged her temples to get rid of the ache in her head. *I can't continue like this*, she thought to herself. But she could think of no way out. So when Lamoon and Mai showed up at her window to visit, they found her again gazing morosely out at the jungle.

"Essmay!" they called softly to her. "Essmay, what happen your house? *Mem* Mil send us away when we come yesterday. She say, 'Go away. You cause much trouble already!' But we come back anyway. Tell us what happen!"

Esme pounded her fists on the sill. "It's terrible! Aunt Miriam learned I went to Loy Krathong. She found out about the sailors and everything! Now she and my father are making me marry Mr. Michaels."

The two girls exchanged guilty looks, but Esme was so wrapped up in her own troubles that she dismissed their uneasiness.

"That very bad for you," they told her, speaking

English as they always did. Esme would have preferred to speak Siamese, but the two girls insisted
on practicing their English whenever possible.
"What you going do? You really going marry that
ugly Mr. Michaels?"

"I can't. I just can't. But they'll make me do it!"

"They make you marry Mr. Michaels because you
go out with us? That silly. Foreigners so silly sometimes."

"That's not the only reason." She debated
whether to tell them and finally decided to relate
what had happened at the ball, the rumor that her
aunt had heard and the one she had created, leaving
out nothing.

They looked at her in shock. "Who say such terrible things?" Lamoon asked. "Surely nobody believe them? You always modest. You wear much
clothing and you not meet men for walks."

Esme wished everyone else knew her as well as
her two friends did, for if that had been the case,
no one would have countenanced the rumors. Not
that Esme hadn't wanted to be courted. It was just
that none of the men who'd ever approached her
had touched her heart.

One man had managed to capture her interest,
she had to admit. But she put Lord Winthrop out
of her mind. She'd never forgive him for making
her situation worse by telling her aunt about Loy
Krathong. She wasn't going to start dreaming
about him again after he'd been so despicable.

"Maybe we not know Esme so well as we think,"
Mai said wickedly.

"Mai!" Esme and Lamoon shouted in unison.

"She do like one man," Mai asserted, and then
giggled. "You marry him, that handsome man who
save us. He make fabulous husband." Mai nodded

at her sister, and the two of them burst into peals of laughter.

"That's what you think. There's more to a good husband than handsome looks," Esme muttered, annoyed that Mai had so effectively read her thoughts. What's more, she disliked the simplistic way her friends approached the business of choosing a husband. But she acknowledged to herself that she wouldn't be fighting quite so hard if she were being forced to marry the envoy rather than Mr. Michaels. "He won't marry me anyway," she continued. "He's from a higher class than I am."

"You can make him marry you," Mai said slyly, a twinkle in her eye. "Go to his bed on ship. Then he have to marry you!"

"Mai!" Esme said, scandalized. "I wouldn't do such a thing! Besides, even if I did 'go to his bed,' he wouldn't have to marry me. I mean, Father and Aunt Miriam already think I've been to his bed and another man's, and they're still making me marry Mr. Michaels."

"It is your karma," Lamoon said with a shrug, espousing the Buddhist philosophy. "You accept and learn to love Mr. Michaels. Will be better later when you have children. You see."

Esme frowned at them both in irritation at their acquiescence. "If I weren't a woman," she told them fiercely, "I could run away to sea. I wish I were a man. Consider Lord Winthrop. He does as he pleases and then just leaves town when life becomes uncomfortable for him. If I could go to Chiengmai as he's doing, I'd be just fine. I could get a job teaching at one of the British schools. Remember that widowed schoolteacher, Mrs. Calvert, who taught here before? She went there. She even sent me a letter describing how beautiful Chiengmai is."

Deborah Martin

"Perhaps you ask Lord Winthrop take you there," Lamoon offered helpfully.

"Ha! There's little chance of his doing that. He's a diplomat. Do you think he'd risk his reputation by helping me escape this marriage? Absolutely not. The monster! Why, I hope he hasn't found anyone to interpret for him. I hope he's stuck here for months looking for an interpreter!"

"Why not you be interpreter?" Mai asked gently. "You speak velly good Siamese, more better than any foreigner I know. He will pay you and you go Chiengmai."

"No, no, don't you understand? He wouldn't take me unless Father let me go, and Father wouldn't do that. It's a shame, because I'd be a good interpreter. Oh, if only I were a man!"

Lamoon and Mai began to offer other suggestions, but Esme no longer noticed what they said. She was thinking. Why couldn't she dress as a man and offer to be Lord Winthrop's interpreter? Perhaps if she cut her hair and ... No, what was she thinking of? The fear of marrying Mr. Michaels had her entertaining outrageous thoughts. Dress as a man indeed! And yet ... She shook her head. It wouldn't work. Even if she could successfully disguise herself as a man and persuade Lord Winthrop to hire her, he'd wonder where this foreign man who spoke fluent Siamese had come from.

But suppose she weren't a foreign man, but a Siamese one? Could she disguise herself as a Siamese man? After all, she'd sent Lord Winthrop to the orphanage to find a suitable Siamese boy. Why couldn't she be that boy? Her brow furrowed in thought, she tried to think of a way it could be done. If she wore the orphans' uniform—the loose cotton jacket and white trousers ... She blushed. How

104

could she go about so wantonly dressed? Then she thought of Mr. Michaels's hand on her arm, and stiffened. Determinedly, she thrust her maidenly modesty aside. She must do something. If escaping meant dressing like a boy, then she'd dress like a boy!

She could braid her hair back in a queue like the orphan boys did ... No, there was her face to consider. In the dark at Loy Krathong, it had been easy to masquerade as a Siamese woman, but how could she pass for a Siamese boy in the daytime in front of Lord Winthrop who'd seen her up close?

Maybe she wouldn't have to be near him much, she told herself. Surely he wouldn't need an interpreter often on the trip. She'd only have to translate a few instructions and direct a few crewmen. In fact, she thought with a surge of excitement, Lord Winthrop probably had some underling to give those instructions for him. She could travel with the entourage to Chiengmai, and stay out of his way as much as possible. As for the discussions in Chiengmai ... Once she was there, the Siamese boy would disappear. She'd become a schoolteacher and no one would be the wiser.

But what if she were found out? She'd deal with that when it happened. At least she'd be away from Michaels and she'd have time to come up with another plan to elude him. And if she were successful, then she'd be free, able to do what she wanted. Wouldn't it be wonderful to live in Chiengmai and be her own person? She could go to Loy Krathong every year if she wished!

She leaned her arms on the windowsill, and stared idly out at the jungle. What if it didn't work out that way, though? What if she and Lord Winthrop *were* in close quarters? What if he recognized her?

If she could just stay disguised long enough to fool him for the first few days of the trip, what could he do? she told herself. He wouldn't have time to turn around and return her to Bangkok. And he wouldn't send her back alone on another boat. Of course, if she were lucky, he'd never know she'd traveled to Chiengmai with him in the first place.

Lamoon and Mai had stopped talking, intent on watching Esme as she thought through her alternatives. With a start, she noticed they were still there, observing her curiously.

"Lamoon, do you think that you could make me look like a Siamese boy?"

Lamoon's astonishment was evident in her face. "Why you want look like Siamese boy?"

"Don't you see? It's the perfect plan! I can be Lord Winthrop's interpreter, but he won't know me! Can you do it?"

Lamoon pursed her lips as she thought. "No, I not think so."

"But surely you could? I have straight black hair and dark eyes. My skin is light, but plenty of Chinese have skin almost as light as mine." Her pleading voice had some effect on Lamoon.

"'Almost' not good enough, Essmay. Lord Winthrop velly smart man. He can tell who you are."

"The sailors were fooled, even when I told them I was English. Different clothing and hair can fool many people."

"Maybe. I not know. Better if you half-and-half."

"Eurasian?"

"Yes, Eurasian."

Esme thought about that for a moment. That would be easy enough to manage. Many of the boys at the Jesuit orphanage were Eurasian, the despised offspring of Siamese mothers and their European "friends."

"I could be Eurasian," she told Lamoon. "Do you think you could make me look like a Eurasian boy, maybe like one from the orphanage?"

"Yes, we could!" said Mai who'd been listening carefully.

"She want look like Siamese and boy. That difficult to do. No, we cannot do," Lamoon insisted. "She must accept her karma."

"But, Lamoon," Mai continued excitedly, "her skin is perfect color for Eurasian. With makeup around eyes to make them crooked, she look like Siamese easily."

"Eyes will be problem," Lamoon said, now caught up in the excitement. "Shape no problem. Siamese eyes not like Chinese eyes. They almost round like yours. But your eyes give you away, because this man have looked in them when you kiss, have he not? Yes, he see your eyes and know you." She thought for a minute. "I know! You know those color glasses old Jesuit priest wear, who beat boys all time? He brought from France to protect eyes from sun. You wear glasses like those."

"Tinted glasses..." Esme muttered. "Yes, I could do that, I suppose, but where am I going to get them?"

Mai giggled. "I get them," she said, a mischievous twinkle in her eye.

"How?" Esme asked suspiciously.

"I know boy in orphanage who like velly much to have the revenge on old priest for beatings."

"You don't mean you'd have him steal the priest's glasses?" Esme asked in horror.

107

Deborah Martin

"Borrow them. He borrow them." Mai now fairly danced with delight.

"I don't know . . ." Esme said.

"You want get away or not?" Lamoon asked.

"Won't everyone be suspicious if I show up at Lord Winthrop's boat wearing stolen glasses?"

"That why we do this right before he ready to leave. He not have time to speak with priests. Your family not have time to search for you."

"You're right," Esme said. "But I don't know when he plans to leave. It could be weeks from now. And I don't know when Mr. Michaels wants to be married."

"We need find out these things. I send my little brother to docks to find out." Lamoon paced under Esme's window as she talked. "We speak with friend of Mai about glasses. Mai and I come back tonight to tell you what we find out."

"What about the uniform from the orphanage?" Esme asked.

"I ask our friend give us his," Mai said. "Lamoon make to fit you. Easy for him to tell story about losing uniform. Priests will give him another."

A knock at her door interrupted all their planning.

"Esme!" her father cried sharply from outside her room. "Esme, I want to speak with you."

Esme looked at Mai and Lamoon in alarm. Lamoon pressed her finger to her lips and then ran back into the jungle, dragging her sister along with her.

"Give me a moment," she called to her father, waiting until her friends were out of sight, then she opened the door.

"I think we should talk," he said as he entered the room.

She stared at him. In a flash she realized the implications of her plan to leave home. Her running away would hurt her father so much. Yet it seemed the only solution. She straightened. At least she could try to convince him once more not to force her to marry.

Resolutely, she sat on the edge of her bed, her face showing her determination to make him see sense. She noticed that his eyes were bloodshot and his hands trembled. She wondered if he'd been drinking, something he'd been doing a great deal since her mother's death. A wave of pity rushed over her.

"I don't think you quite appreciate the need for your marrying," he continued when she sat there in silent expectation.

Her heart went out to him, but she couldn't pretend she wanted to marry Mr. Michaels, not even for her father.

"You're right. I don't see the need, I'm afraid. But it isn't what I feel that counts, is it?" Her voice was bitter.

Her father flinched at her honesty, but recovered quickly. "You're making this harder than necessary, but you're not going to change my mind. You know I love you, Esme. And because I love you, I must do what's best for you."

"If you loved me, Father, you wouldn't think it best that I marry a man I detest."

Her father looked away from her imploring gaze. "It's better than never marrying at all," he said slowly.

"Is it?" she asked. "If no one will have me, why can't I just stay here with you for the rest of my life? I could take care of you and teach at the school and—"

"And after I die, live an old maid's life with no one to care for you and no one for you to care for. Do you really think you'd want that?" His voice was harsh.

"It would be better than marrying Mr. Michaels," she responded earnestly. "Oh, Father, he frightens me. I don't know why, but I feel he would mistreat me. When we walked together, he seemed so . . . so obsessed with me. He makes me feel anything but secure." She took her father's hand in hers. "You can't make me marry him, Father, you just can't!"

For a moment, he seemed as if he were about to waver. Then his face hardened. "And if you have a child? Would you want to raise a bastard?"

She thought she would die from the frustration of it all. How could she make him understand she was innocent?

"I won't have a child," she said desperately. "I can't! I'm still a virgin!"

"I'm afraid I can't believe that," he muttered, turning his face from her. "I'm sorry, dear. I've checked on the rumor your aunt heard and it seems to have substance. It can be traced right back to Emory Lawrence, and he stands by what he said. He said he let the information slip and he truly regrets it now, but he claims every word is true."

"Lawrence?" she asked in confusion. "Mr. Rushton's secretary? I scarcely know him. How am I supposed to have had an affair with him?"

Her father's face grew angry and he gripped her arms. "Stop this deception! Do you hear? I know you've been seeing Rushton. And I've cursed myself a hundred times since yesterday for allowing you to visit Blythe so often. But I never dreamed you were meeting a man there."

Shame and horror washed over her. Mr. Rushton? He was the man the rumor linked her to? "I'm supposed to be having an affair with my friend's husband?" she asked incredulously. "My father's closest friend?" She buried her face in her hands. The situation was even worse than she could have imagined. Someone who knew her well was deliberately spreading this lie about her—a lie that could easily be believed.

"Lawrence said that Rushton himself had told him," her father remarked stiffly.

"Have you talked to Mr. Rushton?"

"Of course. I didn't tell him who told me. Lawrence begged me not to. He fears for his job."

"What . . ." She swallowed, hardly able to venture the question. Then she forced herself to hear it all. "What did Mr. Rushton say?"

"He denies everything."

Relief rushed through her. She'd have been devastated if Mr. Rushton had backed up the gossip. "You see?" she said triumphantly. "I told you!"

But her father merely stared into her eyes, and shook his head. "What else would he say? 'Yes, James, I seduced your daughter? Yes, we've met secretly for months? The man's not crazy. He denied it, but I know his reputation. Lord knows I've counseled him often enough about what to do with his disgruntled paramours once he tired of them. Until now he never toyed with maidens, however."

Her father's voice was so bitter Esme wanted to cry for the pain he was suffering, all because of some gossipmonger.

"Lawrence is his secretary and close friend," he continued. "If he says it's true, then it's true. He has no reason to lie about it. In fact, he said he was

111

relieved I knew because he felt guilty always shielding Rushton.''

"I can't understand how you'd believe such things of your own daughter. Or of your good friend," she murmured, the words catching in her throat.

"My *once* good friend. I've always known how Rushton was with women. Apparently, I didn't know my daughter quite as well. You've given me reason to doubt you lately. Otherwise, I'd be more inclined to believe you.''

She didn't answer for fear she might say something she'd regret later.

"You're going to marry Michaels, aren't you?" her father asked sternly.

"Now that you believe this disgusting lie, and Aunt Miriam's revolting conclusions are all over town, what choice do I have?''

"None.''

His unfeeling response banished any remote hope she'd had that he might change his mind. She didn't want to run away to Chiengmai. Truly, she didn't. But there was no other way, she realized.

She lifted her chin bravely. "Then I suppose I'll do what I must do." She held her breath, hoping that her answer would suffice, for she didn't really want to lie to her father.

"All right then," he replied. "Your aunt will make all the arrangements for the wedding. Mr. Michaels wants to be married quickly, in a week if possible, in case there's a child.''

Esme stiffened but didn't reply. A week! She hoped Lord Winthrop planned to leave Bangkok before then.

"In the meantime, he'll want to visit regularly. I

hope the scene I witnessed yesterday won't be repeated."

"Of course not," she replied. She could swallow her pride now that she knew she'd soon be free.

"Well, then, I'll see you at breakfast."

He left Esme wondering how many more breakfasts they would have together. But she refused to think about that and turned her thoughts to planning her escape.

Chapter Six

The night was black. The moon had abandoned the sky, leaving only the stars for light. In her bedroom, Esme paced restlessly, wearing only her camisole and drawers. She threw open the shutters, not caring that the mosquitoes would swarm around her in seconds. Peering into the darkness, she wondered for the hundredth time when Lamoon and Mai would come. All day she'd been unable to think of anything but her escape. She didn't know how many more days she could stand the waiting.

Suddenly she heard a rustling nearby.

"Lamoon! Mai! Is that you?" she called softly.

"It's Mai," a voice answered. Her friend was alone. Esme could scarcely make out Mai's familiar face. "Sorry I so late, but we do everything tonight. Englishman leave tomorrow!"

"Tomorrow! So soon? But...but..."

"No time to think about it. If you leave, must be

tonight, so make up your mind. Boats sail early."

"Is everything ready?"

"We have uniform, glasses, and makeup. You go with me to Lamoon house. We change you into boy there. Her brother take you to docks early in morning to meet Mr. Chan, secretary of Lord Winthrop. He decide if to hire you."

Then Mai lifted a large, gaily striped cloth bag above her head. "You pack your things in this like Siamese peoples."

"What should I take?" Esme asked as leaning over the windowsill she took the bag.

"Money, for certain. You have money?"

Esme nodded. "I have what I was saving to buy Father a special birthday present. It's not much but it will help." Later, when things were settled, she could buy him any present she wished with the money she earned teaching. That is, if he ever forgave her for running away.

She searched in her drawer until she found the box she kept her money in. She'd used a box of her mother's, knowing that the maid wouldn't disturb it for fear of the wrath of her mother's ghost. When she opened the box, Lord Winthrop's handkerchief at the bottom caught her eye. She'd managed to retrieve it from the garbage, along with her silk sarong and scarf. Why it had seemed so important to keep these reminders of her troubles she didn't know, but she'd done it nonetheless. Now she fingered the handkerchief, wondering if it was time to discard it once and for all.

"Essmay!" Mai called softly, interrupting her thoughts. "You still have sarong we make for you?"

Esme snapped the box shut without removing the handkerchief, then placed the box in the bag. With

Deborah Martin

a sigh, she returned to the window, and answered Mai. "Yes, why do you ask?"

"You should wear sarong until we reach house, so people not notice you."

Esme groaned, but went to retrieve her native costume from its new hiding place. Once more she'd be donning the clothes that got her into so much trouble before. But she knew it was the best choice of apparel for her escape. She'd be among the Siamese, so she needed to blend in if she didn't wish to have her steps traced later.

Quickly, she removed her camisole and tied the scarf around her breasts. She put the sarong on over her drawers, thinking to herself how odd it was that she always felt more comfortable in native dress than in her own clothes.

Then she hurriedly gathered the other items she'd need for the trip and for her new life as a teacher. She decided to take her gray dress, the one that made her look so severe. Once she had a job, she could buy more clothes in Chiengmai. In addition to her dress, she placed in the bag a few essentials and a book of poems—a gift from her father. She added her small sewing kit, so she could mend her clothes until she could buy new ones.

Her bag packed, she sat down at her dresser. She must leave a note to let her father know she was all right. With shaky hands, she lit the oil lamp. Now that she was really leaving, she was becoming nervous.

As she took out a piece of note paper and dipped her pen in the inkpot, she wondered what she could say that would make her leaving any less painful for her father.

"Father," she wrote after several minutes, "I'm truly sorry, but I couldn't marry Mr. Michaels.

Please don't worry about me, for I'm quite safe. I'll return eventually, I promise. But you mustn't worry. I know you won't believe it, but I do love you. I'm only sorry to have caused you so much grief. With love and regret, Esme."

She folded the note with trembling hands, wrote her father's name on it, and placed it on her bed where the maid would readily spot it.

Then with a last quick glance at her room, she threw her bag outside to the ground and climbed out the window, hanging onto the sill only a moment before she dropped to the ground below. As she stood, brushing the dirt from her clothing, she pivoted to look back at the house that had always been her home.

She gazed at the wooden structure built on stilts to keep the water out during the monsoons. With a twinge of fear, she suddenly didn't want to leave its comfortable security. Its open windows stared back at her, warning her not to go, not to try this crazy thing. She hesitated, half wondering if she could get back into the house the same way she'd left. She turned to Mai.

"We go now," Mai said insistently.

Her words broke the spell. When Esme looked again, her home was just a house, a collection of wooden planks that had nothing to do with her, the windows only dark holes.

"Yes," she answered. "Let's go."

Again she found herself following Mai through the jungle. But this time no moon lit their way. They had to move carefully and slowly along the path. Once more they were at the dock, but this time they passed it to tread one of the muddy streets leading out of the city's foreign quarter.

After a few minutes of walking, they passed into

the Siamese section of Bangkok. Here the streets weren't silent as they were in the foreign quarter. Although it was already eleven o'clock, shop doors stood open, their proprietors squatting in front to eat bowls of rice and curry or to beckon customers inside. Old Siamese men chewing betel nut played with dice in the dirt. The scent of curry and garlic lay heavy on the air, mingling with the sweet smell of jackfruit. Esme heard the haunting voice of a singer performing to the accompaniment of a Siamese orchestra. A curious sense of freedom made her heart race.

A few of those she passed gave her curious looks, but most didn't spare her a glance as they amused themselves. Yet Mai hurried her along, whispering that the less anyone saw of her the better, for it wouldn't do to have a hundred witnesses telling her father and aunt where she'd gone.

At last they reached Lamoon's house on the river. Lamoon's husband was one of those who still chose to live in houseboats to avoid the cholera that rampaged through the city periodically. As they stole aboard the flimsy craft, Lamoon emerged from one of the cabins to greet them.

"I thought you never come!" she cried. "We have only few hours before they leave. Hurry! Hurry!"

Quickly, they followed her into the cabin. Inside, Lamoon's "little" brother, who actually was about fourteen, lay on a mat in the corner, apparently asleep.

"Where's your husband?" Esme asked, for it occurred to her that he probably wouldn't approve of what they were about to do.

"I sent him away," Lamoon said with a laugh.

When Mai laughed too, Esme said, "What do you mean?"

"I start argument with him. I tell him he not make enough money. He get very angry and say I greedy, that he make enough money to make second wife happy even if not make me happy. I tell him that he go sleep with second wife if he wish talk like that. He leave. He not be back till tomorrow, I promise."

"He probably get velly drunk at her house, too," Mai told her sister with a grin. "You his favorite. He not like it when you angry."

Esme struggled to keep the horror from showing in her face. She'd always known that most of the Siamese men had more than one wife, often more than one household if they were fairly wealthy. Yet hearing Lamoon talk so casually about it upset her. Esme couldn't imagine knowing that one's husband shared his affections openly with someone else.

"Then we'll be alone," Esme said as she tried to make her voice sound natural.

"Yes. Now come," Lamoon told her. "I made our friend uniform better for you. I think will fit."

Esme took the jacket and trousers from her, having no doubt in Lamoon's ability to alter it. The Siamese were notoriously adept at dressmaking, and Lamoon, in particular, had a good eye. She could judge someone's size and shape without even using a measuring tape.

Peering at Lamoon's brother to make certain he was asleep, Esme stripped down to her drawers. She donned her camisole and then the coarse white broadcloth jacket. The jacket hung loosely, which served to hide her shape. Fortunately, it was designed to reach nearly to one's knees, so it covered Esme's shapely hips very well.

The black cotton trousers were short even for Esme, but Lamoon assured her she'd only been

Deborah Martin

waiting for Esme to try it on before she added a strip of material to the bottom to lengthen them. Esme had no trouble managing the intricate knot that the Siamese used to tighten the loose trousers around their waists, since it was the same knot she used with her sarong.

But in spite of the loose fit of both the trousers and the jacket, her bosom gave her away.

"We must tie up breasts to make them flat," Mai told her sister.

"True," Lamoon agreed resignedly. "And maybe if she slump a little like old Chinese men, her breasts not show so much."

Mai and Lamoon proved to be right. With the binding and the slumping, Esme's shape was transformed. When she saw herself in the mirror that stood against one wall, she grimaced. From the neck down, she looked like a Chinese coolie.

"Not so much slumping," Lamoon said, pulling back on Esme's shoulders. "Just a little. If you do too much, you look like old man, not young one."

When again Esme gazed at herself in the mirror, she saw what looked like a young man with poor posture. That would have to do, she decided.

Now it was time to work on her hair and face. Very carefully, Lamoon and Mai applied kohl to the corners of Esme's eyes, giving them a more slanted look. Then Lamoon smeared a light coating of kohl under Esme's eyes.

"What's that for?" Esme asked.

"Boys at orphanage work velly hard at studies. They always tired, because Jesuit fathers push them to work, work! This make you look sleepy, but also make you look different."

Then Lamoon took one look at Esme's long sooty lashes and drew out her scissors.

"No—o—o, not my lashes," Esme wailed.

"You want look like boy or not?" Lamoon said sternly. "No Siamese boy have such beautiful... What is word?"

"Lashes," Mai supplied.

"Lashes. Must be short. I cut for you." When Esme made a face, Lamoon added, "They grow back. Not to worry."

But that was little consolation for Esme who'd always thought her eyes were her best feature. Lamoon cut the lashes and then placed the glasses on her. Esme peered in the mirror and wrinkled her nose in distaste. Her eyes were barely discernible through the tinted lenses. The glasses fit oddly, giving her an owlish look when coupled with the eye makeup and shortened lashes. Lamoon grabbed her hands and used the scissors to cut her nails.

"Beautiful nails, though not long enough for Siamese woman," Lamoon said regretfully. "But no Siamese boy have beautiful nails." She clipped them squarely, while Mai braided Esme's hair.

"Ouch!" Esme exclaimed.

"So sorry, Essmay," her friend told her, "but hair must be very tight or you not look like boy."

Ruthlessly, Mai yanked and wove the long strands until Esme's head ached. Then Mai paused to look at the effect.

"You see?" She gestured to the mirror. "Look just like orphan boy."

Thank goodness the Jesuits disapproved of the Siamese practice of wearing a topknot and preferred instead the long braid the Chinese wore, Esme thought as she gazed at her reflection. Otherwise, Lamoon and Mai would be chopping off all her hair, too, and tying it on top of her head.

As Esme stood there, Mai undid the braid.

"What are you doing?" Esme asked in alarm.

"You do now. You must undo hair and do again by yourself. You must learn."

Esme groaned. Then she began to plait her hair, pulling it as tightly as she could. She'd have to wear this disguise every morning, she realized. Then she hesitated. She hadn't even thought about what she'd do at night. What could she wear to bed?

As if she'd read Esme's mind, Lamoon scurried to the other side of the room, returning with a long Chinese robe.

"At night," she said, "you dress alone. Try make sure no one see you sleep. Boys sleep with hair down. You do same. But you wear long robe so nobody see you body. Maybe even make loud noise ..."

Esme looked at her quizzically. Lamoon pointed to her brother who was snoring loudly, and Esme laughed.

"You want me to pretend to snore?" she asked, an incredulous look crossing her face. "Why?"

"Men think women never...ah...snore...because men always sleep too heavy to hear. Make loud snore and they think you boy for sure." This time all three women laughed.

"Maybe so," Esme replied. "It's worth a try at any rate."

Now her two friends surveyed Esme critically. They looked her up and down and then nodded, pleased by what they saw. Esme turned to gaze in the mirror. She hardly recognized herself, particularly when she stooped. With the glasses and makeup and her hair pulled back tightly, Esme's face looked thin and gaunt, her eyes haunted and weary under the glasses. She hated the way she looked, but she knew it was necessary.

"What you going call yourself?" Lamoon asked.

"What do you suggest?" Esme countered.

The two girls stood for a moment pondering the matter.

"Goong? That is common name. Orphanage have many boys called Goong," said Mai.

"I'm not going to call myself 'Shrimp,'" Esme replied, wrinkling her nose in distaste at the meaning of the popular nickname Goong, "But a simple name like that would be good."

"You call yourself Lek," Lamoon said. "Very common name."

"Yes. I suppose Lek would be acceptable. I am small, even for a Siamese boy, so that nickname would fit. If I must give a formal name, I'll choose some horrendously long one like Somprasert Khantachanaboon. Then they'll have to call me by my nickname. That would be less confusing for me. We don't want me tripping over my name every time I say it."

"How you going to talk, Essmay?" Mai asked. "You not talk like yourself or everybody guess you not Siamese."

Esme had given a lot of thought to that since that morning. She'd realized she'd have to change her voice. The most obvious solution was to adopt a Siamese accent. Whatever she did, she couldn't speak English like a *farang*, a foreigner. But she could imitate the Siamese accent to perfection after years of helping her father teach English. Unfortunately, that wouldn't be enough, because her voice sounded feminine. Lowering it wasn't only difficult, it also made her sound silly.

So she also needed to change the tone of her voice. After experimenting with various speech styles, she'd hit upon the perfect one—a nasal tone. With

Deborah Martin

only a few hours practice, she'd added a slight nasality to her speech, effectively disguising it.

"I have taken care of that necessity," she responded nasally, placing the accent on *ty* and enunciating her *t*'s and *s*'s as heavily as any Siamese speaker of English would.

The two girls gasped and then clapped their hands loudly.

"Excellent!" they cried. "You not sound the same."

"True," she said, "but any Siamese will be able to tell that I'm a *farang*. Lord Winthrop might be fooled and maybe even this Mr. Chan, but the Siamese people I speak with will know."

Lamoon and Mai's delighted cries had awakened their brother. He now sat up on his pallet and listened to the conversation with interest.

"Maybe...maybe," Lamoon muttered. "But it not matter. If Lord Winthrop could speak Siamese, he not need you, correct? So Siamese peoples can think you *farang* if they want. They can't tell him, can they? Anyway, they will think he already know. But I think you fool them."

"You are right, my sister," said Lamoon's brother in Siamese, rising from his pallet. "If I didn't know she was foreign, I wouldn't believe it. People don't expect to see a woman in men's clothing or a foreigner in Siamese dress, so they won't look for those actions that would give her away."

"But Lord Winthrop knows me...well," Esme said as she turned to the brother, whom she'd spoken to once or twice before.

"He's not expecting you, however, is he? So he won't expect you to look like this. He won't think you'd do such a thing. Men of his kind, who deal with kings, they expect women to be devious only

124

when it comes to love. They think women aren't smart enough to disguise themselves so wisely or to perform the difficult interpreting tasks that you will perform. They expect women to remain in their proper place."

Esme wryly acknowledged the truth of his statement. Lord Winthrop had always made it very clear where she as a woman belonged. He believed she had loose morals, but didn't seem to think she had any sense. No, he wouldn't expect her to do this. In fact, if he knew of her impending marriage at all, with his poor opinion of her, he'd probably assume she'd agree to marry and would then take a lover.

That thought strengthened her resolve. She'd show him, she decided. She'd do her best to keep out of his way, to keep from being discovered. But if by some chance he found out who she was, she'd make it quite clear to him that she'd done the only thing she could, given her wretched situation. After all, he'd been partly responsible for that situation. He'd told her aunt about Loy Krathong. And somewhere along the way, she'd make him pay for that.

In spite of the early hour, the main dock on the Chao Phya River bustled with activity when at last Lamoon's brother escorted Esme to the two large houseboats and launches that were to take Lord Winthrop's entourage to Chiengmai. She waited patiently while he boarded one of the boats. In only a few moments he returned, accompanied by a young Chinese man.

Lamoon's brother introduced her to Chan and then stood back to watch. Chan eyed her critically. Waiting for him to speak, Esme adopted the expression of docility that she knew would help ensure her being hired.

125

"This boy here tells me you speak fluent English. Is that so?" Chan asked.

"Yes, *Khun* Chan," she said, using the Siamese word for "Mister."

"He says you come from the Jesuit orphanage. Were you not there when Lord Winthrop went to look for an interpreter two days ago?"

"I was away from the city. I had a position with an English merchant who went north to buy silks. I returned yesterday."

"The merchant's name?"

"Mr. William Michaels," she said evenly, hoping that Chan wouldn't have time to check her story.

"Do you have references?"

"Yes," she replied as she handed him the letters that she'd hurriedly written before leaving Lamoon's boat. It had been easy to sign her father's name, for she'd signed it many times for him. The other names she'd improvised.

"Somkit!" he called, and a Siamese man who'd been watching them from the boat scurried to the dock.

"Do you know this man?" he asked, pointing to Esme.

Somkit clearly was worried, for he didn't know what he was expected to say. "Do I know you?" he asked Esme in Siamese.

"Who are you?" she asked in Siamese, ignoring the frown that crossed Chan's face.

"The consulate interpreter."

She nearly sighed with relief. She knew just how to get around the man. "I'm the interpreter sent from the orphanage, so if you don't want to go to Chiengmai, you should say you know me." She knew Somkit probably had a family in Bangkok. The last thing he'd wish to do was take a trip for

126

months up north. Like most Siamese, Somkit would have no trouble embellishing her story to suit his needs.

To Esme's relief, Somkit acted true to form. "I know this boy well," he told Chan who'd suspiciously eyed both Somkit and Esme as they talked together. "He is a good interpreter. He has had many jobs in Bangkok."

"What were you saying to him just now?" Chan asked Somkit.

"I inquired about Father James, a friend of mine."

Chan assessed Somkit and Esme, then shrugged. Abruptly, he dismissed Somkit with a nod and turned to Esme. "Why do you wish to work for Englishmen if you came from the French priests' orphanage?"

"The French priests are very harsh," she told him, speaking the truth. "They want me to believe in their religion. But I know that the English do not care so much about religion. They will let me live as I wish as long as I work hard."

He surveyed her once again, uncertain whether to accept her. At last he nodded. "Very well. I would like to know more about you, but we must leave today so I have little choice. You must first speak with his lordship, however." He turned on his heel, beckoning for her to go with him.

Esme tried not to let her nervousness show on her face. This was the true test. If Lord Winthrop didn't see through her disguise, if she could just get on board, she'd be out of danger. Her blood racing, she followed Chan onto the deck of the small houseboat. He knocked on the thin wooden door of one of the cabins, and a familiar voice bade him enter.

Deborah Martin

Before she went in, she prayed silently that Lord Winthrop wouldn't recognize her.

Lord Winthrop's cabin was small, just large enough for a bunk and a rattan table that served as his desk. He sat at it, a pile of papers before him. She stared at him a moment, noting his tired eyes and tousled brown hair. In spite of herself, she felt a sudden surge of pity for him. He looked so weary that she longed to rub away the tiredness in his shoulders as she'd done so many times for her father. His gaze turned from Chan to her, and her eyes quickly darted to the floor as she resisted the urge to watch him while Chan explained why she'd come.

"Your name is Lek, is it?" Lord Winthrop asked sharply.

"Yes, sir," she replied.

For a moment he was so silent she feared he'd already found her out.

"You're certain you weren't at the orphanage the day I went there? You look a bit familiar."

"Very certain, sir. I know I would have remembered you."

He frowned as if struggling to place her. "That's odd. I could swear . . ." Then he shook his head. "Oh, never mind. It doesn't really matter anyway. Chan tells me you have recommendation letters."

She handed them to him. He leafed through them, scanning an occasional word or phrase. Then he looked up from perusing them to assess her. She suffered his gaze with an outward calm she didn't really feel.

At last he placed the letters on top of one of his stacks. "If I weren't in such a bind, I'd need more," he told her. "But at the moment, you're a welcome sight."

"I would be glad to be of service, sir," she replied.

"All right. I suppose I'll hire you. You and Chan may negotiate the salary. Can you be ready to leave right away?"

"Yes, sir," she answered, trying not to sound too eager. "I have brought my bag with me."

"Very well. I'd like to know one thing, however."

"Sir?"

"Are you Siamese? You look a bit . . . ah . . ."

"I am Eurasian, sir. My mother was Siamese, my father French."

His gray eyes narrowed. "Why do you wish to work for the English? You must speak French as well as English. Certainly the French would be more than eager to hire you."

She gave him the same story she'd given Chan. But this time she added what she hoped would be a more convincing element to the story.

"My father was a French sailor. He abandoned my mother, so she died of a broken heart. Thus I have no love for the French."

"I see."

"There is another reason as well. I think the British will soon be the rulers of the world. The French . . . They will never be. So I would prefer to work for the future rulers of my country. Is that not sensible?"

She glanced up at him and for a moment wondered if she'd gone too far. His face filled with amusement. He hesitated and she tensed, waiting for him to laugh and say he knew who she was.

He did laugh, but only briefly.

"Did I say something humorous?" she asked, trying to sound offended.

"No, no. It's just that the Jesuits wouldn't be very pleased to hear you say such a thing, I imagine."

He smiled wryly. "I'm not even sure *I* am as confident as you are about the matter. But only time will tell, won't it?"

"Yes, sir."

"Chan," he said, dismissing her with a nod, "send Somkit home and put Lek in the cabin next door. I'll probably need him to fill me in on Siamese customs, so he might as well stay on this boat instead of traveling with you and the others."

"Very good, sir," Chan replied.

Lord Winthrop turned to the work at his desk as Chan began to lead Esme out the door. Esme had scarcely digested the fact that she was to spend the entire trip at such close proximity to Lord Winthrop, when his voice stopped them.

"Lek, about these letters of recommendation . . ."

"Yes, sir?" she replied, trying not to tremble. Had she come this far only to be discovered?

"I notice that you have one from a Mr. Montrose."

"I do. I have worked with him on occasion, although of course not as an interpreter."

"Have you ever met his daughter?"

Esme's heart skipped a beat. She could hardly keep her voice even as she replied, "Briefly."

"How would you describe her?"

What was she to say that wouldn't alert him to who she was? After a short pause, she murmured, "She knows the Siamese people very well."

"I daresay she probably does," he said dryly, "but that's not what I meant. What is her reputation in the community?"

She swallowed hard. Here was her chance to speak well of herself, but she was angry that he'd ask some boy that question, as if she were so notorious the whole city must know of her.

"I would not know, sir. But I am certain she is

considered to be much as the other *farang* girls are—quiet, modest, and prudish."

"Prudish?" he retorted with a mocking laugh. "Not hardly. Nor quiet and modest. But, as you say, you couldn't possibly know what she's really like, could you?"

"No, sir," she replied, fighting the impulse to throw caution to the winds and slap him.

He flashed her a keen glance, then shrugged. "Perhaps we'll speak more on this later. Good day."

With that, she was truly dismissed. She followed Chan out of the cabin, every muscle in her body tense with fury and fear.

The arrogant beast! she thought to herself. If it took until the end of her days, she'd find a way to wipe that smug smile off his face. She could see now that this trip would be more challenging than she'd ever have wished. She only hoped he stayed locked in his cabin with those papers the entire trip! Because if he didn't, he was likely to find himself floating *in* the river instead of on it!

Chapter Seven

Esme leaned on the rail of the houseboat a short time later, watching as the their boats headed out into the river traffic. Chan had informed her that the two houseboats carried her and six men as well as the Siamese crew.

The boat she shared with Ian had two other cabins. One was to serve as the dining room. The other was filled with gifts for the prince in Chiengmai and provisions for the trip. The second boat also had four cabins. Chan and the cook he'd hired shared one of them. Two military attachés from the Bangkok consulate, assigned to assist Lord Winthrop in his duties, occupied two other cabins. The last cabin belonged to an Episcopal minister who'd persuaded Lord Winthrop to grant him passage.

Glancing up at the sky, Esme realized how much of the morning was gone already. Soon her aunt would call her for breakfast and discover her gone.

Soon her father would find the note. She was over-whelmed by feelings of guilt mingled with a deep sense of regret, but she knew she couldn't go back. Perhaps in time her father would forgive her. At least she was safe from being forced into a wretched, loveless marriage.

But now she was on her own. While the thought excited her, it frightened her more than she'd expected. It was dawning on her how difficult reaching Chiengmai without being discovered would be. Thank goodness Lord Winthrop chose to remain at the other end of the deck, watching the crew, or she was afraid she might change her mind and beg him to turn the boats around.

She stared out at the city as the launches dragged their houseboats laboriously through the crowds of unusual river craft. The river was the main avenue for Bangkok. Aside from those who lived on it in houseboats, merchants cruised it daily, selling their goods from rafts, canoes, and even barges. Around her, young and old men and women pierced the air with cries of "Bananas, sweet bananas!" and "Very fresh fish for sale!."

Eagerly, she stored away memories of the city that would sustain her until she could return. She drank in the sight of temple spires with multicolored tile-and-glass mosaics sparkling in the sun. She inhaled deeply the odor of fish mingled with the scent of pungent *mali* blossoms. And her ears took in the singsong cries of Chinese, Siamese, and Indian men, women, and children that filled the air with a cacophony of sound.

Bangkok was beautiful, she thought to herself. Even with the garbage in the streets and the people who sometimes loved to gamble and drink more than work, she couldn't help but love it. She'd miss

Deborah Martin

it so much: the naked children playing underfoot in the crowded markets and the women ringing gongs and dancing to make merit, thus improving their karma. She'd even miss the shaven-headed and saffron-robed Buddhist priests who skirted her when they passed her in the street because they didn't want to be defiled by touching a woman.

Of course, she'd miss far more than that, for Bangkok held the only family she'd ever known. She squeezed her eyes shut, trying to keep back the tears as she thought of her childhood with her parents. She remembered quiet evenings when her father read aloud to her and her mother from the works of Charles Dickens. She could almost hear again her mother humming a French tune as she bustled about the house. Those days were gone forever, and Esme wished she could have them back.

"Is something wrong, Lek?" a deep voice asked at her elbow.

She opened her eyes with a start to find Lord Winthrop watching her. His face was blank now, but she couldn't help remembering the intense desire she'd seen in it only a few days before. It was all she could do to keep from trembling.

"Not at all, my lord," she replied, trying to keep her voice even. "I was merely remembering my mother."

"Yours is a sad story, I'm afraid," he told her, bracing his forearms against the rail and gazing out at the riverbank.

For a moment she thought he spoke of her real mother. Then she realized he referred to the tale she'd told him as Lek. Once more she felt a twinge of guilt.

"Everyone has a sad story, my lord," she told him honestly.

"I suppose you're right. But I'm sorry yours is the result of the callousness of Western men."

She wanted to laugh at the irony of his words.

"I regret that your experience with Westerners has shown you our worst side," he continued.

That surprised her. She hadn't expected him to care too much about those who worked for him, especially the Siamese. But so far he'd treated her and the crew with respect. The few orders he'd issued through her had been courteously worded. She'd hardly had to change them at all to make them acceptable to the crew, as she would have had to do with some other Englishman. This was a side of Lord Winthrop she hadn't expected to see.

"You seem very young, Lek," he said after a long silence. "Why aren't you still in school?"

"Oh, *Than*," she replied, using the word for "master," "like all *farangs*, you think we are much younger than we are. I am already eighteen years old."

"Really. I wouldn't have thought that. Of course, Siamese men do seem small. That crew of mine doesn't look as if they could handle a boat like this, but they're doing very well."

"The Siamese spend most of their time on the water. Many Siamese live, work, and die on it."

"The British depend on the sea a great deal as well, but not like the Siamese. This certainly is an unusual country."

"But beautiful, don't you think?"

"Yes, sometimes. But I wouldn't wish to live here."

A pang went through Esme. No, of course he wouldn't. He didn't know it as she did, nor feel the thrill that rushed through her every time she glimpsed the majestic grandeur of the temple spires. He didn't understand why she'd risk so much just to see something like Loy Krathong. How could he? Like her aunt and her father, all he cared about was the British social world that she hated with its narrow rules and strict propriety. He didn't understand the carefree innocence of the Siamese.

Then again, that night at the ball he hadn't seemed so concerned with propriety. Now standing so close to him, she was reminded of the furious power of his kiss, the warmth of his hands on her waist. As the feelings that had overwhelmed her then began to stir in her, she grew flushed and was thankful for the light breeze wafting by them.

"With your permission, sir, I shall return to my cabin," she said abruptly, not certain how long she could stand there without her face giving her thoughts away.

He glanced at her and shrugged. "Certainly. But I'll need you later this afternoon. I want to consult you on a few matters."

"As you wish," she replied before escaping gratefully to her quarters.

Once in her cabin, she sank onto the hard mattress of her bunk. Her heart was racing, but with fear or guilt she wasn't sure. She must have been crazy, she thought, to embark on such a mad scheme. It was only their first day and already she'd translated for him once. Worse yet, they'd be alone in his cabin this afternoon! Oh, how was she going to keep up this charade? But she knew she had no choice.

She spent the rest of the morning in the cabin. She'd been up most of the night before preparing to leave and was exhausted. When at last a knock on her door woke her from a sound sleep, the sun had already begun its descent on the horizon.

At first she didn't know where she was. She glanced around the tiny cabin in alarm, not recognizing the uniform hung on a hook or the clay water jar in the corner. Then she remembered and jumped off the bunk with a start.

"Yes?" she called out, careful to use her disguised voice.

"It's Lord Winthrop. May I come in?"

Oh, no, she thought. She'd shed her uniform and unbound her breasts because they were sore. She'd been careful to latch the door, but still she should have at least put on the Chinese robe instead of simply collapsing on the bed in her undergarments.

"I—I'm not dressed," she replied.

There was silence beyond the door.

"All right then," Lord Winthrop finally said. "Come to my cabin as soon as you've dressed."

"Right away, sir," she shouted, relieved, as she scurried about the cabin, putting her disguise back together.

When she entered his cabin a few moments later, he looked up from his seat at the rattan table.

"Sit down, Lek. I'll be with you presently." He then returned to what he was doing.

She sat in the chair he gestured to, while he finished reading some papers. Again she thought how exhausted he looked. An irrational urge to smooth his creased forehead came over her, but it left as soon as he raised his clear gray-blue eyes to find her observing him.

His eyes narrowed. "For a boy who's been raised in a crowded orphanage, you're rather modest, don't you think?"

His question threw her off guard. "I—I beg your pardon?"

"I just thought it odd that you latched your cabin door."

She sat in silence, searching for an explanation. "I relish my privacy, my lord," she finally murmured.

"Really?" he asked, one eyebrow cocked as if to question what right she had to privacy.

She kept silent. Let him think her peculiar, she thought. She'd have to keep her door latched if she was to continue her charade, and she couldn't always be finding some excuse for why she did.

Instead she changed the subject. "You wished to discuss some matters with me, my lord?"

As if he recognized her ploy, he gave her a half-smile, one brow quirking up. Then with a dismissive gesture, he remarked, "I do, as a matter of fact. Before I came to Siam, I talked at length with a previous visitor. He told me some nonsense about not pointing my foot at anyone or touching anyone's head. I can't imagine I'd do either, but he was very adamant about it. Have you any idea what he's talking about?"

"Yes," she answered, and explained that the Siamese ranked body parts, with the foot being beneath contempt and the head almost holy. "If you touch someone's head, you place them beneath you. If you point with your foot, you also commit a grave error by saying they are beneath contempt."

He shook his head. "That's the oddest thing I've ever heard."

"Don't you British do the same? You do not show or discuss certain body parts."

"You mean like a woman's legs and breasts?"

Esme strove to keep from blushing. "Yes, precisely."

"That's so, I suppose, but we don't run around

138

half-clothed and then make rules about our body parts."

"But you see, sir ..." she said before a knock at the door silenced her.

Lord Winthrop went to the door and admitted the Siamese man who headed the crew.

"We stop now," the man said hesitantly in English.

"What?" Lord Winthrop asked. "But why?"

"We stop now," the man repeated.

Lord Winthrop looked helplessly at Esme.

"Why must we stop?" she asked the man in Siamese.

"Ahead is a very difficult spot of the river. We must wait until morning to pass it. It is too late to begin now."

Esme told Lord Winthrop what the man had said.

"Oh, all right," Lord Winthrop said. "You'd better signal the other launch and find a place to moor for the night."

Esme repeated the man's words.

"Lek," Lord Winthrop said, "we'll have tea as soon as we've stopped. I don't suppose you're accustomed to taking tea since I doubt the Jesuits ever served it, but would you join us anyway?"

Esme started to refuse and then thought better of it. She couldn't hide in her cabin the entire trip. Besides, she'd been alone most of the day. She was ready for some company.

"I would be honored," she replied.

The tea provided her with her first chance to meet some of the other members of their group. First there were the two attachés. She'd met one of them before, Godfrey Harmon. They'd scarcely been acquaintances, but she'd had a moment of fright when she'd feared he might recognize her. She need not have worried. He'd stared right through her as he would have done to any Siamese. And his behavior, so typical of most British toward the Siamese, made her dislike him immediately.

But she took an instant liking to the other attaché, Harold Thurwood, whom she'd seen at embassy functions but never actually been introduced to. His warm smile made her feel welcome in a way that she sensed Godfrey could never have done.

The group had chosen to sit on the deck to have their tea, for the slight evening breeze made the deck more bearable than the dining cabin. The food proved better than Esme had expected. She devoured the delectable cakes and scones, having eaten nothing all day. The tea was also of good quality with even a bit of cream to put in it.

"Chan," Lord Winthrop asked as he tasted his first scone, "how on earth did you find a Siamese cook who knows how to prepare a decent tea? Everyone I've spoken to in Bangkok says it's impossible to have it done right by the Siamese."

"The cook isn't Siamese," Chan replied. "I found a ship's cook to go with us. I don't know why he took the job, but he did mention that the ship that hired him before had let him go, leaving him without a means to get back to England. He seemed quite eager to work for us."

"Isn't he going to join us for tea?" Lord Winthrop asked.

"No, apparently not. He seems to think he'd be better off staying to himself."

"If that makes him happy, then fine. But give him my compliments on the food. I hadn't expected to eat quite so well on this trip," Ian said. "And speaking of people who don't wish to join us, where's Reverend Taylor?"

"Sir, you know Americans do not have tea," Chan replied.

"I suppose so. But I would have thought he'd want the company."

"What on earth is a minister doing with us anyway?" asked Godfrey with a sniff.

"He didn't want to travel alone, and I didn't see any harm in letting him join us," Lord Winthrop replied. "He's just returned from a visit to America and was eager to get back to his work in Chiengmai. Don't worry, though, he's paid for his passage."

"But a minister!" said Godfrey. "I hope he doesn't make the trip too tedious."

Privately, Esme hoped *Godfrey* didn't make the trip tedious. He irritated her with his complaints and snide remarks. He was so obviously unaccustomed to hardship that she wondered how he'd ever gotten his position. Unlike Lord Winthrop, who exuded power like an aura around him, Godfrey was almost foppish, with his flaming red hair meticulously combed and his mustache waxed and curled. It was enough to irritate anyone.

They were nearly finished with tea, however, when Godfrey gave her yet another reason to dislike him.

"I say, Harold," Godfrey remarked, "you'll never guess the news I heard at Michaels's house the night before we left."

"Michaels? You mean that wily merchant William?" Harold asked.

"The same. He's getting married and you'll never believe to whom."

"Some widow, I imagine."

"Not at all. He's marrying Esme Montrose, that

141

little filly who's the teacher's daughter."

Esme noticed that Lord Winthrop, who until then had been only half listening to the conversation, paid attention.

"I don't believe it," Harold said. "I saw her dance with him at Rushton's, but I didn't think anything of it. He's not her type at all. Far too old for her, don't you think? You must have misunderstood."

"But it's true. Michaels insists that she's accepted him and everything. I saw the ring." A smug smile crossed Godfrey's face as he imparted that piece of information.

"Why on earth would she want to marry Michaels? I know the man has money, but is she that kind of girl, to covet a man of wealth? I've never met her, but all accounts say she's snubbed anyone who's ever offered for her, no matter how much money they had," Harold said as he took out his snuffbox.

"Yes, but she can't afford to be choosy now, you know."

Esme's hands tightened on the handle of her teacup. So he had heard those vicious rumors, too. And from what she'd heard about Godfrey from Blythe Rushton, he enjoyed spreading such rumors whenever he got the chance.

"Why not?" Harold asked, the snuffbox forgotten.

"You mean you don't know? Half the city knows. I heard it from George Courtney at the ball."

"I'm afraid I'm not quite the gossip you are," Harold said with distaste. "But I see you're dying to tell me, so let it out. What ghastly story have you heard this time?"

Lord Winthrop frowned a warning at Godfrey, but he ignored both that and Harold's contempt.

He leaned forward with a mysterious air, allowing the suspense to build.

"She's been having an affair with Rushton."

Harold's face registered his surprise, and Esme fought to hide her chagrin. She still couldn't believe it. How could Mr. Rushton have said such a thing about her to his secretary? Or had he? If not, why was Lawrence, whom she barely knew, telling his wicked story? Shakily, she set her cup down in its saucer.

"I can't believe it, Godfrey, really," Harold retorted. "Does anyone have evidence or is this just a nasty rumor some jealous woman started?" Harold's skepticism made Esme want to kiss him.

"Aside from the fact that George heard it from Lawrence who says he heard it from Rushton himself, I don't know if there's any evidence," Godfrey said with an injured sniff. "I mean, she's always visiting Blythe, and you know Rushton's reputation for seducing anything in skirts, so it's quite plausible—"

"I don't believe it! I've seen the girl once or twice. She looked the complete innocent, the type to do just as she's told." Harold dismissed the entire story with a wave of his hand.

"Oh, really?" Godfrey said with an air of triumph. "Then let me tell you about her most recent escapade. Half the city knows about that, too. I heard it myself from that little Siamese lad who pretends to be my valet."

"All right, out with it. I can't help it if I ignore most of the gossips in town. Tell me the rest."

Esme groaned inwardly. The other sordid story about her and Lord Winthrop would now be aired. She squirmed uneasily as she waited for Godfrey to impart his gossip.

143

Deborah Martin

Godfrey leaned back in his chair and glanced across the table at Lord Winthrop, giving him a conspiratorial wink.

"Perhaps you should ask his lordship here. Then you can get it straight from the horse's mouth."

Lord Winthrop's answering stare was enough to unnerve anyone. "I don't know, Godfrey, you seem to be doing quite well on your own."

"Well, perhaps I shouldn't say anything . . ." Godfrey's good sense had evidently caught up with his mouth.

"No, no," Lord Winthrop told him dryly. "I'd be very interested to hear your tale. Do continue."

Esme tried not to show that she hung on every word of the conversation, but containing herself was difficult. Apparently, what her aunt had said would happen had. The foreign community was gossiping freely about her as if she were a loose woman. She tried to raise her cup nonchalantly to her lips, but had to set it down again, hoping no one would notice her trembling hands.

"Well," Godfrey said hesitantly, glancing at Lord Winthrop whose expression was unreadable. "Well, the way I heard it, she sneaked out of the house one night with two Siamese girls and showed up at the docks in one of those Siamese ensembles. You know the clothes I mean—the scanty sarong and scarf."

"Surely not!" Harold exclaimed.

"Oh, yes."

Harold frowned thoughtfully. "That certainly puts a new light on things."

"But there's more. While on the docks, they were attacked by sailors who thought they were tarts, understandably enough. God only knows what happened before Ian rescued them."

144

"Not much," Lord Winthrop replied, his eyes shooting daggers at Godfrey.

"You mean she didn't give you a 'reward' for saving her?" Godfrey said, blithely ignoring his friend's irritation. "After the way you asked about her that night, I would have thought she might. And certainly everyone thinks she did. But if what you say is true, then it's a pity you passed up a beauty like that and left her to Rushton and Michaels! Neither one deserves her."

"Someone ought to close your mouth for you permanently, Godfrey," Lord Winthrop told him coldly.

"Sorry, my lord," Godfrey said with a wicked grin. "I didn't mean to imply you weren't a gentleman or—"

"Of course you meant to imply it. But don't worry about it," Lord Winthrop told him, his face rigid as he tried to regain control of himself. "You might do well in the future, however, to remember I'm a far better shot than you are."

Godfrey laughed. "True. You always were."

Ignoring his sarcasm, Lord Winthrop said, "But do continue. Tell us why she's marrying this Michaels."

How could Lord Winthrop be so blind? Esme thought. It should be clear to him that she was being forced to marry because of all the lies being told about her.

Godfrey shrugged. "I suppose her father insisted on it. Michaels has apparently proposed before, or so I hear. I guess her father learned of the Rushton affair and her alleged affair with you and realized that her reputation would prevent anyone else from marrying her, so he jumped at Michaels's proposal this time."

"That's ridiculous," Lord Winthrop replied. "Though I didn't have an affair with her, she is the worst sort of flirt. Surely she's done this kind of thing before. Whatever reputation she has didn't seem to affect her popularity at the ball the other night, and her father hasn't made her marry because of her past transgressions. There *have* been some, haven't there?"

"Not that I know of," Godfrey said thoughtfully. "Until now, she's very rarely been talked about. Though that doesn't necessarily mean anything, does it? Perhaps she's good at hiding her peccadilloes. Now that you mention it, she did get into a bit of trouble last year."

Esme braced herself for the new lie she was certain Godfrey was about to spread.

"I heard some blather about her going to see the king's birthday celebration without her father's permission," Godfrey continued.

Esme almost sighed aloud with relief. Wanting to see the king's birthday celebration could hardly be considered a terrible sin.

Evidently, Lord Winthrop thought the same thing. "You mean to tell me," he remarked in chilly tones, "that Miss Montrose doesn't have the reputation for being a flirt?"

Godfrey laughed. "Esme Montrose? Not hardly. At least not until recently. I hardly know her, you understand. But in the foreign community, everyone talks and, well, they say she's a bit wild. She spends all her time with the Siamese, and you know the natives don't have our ethical and moral sense."

The conversation turned to other things, but Esme could no longer listen. *Don't have our ethical and moral sense!* she thought. *You're no better than they are, telling stories about me like that!* Esme could hardly believe what she'd heard. She wanted to defend her actions, and resented the disguise that prevented her from doing so.

Some of this was Lord Winthrop's fault, she thought. He seemed surprised that the stories, especially the one about him, had gotten around so fast, but he shouldn't be. As she had known would happen, once he told her aunt, the maid was sure to find out, and then it was certain to be spread from servant to servant. So little happened in Bangkok that every tidbit of gossip became a major news item in the foreign community.

She wanted to cry with frustration. How could people be so hurtful? She barely knew Godfrey, but he knew more about her than she'd ever dreamed possible, most of which wasn't even true!

And Lord Winthrop was even worse, calling her a flirt. Surely he'd been able to tell how little she knew about men when he'd kissed her at the ball. Though he had denied their affair, he persisted in believing that terrible rumor about her and Rushton. She struggled to contain her rage. Never had one man been able to get under her skin so much! The merchants' sons and young teachers she'd known had been very polite. A few had courted her, but she'd been too concerned about her father to pay much attention to them. Besides, none of them had really attracted her. They all seemed like such little boys.

But Lord Winthrop was a different matter entirely. He acted as if he had every right to know all about her. She didn't know how much longer she could keep from letting him know just how much she despised him.

Watching him across the table, however, she realized that he seemed a little repentant. The others talked animatedly, but he just stared past them at the riverbank, which darkness was beginning to shroud. She tried not to look at him, wanting to preserve her anger, but she couldn't help herself. Her eyes were drawn to his face. His gray-blue eyes gazed ahead, unseeing, while his lips were set in a grim line.

Out here in the wilderness, the men were in their shirtsleeves and waistcoats, making them look common. Except for Lord Winthrop. He had an air of authority about him that none of the rest did. She couldn't help but notice that the thin material of his shirt clung tightly to his corded, sinewy arms and that his chest was broad and muscular, filling out the waistcoat to perfection. The chestnut waves of his hair did nothing to take away from the rugged handsomeness of his face.

Suddenly, his eyes moved to hers and her breath caught in her throat as she realized she'd been staring at him for some time. She dropped her eyes to her plate, her hands twisting her napkin under the table. She feared that if she looked up, she would see that amused grin and know that he knew who she was. But when at last she glanced at him again, his eyes were once more staring out at the riverbank.

Her heart's pace slowed to normal, but she couldn't stand anymore. "I think I shall retire," she said, abruptly rising from the table. "I'm very tired."

"But what about dinner?" Lord Winthrop asked, turning his gaze to her again. "It's early and we may not eat for a while."

She thought surely he could read her very thoughts. "I'm fine," she responded. "I'm not very hungry."

She knew the men watched her closely as she left, but she didn't care. If she didn't escape them all right away, she'd say something she'd regret.

In her cabin, she breathed a little easier. But as she undid her plait, she thought to herself that this was going to be a long trip—a very long trip indeed.

Chapter Eight

Ian sat in the dining cabin, staring at the wall. The others had long ago returned to their cabins for the evening, leaving him to his brandy and his thoughts. Try as he might to dull his senses with spirits, he couldn't stop thinking about the conversation that had taken place earlier. He knew he wasn't guilty of anything. He'd kept Esme's secret until her aunt had told him some twisted version of what had happened at Loy Krathong. And he hadn't made up the gossip about him and Esme. Still, he could see again Esme standing before him, swearing that something terrible would happen if her family found out about the incident at the festival. Evidently, she hadn't lied, although it sounded to him like her affair with Rushton damned her more than her escapade to Loy Krathong and her supposed affair with him.

He tried to tell himself he didn't care she was

marrying Michaels. After all, she'd already given her favors to Rushton and possibly others. Or had she? He found it odd that she'd never been considered a flirt before. Harold had been stunned by Godfrey's gossip. Was it possible that someone had started the story on purpose? He certainly knew the gossip about him was false.

But what reason could anyone have for maligning her? It wasn't as if she had a fortune that someone could blackmail her for. She wasn't a significant member of the community. Her father was a schoolteacher, for God's sake!

But even if the story were true, what a terrible fate for her—to be married to a balding merchant. Ian sensed that she wouldn't be happy marrying someone just to save her reputation. He didn't know this Michaels, but if the man were anything like the men she'd danced with at the ball, she was soon to be married to a lecher, of that he was certain.

How could James Montrose do such a thing? Ian wondered. He'd liked Esme's father almost instantly, but now he began to wonder if he'd seen the man's true character. On the other hand, the story might not be quite as Godfrey had told it. Esme might have wanted the marriage, despite what she'd said at the ball. Perhaps she'd been attracted by all that wealth and the chance to escape her aunt.

He could hardly believe it, though. As Harold had said, Esme didn't seem the type to marry for money. But Ian had known his share of schemers in his day, including Caroline. Perhaps Esme was just better at hiding her true nature than some. After all, he mused, he hadn't realized until too late that Caroline wasn't what she seemed to be.

A vision of Esme came back to him as she looked

the night of the ball, her eyes wide and innocent as she recoiled from his kiss. He'd desired her then. God, how he'd desired her. He'd wanted to run his fingers through that ebony silken hair, making it float on her shoulders as it had before. Her lips had been so sweet, too tempting to be those of an innocent. And how could an innocent have fired him as she had? He wasn't in the habit of taking virgins. Virginal maidens didn't normally attract him; too much of the schoolroom air clung to their skirts, and their mamas were usually close behind, eager to capture an earl's son for their daughters. No, he'd steered clear of younger women, especially after Caroline.

Esme was no virginal maiden, though. Her body had Eve's guile, even if her mind didn't, for she'd enslaved his thoughts far more than Caroline ever had. He tried to put her out of his mind, but he couldn't, for now an image of her whirling around the ballroom in that wretched merchant's arms assailed him, and his fingers tightened on the stem of the glass he held.

Damn that Godfrey! Why had he mentioned Michaels? Now all Ian could see was another man's hands holding her, bending that lovely body of hers to his will.

"No!" he cried aloud, hurling the glass at the wooden wall opposite him as he started out of his chair. He'd go back, he'd get her father to change his mind, he'd . . . He'd do what? Marry her? He frowned. With Esme as his wife, his career would be over. She'd never be able to control her impulses, which was absolutely essential for a diplomat's wife.

Those were the practical reasons. But there were private ones. His pride wouldn't allow him to marry a woman whom everyone knew had been promiscuous—even if they had counted him as one of her lovers. It was out of the question. He would be marrying another Caroline and that was the last thing in the world he wanted.

He sighed. He could do nothing. She'd have to marry the merchant. Worse yet, with her twisted logic, she'd probably blame him for it. But better that she blame him, that she refuse to see him when he returned, than that he should find himself tied to her in some bedeviled union.

Or so he told himself. And later on he continued to tell himself he was better off without her, as he tossed and turned on the hard mattress before sinking into a drunken, troubled sleep.

"Damn it, Chan, where are the letters you wrote for me?" Lord Winthrop shouted as he threw papers across his desk.

"They are here before you, sir," Chan answered quietly, trying to point at the right papers while keeping well out of the way of his irate master. Chan didn't know what had happened to put Lord Winthrop in such a foul mood this morning, but he knew he'd better keep his distance.

It would only be a matter of time before Lord Winthrop discovered the absence of the maps and letters Chan had stolen, but perhaps if Chan were lucky it would be long after his bad mood had passed. Otherwise, Chan would have to tread carefully.

In all of his previous assignments, Chan had worked with weak men and fools. Gathering the information he needed for Michaels had been easy. No one had ever suspected him, because he was always careful to incriminate someone else with pieces of damning evidence. But this time, he'd been alarmed to find that his lordship was neither weak nor a fool. This would have to be his last job, he decided. The risks were too great. He would do only so much for money. Before long the British would start making some connections, and then he wouldn't be safe anywhere, perhaps not even in France.

Besides, there was the mess with Michaels and the Montrose girl. If Michaels's plan succeeded, perhaps everything would be all right. But Chan worried about it nonetheless. The girl probably wasn't a threat, but one never knew for certain. Chan watched Ian stoically. Yes, it was certainly time Chan got out of the business.

"Do they meet with your approval, sir?" Chan asked as Ian perused the letters.

"Yes, they're fine. But I need to refer to the copy of the last one we sent," he said, reaching for the key inside the pocket of his waistcoat.

Chan willed his expression to remain fixed as Lord Winthrop unlocked the strongbox and reached for the leather satchel inside. Opening it, Lord Winthrop thrust his hand into the case, but the sheaf of papers he removed looked thin indeed.

"Where are the others?" he muttered half to himself. He emptied the satchel on the table, then searched through the documents piled there, but no other papers turned up. "These aren't the letters I need," he said, pivoting to stare at Chan. "Where are the others?"

"I don't know. Only you have the key to the box."

"Yes, but where I keep it is no secret. Godfrey and Harold have both seen me use it. So have you and Lek."

"Are you suggesting that someone has taken the papers?"

"Of course I'm suggesting that. I certainly didn't misplace them myself." Lord Winthrop slammed the strongbox shut, his face grim. "They're definitely gone, along with the maps I require for this mission."

"Then perhaps you should search the cabins. There isn't much room on the boats. Such papers would be difficult to keep hidden." *Unless they're already off the boats*, Chan thought, as he knew they were. The entourage hadn't moored where it had by accident. Having been bribed by someone else so that Chan wouldn't be implicated, the crew had docked conveniently near a village where Chan's accomplice waited to take the documents northeast.

Lord Winthrop didn't seem to have heard him.

"Sir?" Chan asked.

"Yes, I suppose you're right. But I can hardly tell Godfrey and the others why I want to search their cabins. If they're innocent, as I'm sure they are, they'll be highly indignant. I have enough trouble without having to deal with Godfrey's hurt pride. Besides, it's just as likely that someone not of our party crept on board last night while we dined and then picked the lock on the box."

"But we're in the midst of the jungle. No one is nearby."

"It's not that deserted. We were at a popular mooring spot. In fact, there was a village not too far from where we were. Didn't you notice?" Lord Winthrop asked in irritation.

So Lord Winthrop had noticed the village, had he? "Not really. I spent most of my time writing those letters for you."

"At any rate, I'd rather be secretive about this."

"I could keep the others occupied, sir, while you search the cabins."

Lord Winthrop eyed him skeptically, dropping into the chair behind the table. "How will you do that?"

"I will engage them in a game of cards this evening after we stop. If we play on this boat, you can search the cabins on the other without difficulty."

"And what about Lek's cabin?" Lord Winthrop asked with a scowl.

"We will be making plenty of noise. If you're quiet, I do not think the boy will notice."

Lord Winthrop's eyes grew thoughtful as he rubbed his chin. "I don't know that I like this plan of yours, Chan." He looked down at the piles of papers, and his gaze hardened. "But I suppose I've no better alternative. We must find those maps. The others I have aren't nearly as accurate. And if the letters get into the wrong hands, it could be disastrous."

"We will find them, sir. Or find the spy who has taken them."

"I hope you're right," Lord Winthrop replied, waving his hand in a gesture of dismissal.

As Chan left the cabin, he congratulated himself. Nothing would be found yet, but he had the maps and letters and had also been able to plant a few seeds of suspicion. Now all he had to do was wait.

So the game has begun, Ian thought to himself as he watched Chan leave. Ian had wondered how long it would take Chan to pilfer the documents in the strongbox. He was surprised that Chan had moved so soon, but perhaps the spy hadn't expected the robbery to be discovered just yet.

Ian smiled to himself. Chan's contact would be infuriated when he discovered that the documents contained nothing of value. The valuable ones had been hidden safely somewhere else, shortly after he'd made an elaborate show of locking them in the strongbox. What Chan had stolen were old letters of little consequence and maps of seldom-used trade routes in north Siam.

Ian wondered if he'd find anything when he searched the cabins. He didn't think so. He doubted that Chan would start implicating anyone so soon. He never had before. In all the cases Chan had been involved in, the stolen material had never been recovered, but unimportant bits of it had eventually turned up in minor consular officials' quarters or offices.

At first, the British had been fooled. The men had been arrested. But in every case, the men had committed suicide before they could be questioned. That hadn't seemed unusual, since spies often killed themselves to prevent being questioned. But the latest case had made the British suspicious. This man's death had seemed less like suicide and more like murder. This, coupled with the fact that none of the men had seemed to profit from their activities (no secret monies found, no evidence of ties to the French), had forced the British to reconsider the cases. A careful scrutiny of all the people who might have had access to the stolen papers in each case— and there were hundreds—had finally allowed them to narrow the suspects down to two or three men and then down to one. Chan.

Now it was up to Ian to trap him, and more important, to track down Chan's contact, the one responsible for transporting the stolen documents to the French government. With the papers missing and Chan's hints that someone on board might be responsible, Ian felt certain he was getting close to capturing the elusive spy. All he needed was to catch Chan in the act and force him to reveal his contact.

For the moment, Ian had to go along with Chan and search the cabins. He might not find anything, but if by some chance Chan wasn't the spy and the papers were in someone else's possession, Ian needed to know that. Besides, if Chan had planted incriminating evidence, it would look odd if Ian didn't find it.

The hours before nightfall passed swiftly, since Ian was preoccupied with assessing just what Chan had taken from the strongbox and what he'd left. Then Ian dealt, through Lek, with some squabble among the Siamese crewmen. As he watched Lek speak animatedly to the boat crew, Ian wondered again where he'd seen the boy. Something about his gestures seemed so familiar. But Ian couldn't place him, and finally gave up trying.

When at last they moored for the evening, Chan wasted no time in urging his companions to join him in a game of cards. Lek seemed about to hesitate, but Chan was so insistent that Lek finally agreed, stating that he'd have to learn how to play. Feeling like a fool, Ian slipped into Lek's cabin, deciding he might as well begin with the most difficult one. His movements were stealthy as he closed the shutters of the cabin and lit the small lantern.

The boats were built in such a way that all the passenger's possessions were kept in compartments under the deck, so Ian looked there first. He drew out Lek's bag and began to remove the items in it, intending to glance quickly through the contents.

The first thing he found was a tortoiseshell comb. He thought to himself that was a rather odd thing for a poor orphan boy to own. Then he came across a cedar box, carved with intertwining *fleur de lis*. That struck him as being even odder than the comb. Inside the box he found a small sum of money and some women's jewelry resting on a man's handkerchief. His curiosity increased as he dumped the rest of the items onto the cot. He noticed a European-style dress and petticoat. Why did Lek have foreign women's clothing and jewelry?

Determined to find the answer to the mystery, he passed the lantern quickly over the other objects on the bed. A sarong and scarf of blue silk material drew his attention. He spread both pieces. One piece had a tear in the middle where a pin had held it; the pin was still attached to one end. And suddenly he remembered where he'd seen such material and a gold filigree pin. He snatched up the curious box again, dumping its contents out and holding up the man's handkerchief. It was his.

Now faced with the facts, he was forced to make the logical conclusion. The tinted glasses, the shy behavior whenever he was in the room—it all made sense. No wonder Lek looked so familiar to him. Confronted with the evidence, Ian had to admit that Lek wasn't a poor orphan boy at all, but the same girl who'd kept him up half the night regretting his actions.

Damn her! he thought in a burst of rage. He'd been right to think her guilty of all that she was charged with, for she was truly the most devious woman he'd ever known! She'd probably been laughing at him all along, delighting in fooling him! But she must have been out of her mind to go this far, he thought.

His hand clenched the blue silk unconsciously. No doubt she knew what position she'd placed him in. She knew that if he should discover her and send her back, her family would be as furious with him as they would be with her and would no doubt try to force him to marry her. They wouldn't believe he hadn't brought her along purposely.

Well, if that was her plan, she'd soon learn she was wrong to cross him. He was certainly not going to marry some conniving flirt who thought to force his hand by insinuating herself into his camp!

The more he thought about it, the angrier he became. And he'd been feeling sorry for her last night! He certainly didn't feel sorry for her now. She was a devious schemer who deserved to be thrashed within an inch of her life for what she'd done! That was what she needed, a sound caning, and he'd take great pleasure in giving it to her when he confronted her.

Then his anger turned into a cold fury as he contemplated the clothes spread out before him. Perhaps there were better ways to punish her. Yes, there certainly were. He stuffed his handkerchief in his pocket. Then he placed everything else back in the bag, setting it into its original position. He left the cabin, noting with satisfaction that Chan had kept the other members of his party occupied since the deck remained empty and no lights shown from the other boat.

He thoroughly searched the other cabins, but he found nothing. Of course, he hadn't expected to find anything. Chan wouldn't make it too easy or it would look like a setup. But at the moment, Ian wasn't concerned with Chan. His entire being was filled with rage at one person only, and he eagerly anticipated venting that rage.

He returned to where the men were playing cards.

"May I see you in my cabin for a moment, Chan?" he asked, doing his best to avoid looking at "Lek."

When they were both in the cabin, Ian slammed his hand onto the desk in frustration.

"I take it you did not find the letters?" Chan asked.

Ian nodded.

"As you said before, it's possible that the culprit isn't on this boat," Chan continued.

"Yes, yes," Ian said impatiently. "I must find those papers, though, and the possibility remains that one of the men on board has them. I've no choice but to search the men themselves."

Chan gave him a startled look before he once again gained control of himself.

"Is that really necessary, sir?" he asked. "It might alert the spy to what you are doing. Why not just observe them all closely for the next few days? Perhaps one of them will slip and give you a clue to where the papers are hidden."

"Trust me. I know exactly what I'm doing. And I'll start with the interpreter. Tell him to come to my cabin."

"Yes, sir," Chan replied meekly as he headed for the door.

Ian smiled to himself as the door closed behind Chan.

Oh, yes, he thought, *Miss Montrose is about to learn just what it's like to attempt to deceive Ian Winthrop. And I don't think she's going to enjoy the lesson.*

Chapter Nine

Esme entered Lord Winthrop's cabin behind Chan, wondering what on earth his lordship wanted with her now. He stood at one end of the cabin, his profile clearly outlined by the light spilling from the lamp that hung on the cabin wall.

"Leave us," Lord Winthrop told Chan.

The secretary gave a quick bow and left the room. When the door closed behind Chan, Lord Winthrop didn't turn toward her but continued to stand beside his desk. He seemed engrossed in reading a file, but she got the uncanny feeling he was also observing her.

She asked herself yet again how she could have been so stupid to think she could pull off her charade. Granted, she'd assumed she wouldn't have to deal with Lord Winthrop every day, but even once in a while was too often. Maintaining her nasal voice and accent had become tedious, if not painful.

And knowing that only a flimsy wooden wall separated her cabin from his had certainly worsened matters.

Then there was the constant fear he might discover who she was. It was one thing to believe during her planning of this fiasco that he could do nothing to her on the trip, but quite another matter to contemplate facing his wrath when she saw him every day.

What could he possibly want with her now? No Siamese were in his room, so he didn't want her to interpret for him. And he didn't seem to need her advice on Siamese custom, for he wasn't saying a word, just staring ahead of him at the desk.

Finally he turned to fix her with an insolent stare, making her heart leap in her throat.

"I called you in here, Lek, because some very important letters and maps are missing. Did you notice any such papers while you were in here yesterday?"

Esme kept her eyes riveted on the floor so that he wouldn't detect the consternation in her face. Now she really was in a pickle. He thought she was a spy, of all things!

"No, sir," she answered with the meekness of the Oriental.

"I see. I also remember that you lived with the Jesuits for many years and speak French. Could you perhaps be more partial to the French than you led me to believe?"

He moved to stand in front of her, his arms folded across his broad chest. She tried to control the anxiety threatening to affect her voice.

"No, sir. As I said before, I was not happy at the orphanage and thus was glad to receive this position in your service." At least she didn't have to defend the priests, for they had a reputation for being overly strict with their young charges.

"You mean to say you don't feel gratitude to the very people who saved you from dying in the streets?"

Esme saw her mistake instantly, but didn't know how to answer.

"Lek?"

"I think you misunderstand, sir. Is it not possible to be glad to be alive, but not happy about the life you are supposed to live?"

"All right then. We'll assume you have no love for the Jesuits. Perhaps you can tell me what Father Joseph, in particular, has done to you to make you dislike them so."

Esme searched her memory. Was there a Father Joseph? She'd been to the orphanage several times, and she didn't think there was a Father Joseph. Yet, it had been three or four weeks since she'd last visited it. Suppose someone had come in on the latest ship? There'd been talk that a new priest was on his way. Or was that a new missionary for the Baptists? Oh, dear, if only she could think! But he was making her too nervous to think.

"Well?"

"He's been very kind to me, unlike some others."

"There isn't a Father Joseph."

Esme felt a surge of anger at the way he was trying to trap her in a lie. She decided to strike back. She raised her head to look him straight in the eye. "Then why did you ask about him, *Than*?"

Was she wrong or did a glint of amusement briefly light those cold silvery eyes? No, she must have imagined it, for now his face was blank.

He leaned forward, the muscles in his arms tensing as if he were controlling some violent impulse.

"I think you're lying, Lek. I think you're a spy planted by the French, who'd love to get their hands on those papers. How much did they agree to pay you? A thousand *baht*? Two thousand?"

"I'm not a spy!" she protested, forgetting to disguise her voice. "Would a spy come to you from a French orphanage, sir? Wouldn't a good spy have apparent loyalties to your government?"

"Perhaps," he said, his eyes now piercing her with a look that made her knees shake.

She struggled against the desire to confess everything to him, to throw herself on his mercy. She remembered instead the many insults he'd given her, and her chin jutted out stubbornly. Her temper got the better of her, making her forget to be as cautious as a Siamese would be.

"Why do you accuse me, sir, and not the others? Is it because I am not of your race and the others are?"

He shrugged. "Chan—an Oriental like yourself, I might add—felt you were the most likely suspect. After all, your ties to the French are much closer than anyone else's on board."

"And, of course, I am less likely to make a fuss. Is that not part of it too, sir?"

"All of that is beside the point," he stated as he advanced even closer to her so that scarcely an inch separated them. "You've only tried to skirt the issue. You haven't convinced me you're not a spy, so I'll have to take measures myself to ensure it. You could have those papers anywhere on you. If you're not a spy, then you won't object to a search. You won't mind letting me examine your clothing or what's hidden underneath, will you?" An unmistakable expression of triumph lit his face.

For a second, her heart seemed to stop beating.

Could it be he knew? No, how could he? At breakfast he'd acted quite normally toward her. She hadn't seen him at all in the meantime, so how could he have learned anything?

"You cannot examine my clothing," she told him, her voice noticeably quavering.

Her reply didn't seem to surprise him. "As your employer, I may do as I please. And at the moment, I wish to remove your uniform and search you."

Her breath came in short gasps. He couldn't do this to her, he couldn't! Her desperation carried into her voice as she said, "You have no proof I stole the papers. I will not allow you to search me unless you produce some evidence of my guilt. I will not remove my uniform for you." She didn't know what else to say to dissuade him.

"But you see," he said, his voice now almost menacing, "*you* won't be removing your uniform. *I* will."

At the thought of his hands moving over her body, Esme couldn't help but blush. To her relief, he seemed not to notice, however, as he circled her to stand at her back.

"It is the same thing as far as I'm concerned," she answered him, his presence behind her upsetting her even more. "I will not let you search me."

"It seems to me, Lek," he replied, his voice sarcastic as he said the name, "that you have only two choices. Either let yourself be arrested for the spy that you are or allow me to search you. Which is it to be?"

Now was the time to tell him, she thought. She might as well get it over with. But she couldn't bring herself to do it. She'd almost rather be arrested as a spy than admit to him what she'd done and risk facing the unknown extents of his cold fury.

"Have you decided?" he asked behind her.

"I cannot let you search me, sir," she mumbled.

"Indeed. Perhaps I should tell you I've already taken the liberty of searching your belongings. Regrettably, I didn't find the papers among them, which is why I must search your person."

At first, the full implication of what he said didn't hit her. Then her heart sank as she realized he must have seen her dress.

"You know!" she whispered.

She felt his fingers at the back of her neck release the black ribbon that tied her braid together. Slowly, he unraveled her plait.

"What do you think I know?" he asked in a hard voice as with one hand he toyed with the strands of her hair while his other hand rested on her shoulder.

"You unconscionable wretch!" she cried. Then she whirled to face him, swinging at his hands and throwing her shoulders back. "You've known all along."

His eyes were now unfathomable as he stared her down. With a roughness born of anger, he removed her glasses, tossing them behind her onto the desk as he spoke. "Not quite. Not until I searched your room."

"To find the supposedly 'missing papers?'" she bit out, furious at the way he'd played with her emotions.

"Oh, the documents are missing all right. I still have to search you." His jaw firmly set, he started toward her.

"Not if I have anything to say about it," she retorted, darting around his desk, putting it between them. "You'll have to take my word for it that I didn't steal them."

His face was now rigid with anger. It was all she could do to keep from quailing in front of him as he advanced on the desk. "The word of a scheming little brat who thought to use me as cover for her devious purposes? Why should I take your word?" He slammed his fist onto the flimsy table, making it shake.

"You—you monster!" she cried as they both circled the desk. She tried desperately to keep him away from her. "You promised you wouldn't tell anyone about what happened at Loy Krathong. Then you turned around and told my aunt anyway without so much as a pang of conscience and made her think the worst of me. Now you accuse me of being untrustworthy? You have some nerve!"

Ian's face tightened as he stopped dead in his tracks. "I didn't reveal anything that wasn't already known."

"Of course you did!"

"You were foolish enough to trust your little Siamese friends, so they gossiped about the whole thing in the markets and Harriet Bingham's maid found out. Harriett told your aunt. I only confirmed it was true and corrected the version she'd heard. I cannot be blamed for your aunt's refusal to believe me and to think we had a dalliance."

"You're lying!" she cried out.

He ignored her outburst. "By the time the story had reached your aunt, the gossips had you willingly cavorting with sailors by the riverside and had added me to the list!"

Esme gazed at him, stunned. Was he telling the truth? Had Lamoon and Mai really betrayed her? She remembered now the curious looks they'd given each other when she'd told them what had happened. Curious guilty looks. She knew how much they loved to gossip. How often had she discovered the most intimate details about other *farang* households just by listening to them?

Suddenly a terrible thought occurred to her. If they'd revealed that secret, what about the more important one of where she'd gone? Her heart raced as she wondered if even now Michaels was on her trail. No, she tried to reassure herself, her friends certainly wouldn't reveal that secret, for she'd sworn them to secrecy on her mother's grave. The Siamese belief in ghosts was so strong that Esme doubted they'd risk being haunted just to spread idle gossip.

Her shoulders slumped as she realized that Lord Winthrop probably told the truth.

As he saw her expression change, he said arrogantly, "I told you the first night we met what a risk you were taking. You should have listened to me."

Coming from him, that advice only angered her more. "Lamoon and Mai may have revealed that secret," she countered with eyes flashing black fire, "but they didn't know about the night on the gallery at the ball. Did my aunt happen to mention that?"

"Oh, come now, what could she have known of that?" he said with exasperation in his voice.

"She found your handkerchief with my ball gown. Besides, she isn't blind, you know. As my chaperone, she watched my every move. In spite of your attempts to be chivalrous and protect my reputation," she said in a voice that implied he'd really done no such thing, "she knew where and with whom I'd been while I was gone. My aunt accused me of having...having been compromised. She said we were having a 'liaison' at the ball. And you heard Godfrey say everyone believes we did."

169

"You're not going to imply that this entire misbegotten scheme is my fault now, are you?" His eyes glinted like cold steel as he spat out the words. "Tell me, are you also going to claim I forced you into your affair with Rushton?"

She stared at him in astonishment, momentarily at a complete loss for words. "You—you—" she sputtered. Then she matched his rage with her own. "You can't tell me you believe that vicious lie!"

His expression was implacable.

"You *would* believe it, wouldn't you?" she said bitterly. "You've been certain from the moment you met me that I was . . . that kind of woman."

Lord Winthrop darted around the table, catching Esme off guard. Now stung by her accusations, he grabbed her arms in a determined grip, thrusting her back against the hard teak cabin wall. His eyes raked her.

"You amaze me," he said, sarcasm lacing his words. "You're truly a consummate actress. You expect me to believe that you put on this disguise and acted the part, lying whenever it suited you, because you were an innocent and put-upon virgin. Let me tell you something. Innocent maidens don't slip out of the house at night, clad only in a piece of silk. Innocent maidens don't sneak aboard boats and pretend to be boys. You really have lost your mind if you think I'd believe anything you say now."

"I don't care if you believe me or not," she cried, struggling to escape his grasp, her hands pressing hard against his chest. "Why, you already think I'm a spy," she said as if the entire idea were ridiculous. "How can I expect you to believe the truth about anything else?"

"Oh, yes," he said with deadly calm. "I'd forgotten you're a suspect. I should be searching you. I

170

admit I'm curious to see how you managed to hide your rather unboylike physique. Of course all you need do to keep me from searching you is admit the truth—that you intended to use this silly escapade to trap me into marrying you and to save your reputation. Admit it!''

Trapped against the wall, she felt helpless under his onslaught. But if he thought to make her say what wasn't true and beg his forgiveness, he was in for a surprise. She glared at him and threw her shoulders back proudly, dropping her hands from his chest.

"Search me then if you must, you cad, because I can't confess to what I haven't done," she challenged him, her jet-black eyes defiantly clashing with his ice-blue ones.

Her stubbornness seemed to infuriate him. "I certainly will, since you've decided not to be sensible," he retorted, his mouth hardening into a thin line.

She willed herself not to move as he slid both hands under her arms. His cool gaze raking her body, he patted her sides as if he expected any minute to find the incriminating papers. When his hands reached her waist, they paused. He glanced at her face to see if she was ready to say what he wanted to hear. She put as much withering contempt into her expression as she dared. Stony with rage, he returned his attention to his search.

Deliberately, he slipped his hands over her hips, hesitating a moment to make her aware of the intimacy of his touch. Then his hands slid to the sides of her thighs and down her legs. He stood up, waiting for her response. But she closed her eyes, fearing what he might do next. His steely gaze never leaving her face, he lifted one hand to the wooden buttons at the collar of her jacket. With decisiveness, he unbuttoned the top button and slowly moved on to the next.

When his fingers reached the fourth button, she couldn't stand it anymore. Try as she might to hold them back, tears flooded her eyes. One of them slipped slowly down her reddened cheek to drop off her trembling chin.

His hand hesitated at the collar of her jacket as he watched in horror the tears that began to stream freely down her face. He reeled away from her, his face registering both surprise and anger. He jerked his handkerchief from his pocket and offered it to her.

The sight of it reminded her that he'd gone through her things. She thrust his hand away in disgust, releasing the breath she'd held as she waited for him to remove her clothes.

His chiseled jaw tightened as his anger returned for a fleeting moment. "No, I don't suppose you'd want to dry your tears. That would destroy the affect, wouldn't it?"

Fury and humiliation warring in her face, she snatched the handkerchief and used it, struggling to force her tears back.

They stood in silence as both tried to gain control of their emotions. Her breath came in short gasps as she realized how close he'd come to stripping her.

After a long silence, he spoke, "How long had you planned to continue this charade?"

"Until we reached Chiengmai," she answered, forcing her eyes away from him as she tried to compose herself. "I planned to get a job as a teacher there."

"And you really thought I'd be fooled that long?"

he asked, his words harsh as he flashed her an accusing glance.

"I—I didn't think I'd have to interpret very much until we reached Chiengmai. I didn't realize you needed someone so often during the trip."

"So you planned to leave me without an interpreter in Chiengmai."

Her eyes avoided his as a quick pang of guilt shot through her. "I'm sorry," she murmured, a hint of shame in her voice. "It was a stupid idea. But you must understand I couldn't stay in Bangkok."

He lifted a hand to her chin, stroking down and beneath the mandarin collar until the tips of his fingers traced tiny paths down her neck.

"Poor Esme, forced to marry that fellow Michaels," he said, his voice slightly bitter as his hand closed on her shoulder, drawing her nearer to him.

She twisted away from his hand, turning her back to him. "I couldn't do it. I couldn't marry a man I found so repellent. He said he'd treat me well. But I couldn't believe him—he frightened me so. I couldn't stand to have his hands on me. And I certainly don't care enough about my reputation to marry him. Actually, I'm surprised he still wanted to marry me, after everything that's been said of me."

He took in what she was saying in silence. Then he said, "That doesn't surprise me at all. You're a beautiful woman."

"And faithless and deceitful," she added acidly. "Quite a bargain for any man. Between you, my father, and half the population of Bangkok, I've changed overnight from a slightly unconventional girl into a—a whore. Amazing what a few well-placed words can do to a woman."

173

He sucked in his breath. "You insist you've never been to Rushton's bed?"

"What does it matter if I tell you the truth? You won't believe me anyway." She clenched her fingers into a fist.

"You must admit I've good reason for finding it all hard to accept," he said, his lips tensing. Clasping her arms tightly, he forced her to face him. "Why would anyone spread a false rumor about you? Have you any idea?"

Her father had asked the same thing. She'd sought the answer over and over, but could think of nothing.

"I don't know," she said softly. "Father said Mr. Lawrence insisted that Mr. Rushton told him the story. I can't believe Mr. Rushton would invent such a lie. Yet I don't know why Mr. Lawrence would say such a thing either."

"Or you can't think of any reason to give," he retorted, ignoring her consternation. "Perhaps I was wrong. Perhaps you're not as good at lying as I thought. If you're attempting to save your lover's precious reputation by insisting you've both been falsely impugned, I'm afraid you won't be too successful. From all accounts, his shenanigans are already widely known. Still, your affair seems to have surprised even the gossips."

"I won't defend myself to you anymore," she said with a regal air, "since you're clearly determined to believe what you wish."

"I think it's a bit too convenient that you ended up on *my* boat. But I'm sure you thought that out. You knew your presence here would make things difficult for me, especially after you knew your aunt's accusations had become well known." His eyes searched her face as if hoping to read the truth there.

She swallowed as his gray-blue gaze bore into her. "I'll admit," she said with some hesitation, "that the thought occurred to me. But I truly hoped you wouldn't find out, that I could escape to Chiengmai unnoticed and begin a new life there."

"And that's why you decided to run away," he said flatly.

"Yes. What other choice did I have?"

"You might have come to me openly. You might have declared your innocence and asked for my help. I would have gladly aided you."

Her answering laugh was bitter. "Like you aided me before? Forgive me if I didn't think you had my best interests at heart. I told you terrible things would happen, but you didn't believe me. I thought I'd be better off taking care of myself than relying on you. I still think that."

"If taking care of yourself is so important, why stow away on my boat? You must have known I'd guess who you were eventually." Then he answered his own question. "Admit it. You assumed I'd take care of you, possibly marry you to save your reputation and mine." This time his tone was matter-of-fact, the anger gone out of it.

Her frustration mounted, for she didn't seem able to make him see how things really were with her. All he was concerned about was his own neck. "You would see it that way, wouldn't you? But, no, that's not what I intended. I already told you. I thought I could get to Chiengmai without your noticing me."

That statement really got his attention. His hands reached for her hips, pulling her against his body. She stood mesmerized by his smoky gaze.

"Did you really think I could avoid noticing you, Esme?" His fingers slid sensuously up the jacket to rest on her waist, his thumbs caressing the silky smoothness of her camisole-clad skin.

"Please don't," she said, her breath catching in her throat.

"Don't what?" he murmured before he lowered his head, and in the moment before his lips touched hers, she knew she wouldn't be able to resist his kiss. She shouldn't even try. She'd relived that first kiss too many times not to want to experience it once more. But she knew she ought to fight the creeping warmth that stole through her body.

His lips played with hers, teasing them into opening for him. But once her soft lips admitted him entrance, he abandoned all semblance of gentleness. He crushed her against him, one hand sliding around to her back as the other fiercely gripped her waist. His tongue darted boldly in and around the delicate contours of her mouth. She felt as if he consumed her, devouring her very soul. And she let him, reveling in the possessiveness of his kiss. Against her will, her body responded, arching against him as her hands crept around his waist to cling to the firm muscled body separated from her by two thin pieces of cloth.

His hands slid beneath her jacket to climb the smoothness of her back. When he encountered the linen cloth that bound her breasts, he lifted his lips from hers. Amusement crossed his face as he gazed into her dark eyes glazed with desire.

"What did you do, my little runaway?" he whispered huskily. "Bind yourself? Isn't that rather extreme?"

She felt his hand grope along the material, searching for the pins that held it in place. In a panic, she realized she couldn't let him find them or she'd be lost to his desire. Reluctantly, she tore herself away from him, leaning against the wall to regain her breath as he stood there, his eyes still smoky with desire riveted on her face.

He reached for her again, but she slipped away from the wall and across the room, putting as much distance between them as she could in the tiny cabin. When at last she brought herself to look at him, he was leaning back against the wall where she'd been. He stared at her, his entire body rigid, as if he sought a way to regain control.

"What am I to do with you now?" he asked, one hand gripping the chair in front of him so tightly she thought it would crumble.

"I—I don't know," she answered, her breath still coming quickly. "You've every right to put me off at the next stop."

A muscle worked in his jaw. "Don't be silly. I'm not in the habit of leaving homeless urchins to fend for themselves in foreign countries."

"Siam is my home."

"Yes, I know," he retorted, his sarcastic tone returning. "But we're presently in the middle of a jungle. You wouldn't last two days out there. Even in the villages, you wouldn't be safe. The Siamese are very suspicious of foreigners, particularly now that the French are advancing in the north. No, I suppose I must take you to Chiengmai."

"And what will you expect me to do in the meantime, my lord?" she asked, her body stiffening as she prepared to do battle if his suggestion didn't meet with her approval.

His lips curled in a grin at the obvious rebelliousness in her voice. "Do call me Ian, won't you?" He paused. "Now what did you ask? Oh, yes. What do

I expect you to do? I don't suppose you'd want to be my . . . ah . . . companion for the remainder of the trip, shall we say?" At her look of outrage, he chuckled. "No, I didn't think so. At least not yet."

"Not ever!"

"Of course," he said lazily. "Then, unless we want to cause an enormous scandal, you'd best remain disguised as my interpreter. After all, I still need one. When we reach Chiengmai, I'll relinquish you to the consulate, and they can give me their interpreter. They'll take charge of you until I return to Bangkok and inform your father where you are. Then he can come and fetch you if he likes."

"What a tidy plan," she said bitterly. "No hint of scandal touches your name, since no one need know how I got to Chiengmai. Of course it doesn't do too much for me. I'll still have to marry Mr. Michaels, and I'll be no better off than I was before!"

He shrugged. "It's not as bad as it sounds. Nothing can stop you from searching for a teaching position while you wait for your father. By the time he reaches Chiengmai, you could be well established at some school. Besides, by then I'm sure your Mr. Michaels will have changed his mind about marrying you. Who wants a bride so reluctant she'd run off with the very man she supposedly took as a lover?" His face showed he clearly thought she'd exaggerated the gravity of the situation.

"And what if you're wrong? What if my father insists on bringing me back? What if Mr. Michaels still insists on marrying me?" she asked in despair, feeling her throat constrict at the thought of being sent back to be married.

"I'm sorry, Esme. That's the way it must be." His voice was full of pity, which only upset her more.

"Men like you are always sorry, but that doesn't

stop you from hurting people. If it weren't for men like you, I wouldn't be in this mess."

He flinched, then took a step forward, glowering at her. "You're angry because at last you've been found out. Well, you'd best learn to place the blame where it really lies—on yourself. I don't need a sulking woman upsetting my plans. Do you understand me?"

"Quite well," she said icily. "Now may I have your permission to retire, my lord, or do you still have to search me to determine if I am a spy as well as a prodigal daughter?"

"No, you little—" he started, and then thought better of it. "No, I don't need to search you. I didn't think for one moment you might be a spy. Don't worry about that. But I won't have you pulling any more crazy tricks. You may bloody well leave."

She began to open the door, then was stopped by his voice. "I think you'd best put your glasses back on and plait your hair again before you go out, unless you want everyone to get the wrong idea."

She gave him a murderous look as she reached back and braided her hair. Then she moved stiffly toward the desk. But as she reached for her glasses, his hand closed over her wrist in a steely grip.

"I might point out something you clearly haven't considered. When you left Bangkok, you left everything behind. Anything could happen to you and no one would know. I'm the only one standing between you and that jungle. I can't afford the trouble that would ensue if you were found in my camp, so you'd best play your game well or I might just abandon you after all."

"I'll do my best, don't worry," she retorted, trying to wrest her hand away from him.

"I'm not worried. Because if you don't do as I say,

if you defy me at all, I'll send you back to Bangkok as a prisoner and claim you're a spy."

"Are you saying, my lord, that you would take advantage of my situation to make me do whatever you wish?"

"No. Nor did I mean what you're implying. I don't force women to lie with me, despite what you think. In everything else, however, I'll have your complete obedience. And my first command is that you stay out of my way as much as possible."

"Gladly!" she retorted as she wrenched her hand loose from his grip. Then she stormed out of the cabin and flung the door shut behind her.

Chapter Ten

Esme awakened with a start, some slight noise having intruded on her already restless sleep. She heard it again. Splashing sounds in the river. She recognized the noises, for she'd often seen the jumping fish that came out at night. But why had they awakened her tonight? And why had she tossed and turned so violently ever since she'd gone to bed?

Then she remembered what had happened the night before. First, Ian had confronted her in his cabin. Then she'd been forced to endure a torturous dinner with him glaring across the table while the others looked quizzically at both of them.

Now she lay staring at the mosquito netting that surrounded her bunk. She knew it wasn't yet near dawn, because no bird cries marred the night's stillness. She began to feel hemmed in by the silken threads of the netting, as if Ian himself had woven the cocoon that encircled her, cutting her off from the world. She clawed at the thin material as she searched for the opening until at last she was free and out of her bunk.

Her breath came quickly as she glanced about the room. The cabin that before had seemed her conduit to freedom was now her prison. She darted for the door, unconcerned that her hair still hung freely down her back and that she wore only the thin Chinese robe which served as her nightdress.

All was dark and quiet as she stepped outside her cabin. The others would be in bed for quite some time, so she felt certain she'd be alone for a while. She crept to the back of the boat and sat down in one of the rattan chairs.

She wondered how she'd endure the next few weeks, knowing that once they reached Chiengmai the consulate would take over for her father. Once the authorities learned who she was, they'd undoubtedly refuse to help her find a position until they heard from her father. And until she reached Chiengmai, she was trapped. Ian had been right, of course, about her not being able to survive alone in the jungle.

So how could she convince Ian not to tell the consulate who she was and not to tell her father where she was? If he only understood how serious everything was, perhaps. . . .

No, he chose not to understand, just as he chose to believe that evil rumor. In his eyes, she'd brought all of this on herself. To a certain extent she had, but she wasn't the scheming flirt he thought she was. Perhaps if she could prove to him she could be responsible. Yes, that was it. If she acted the part of dedicated interpreter to perfection, perhaps he'd be impressed enough with her maturity to let her do as she'd planned once she reached Chiengmai.

She felt a little better having made that decision. She knew keeping to it would be difficult, for she wanted nothing more than to thwart him every way she could. But acting responsibly seemed the best approach to her problem. She'd endure the humiliation and do whatever he asked. Except of course for certain unmentionable things. Her cheeks flamed as she thought of what he'd like her to do. Well, she'd certainly never do *those* things.

After a moment on deck, she told herself she should return to her cabin. But the night was so peaceful she continued to sit there, gazing around at the quiet calm of her surroundings. Suddenly tiny lights flashed on a tree opposite her as if a million miniature candles had been lit at once. She smiled. It never ceased to amaze her that the fireflies could be so attuned to each other that they flashed their lights in unison. The points of light extinguished themselves after a few seconds of glory. Moments after that, they lit up again, sprinkling the tree with light.

She watched the lights pulse on and off for some time. Then she glanced at the other bank to see if it too had trees lit by fireflies, but it was dark. As her eyes became accustomed to the darkness, she could see the hulking shapes and floating shadows of the jungle trees lining the other bank. They seemed to keep a silent vigil over her, and she settled more comfortably in her chair as the boat rocked softly. Her eyelids drooped, so she closed them for a moment....

A loud creak made her sit up abruptly. She realized her eyes had been closed far longer than a moment, because the sky was beginning to lighten. Frantically, she glanced around. Then she saw who'd made the noise that had awakened her. Sitting next to her in one of the other chairs was Ian.

"I know the bunks are uncomfortable," he said dryly, "but these chairs are hardly better."

"I didn't mean to fall asleep—" she began, darting out of the chair.

"Don't worry about it. You look lovely when you sleep."

Color suffused her cheeks. "How long have you been sitting there?" she demanded.

"Long enough to notice that you sleep with the most girlishly innocent expression on your face. As if nothing horrible in this world has ever touched you."

She couldn't stop the words that came tumbling out. "But we both know how deceptive such an expression is. I'm a consummate actress, remember?"

A smile flickered across his face. "Of course. Actually, if you continue to doze out here, you're going to need far greater acting abilities than even you have."

She stared at him in confusion. "What do you mean?"

"I'm merely trying to point out, that if any of the others came upon you sleeping on the deck, they might wonder why Lek looks so feminine. Especially since you seem to wear very little under that robe, if anything."

If he expected her to blush, she didn't oblige him. She was too angry at being chastised yet again. Her chin came up proudly. "I thought, my lord, I'd be alone. If you'll notice, no one else is up but you. How was I to know you'd be spying on me so early? But don't worry. I'll do my best to remain closeted in my suffocating little cabin for the rest of the trip."

She started to pass him to get to her cabin, but his hands grabbed her waist, yanking her onto his lap so quickly that the rattan chair threatened to dump them both on the floor.

"If you didn't wish me to spy on you, my dear, you shouldn't have come on the voyage," he hissed in her ear as she struggled to escape his grasp.

"Release me at once!" she cried, her hands beating at the arms that held her as easily as if she were a child.

"Shh, shh!" he whispered against her cheek as his arms encircled her, pinning her arms at her sides. "You don't want the others to wake up, do you? Sound carries out here."

She glanced up to find his eyes twinkling merrily at her, making her even angrier. "If you don't want the others to hear me," she hissed back, "then you'd better release me!"

But he only tightened his iron hold. His lips brushed the corner of her ear, then trailed tiny kisses on the lobe and down her golden neck. She didn't move as she felt him bury his face in the curtain of her hair. His arm around her waist pressed up against the undersides of her breasts, making them tingle with a strange sensation she'd never before experienced.

Slowly, through the thin silk of her robe, she became aware of his arousal, of the hard bulge that pressed against her bottom. This time she did blush as the blood rushed through her body. Feebly, she struggled against him again, but he only bent her back across his arm as his eyes, oddly colorless in the dim morning light, captured hers in a gaze so intense with longing she couldn't tear herself away from it.

"I don't know how I'm going to stay away from

185

you these next few weeks, Esme. If you insist on denying us both what could be a very pleasurable experience, you'd best not let me see you again with your hair down and loose. Or I swear I'll carry you off to my cabin and lock you up there for as long as I can keep you. Which wouldn't be wise for either you or me."

"Yes, Ian," she whispered, unable to say more.

At her use of his first name, a ragged breath escaped his lips. He began to lower them to hers, but the sudden movement of the boat that stopped him also made her wriggle out of his arms in alarm. Someone had stepped on board.

They froze as they heard a loud knock at one of the cabin doors. After a moment, a voice called out, "Lord Winthrop! Are you awake?" It was Chan.

She glanced at Ian in terror. She couldn't get back to her cabin without being seen by Chan because it was next to Ian's. Ian drew one finger to his lips and motioned her to move out of sight to the opposite side of the boat.

"I'm back here!" he called out to Chan as she obeyed his order.

"I have brought the cook with me," Esme heard Chan say as he rounded the back of the cabins. "I am very sorry to disturb you so early, but he says we must find a village before we leave if you want fresh fruit and vegetables for the next few days. He did not have time to gather sufficient provisions in Bangkok. I thought you should speak with him."

The voice that spoke next sent a shiver through Esme.

"I tole 'im not to bother you, sir, but 'e says as you ought to know that we need the interpreter to go with us."

Esme would have recognized that voice anywhere, for she could still hear it saying, "I'll teach you, bitch, to claw your betters!" She smothered her horrified moan behind her hand. The sailor! What was that awful sailor doing on board the boats?

Ian evidently wondered the same thing. "I'm surprised to see you here, Henley," he said after a painfully long silence.

"I hired him," Chan broke in, his voice sounding quizzical. "Is there a problem?"

"Did you know this man was fired from his last position?"

"Now lookee 'ere, guvnor," the sailor interjected. "I'm truly sorry about wot 'appened that night. I was stewed to the gills, I was, and I promise it won't 'appen agin. But I'm a good cook, sir, and I need a job. Chan 'ere gave me one and I'm grateful to 'im. I don't want to cause no trouble."

"No one wants that more than I do," Ian replied.

"I tell 'e I won't be no problem. I'll jist cook y'r meals and keep to meself. You won't even see me at all after t'day."

"The less I see of you the better, Henley. But we do need a cook, and I'll admit you're a good one. All right, we'll keep you for the moment. But keep out of the liquor or you'll find yourself left at the next stop. Now what's this about the provisions?"

Esme couldn't bear to hear anymore. She had to escape before she showed herself and did something she'd regret. Quietly, she inched along to the dining cabin. The door was locked as was the door of the next cabin. She continued stealthily around the bow of the boat to the other side. She peeked around the corner. Both men seemed to be out of sight at the back of the boat. Without pausing to think, she slipped quickly through the door of the cabin closest to her, which happened to be Ian's.

Only then did she breathe easier. But her heart wouldn't stop racing so furiously. How could Ian allow the sailor to remain with the entourage? After everything Henley had done to her, the thought of his being so close sent chills through her body.

She eased down on the nearest piece of furniture, not even caring it was Ian's bunk. After hearing a few moments of muffled conversation, she heard footsteps pass Ian's cabin and the boat lift as people left it. She tensed when Ian's door opened, but on seeing it was Ian and that he was alone, she released her breath in a rush of relief.

His eyes widened as he saw her perched on his bunk. "May I flatter myself you're waiting for me so we can continue what we started on deck?" he teased.

She ignored his comment and got right to the point. "You're not going to let that man stay with us, are you?"

"I suppose that means no," he responded dryly.

"Ian, be serious!"

"I was serious. As for 'that man,' I can't really leave him stranded in the midst of the jungle, can I, without a good reason? And his past transgressions are not reason enough at this point, I'm afraid. Not if we want to avoid your being detected. Chan and the others will wonder why I'm throwing a man off the boat for accosting a Siamese girl in Bangkok."

"But he might recognize me!"

"I doubt that. To him, all Siamese look the same. And he's certainly not going to connect my boyish interpreter with the woman he met on the docks." He cast her an assessing glance. "I certainly didn't," he added, his jaw stiffening.

"What if he does?"

He stared at her with an unfathomable expression on his face. "Then you can twist him around your little finger like you've twisted me."

She recoiled as if he'd slapped her. Rising to her feet with as much dignity as she could muster, she walked past him to the door. But before she opened it, she paused, turning her head toward him slightly.

"I certainly had him twisted around my finger that night on the dock, didn't I? I don't even know why you bothered to come to my aid."

He reached out to clasp her shoulders from behind. "I'm sorry, Esme, but I'm under a great strain. I don't have time to worry about whether you'll be discovered. To be honest, it's hard to sympathize with you when you brought all this on yourself and made it worse for us both by joining my entourage."

"We've had this discussion before," she retorted, wrenching herself away from his hands. "As I recall, you didn't agree with my view of the situation. So there's no point in discussing it further."

"All right, then," he said curtly. "We won't discuss it. But I'm afraid you'll have to do one thing for me. You'll have to accompany Henley and me to the market to buy provisions."

"What?" she asked pitifully, wondering how he could be so callous as to expect her to be with Henley. The very thought of that man gave her chills.

"We need an interpreter," he said in explanation.

She thought about that for a moment. Being near Henley wouldn't be a pleasant experience, she knew. But she was forced to admit that Ian had no choice but to send her with the man.

Then it occurred to her that Ian didn't need to go, however. "Why are you going?" she asked softly.

Deborah Martin

"Let's just say I'm curious to see a Siamese market."

But, still, she wondered about it. With a start, she realized that despite all he'd said, he didn't want her to be alone with Henley if he could help it.

He ignored her quizzical expression and turned away from her to his desk. "Meet me on the bank as soon as you're dressed," he commanded.

"Certainly, my lord," she replied with a sudden meekness and left him to return to her cabin, feeling infinitely better than she had for some time.

Esme glanced at Henley for the tenth time that day as they passed through the market. To her relief, he hadn't yet seemed to have the slightest inkling who she really was. For the most part, he'd ignored her all morning. Even now as he rattled off a list of the fruit he wanted, he spoke only to Ian, even though Esme made all the transactions, bargaining in Siamese for every item.

Ian had certainly assessed the sailor correctly, she thought to herself. To Henley, she was only another Siamese, to be used as necessary.

"Ask him how much he wants for that curious-looking fruit there," Ian said at her elbow, gesturing to the wizened old Siamese man who squatted in front of a mound of large spiny balls with a pungent odor that permeated the air.

"Me lordship, what do you want with 'em?" Henley broke in. "Them are durians and no white man likes 'em. Taste like rotten onions, they does."

"I shall have to agree with Mr. Henley," Esme told him in her usual stilted accent. "Few white people find the fruit palatable. I do not think you would wish to spend your money on them."

"Do you eat them?" Ian asked.

"Of course," she replied, meeting his gaze steadily. "I find them quite delicious. But I am not a white man."

She could tell he was struggling to keep the amusement from showing on his face.

"That's certainly true," he quipped.

She didn't reply, knowing that the sailor watched them both with a curious expression on his face.

Noting the sailor's gaze on them, Ian sobered. "Well, then, Lek. I suppose we'll leave the durian alone. But I'm determined to try one of the exotic fruits in this market. Choose one you think a white man would like."

She ignored his baiting of her and pointed to the small deep purple globes called mangosteen. When he nodded his approval, she began bargaining for the fruit.

"Guvnor, you ain't gonna take what that Siamese boy tells you to, are you?" Henley asked in a loud whisper. "Them Siamese would just as soon poison you as not."

Esme couldn't help but overhear Henley since he'd obviously intended her to. She stopped bargaining and pivoted to face him.

"His lordship has been most kind to me," she told him, her dark eyes flashing behind the tinted glasses. "Why would I wish to poison him? If I were to use the secret poisons of the Orient on anyone, I assure you I could think of a better victim."

She hadn't meant her words to sound like a threat, but the palpable fear that lit the sailor's eyes for a moment told her Henley had taken them as such. His response worried her, for she didn't want to make an enemy of him.

But Ian laughed. "Better keep a civil tongue in

Deborah Martin

your head, Henley," he said, his eyes twinkling, "or you might find yourself choking on your tea one day."

Henley was not amused. He threw a glance at Esme that made her shiver and curse herself for being so quick to take offense. Her fear of the man was heightened by the sheer evil of that look. Her eyes flew to Ian's face, but he didn't seem to have noticed the exchange.

As Ian moved ahead of them down the bumpy dirt path, Henley drew Esme aside. "Lookee here, boy," he muttered in her ear. "I need this job an' I'll not be 'aving you make a fool of me in front of 'is lordship. So I'm thinkin' it's you who'd best be keepin' a civil tongue in your 'ead, you 'ear me?"

The wicked cackling chuckle that followed his statement filled Esme with terror far more than his words. All she could do was nod.

"Good. Then we 'ave an understandin'."

He pushed her just enough to make her stumble ahead of him. She followed behind Ian, her mind racing wildly. She must tell Ian. But what could she say? That the sailor was evil? She'd already said as much that morning and he'd ignored her. He didn't believe the cook was more than a harmless sot who got rowdy when he'd had too much to drink.

It certainly didn't help that Ian was more likely to believe anyone than her at the moment, convinced as he was that she was a manipulative flirt who always exaggerated danger. She squared her shoulders determinedly. She wouldn't let Ian have the satisfaction of knowing she was frightened. He'd just say yet again that she'd brought it on herself.

But she wouldn't let herself be bullied by that slimy sailor, either! Let him think her capable of

192

poisoning him in his sleep. He'd soon steer clear of her if he believed she'd do it.

She stopped abruptly in front of a pile of baskets filled with leaves and roots. When Ian noticed no one was behind him, he too stopped.

"Yes, Lek, what is it?" Ian asked.

"I wish to buy a few herbs, sir, if you do not mind."

He looked at her questioningly.

"For medicinal purposes, sir," she added, glancing meaningfully at the sailor. "In case one of us becomes ill on the journey."

The sailor's eyes narrowed.

Ian gave her an intent look, then shrugged. "As you wish."

She had no idea what properties any of the herbs possessed, but she doubted the sailor did either, so she made a pretense of searching through the baskets until she'd found just the right root. Then she lightly gathered a few other leaves and roots and bargained for them judiciously.

By the time they were ready to leave the market, the sailor looked uncomfortable and Esme felt a little better. She felt certain he'd think twice before tangling with her.

They might have left the village without incident had it not been for a rock in their path that made the sailor stumble and drop the coins in his hand. Ignoring the fallen money, Ian turned to right Henley, but the sailor, seeing a small child head for the coins, put his foot on them. The child merely toddled off to find something else to play with. Esme glanced around, hoping no one had witnessed what had happened, but two men with hands on their machetes were already starting their way.

"Get your foot off the money," she hissed. Henley

was so startled that he obeyed. She scooped it up swiftly. The sailor began to say something, but Ian, who'd assessed the situation correctly, gripped the man's arm.

"Be still and shut up, you fool," he said as he looked warily at the two Siamese men facing them.

Esme bowed and *waied* as low as she could several times. "We are very sorry that our friend has offended," she said rapidly in Siamese. "He doesn't understand the ways of the Siamese. He's but a foolish foreigner and wasn't thinking. He would apologize himself, but he doesn't speak your tongue." She took the coins out and held them reverently. "He meant no disrespect to His Majesty, I assure you. The tall man is his master. He'll make sure the offender is punished severely for the insult."

She waited with baited breath for the men to seize them, but evidently her explanation pacified them somewhat.

"We must leave now," she told the Siamese. "Thank you for your understanding."

She backed away, bowing low and *waiing* the entire time, while in front of her Ian propelled Henley forward. Only when they were completely out of sight did Esme turn her back on the men.

"We'd better move quickly," she told Ian. "They may change their minds and come after us anyway."

"Wot the bloody 'ell is goin' on 'ere? Why're them bastards so eager to 'ave our 'eads?" Henley asked.

"Because people like you don't bother to find out about their customs before they barge into things," Esme muttered.

"Bloody fools, that's wot," Henley replied, but by this time they'd reached the boats and Ian was pushing him toward the second boat. Ian barked orders to the crew that Esme translated as fast as she could. The others shouted to them from the second boat, asking what was wrong, but they were ignored as Ian tried to get the boats moving. When the launches and houseboats were safely out on the river, he relaxed his guard.

"Come with me," he commanded, dragging Esme inside his cabin before she could protest. Running his fingers through his hair, he sat down at his desk. He motioned for her to sit in the chair opposite him.

"I don't really understand what just went on. Would you mind explaining why we were nearly murdered a few minutes ago?"

Esme drew one of the coins out of her pocket and placed it on the table. "Whose picture do you see there?"

"King Chulalongkorn's. But I don't quite see—"

"Knowing what I told you about the foot and the head yesterday, try to imagine what went through the minds of those Siamese when they saw Henley put his foot on top of an item that bore the king's picture."

"Oh, God," Ian groaned. "I thought it had something to do with that foot business, but I wasn't even thinking about what was on the coin."

"To a Siamese, the king is a god. Literally. As you may have noticed in your audiences with King Chulalongkorn, the Siamese grovel on the floor in his presence, so that they won't show him disrespect. That respect extends to his likeness as well. Paintings of him are placed at the highest point of every house. Nothing can be put above his picture. When Henley put his foot on that coin, he—a terrible *farang* in their eyes—was showing the utmost contempt for a man whom the Siamese revere. I suppose it would be like an Indian student slapping Queen Victoria in the face when she's surrounded by loyal townspeople. We're lucky we got away at all."

He was silent for a long time, his fingers toying with the coin that lay between them on the desk. "What did you say to them?" he finally asked.

"The only thing I could say. I apologized profusely for the monstrous error of the ignorant foreigner. Then I told them you were the offender's master and would punish him severely."

"I certainly will." He clenched the coin in his fist. Then his brow, which until that point had been stern and frowning, smoothed out as he relaxed in his chair. Lazily, his eyes studied her, as if searching for some clue to her character. "Having you along may turn out better than I thought."

She kept silent.

"You think we're all fools, don't you?" he continued as he noticed the disgust on her face.

"I think anyone who sets out to negotiate with a foreign power without having the slightest idea of the rules that govern the people's behavior is being foolish, yes." She lifted her chin, daring him to contradict her.

"I'd agree with you, since I assume you mean me. Unfortunately, I didn't have much choice in the matter. I was sent here by those over me."

Again the weariness she'd noticed in his face two days before was there again, sharpening the angles of his jaw so that he appeared older than his years.

"Why not send Mr. Rushton?" she asked without thinking. "He's the minister resident. He's been in Siam for years and knows how the Siamese think."

"You would have liked that, wouldn't you? Think of all the hours you could have spent with him.

Why, you wouldn't even have had to disguise yourself," Ian said, his face suddenly implacable.

When she refused to respond to his barbs, he answered her question. "Rushton would have been the logical choice. Unfortunately, there were other reasons for choosing me besides familiarity with the country. Reasons I can't explain." He sighed. "Just be assured I'm as aware as you are of the volatility of the situation. I feel like a blind man groping through a maze. If you hadn't been with us this morning, I shudder to think what might have happened."

"They would have killed you," she stated.

"No. That's the worst of it. More likely I would have been forced to kill them," he said, drawing an intricately carved Oriental dagger out of a sheath inside his waistcoat and placing it on the table. "And that would have been difficult to explain, to say the least."

She shuddered, her eyes fixed on the weapon in horror. "Do you always carry that thing?" she whispered.

"Yes. I quickly learned I wouldn't survive in the East without it. But it's not as much help here as it was in Hong Kong. Here there are so many nuances, gestures, and innuendos I'm not familiar with that I don't know when I should be on my guard. I know the Chinese. I've worked with them for years and speak three of their dialects. But the Siamese are entirely different. For one thing, they've never been colonized, so I can't put the fear of the British Crown into them. And their logic eludes me, which makes it hard for me to do my job."

"I can help," she said, leaning forward eagerly.

"You've already helped more than I should have

let you. The minute I found out who you were, I should have confined you to your cabin until we reached Chiengmai. But I couldn't do without an interpreter."

"I can help even more," she persisted. "And it won't be dangerous. We've got two or three weeks ahead of us, haven't we? Why don't you let me teach you about Siam? I can tell you a great deal you wouldn't find in travel books. I was practically born here."

The drawn look left his face for a moment. "That would be a help indeed." Then he surveyed her coolly and his eyes hardened. "But why should you aid me? Unless, of course, you've a reason for offering this help."

She met his gaze defiantly. He could read her so well. "I do, but keep in mind I have a lot to offer. Surely you could give me something in return that wouldn't cost you much."

"Such as?"

"When we reach Chiengmai, let me go. Don't leave me at the consulate, and don't tell my father where I am. Let me do as I'd planned from the beginning."

His jaw tightened. "I thought those might be your terms."

"Why do you care what I do anyway?" she cried. "I won't disgrace you, and I won't tell anyone where I've been. There's no reason for you to be so adamant about interfering in my life."

"I have only your welfare at heart. No woman should be left to fend for herself in a foreign country. I haven't seen Chiengmai, but I gather it's not any safer than Bangkok. I won't leave you there without the protection of the consul who will demand in any case that your father be told where you are."

She tossed her head angrily. "Everyone has only my welfare at heart—my father, you, even Mr. Michaels. Strange how no one has seen fit to consult me while they rearrange my life. This time I won't allow it." Her voice became earnest. "You need me, Ian, and you know it. If you don't agree to leave me there, I'll not tell you anything. More than that, I won't interpret for you, either. You'll have to muddle by with what little English the crew knows."

He stood up and walked around the desk. Then he leaned down to brace his arms on either side of the armchair she sat in, trapping her there.

"For a woman who's in danger of being abandoned in the jungle, you're suddenly very brave," he said, his eyes narrowing.

She met his gaze with a triumphant look of her own. "You don't frighten me, Ian. If you were going to abandon me in the jungle, you'd have done it before now. But you won't. You're too much of a gentleman for that. So what good will it do you to keep me prisoner until we reach Chiengmai when I can be helping you on the way?"

When she saw his jaw tense and his face cloud ominously above her, she wondered if she'd been too bold. He lifted her out of the chair as if she were a rag doll. Setting her on her feet, his hands tightened painfully on her arms.

She stared at him in terror for what seemed like hours, but was probably only a few seconds. As she stood there, she became aware of a subtle difference in his expression. The anger had ebbed, replaced by an indefinable intensity of emotion. He released her arms so suddenly she swayed against him. He steadied her and then held her at arm's length.

"No games, Esme. I'm tired of your games. Either you help me or you don't. That's your choice. But

Deborah Martin

I won't be blackmailed. If I were you, I'd consider a few things. First of all, if you refuse to interpret for me, you'll have to explain why to everyone on board. And if you reveal your real identity, I'll no longer have a reason to put up with you. The scandal will be just as bad for me if I take you with me or if I send you back. I wouldn't think twice about sending you back to Bangkok under hired guard if need be. So you either play along and take the chance that you'll buy enough time to thwart your father's plans for a marriage, or you return. You'd be back there in three or four days at the most, which shouldn't stop Michaels from marrying you."

"You couldn't be so cruel!" she cried.

"Try me."

For a moment, their eyes locked. She wanted to call his bluff, to end the masquerade once and for all.

But she dared not. "You give me little choice."

"None at all. If you'll recall, you gave me no choice in taking you with me. But in doing so, you made me responsible for you, and I don't shirk my responsibilities."

"You're a monster!"

"So you've said before," he responded, shrugging his shoulders as he released her arms.

She wanted to fight him but she realized he was right. If he sent her back now, she might still have to marry Michaels. If she waited for her father to come to Chiengmai, however, she had a better chance that Michaels would have given up on her.

Then another thought occurred to her. "All right," she said resignedly, though her eyes glowered at him. "I'll help you, Ian, but not out of the goodness of my heart. I have another condition— one you might find more manageable."

200

"I doubt it," he said evenly. "But let me hear it anyway."

"I'll help you if you swear you won't touch me again. If you promise we'll work together as if I really were your interpreter, I'll do all I can to help you prepare for Chiengmai."

His first response to her request was to look startled. "I don't know if I can promise that," he said, his eyes searching her face. "I'm not even sure you really want me to."

"I assure you I mean every word. I don't want you, Ian, and I'm already regretting that I've placed myself in your power. If I had my way, you'd be back there battling the men with the machetes at this very moment."

"No doubt," he said, the beginning of a smile on his face.

"It's not funny," she said crossly as she moved out of his reach and headed for the door. "You won't take me seriously, but I mean what I say. I don't care what happens to you, so you'd best watch your back. I hate you."

"You hate me, do you?" he replied. Then he moved to block her way to the door. His fingers cupped her chin, while his other hand clasped her waist. With his thumb, he traced the outline of her lips before lowering his own to hers for the briefest of kisses. In spite of herself, she trembled.

"I like your hatred, Esme Montrose, if the way you respond when I touch you is any indication of it," he murmured.

She shoved him away from her, inwardly cursing the fact that she always seemed to lose her nerve to resist him when he came anywhere near her. Then she slapped him as hard as she could.

"Maybe that's a better indication," she told him sweetly.

He gave her a hard stare meant to cower her. But she wouldn't be intimidated and returned the stare.

"I agree to your condition, Esme," he said coldly. "I won't touch you. You have my solemn promise. But I think this is one promise you'll soon wish me to break."

"I doubt it," she answered softly, then fled his cabin.

Chapter Eleven

Esme sighed as she watched the dying sun stretch fingers of lavender and pink across the sky. Her gaze shifted to the other boat.

"Do you wish you'd joined the others for tea, Lek?" a gentle voice asked beside her.

She glanced at the little group who sat on the other boat and shook her head. "Not at all. I enjoy conversing with you."

It was true. The minister's presence had made the trip more bearable than it might have been otherwise. Reverend Horace Taylor had surprised everyone when he'd finally made his first appearance at dinner. Like a stereotypical puritanical preacher, he was gaunt, solemn, and angular with stringy gray hair slicked back from a high forehead. But his brown eyes were warm and friendly, and he frequently bestowed a generous smile on his companions. And unlike some American missionaries in Siam, he was well educated and had gentlemanly manners.

He'd taken to her almost immediately. She knew it was because he pitied Lek, the poor orphaned Eurasian who wasn't quite part of the whole entourage. But she liked to think there was more to it than that. He seemed to sense she wasn't what she appeared to be, for he treated her kindly, as if to make up for any hardships she encountered. She felt guilty for deceiving him, sometimes wishing she could just abandon all caution and confide in him. But her fear of Ian always stopped her.

"You seem distracted this evening, Lek. Is something wrong?" Reverend Taylor asked, his voice filled with concern.

"No, of course not," she replied as she shifted her body so that her back was to the other boat. She tried to give him a bright smile she didn't really feel.

"I hope I'm not boring you with all my questions. It's just that so much has changed since I left here a year ago, and you seem to know so much about the political situation."

"You do not bore me, sir, I assure you. I am grateful to be of service."

"Then I suppose it's the leader of your little expedition who's bothering you," he said, settling his lanky frame back against the rattan chair.

She glanced at him in surprise. "Wh—what do you mean?"

"It's not difficult to see that the two of you don't get along," he said, giving her a fatherly smile. "He acts distant around you, almost as if your presence annoys him."

"Yes," Esme said pensively. That was exactly how Ian acted around her. And not just when they were with the others. He was aloof even when they were alone together. But she told herself she didn't care as long as he refrained from touching her.

"Does he abuse you?" Reverend Taylor asked quietly.

Esme's startled look seemed to answer his question.

"I didn't think so, but I wasn't sure," he continued, "although he doesn't seem the type to beat his servants."

"He has been very kind to me. But I do not think he particularly likes me."

"He works you too hard."

She thought a moment, then gave Reverend Taylor a half-smile. "No, not really. I do spend most of my mornings discussing Siamese customs with him, but I can do as I wish with my afternoons and evenings. The only interpreting I do is for the crew, which is not much."

"But something about your duties disturbs you," he persisted.

She sighed and looked down at her hands. How much could she say about her situation without saying too much? "It's just that . . . that he feels I am a burden to him because I am so young. He feels responsible for me."

"And that bothers you?" he asked with the tone of one accustomed to being confided in.

She nodded, straightening her shoulders with an unconscious air of independence. "I am old enough to care for myself. I do not need him to tell me what to do and how to behave."

"Surely that's his right as your employer."

"It is, as long as he confines himself to my duties. But he wants to control the way I live as well. He has no right." She tilted her chin up stubbornly.

The minister laughed. "Somehow I can't see Lord Winthrop in the role of busybody."

An exasperated sigh escaped her lips. "I cannot explain it," she muttered.

"Perhaps what you're trying to say is that he's condescending. I can't blame you for disliking that. But you must understand. He's older and more experienced than you. He's probably better educated. I'm sure he just wants what's best for you."

"That is precisely what *he* said," she retorted, crossing her arms across her chest. "Oh, talking about it serves no purpose. He and I just do not suit."

"Whatever you say, Lek. But don't let it spoil your enjoyment of the trip. Look at this lovely countryside we're passing through." He waved his arm around them. "Accept that your presence here is God's will and you'll be much happier."

Esme was silent. She liked the older man a great deal—even when he became too religious. After all, she thought, if not for Reverend Taylor, she didn't know how she'd have endured the past two weeks. It wasn't that her morning discussions with Ian had been dreadful. In fact, sometimes the hours in his cabin had slipped away so pleasantly she'd wondered where the time had gone. She'd told him everything she knew about Siamese customs, particularly those things he'd need most in dealing with a prince. He, in turn, had listened carefully, although he hadn't resisted commenting on the peculiar nature of some of the customs.

But she'd always felt ill at ease with him. Since the day of their agreement, he'd been civil to her but no more, treating her as a bothersome nuisance. Occasionally, the civility had given way to outright hostility, forcing her to grit her teeth to keep from snapping at him. But for the most part, he'd been aloof, and she'd responded with equal coolness, so that their sessions together were polite but tense.

Yet she knew he wasn't entirely oblivious to her as a woman, for at times she caught him watching her with a look of such intense desire it frightened her. Sometimes when her fingers accidentally brushed his hand or she bumped into him in the tiny cabin, she knew only his strength of will kept him from clasping her to him.

She wished she could feel glad he'd upheld their agreement. But that was the worst part. As much as she wanted to deny it, as much as she fought it, she found herself more strongly attracted to him every day. First of all was the physical attraction. Who could resist those smoky eyes that changed from blue to gray seemingly at will? He'd promised not to touch her, but he hadn't promised not to look at her, and more than once his eyes had spoken more than she wished to hear.

In their two weeks together Esme had memorized every inch of his face: the broad forehead sometimes creased with lines of weariness; the aristocratic nose; and the square jaw with the muscle that twitched whenever he was angry. Her tinted glasses had enabled her to study him without his realizing it, and as the days went by, her eyes had lingered whenever she looked at him.

Oh, yes, physically he was a fine specimen of a man, she thought. But it was more than that, for he'd proved to be quick at grasping the odd quirks of Siamese thinking. He'd discovered more similarities between the Chinese and Siamese ways of thinking than he'd previously thought. Eight years of dealing with Orientals in Hong Kong, Singapore, and Saigon had sharpened his knowledge of the

Oriental mind, so he easily understood the peculiar reasons behind Siamese behavior. Their discussions had enlightened her as much as they had him, because his extensive travels allowed him to describe to her other worlds and ways of thinking than the ones she'd grown accustomed to.

In all, her trip had been more enjoyable than she'd anticipated. She'd spent her mornings with Ian, but in the afternoons she'd been left to her own devices, since Ian spent most of that time poring over maps and documents. Some days she'd just sat on the deck, watching as the landscape that bordered the huge river changed from flat stretches of rice paddy to gently swelling hills and then small mountains blanketed with rich luxuriant jungle as they'd moved north. Occasionally, she'd borrowed one of Harold's books. Then she'd sat in one of the deck chairs, reading, grateful for the tinted glasses that shielded her eyes from the merciless tropical sun.

Mealtimes had been difficult, however. She'd done her best to stay out of the conversations, for she hadn't wanted to risk making a slip. Ian had seemed to realize what she was doing, so for the most part he'd ignored her at meals. Godfrey and Chan, too, had treated her as if she were invisible. But Harold hadn't been so accommodating. He'd found the little Siamese interpreter intriguing and had constantly tried to draw her out. Generally, she'd resisted his attempts, but sometimes she found a perverse enjoyment in repeating for his benefit some of the outrageous tales that Lamoon and Mai had told her about Siamese life, thus shocking his delicate sensibilities.

In fact, she hadn't often minded her charade. Instead of imprisoning her, her disguise had liberated her in many ways. As Lek, she'd been able to ask questions that wouldn't have been taken seriously if Esme Montrose had asked them. She'd heard men discuss ideas they would never have discussed with a woman, topics even her father would have shunned in her presence.

Even physically, her disguise freed her, for although her breasts were bound, her clothing confined her less than her corset had. In fact, the loose-fitting pants and jacket allowed her more liberty of movement than she'd ever experienced with her voluminous petticoats and tight skirts. She wouldn't want to dress as a boy all the time, but for the moment she basked in the freedom it afforded.

Yes, all in all, the trip had been pleasant. The only thing limiting her pleasure was Ian's coldness, and she couldn't really change that. Much as she wished to give in to his desire, she knew she mustn't. He only wanted her body, and he believed awful things of her. She'd never allow a man close to her who couldn't or wouldn't see her for what she was. If she did, she'd regret it, for he might make her his mistress but never his wife.

Yet being with him day after day made it difficult not to wish to be closer to him. In the beginning, she'd just forced herself to remember that he intended to send her back to marry Mr. Michaels. That had rekindled her anger and kept her from wanting more. But, lately, not even her anger could subdue her desire. Wistfully, she gazed out at the shore, wondering how much longer she could continue to act like a stranger toward him.

Esme would have been surprised to know that while his behavior was cold toward her, Ian himself was not. He sat at the table with the others as tea was poured, but his mind was elsewhere. His gaze rested on Esme and Reverend Taylor as they sat on the boat moored next to his.

What did she see in the old minister that made her spend so much time with him? he wondered irritably. Probably someone else she could manipulate into doing her bidding. Had she revealed her identity to the good reverend and told him about her past? Ian didn't think so, for surely the man wouldn't have been so kind to her had he known everything.

With a scowl, Ian waved away the tea Godfrey tried to pour for him, reaching instead for the brandy and pouring himself a generous amount. Esme certainly was enjoying herself these days, he thought. He hadn't failed to notice the satisfaction her masquerade seemed to afford her. For some reason it galled him that she was making the best of the situation. He'd expected her to be more of a child about the whole mess. Instead she'd played her role to the hilt.

Worse yet, his presence didn't seem to affect her at all. After she'd reacted so violently to him that day, he'd thought she felt more for him than she had admitted. Since then, however, she hadn't so much as trembled when he was around. He was struggling to keep from touching her, and she was completely oblivious to his distress. Ian frowned at no one in particular. Judging from the gossip, she was accustomed to putting men through this torment. And torment was the only word for it, since it had been all he could do to keep from kissing her again, from seizing those sweet lying lips with his own.

But he'd kept his promise, not only because he'd found her assistance invaluable and was loath to lose it, but also because he'd wanted her to come to him, to admit she desired him, too. Increasingly that mattered a great deal to him. To his surprise, he looked forward to seeing her every morning for their discussions of Siamese culture. But their daily meetings made it harder and harder for him to keep her at arm's length.

He knew she still hoped he'd relent and let her do as she wished in Chiengmai. God knows he wanted to. He didn't want to involve himself with her any more than was necessary. But he just couldn't abandon her. If something were to happen to her, he'd feel responsible and her family would no doubt blame him, even though he hadn't asked her to travel with him.

He knew he was right to remain aloof around her for more reasons than one. He shouldn't get too close to her, because if he did, it would be difficult to leave her in Chiengmai. And he certainly didn't need this girl toying with his mind at a time when he must be alert. Once Esme was settled at the consulate, he'd have nothing more to do with her except to visit her family upon his return to Bangkok.

Or so he told himself.

"Why do you know so much about Siamese customs, Esme?" Ian asked as they worked in his cabin the next morning.

His question surprised Esme. Recently, he hadn't expressed much interest in her life. "Father has always taken an interest in them. When we came to Siam years ago, he thought it important to understand the culture of those he planned to teach. Few books were written about Siam, so he learned the culture by spending time with the Siamese themselves. When I was small, he took me with him sometimes."

"Your mother allowed him to do that?"

"Yes," she said, growing pensive. "She thought I should learn as much as I could about the world."

"Your mother must have been an unusual woman," he said as he watched the emotions flit over Esme's face.

She smiled wistfully. "I suppose she was. Her thirst for everything infected the whole house. She was as vibrant as the tropical flowers she loved. I adored her. She was the most beautiful, kind woman I've ever known."

"So you take after her in looks," he remarked, his gray eyes warming her with their appraisal and sudden flash of interest.

"Do I?" she asked, her heart skipping a beat at the way he regarded her with a gaze that was anything but aloof. Then realizing she sounded coy, she plunged on. "I never thought so, but Father always said I did. I certainly don't resemble him."

"That you don't," Ian said with a grin. Slowly, the smile faded from his face. "He must be very worried about you. Doesn't that bother you at all?"

He couldn't have hurt her more if he'd struck her. Her dark eyes filled with unshed tears. "What kind of woman do you think I am? Of course it bothers me. I nearly didn't leave because I knew how much it would hurt him. But he insisted he'd make me marry that horrible Michaels. I couldn't marry him! Can't you understand that?"

The tears began to fall then, hard as she tried to hold them back. Her tears seemed to startle him. He rose from his chair, coming out from behind the desk to gather her in his arms, unconcerned that

212

he'd promised not to touch her and had kept his promise so far.

"I'm sorry," he murmured soothingly. "I shouldn't have brought it up, I know."

"But you still take his side, don't you!" she accused, pushing away from him. "You believe he's right to marry me off. You're just like him. You think I need a firm hand to put me in my place and keep me there so I don't start any more scandals."

He remained silent, at a loss for what to say.

She met his searching gaze with a look of defiance. "I wish you knew how hard it was to leave. It took every ounce of my courage. I hate pretending to be what I'm not. I hate deceiving good people like Reverend Taylor. And most of all, I hate your treating me like some sly flirt!"

His eyes turned to stone as he gave a mocking little laugh. "If the shoe fits ..."

Her face showed her outrage. "You're the most horrible person I've ever known! If we reach Chiengmai without my pushing you overboard, you're going to wish you'd never laid eyes on me."

"Oh? How are you going to make me wish that?" he asked, his eyebrows raised in obvious skepticism.

"I—I don't know. I'll think of something," she told him, wanting more than anything to be able just once to disconcert him. She dropped back into her chair, a frown on her face. Then incensed at the blatant amusement showing in his expression, she added, "Perhaps I'll tell the consul in Chiengmai that you kidnapped me. Yes, that's what I'll do."

To her chagrin, her threats didn't seem to alarm him in the least. "It won't work, my spiteful little girl," he said as he moved to stand behind her chair, his eyes sparkling with mischief. "You see, everyone

213

on board has seen you prancing about as Lek, the poor orphan child. They'll be quick to tell their side of the story, and I'm sure it won't contain any mention of your being kidnapped."

"They won't know I'm Lek unless you tell them, and you've already said it would be to your disadvantage to let them know you knew my identity. So I can claim you kept me hidden and dragged me to Chiengmai against my will."

His warm chuckle behind her increased her frustration. "And where am I to have hidden you? Under this poor excuse for a desk?" he said, circling past her to strike the wicker table lightly. "Or perhaps under my monstrously large bunk," he added, striding across the room and throwing himself on it to demonstrate that he barely fit on it himself.

She glowered at him.

"No one would believe such a ridiculous story, Esme. You're a good liar, but that lie won't wash and you know it. Just like your tale of why you needed to embark on this scheme. You've exaggerated this Michaels business, I'm sure, to convince me to let you get away with your masquerade. And I don't for a minute believe someone invented a story about you. Why should they?"

She sat rigidly straight in her chair, trying not to lose her temper. "I'm not a liar," she said through clenched teeth.

"Oh. Then all that wonderful business about your poor Siamese mother and her French sailor was true, was it?"

"That's different!"

"I'm quite sure it is," he said dryly, leaving the bunk to pace the room behind her.

She leaned forward, her voice earnest in her desire to convince him. "Ian, I did what I had to. But

214

I'm not lying about what happened and why I'm
here. I don't generally tell tales. I only said I'd tell
that the kidnapping story to the consul in Chiengmai because you've been so awful to me. You know
I wouldn't really do it."

He moved between her chair and the desk, standing so close that he forced her to lean back to see
his face. His lips held a smile that didn't quite reach
his eyes.

"I'm not so sure. Fortunately, I'm not worried
about it, either. Right now I'm far more concerned
that, despite your lying, I want you so badly I could
easily forget how you've complicated my mission."

She started to speak, to remind him of his promise, but his finger touched her lips, bidding her be
quiet. He drew his fingertip to the point of her chin,
then traced a line down her neck to the collar of
her jacket. When she swallowed nervously, he
brushed the back of his finger over her throat. Then
he slid his hand to the back of her neck, twining
his fingers in her hair as he bent down, catching
her up to him roughly with his other arm.

Just as he was about to kiss her, however, she
stepped back and in doing so heard something
scrape the floor under her foot.

Ian ignored the sound, but she pounced on it as
an excuse to get away from him. "What is that? I—
I've stepped on something you must have dropped
on the floor."

"Leave it be," he murmured, but she squirmed
out of his arms, reaching down to pick up the object.

"It's a key," she said, trying to regain her composure, which he'd easily shattered. "You must
have dropped it."

Ian snatched it from her irritably and started to

toss it on the table, when a glance at it arrested him.

"What's wrong?" she asked, worried as she saw him pale. She took the key from him. It looked ordinary enough, with a slender chain threaded through a hole at the top, although the chain had obviously broken.

"Do you keep this around your neck?" she asked, wondering why he continued to stare unseeingly ahead of him.

He reached inside one of his waistcoat pockets and drew out another key. He took the one she held, then placed the two keys together. They were identical.

"Where was this?" he asked sharply, holding up the key with the broken chain.

"Right under my chair. Why? What lock does it belong to?"

"The one on my strongbox," he answered, his hand closing around both keys in a fist as a troubled look crossed his brow. Then he threw the two keys on the desk.

"What's in the strongbox?"

He didn't look at her as he answered, "The missing papers were in there."

A sense of dread gripped her. "Why was the key under my chair?" she asked, suddenly afraid of his answer.

His lips formed a grim line as he grasped her shoulders tightly, his eyes holding her with the strength of their silver gaze. "Listen very carefully to me, Esme. You're not to mention this to anyone and I mean *anyone*. Not the reverend, not Godfrey, and especially not Chan. I'll have to deal with this myself. And it may involve telling Chan who you are."

She felt such relief as she realized he didn't believe the key belonged to her that she didn't at first notice what he said.

But as his last words hit her, she became confused. "Why? What's going on, Ian?"

He hesitated a moment. Then a glance at the two keys on the desk seemed to decide him. "Under the circumstances, you've a right to know. Can I trust you not to reveal to anyone what I'm about to tell you?"

"Of course. But if you don't want to tell me, don't. I'll understand." Her chin came up stubbornly.

He looked at her with what was nearly a smile. Then the smile faded. Gently, he pushed her away from him, turning to face the window. "The British government has long suspected that Chan is a spy for the French. Part of the reason I was sent here was to trap him so we could force him to reveal his contact."

"Do you really think he'd do that?"

"If we have concrete evidence that he's a spy, he'd be a fool not to gain some leniency by telling us who's been transporting the information from country to country. We're not so much interested in Chan. He's a paid worker. No, we need him to lead us to the more dangerous spy, the one who pays him."

It flattered her that he trusted her enough to tell her this. But she was still confused. "What has all of this to do with the keys?"

Ian turned back toward her, his face hardening perceptibly. "Chan's pattern in the past has been to steal documents over a period of time while carefully incriminating someone else. He makes insinuations and plants inconsequential bits of evidence until someone finally arrests the wrong person, leaving Chan free to move on to another area with the truly important documents."

"But what—" she began. Then the full implication of what Ian was saying struck her. Chan had said *she* should be searched. The key had appeared beneath *her* chair. Oh, no. She was the one Chan planned to incriminate.

"It's only the beginning," Ian said as he saw comprehension in her face. "Right now he'll plant only enough to make me suspect you. Eventually, however, when he's gathered all he needs, he'll choose something very important to leave in your cabin or room or clothing and set it up so the evidence will be found before you even realize it's there."

An involuntary shudder went through her. "Why me?" she asked in a small voice.

"You mean, 'Why Lek?'" he said bitterly. "Now you see why your presence on this boat has complicated everything? Chan thinks you're a poor Eurasian orphan whom no one would champion. You're the perfect scapegoat. But it's going to end here."

"What will you do?" she asked, trying to ignore the whisper of fear that echoed in her mind.

"Reveal your true identity to him. I won't let him use you this way, so I must tell him who you are. He's not so stupid he'd set up a young girl who's simply running away from home. He knows no one would believe that you could be a spy."

Esme's blood ran cold as she realized Ian had known about Chan from the beginning and had been aware that she was being set up. "Why didn't you tell him before?" she asked bitterly. "You must have known."

"How could I have known?" Ian asked, an odd

expression on his face. "He hasn't tried to implicate anyone yet."

"You said he told you to search me."

Ian looked away from her, clearly uncomfortable. "That was a lie, dear girl. I wanted to make you nervous. No, he didn't want me to search anyone. I'd begun hoping Henley was his choice or even one of the Siamese crew members."

His confession should have angered her, but she was relieved he hadn't willingly allowed Chan to set her up. "If you tell him who I am, what will happen?"

He shook his head. "I don't know. Most likely he'll decide the entire project is too risky, now that he's taken definite steps to implicate you. He won't want to change scapegoats because that would look too suspicious."

"Then all your planning will be for naught," she murmured, a shadow crossing her face as she felt a pang of guilt. She'd never wanted to do anything that would harm her country.

"I'll have to take that chance. I can't risk endangering your life."

Alarm bells went off in her head. "My life? What do you mean?"

His hands tightened into fists as he looked at her. "All of Chan's previous scapegoats died in prison before they could be questioned. They supposedly committed suicide, but I don't for one minute believe they died willingly."

Esme trembled with fear as she realized Ian was afraid for her. And with good reason. But she also didn't want to be responsible for Ian's mission going awry.

At that moment, she made a decision. "They died

only after they were arrested?'' she asked, her eyes narrowing.

"Yes, why?"

"Because that means I'm in no danger."

"Yet."

"Yet," she agreed. She bit her lip, then went on with firm resolve. "So there's no reason you can't continue in your plans to trap him."

Ian moved to stand in front of her, his face showing his surprise as he clasped her shoulders. "What are you saying?"

"I'm saying I should continue the charade so you can catch him."

"You're mad," he muttered, his eyes searching her face for some sign of why she'd do such a thing.

She dared not tell him all her reasons. True, she did want to rid herself of any guilt she might feel from having ruined his trap for the spy. But she also hoped her willingness to help would convince Ian she was mature enough to be on her own. Perhaps if he witnessed her taking such a risk for her country, he'd release her once they reached Chiengmai.

"No, I'm not crazy," she said softly. "But you've said many times that my presence has made things difficult for you. I'll admit I hoped, when I joined your entourage, to do just that. But I won't be responsible for letting a spy escape."

"You've no choice," he said fiercely, his jaw set.

"Yes, I do," she replied, her nose tilting up in the air haughtily. "I swear I'll tell him everything you know, Ian, if you don't let me do this. Then he'll probably murder both of us in our sleep."

His eyes were like stone as he stared at her. But she met them with a steady gaze, refusing to relent.

"And if by some chance he discovers who you are?"

"Then you can watch how he reacts. Who knows? He might lead you to his contact. And if he doesn't discover my identity before we reach Chiengmai, the problem will disappear with Lek. He can pin any crimes he wishes on the poor interpreter and still feel safe. Then perhaps he'll contact his employer. When he does, you can catch him."

"I wish it were that simple," Ian remarked, his face suddenly looking very weary.

"At least you'd be better situated to catch him than you'll be if you reveal my identity to him now."

He was quiet for a moment, his gaze thoughtful. She could tell just when he'd decided to accept her proposal, for he nodded to himself, then kneaded her shoulders gently.

"There's one thing I can do to protect you," he said firmly.

"What's that?"

"Steer him in another direction and force him to implicate someone else. Henley, for example."

Esme smiled as she thought how appropriate Henley would be as a scapegoat. Ian's worried frown faded as he noticed her smile.

"Can you do it, my little actress?" he murmured, his hand moving up to stroke her neck.

"Of c—course," she replied unsteadily, her pulse quickening under his touch. "I've done well until now, haven't I?"

"That you have."

Then before she could stop him, his lips were on hers. But she didn't resist, for her longing for him had been building for two weeks. She reveled in the taste of him, opening her mouth in surrender as he plundered her velvety softness. His hands snaked

221

around her waist, clutching her to him as if he were afraid to release her. She lifted her fingers to caress the rough stubble on his cheek, and he groaned.

"You've missed me, too, haven't you?" he said in a husky voice as his hands stroked the contours of her back and hips.

"Yes," she said breathlessly, forgetting about her promises to herself not to relent, forgetting about everything except the way he made her entire being vibrate with excitement.

His eyes glowed in triumph. Then his mouth rained kisses on her face, her hair, her neck. His lips were whispery soft over her skin, and she arched against him, her hands clutching his muscular arms. That only increased the urgency of his movements. One hand cupped her breast, then caressed it. At her low moan of pleasure, his lips sought hers again with fierce insistence.

Just as he slipped his hands up under her jacket, however, a sound at the window made him abruptly stop kissing her. His face went rigid as he thrust her away and walked swiftly to the window where he stiffened in alarm.

"I think we've done enough for today," he said curtly. "I'll see you this evening at dinner."

She rebelled at being dismissed so abruptly, while her body still tingled from his caresses. "Ian—"

"I'll see you at dinner, Lek. Good day."

Only after she'd left the cabin in confused anger did she realize he'd used her Siamese name.

Ian watched her leave and then released a pent-up breath. Again he glanced out the window. He could have sworn he'd seen one of the Siamese crewmen near it, but he couldn't be certain. If so, how long had the man been there? Had he heard any of the conversation, or worse yet, seen Ian kissing Esme?

Ian went cold at the thought. Thank God he'd kept his distance until then, treating her as if she really were his interpreter. Too much was at stake now for her disguise to be discovered. He'd have to keep his hands to himself for her sake as well as his own.

That was going to be incredibly difficult. Despite her disguise, Ian found himself wanting her more every time she was near him. He pictured what it would be like to have her gleaming golden body lying on his bunk, her soft breasts free of the binding, and her slender arms beckoning to him. He knew her skin would be the color of polished ivory, for although he'd only seen her neck and bare shoulder, it had been enough to fire his imagination.

He slammed his fist into the flimsy wooden wall. What he wouldn't give for one night with her when she was loving and willing instead of angry, one night when he could forget about Chan and the troubles of the British Empire.

But he knew peace was nowhere at hand with Chan setting his trap for her. Chan had probably chosen Esme because she spent so much time in Ian's company. Ian would have to change that so he could deflect Chan's interest in her as a target.

In the meantime, he must tell Chan about finding the key. But he needed to do it without incriminating Esme. He walked back to the chair where Esme had been sitting, an idea forming in his mind.

Late that afternoon, they moored at a spot where heavy vines formed an impenetrable curtain separating the river from the land. As soon as the boats were anchored, Ian stepped onto Godfrey's boat, surprising the young man as he left his cabin.

"I need your advice about something, Godfrey," he said in a voice that carried to the other cabins. "Come back to my cabin for a moment, will you?"

Godfrey shrugged and followed Ian, used to being abruptly summoned whenever his friend wanted something. In the cabin, Ian chatted with Godfrey about the political situation in north Siam. He kept Godfrey there until dinner. Then after dinner he invited Henley back to his cabin to consult with him about their provisions, something he'd done on previous occasions and knew wouldn't look suspicious.

After Henley left, Ian settled down at his desk to wait. He wasn't surprised when Chan entered the cabin moments later. Nor did he miss the surreptitious glance Chan gave the deck in front of the table and the marked dismay that crossed his face.

"You wished to see me about something?" Ian asked, noting that Chan perched carefully in the chair opposite him.

"I thought we should discuss what you plan to do when we don't reach Chiengmai by the deadline you set for the crew."

Ian stared coldly at his secretary. "What makes you think we won't make it?"

"I—I believe Lek was saying something to that effect yesterday." Chan's nervousness was only slightly apparent, but Ian saw it because he was watching for it.

"You must have misunderstood him. We're right on schedule if I'm to believe the boat crew's leader. We should be there in a few days." Ian turned back to the papers he'd been perusing, but Chan didn't move.

"Was there something else?" Ian asked. "If not,

I really have a great deal of work to do."

"No, nothing else," Chan said. "I'll leave you to it."

As Chan stood, Ian heard a familiar scrape and nearly smiled.

"What's this?" Chan asked, bending down to pick up the key Ian had planted back under the chair.

"Who knows?" Ian said, pretending to be irritated. "Probably something I knocked off the table."

"I don't think so, sir," Chan replied. "It's a key with a chain. Do you leave keys lying about on the table?"

"Let me see that," Ian told him, taking it when Chan handed it to him. He drew out the key in his waistcoat pocket, compared the two keys, and frowned.

"What is it?" Chan asked innocently.

"It's the key to my strongbox. Or an excellent copy."

Chan's attempt to look disturbed was thinly disguised. "Whoever carried it must have kept it around his neck. The chain broke, and he did not realize it had dropped on the floor."

"I'm sure that's precisely what occurred. Now all we have to determine is who dropped it."

"Lek spent most of the morning in here, did he not?"

Ian tossed the key in his hand as he pretended to think, allowing the tension to build in the room. "Lek wasn't the most recent visitor to my cabin," he stated carefully. "Both Godfrey and Henley have been in here today. It could have been one of them as well—or even you."

He stared at the man across from him.

Chan's face betrayed nothing. "Yes, of course

225

we're all suspects. But surely you don't suppose Godfrey would do such a thing? And why would I point it out if I'd dropped it myself?"

"No, no, you and Godfrey are out, of course," Ian said nonchalantly, fingering the chain in his hand. "But Henley would be a good choice. He dislikes me for getting him thrown off the ship he worked on and since it was also the ship we came here on, he had ample opportunity to make a copy."

"But he's never seen you use the key," Chan said quietly, "and Lek has."

"Consider also that Lek came on board the day we left. How could he have made a copy while we've been traveling? None of the villages we've seen has had a locksmith."

"Lek must have had someone working with him. How else did he know to present himself for employment just as we were leaving and not a day before? He knew we'd check his references if he joined us earlier, so he must have planned to force us into a corner as he did. I don't know what he said to the other interpreter, but I don't think it was what he claimed to have said. No, that copy must have been made some time before we departed."

"You've been thinking about this a great deal, haven't you, Chan?" Ian said, catching the young man off guard, for Chan looked startled for a moment before he controlled himself.

"I suppose I have. It just seems unwise that you place so much trust in this Siamese boy."

Ian's eyes narrowed for a moment, before he nodded. "You're right. I must be more circumspect in my dealings with Lek. It wouldn't do to have our mission undermined by the work of a spy, would it?"

"No," Chan said, his shoulders relaxing imperceptibly.

"But I can't rule out the possibility that one of the others is at fault in this thing, can I?"

"No, of course not. Just be careful, sir."

Ian's mouth twisted in a bitter smile. "Certainly." Then his face wiped clean of all expression, he added in a voice that brooked no argument, "Well, then. Now that's settled, why don't you join the others and leave me to my tedium."

Chan hesitated but at last left.

Ian stared at the key in his hand before rising to place it in a secret compartment under his bunk. He'd hoped to end Chan's determination to implicate Esme, but he didn't think he'd been successful. He groaned aloud as he thought of the mess she'd entangled them both in. But he had to admit her desire to continue her charade made him admire her, even while it frustrated him.

He'd feel better if he thought this would be the only incident to happen before they reached Chiengmai. Then Lek could "disappear," becoming Esme Montrose at the consulate.

And if something else did happen? He could only pray nothing else did.

Chapter Twelve

In the middle of Esme's nap, the boat lurched to a sudden halt, throwing her against the wall beside her bunk. Swiftly, she darted out of bed. She plaited her hair and wrapped the binding tightly around her breasts. Before she'd even finished buttoning her jacket, however, she heard a pounding on her door.

"Get out here!" shouted Ian.

She unlatched the door to find him with his waistcoat unbuttoned and his hair mussed, as if he too had been sleeping. Without a word, he dragged her out and along the deck to where the Siamese crew captain barked commands to two of his men.

"Excuse me," she said in Siamese, tugging at the captain's arm as Ian stood beside her, his fingers squeezing her other arm. "Excuse me!" she repeated more loudly. "Why have we stopped?"

"The launch hit a mound of sand a short distance

back," the captain answered. "It shouldn't have injured the boat because we slid over it easily. But a log under the sand caught and ripped off our rudder. I lost control of the launch and we hit that rock there."

He pointed to a mammoth stone to their left that jutted up out of the river.

"I managed to bring both boats to the bank," he continued, "but it was hard. We must camp here and make repairs."

Esme translated what he'd said for Ian.

"Ask him how long it will take," Ian told her.

"The hull has been weakened there," the captain said in answer to her inquiry, pointing to a spot at the front of the launch. "And we'll have to install a new rudder. Tell him two days, perhaps three."

"Two days!" Ian retorted when she repeated the captain's words for him in English. He climbed out of the boat into ankle-deep water and made his way to where the launch bumped up against the bank, one side listing to the left. He stood watching the Siamese crewmen who were already in the water, assessing the damage to the hull.

Then Ian whirled around, his entire body tense as he boarded his boat again, striding past the captain to where Esme stood. Scarcely pausing, he grabbed her arm, pulling her behind him to his cabin.

When they were in the cabin, he slammed the door shut behind them. "Sit!" he commanded.

Meekly, she lowered herself into the chair farthest from him, wary of his surly mood. She watched as he paced the room, his jaw set and his mouth in a severe line.

"Do you ever talk to the crew when you're not interpreting for me?" he asked, pivoting to face her.

His legs were planted wide as if he were beginning a long interrogation, and she swallowed nervously, wondering what she'd done this time.

"Sometimes."

"About what?"

"Mostly what part of the country we're passing through. Why?"

He ran his fingers through the unruly waves of his hair. When he spoke again, his tone was less menacing. "Have any of the crew ever mentioned we might not reach Chiengmai on schedule?"

"Not that I can remember," she answered. She searched her memory and then added more positively, "No, I don't think so."

His brow was furrowed as he searched her face. Then a glint of satisfaction lit his eyes, and his body seemed to relax. "So you've never told anyone our arrival might be delayed."

"No, of course not," she said, wondering what on earth he was thinking.

To that response he said nothing, turning once more to pace the cabin.

"Ian," she asked after he was silent for several minutes, "what is going on?"

"I'm not sure. Perhaps nothing." Then he stopped his pacing to sit down at the table, leaning forward across it to study her once more. She met his searching gaze confidently, pleased that his expression held no suspicion.

Finally he spoke again. "Esme, I need you to do something else for me. I shouldn't ask it of you— God knows I shouldn't—but I'm hampered by my inability to speak Siamese."

When she didn't answer, he continued, "I want you to ask the crewmen some discreet questions. Make them think you're simply curious, that you're acting on your own and not at my request. Can you do that, do you think?"

"What kind of questions?" she asked hesitantly, worried by Ian's serious tone.

"I want to know anything you can find out about this accident, every detail of how it happened, if such an accident occurs often, why they didn't see the sand bar in time to avoid it. Find out as much about the whole incident as you can."

"Why?"

"Will you do it?"

"Yes, of course, but why do you want to know all this?"

He delayed a moment before answering her, and she realized with alarm that he looked uncharacteristically anxious.

"Understand that I tend to believe the wreck was accidental. But I don't know for certain Chan didn't plan it."

"Plan it? How could he plan it?"

The harsh planes of his face softened as he contemplated her question. "For one thing, he could bribe a member of the crew, even the captain, to 'make an error,'" he replied, the faintest hint of a smile on his lips at her naiveté.

"I—I suppose so," she said, somewhat irritated that he found her innocence amusing. "And I guess delaying your arrival in Chiengmai would be to the advantage of the French."

"Most assuredly," he said as he leaned back in his chair. "You see why I need your help."

"I'll do what I can," she told him, gratified that Ian both trusted and needed her, even if it was for something as minor as this. She wanted to thank him for his trust since she hadn't the chance to do so before. But whatever she might have said was cut off by knocks at the door.

Ian opened the door to admit Harold, Godfrey, and Chan, who crowded into the tiny room demanding to know what had happened. Ian explained what he could, but they weren't satisfied until "Lek" gave them a detailed translation of the captain's words.

"Oh bother," Godfrey said, plopping down on Ian's bunk when all the explanations had been made. "Here we are in the middle of nowhere, stuck for God knows how long. You know if they said two days, it could be two weeks."

"They assured me it would be no more than three days," Esme cut in.

"Even if it is," Harold said, "we're still trapped here without a village in sight. And tomorrow's Christmas! What a dreadful place to spend it in!"

"What!" they all said nearly in unison.

Harold glanced at the surprised faces surrounding him and frowned. "You don't mean to tell me I'm the only one who remembered? I realize we're miles from civilization, but at the very least I expected a goose or something for dinner tomorrow. We *are* going to have a celebration, aren't we, Lord Winthrop?"

Ian groaned when everyone's eyes turned his way. "Damn it, Harold. I can't be expected to remember everything."

"But Christmas!" Harold said in dismay. "How could you leave Christmas out of your plans?"

"Now, Harold—" Ian began.

"We shall have a celebration," Esme said quietly, the assurance in her voice silencing them all. "Lord Winthrop can tell Henley to prepare a ham. I know he brought one in our provisions." She ignored Ian's sardonic half-smile as she set tasks for them all. "Godfrey can lead us all in a few Christmas songs. What do you English call them?"

"Carols," Harold supplied helpfully.

Ian raised one eyebrow in frank amusement.

"Ah, yes, carols," she said, avoiding Ian's gaze. "Harold and I will find something to serve as a tree. The rain forests have little undergrowth, so we can easily search for a bush or small tree and perhaps some berries to decorate it with."

"We don't need all of that," Ian said. "The ham is plenty."

"Don't be absurd," Godfrey retorted as he leaned leisurely against the wall. "It won't be Christmas without a tree. We're stuck here anyway, so why not let them get us one? I want to see what they come up with."

"All right then," Ian said firmly, his jaw set. "But you and Harold will go. I need Lek to help me here."

Esme's eyes flashed defiantly as she glared at Ian. "I would like to go."

"Of course you're going with us," Godfrey said, ignoring the angry glance Ian shot him. "The old slave driver can do without you for a day. I'd feel much safer with a native beside me anyway."

Ian refrained from retorting, but Esme knew from the way the muscle worked in his jaw that he was unhappy about her being out alone with Godfrey and Harold.

"Let's go," she said, darting out of her chair and hoping the others would follow before Ian could stop them.

Ian strode after her and out the cabin door, but when Harold and Godfrey pushed past him and grasped her arms on either side, he let them leave. She thought she felt his eyes following them off the boat as they stepped to shore. But when she glanced back, he wasn't on deck, so she decided she must have been mistaken and was just nervous about defying him.

Godfrey let out a low whistle as he looked around them at the towering teak trees that crowded out the sunlight, leaving below them a dark and musty forest floor. He shivered as a snake slithered into a bush only a few feet from them.

"I think Ian's right," Godfrey said. "We don't need a tree." He started to turn for the boat.

Esme's hand restrained him. "Are you afraid?" she asked, knowing Godfrey would be horrified to be considered a coward.

"No, no, certainly not," he said, drawing himself up. "But we might...uh...might get lost in that jungle."

"Not if we keep the river always in sight," she said. "Come along, sir."

"How do you know so much about Christmas anyway, Lek?" he asked, trying to delay her. "I mean, the Siamese don't celebrate it or anything."

"I'm half-French, remember? Besides, the British aren't the only *farangs* who observe Christmas. The orphanage always had a lengthy celebration."

"Ah, yes, your sentimental childhood," Godfrey said dryly.

"Come now," Harold said with a smile, "we can't disappoint the boy, can we? He longs for the days of his halcyon youth, so we must aid him in recapturing the past." Pointing into the forest, Harold lifted his head high. "Onward, Lek, onward! Let us sally forth to find a tree!"

Godfrey still seemed uncertain of the wisdom of their enterprise, but he followed behind Lek and Harold just the same.

It didn't take them long to find a suitable tree, for the dense forest along the river soon gave way to a clearing edged with growing seedlings, a few of them even evergreens. They argued a short while about which one was best, but at last they settled on a spindly five-foot sapling with sturdy little branches that Esme said would hold whatever decorations they found. Harold returned to the boats for a hatchet and was back a short time later.

As he chopped at the tree, Esme scanned the woods and clearing for things they could use as ornaments.

"Look!" she cried, running to a bush covered with hard red berries. "These are perfect! We can string them to make garlands."

Harold and Godfrey exchanged glances. When she realized that in her enthusiasm she was acting very unlike the Siamese boy she was supposed to be, she sobered a bit.

"Who's going to string these jewels?" Godfrey asked in a bored tone. "I couldn't use a needle if my life depended on it."

"Well, I can," Esme remarked. When both men flashed her strange looks, she added hastily, "All of the orphans were taught to sew, so that we could be self-sufficient."

Godfrey and Harold looked unconvinced, but they didn't argue with her.

In no time at all the tree was down, and Esme had filled her pockets and theirs with berries. Then the two men started to leave.

"Aren't you coming?" Harold asked as she continued to stand in the clearing.

"You go on with the tree and put it in my cabin. I'll be back shortly," she replied. "I wish to look around."

Deborah Martin

But as soon as they'd disappeared into the woods, she ran across the clearing and through a brace of trees toward the sound she'd heard not too far away. To her delight, her ears hadn't deceived her. Bubbling over rocks on its way to the Chao Phya was a clear stream.

She gazed at it with longing. She wanted desperately to immerse herself in the refreshing water. It had been so long since she'd had a real bath. She was tired of only being able to dab herself with water from the small clay water jar in her cabin. The others had bathed daily in the Chao Phya, but she'd been unable to since she hadn't dared remove her uniform.

She knew she shouldn't let the fresh water tempt her. Tigers and poisonous snakes were common in the jungle as were bandits who accosted lonely travelers in the hill country. But the water was so inviting, much cleaner than the muddy waters of the Chao Phya and certain to be cool.

She made her way up the stream until she was out of sight of the river. Coming upon a tiny waterfall, she stopped. *What a perfect spot for bathing,* she thought. She shed the uniform she'd worn for so long, feeling uncomfortable removing everything, but the thought of being thoroughly clean persuaded her. She wished she had time to wash her clothes, but that was out of the question, so she'd settle for a bath. She thought she heard a twig snap, but when she whirled around, she could see nothing but the wild growth around her. She decided that undressing in broad daylight had just made her nervous, for she'd never bathed outdoors before.

She dropped her clothes on a rock and unplaited her hair. Hastily, she darted into the water, shivering as the icy liquid hit her skin. It was colder than she'd expected. In spite of the warm sun, it was the cold season in Siam and like all the streams in the area this one came from the hills of the north. But she ignored the cold in her eagerness to bathe.

The stream was shallow, running over rocks and pebbles that shifted as she tread over them. But the hollowed-out pool beneath the waterfall was deep enough to bathe in, and its water was slightly warmer because it was in the sunlight. She sank down gratefully into the bracing water, throwing her head back to let her raven locks trail in the gentle eddying movement. She knew she shouldn't linger, but nonetheless her movements were lazy as she twirled her hair in the water.

She stretched out, letting the cool swirling liquid caress her skin. She enjoyed the lonely wildness of the little stream as she stared up into an azure sky and pretended she was free of restrictions and troubles. The water swished over and under and around her thighs, dancing down her calves and over her feet. She relaxed, letting the water lull her as she tried to forget everything. She felt as if her mind as well as her body were being washed clean.

Then she swam leisurely to the falls to stand under the cascade. After splashing in the pool a few more minutes, she rose from the water with regret. She didn't want Godfrey and Harold to come back for her and find her there.

As she waded through the stream toward the rock where her clothes were, a movement in the corner of her eye stopped her. She froze in terror as Henley emerged from the trees heading straight for her. She sank down into the stream, but it was too shallow to offer her much protection from the sailor's leers.

"Well, well," he said, his eyes gleaming with satisfaction. "Lookee what I've found. So our little Lek ain't a boy. I should've guessed by the way 'is lordship was always closed up in 'is cabin with you. Right smart of 'im to bring 'is mistress along. And in disguise too so 'e wouldn't 'ave no competition."

"How did you find me?" she asked, trying to gain time as her eyes scanned her surroundings for a way to escape.

"I followed you and them two idiots out 'ere, 'oping to catch you alone so I could get some of me own back on you for y'r insults in the market t'other day. But when I saw you takin' off y'r clothes, I decided to wait and watch. Got more than I bargained for, didn't I?" He sidled closer to the water's edge.

Horror filled Esme as she realized he'd watched her bathing. But that thought occupied her only a moment, for she knew she had to get away from him. She glanced frantically around. The bank behind her was too steep to climb, and ahead of her was the sailor. To her left was the waterfall. The only way remaining was downstream.

Henley grinned as he saw her make her decision. As she darted to the right, he strode into the stream ahead of her. He had the advantage because her feet were bare and couldn't move swiftly over the shifting pebbles and jagged rocks. But his heavy-booted feet easily trod the stream bed, so in moments he'd cut her off.

She struck out to the left, but he was upon her before she could even reach the muddy bank.

"Got you now, my pretty," he snarled as his hands closed over her shoulders. Twisting her around to face him, he lifted her over his shoulder and strode toward the bank. She beat on his back with her fists, screaming in rage as she tried to wriggle from his grasp.

He tossed her down in the grass so hard he knocked the wind out of her. Before she could gather her breath for another scream, he threw his body across hers and clamped his beefy hand over her mouth. With his other hand, he grabbed her hair, jerking her head back so she was forced to look up into his cruel, cold eyes.

"Are you the girl what was on the dock that night?" he asked her, yanking her hair until she thought it would come out of her head. "Just nod if you are."

She didn't move, but her terror of him must have given her away, for he gave her a sick leer that showed his rotting teeth.

"I'd be willin' to bet you are. It makes me blood boil that 'e got what 'e wouldn't let me 'ave. Still, things is falling nicely into me hands. I got that Chinee Chan to hire me so's I could find a way to teach the guv'nor a lesson. Now you land in me lap, makin' it easy fer me." He moved his lips to within an inch of hers and grinned cruelly. "I don't believe his lordship 'ud take kindly to 'aving me take what's 'is, do you? 'Specially if I was to make sure 'e couldn't 'ave you ever again."

Her body went still as she realized he intended more than rape. He planned to kill her or to kidnap her, either of which would be equally terrifying, for she had no doubt he'd abuse her if her allowed her to live.

He took away his hand when she quieted, but when she started to scream again, he thrust it back over her mouth.

"I don't know why y're botherin'," he said, his mouth twisted into a brutish grin. "No one'll 'ear you over the sound of that water, even if we was close enough to the boats to be 'eard.''

With a sinking heart, she realized he was right. He laughed as she renewed her struggles against him, fighting vainly to wriggle out from under his body.

"I'm goin' to let your mouth go now. You can scream if you like, but it won't do you no good, so maybe you'd better put y'r energy into beggin' me to spare you.''

The chuckle that followed this pronouncement told Esme that words wouldn't change his mind. But she had to try to convince him to release her.

"I'm not Lord Winthrop's mistress,'' she said in a rush once her mouth was free. "But he knows about the disguise. When I don't return with the others, he'll come after me, so you'd best let me go.''

Henley threw his head back and laughed heartily. "I almos' wish you was right," he said as he moved his free hand down to knead her breast. "That bastard left me stranded without a berth in Bangkok because o' you. I'd like to 'ave 'im see me take you and not be able to do anythin' about it.''

The pressure on her breast eased as he reached down to pull something from his side. Her eyes widened as she glimpsed the knife in his hands.

"Yes, that'd be a picture," he said as he grinned wickedly. "If 'e showed up, I'd cut 'is gullet with this 'ere pigsticker. Then 'e could watch me 'ave 'is whore while 'e's dying. But 'e ain't gonna show up anyhow. 'E was in 'is cabin when I left, most likely caught up in those papers of 'is or sleepin'.''

Esme swallowed as she remembered that Ian had looked like he'd been napping before. What if he'd gone back to sleep? His face had been etched with lines of weariness the last time she'd seen him. He might sleep for hours!

"I see you take my meanin'," Henley said with a satisfied grunt as he held the tip of the knife to her throat. "By the time they figure out y're missin', I'll be long gone on one o' them rice barges 'eadin' for Bangkok, and there'll only be y'r body to show 'im I 'ad my revenge."

"They'll find you," she said in a strangled whisper. "Ian will find you."

" 'E won't turn back from 'is bloody mission, not even for a bit o' fluff as pretty as you." Then his eyes grew menacing. "But enough o' that. I want to 'ave a taste of what 'e's been enjoyin' in 'is spare time."

Without warning, he released her hair, swinging a huge meaty hand down to grab both her wrists while he held the knife tight against her throat. Jerking her arms above her head, he raised himself up on one knee. Then he raked her body with a long lecherous stare. She thought she'd die of shame as his eyes greedily devoured her. Tears streamed uncontrollably down her face, but he only laughed when he saw them.

She closed her eyes, unable to bear the sight of him hovering over her. Then he dropped on her again and covered her mouth with a wet, loathsome kiss. She twisted her head away, trying to escape the fat lips that groped for hers.

Suddenly the lips were gone and the weight lifted from her body. She sprang to a crouch, ready to run, but as she opened her eyes she saw Ian standing at her feet, his arm clamped around Henley's waist. His other hand held a knife to Henley's throat.

"Shall I kill him for you?" he asked her in a voice cold with rage. His face was livid and his eyes blue fire as he held the sailor in an iron grip.

Henley's face paled. She watched speechlessly as Henley's mouth tightened. To her horror, she saw him lift his own knife.

"Ian!" she cried, but too late, for Henley was already slashing wildly at Ian's arm which held the knife to his throat.

The pain was enough to make Ian release him and the sailor took advantage of the brief respite to lunge toward Esme. She ran for the woods when she realized that he meant to use her as a hostage to make good his escape. She stumbled as her foot fell in a hole. Pain shot through her ankle, and she felt her leg twist from under her. As she fell, she looked back and saw Ian lift his arm and a flash of steel split the air.

Henley let out a terror-filled cry from right behind her. Then he fell on top of her, and she screamed. Instinctively, she pushed him away, staring down in disbelief at the red liquid smeared across the top of her shoulder. She looked at him and shuddered as his eyes fixed on her in a shocked stare before becoming blank. Her breath came in ragged gasps as she stared at his lifeless form, unable to tear her eyes away from the blade that protruded from his back.

Slowly, she lifted her eyes to find Ian standing stock-still, his right arm now limp at his side. His face held a curious expression of mixed anger and guilt as he stared at Henley's body. Then he strode toward her, blood still dripping from the slashes Henley had made in his arm. Kneeling beside the sailor, he withdrew his knife, wiping it on the grass before replacing it in its sheath. Then he put his fingers against the man's throat.

"Is he—"

"Yes, he's dead," Ian replied in an emotionless voice.

She collapsed into hysterical sobs. He gathered her to him, stroking her back and whispering soothing words as she wept. She scarcely heard what he said, since she was still gripped in the terror of seeing a man killed. It was some time before her weeping subsided to occasional sniffles and she could concentrate on what Ian was saying.

"I'm sorry, love," he murmured in her ear. "I should have listened to you when you said he was dangerous."

She raised her tear-filled eyes to meet his sorrowful gaze. "You're not angry with me, are you?" She didn't pause to hear his answer before she rushed on, "I—I only wanted to bathe. It's been so long and ... Oh, Ian, I couldn't bear it if you thought that I encouraged him or—"

His mouth hardened as his eyes filled with remorse. "God, Esme," he said with a strangled cry, his arms tightening around her. "Do you really think me that much of a beast? Of course I don't think you encouraged him. If it hadn't been for your screams, I might never have found you."

Her heart gave a tiny leap as she realized he'd come looking for her. Gradually, she became aware that his hands rested on her back and his eyes were staring at her face as if to keep from looking elsewhere.

With a jolt, she remembered she was naked. Thoroughly and completely naked. She couldn't look at the man who was holding her and who so often had said he wanted her. Hiding her face from him in open embarrassment and clasping her arms to her breasts, she blushed crimson.

Noting her discomfort, Ian released her and stood

243

Deborah Martin

abruptly to his feet. As he walked back toward the stream, she noticed for the first time a basket and a blanket on the ground a short distance from them. Throwing the blanket over his shoulder, he returned to sit beside her. Without a word, he draped the blanket around her shoulders.

"What—" she began.

"When Godfrey and Harold returned, I asked about you. They said you'd requested to be left alone for a while. I decided . . . That is . . . I thought—"

"You thought you'd catch me out here alone," she finished for him, "and ply me with food. Am I correct?"

"Not much of a picnic, was it?" he said by way of answering her, casting a bitter glance at the body on the grass so close to them. "Come," he said, wrapping the blanket more securely around her. "We'd better return and tell them what's happened."

He rose from the grass. She tried to stand but the sharp pain that pierced her leg made her cry out and sit down again. Ian dropped to his knees, his face filled with concern.

"Did that bastard hurt you?" he said through clenched teeth as he noted the way she moved her leg gingerly from beneath her.

"No," she said, "I think I hurt my ankle when I ran from him."

He lifted her calf gently in his hand, carefully turning it so he could observe it from all angles.

"It doesn't look broken, so you've probably just twisted it." He rose to his feet and reached down to scoop her up in his arms, blanket and all.

"I'm sure I can walk with just a little help," she said as she glanced up into the chiseled planes of

244

his face, her every nerve aware that only a thin blanket separated her body from his.

"I'm giving you a little help, Esme."

"But you're hurt, too," she protested weakly.

"I assure you they're just scratches."

When she started to retort, he said, "Lie back and relax. You shouldn't put weight on that foot. You'll need to be able to walk in a few days when we reach Chiengmai."

His comment reminded her of what she was doing on this trip in the first place. She stiffened in his arms, suddenly remembering that her clothes were on the rock.

"Stop!" she told him. "My clothes are back there and I don't have another uniform!"

An ironic smile crossed his face. "I'll return for them later, but I'm afraid you'll have to abandon your disguise now, my dear, for that lovely little gray dress you brought with you. I don't think anyone will be convinced if I tell them I knifed Henley to stop him from raping Lek. As wicked as Henley was, his tastes never ran to boys."

She couldn't help but notice how grim his face had become.

"This won't help your career, will it?" she asked, wondering how she could make up for all the trouble she'd caused him.

For a moment, his eyes glittered with amusement. "What a lovely way to put it. To be truthful, I haven't really thought about it." He paused briefly before continuing, "Believe it or not, killing Henley won't damage my career much. After all, I saved a damsel in distress from a rapist. Anyone who hears the story will applaud me. But they won't approve of your presence here in the first place. No, I'll not be applauded for that."

245

She swallowed nervously, unnerved by the unexpected stoniness of his expression. "And what about Chan? Now he'll know about me."

A muscle throbbed in Ian's jaw. "We'll just have to see how Chan reacts to the news, won't we?"

Remorse flooded Esme at his serious expression. "I'm sorry, Ian, truly I am," she said softly as her delicate brow creased in a frown. "I never expected to be such a thorn in your side."

"But you are, my lovely girl, you are," he replied, his glance fleetingly piercing her as her eyes shone up at him like lustrous black sapphires. "In more ways than one."

With that enigmatic statement, he lapsed into silence. As he pressed on through the woods, swerving around trees and stepping over rotten logs, she clung to his neck to keep from falling out of his arms. Looking up at his harsh expression, she worried that her weight might be too much for his wounded arm.

As if he guessed her thoughts, he tightened his hold so her face was lifted to within inches of his. She stared at the light stubble on his chin and the set lines of his jaw, wishing she could brush his troubles away. But she knew she couldn't, and guilt assailed her because she knew she was partly responsible for them.

Within a few minutes they had emerged from the forest to where the boats were docked. No one but Harold was in sight and he lounged in one of the chairs on the deck of Ian and Esme's boat. He rose to his feet and hurried to the front of the boat when he saw them approach.

Ian handed her up to Harold, giving him no choice but to take her in his arms as Ian boarded.

The startled look he gave her as she clung to his neck nearly made her laugh.

"Hello, Harold," Esme said calmly.

"Lek!" he exclaimed as Ian took her back. "What the hell is going on here?" he asked, following Ian to Esme's cabin.

"You'll get a full explanation later, Harold," Ian called back to him. "As soon as I take care of Esme."

"Esme?" Harold asked, but Ian was already elbowing her cabin door open.

"Damn it! What is this bloody tree doing here?" Ian shouted as he nearly stumbled over the tree spread across the cabin deck, blocking his way to the bunk.

Esme couldn't help it. Coming upon the heels of Harold's confusion and the horrifying events of the day, Ian's statement was enough to send her into hysterical laughter.

"Oh...oh," she gasped as Ian glared at her. "It's the Christmas tree!" When he started to kick at it, she cried out, "No, don't! Don't destroy my beautiful tree!"

He grumbled at her pleas, but he stopped kicking. "Harold!" he shouted louder than he needed to since Harold was right on his heels.

"Ye—es?" the poor man asked, totally bewildered by what was going on.

"Move her precious tree, will you, so I can put her down?"

Quickly, Harold did as he was told. Taking care not to dislodge any of the folds of the blanket that encased Esme, Ian lay her gently on the bunk.

"Tell the others to meet me on the deck in half an hour, Harold," Ian said, his eyes never leaving Esme's face. "And close the door on your way out."

Harold hesitated.

"If you don't get out of here," Ian said coldly, "I'll—" He didn't have to say more, for Harold was already walking out.

She stared helplessly as Harold shut the door, leaving her alone with Ian. He slid past the tree to the water jar in the corner of her cabin. Without a word, he lifted it and the cloth draped over the jar, as well as the soap, and returned to her bed.

"Wh–what are you doing?" she asked as he sat on the edge of the bunk.

"You've blood all over you. I'm going to wash it off."

She flushed. "Ian! Don't you dare! I can wash myself well enough, thank you, if you'll just hand me that cloth."

He ignored her protests, none too gently shifting her onto her side so she faced the wall. "You can't reach your back even if you could walk to the water jar."

He tried to pull the blanket down, but she held the ends of it tightly in her fist.

"Look, love," he cajoled, "I've already seen you naked, and I conducted myself quite admirably, if I may say so. I'll only see your back. After today's events, I hardly think that's much cause for alarm."

She had to admit what he said made sense. And the thought of having Henley's blood on her and not being able to wash it off was enough to make her relent. She uncurled her fist.

"Thank you," he said, lowering the blanket to bare her upper back and neck.

His hands were gentle as they rubbed her skin with the soapy cloth, stopping every few seconds to rinse the blood out in the jar. The occasional touch of his fingers on her back made her shiver, for they were almost caressing as they brushed her skin. She felt his hands follow the trail of blood up, moving to scrub her softly rounded shoulder. Then he turned her onto her back.

She held the blanket clasped loosely over her breasts, though it barely covered the soft mounds. He continued to wash her, but now he washed areas she could have reached easily by herself. His hands moved down her collarbone, wiping the blood away with strokes so tender they made her throat constrict.

She gazed up into the liquid blue warmth of his eyes, and she couldn't look away. She knew she should mind what he was doing, knew she should stop him from touching her so intimately, but she didn't. His gentle washing of her made her forget Henley's degrading touch and feel whole and clean again. Whether this was Ian's intention, she didn't know. She only knew she didn't want him to stop.

He suddenly went very still as he realized she hadn't halted him. He stared at her, mesmerized by her eyes that shone like a doe's, innocent and trusting. Then his gaze traveled down to where her hand held the blanket close against her breasts. He drew his breath in sharply at the sight of the smooth creamy flesh that rose and fell with each breath she took. By the stream he'd been too concerned about saving her to notice how truly lovely she was. But now his eyes drank in her beauty.

Then a spot of blood on her shoulder that he'd missed caught his attention and he released a long drawn breath. What could he be thinking of to desire her when she'd scarcely escaped the lust of another man? Through a force of will, he dragged his gaze from her and threw the cloth into the jar. Turning away, he picked up the jar and moved without a word toward the door.

"Thank you, Ian," she said in a soft voice as his hand hesitated on the door handle.

"Get some rest," was all he could manage. Then he was outside, cursing all that made him desire her so much.

Chapter Thirteen

"Then we're agreed?" Ian asked, staring at the
group who circled the table. "No one will mention
to anyone that Miss Montrose was on this boat?"

Ian had spent the entire afternoon assembling
everyone for a discussion. Chan had been searching
for Henley to discuss the Christmas ham, and the
reverend had convinced Godfrey to go for a swim
up the river some distance from where they were
moored.

Now they sat pondering Ian's question. Harold
nodded his head almost immediately, but everyone
else remained quiet.

"Reverend?" Ian asked, inclining his head toward
the cabin. "Won't you aid the poor girl? She won't
be able to get a teaching position in Chiengmai if
they think she's anything but a lady, and they're
certain to think that if they know she's been traveling unchaperoned with six men."

Deborah Martin

"Of course I want to help her," the minister hastened to assure him. "But what if I can't? While I don't wish to tell anyone she was on board, if I'm asked about her presence to my face, I can't lie. Surely you understand that."

"Yes, yes," Ian said irritably. "But if no one knows she was here, who will ask? All I want is your promise that you won't reveal her secret of your own accord."

"You have my promise," the reverend said.

"Godfrey?" Ian asked next.

"I've no quarrel with saving the girl's reputation, such as it is."

Ian flashed Godfrey an angry glance that his friend ignored.

"But what about Henley?" Godfrey continued. "What are we to say about that without bringing her into it or telling more lies?"

Ian knew that Godfrey only balked because his pride was stung at having been fooled by the very woman whose reputation he'd disparaged. But Ian had to acknowledge the legitimacy of Godfrey's question.

"Why do we have to mention Henley at all?" Harold broke in. "Possibly no one except us knew of his presence on these boats. And from what Ian tells us of the scoundrel's behavior today, he won't be missed—here or in England." Harold leaned back in his chair, satisfied he'd effectively dealt with the problem.

Reverend Taylor frowned, but Ian answered Harold before the minister could object. "I can't keep the entire episode a secret, much as I might wish to. If Miss Montrose or one of you should chance to speak of it, the incident would look far more suspicious for having been covered up. But I see no

252

reason I can't say he attacked me because of my role in getting him thrown off his ship. Then I was forced to defend myself. All of that is true. Miss Montrose's part in it need not be mentioned at all. Does that meet with your approval, Godfrey?"

Godfrey shrugged and then nodded.

Ian at last turned his attention to Chan, wondering what tack the spy would take now that his scapegoat had become a woman. "Chan?"

"Of course I will preserve the girl's reputation. It has occurred to me, however, that Henley might have been the one who took those papers."

"You mean the ones Ian had us all searched for?" Godfrey said bitterly.

"Yes," Chan answered. "If such is the case, then we are better off rid of him. But perhaps the girl can tell us if he said anything that might reveal whom he was working for."

"Perhaps," Ian said, so immeasurably relieved that Chan had chosen to turn the events to his advantage without harming Esme that he was willing to play along with Chan in whichever way the spy wished for the moment.

"In any case," Chan said coolly, "no one shall mourn his death. Except the French, that is."

"Yes," Ian said, struggling to keep his face expressionless.

"But, Ian," Godfrey said, "no one knows for certain if he's a spy, and you can't allege such a thing without proof. So shan't you get into trouble for having killed the man?"

Ian's voice held a slight tinge of irony as he answered. "Ah, but I have diplomatic immunity—not that the Siamese care about a foreigner's death. No one's going to question my right to kill a lowly sailor who engaged me in a fight, not even in these

253

enlightened times. So I doubt his death will damage my reputation or my career, if that's what you mean."

"But he's still a man," Reverend Taylor gently admonished. "And his death deserves some attention."

Ian's steely gaze didn't falter as he stared at the reverend. "If you think I don't regret being forced to kill him, Reverend, you're mistaken. I don't like killing, and I certainly don't make a practice of it. As for his being a man, all I can say is that real men don't assault innocent women to exact petty vengeance. So I don't see why we should pity a man whose despicable actions brought him to his own death, do you?"

The minister seemed taken aback by Ian's candor. But he wouldn't allow him the final word. "Nonetheless, I think we should bury him and not leave his body for the animals."

"That's acceptable to me," Ian said.

"And I shall say a word or two over the grave," Reverend Taylor added.

"Certainly," said Ian, although he couldn't help hoping the reverend wouldn't also insist on flowers and a gravestone.

"Now that you've disposed of Henley," Godfrey said with his usual lack of concern, "what are you going to do with the girl?" Godfrey's lips turned up in an insidious smile. Then he nodded his head meaningfully toward Esme's cabin and lowered his voice to a stage whisper. "I have to wonder what you've done with her until now, old boy. Her disguise thoroughly fooled the rest of us, but surely not you, since you saw her in your cabin for long hours at a time. Getting her into your bed shouldn't have been too difficult. I mean, Rushton paved the way for you. After all those days alone, did you convince her to succumb to that lady-killing charm you're so notorious for having?"

Ian looked at Godfrey with utter contempt and started to retort, but he didn't get the chance, for Godfrey's knowing expression was quickly replaced by one of chagrin as a decidedly feminine voice answered him.

"The lady hasn't succumbed, I assure you," Esme replied from where she stood behind Godfrey's chair, having just moved up the deck from her cabin a few feet away. "I think, Godfrey, that you're possibly the nastiest person I've ever known. And I still haven't forgiven you for spreading all those terrible rumors about me, especially the ones that aren't true."

Godfrey's face reddened, tempting Ian to smile at the poor man's mortification. But his attention turned to Esme. Somehow she'd managed to dress herself. After days of seeing her in her ghastly glasses and uncomplimentary uniform, he was astonished to realize once again just how lovely she was. The gray cotton day dress she wore was simple with only a touch of lace at the high-neck collar and the cuffs. But the tight bodice showed to advantage her hourglass shape that even a corset couldn't improve. He could tell she wore only a single petticoat, for her skirts swung loosely about her legs and the shape of her hips was well defined.

Her face was transformed as well. She wore no traces of the makeup that so distorted the shape of her eyes. Without it, her ebony eyes were large and luminous, and her oval face fuller and more lively. But her hair held most of his attention. Unable to pin it up, she'd left it cascading down her back, evidently choosing not to braid it again. Its satiny

Deborah Martin

sheen reminded him of the morning he'd found her
on deck in her robe. It was all he could do to tear
his eyes away from her.

He wasn't alone in his observations, he realized
after glancing around the table. With an unexpected twinge of jealousy, he noted that Harold was
clearly smitten. And Godfrey's awed gaze made him
look like a foolish schoolboy as he twisted around
in his chair to look at her. Even Chan seemed intrigued by the transformation, and a trace of admiration crossed his face for a moment. Only the
reverend was unmoved, although the smile he gave
her was as kind as ever.

But Esme hadn't noticed the glances, so hurt was
she by Godfrey's accusations. Clearly, they'd been
gossiping about her. She should have realized what
they would think of her after all the stories going
round. Still, it wounded her to find the men speculating about whether she was Ian's mistress, especially considering what she'd been through. And
Godfrey's final comment reminded her of Ian's reputation as a rake. Although Ian had done the gentlemanly thing and saved her from Henley, she should
guard against taking that as a sign that he cared
for her beyond desiring her. It wouldn't do to assume he felt more for her than he did.

"You should be lying down," Ian said kindly. "I
thought I told you not to put any pressure on your
foot?"

Ian's concern mollified Esme somewhat, but she
was still piqued at Godfrey's words.

Harold rose hastily as he realized she'd been leaning against the wall for several moments. "Sit
here," he begged, pulling out his chair for her.

She sank gratefully into it before answering Ian.
"Like everyone else here seems to be, I was curious

256

about what you planned to do with me. You've said before that, if I were found out, you'd ship me back to Bangkok on the next boat we passed. Is that still your intention?"

The others listened with great interest, happily seizing on the information that Ian had known who she was for some time. Esme noticed with alarm that Chan in particular had taken note of what she'd said. She regretted her quick tongue as she remembered what Ian had told her about Chan. Oh, why must she always speak her mind without thinking?

But her statement didn't seem to alarm Ian. Instead he looked amused.

"What do you think, Godfrey?" he said, leaning back in his chair with a grin. "Shall we ship her back on one of the lumber barges that pass us daily? Or shall we wait until a nice rice merchant comes along?"

"You wouldn't!" she cried.

"Of course he wouldn't," Reverend Taylor answered, flashing Ian a disapproving glance. "He'd have to answer to all of us if he did."

"Hear, hear!" Harold shouted. "Tell the villain to leave the lady alone, Reverend!"

"Come now," Ian responded, his eyes twinkling with mischief, "don't you think she'd make a lovely rice merchant's wife?"

But Esme didn't think his teasing was funny, for she truly was worried he might send her back. And her last encounter with the sailor had brought home to her how potentially dangerous it could be to travel unescorted in Siam. She stood up with as much dignity as she could muster given the soreness of her ankle. Ian's face seemed to cloud over immediately.

"I should have known there was no use talking

to you," she responded quietly. "When you're ready to behave like a gentleman, which I realize may be no time soon, I'll be in my cabin."

"Sit down," Ian said softly as she turned to go. "Please sit down," he repeated when she hesitated.

She acceded to his request, placing her hands demurely in her lap as she waited for him to speak.

"Nothing has changed," he said, oblivious to the others. "I still intend to leave you at the consulate in Chiengmai."

Godfrey snorted. "How will you explain how she got there?"

"That's up to Miss Montrose," Ian replied, his gaze locking with hers. "If she wishes to ruin her chances of getting a position by telling them she's been on this boat with us, she's welcome to do so. But I won't hesitate to give them the details of how she got here, thus ensuring that they'll telegraph her father of her whereabouts and hold her until he arrives."

"They can't do that!" she cried. "I'm old enough to do as I wish with my life!"

"First of all, dear girl," he said acidly, "no school will hire you if you have a damaged reputation. Secondly, I'm sure the consul will be more willing to meet the requests of your father, the close friend of Minister Resident Henry Rushton, than the pleas of a runaway daughter who's all of eighteen. If your father asks them to hold you, they most assuredly will."

She had to admit grudgingly that he was right.

"If, however," Ian continued, "Miss Montrose chooses to say she booked passage on some passenger boat and needs their aid in acquiring a position, leaving them to assume I escorted her from the dock, then she'll be free to pursue her aims in

Chiengmai. She can only hope the rumors circulating in Bangkok don't reach that far. I think I can speak for Godfrey and Harold," he said, flashing the two men a warning glance, "when I say none of us will speak of them."

"Do you still plan to tell my father where I am?" she asked.

"Of course. As soon as I return to Bangkok. But I'll also try to convince him to refuse Michaels's marriage proposal."

"Father won't refuse it," she said with conviction.

"That's not my concern," Ian replied, but she could tell he didn't entirely mean it.

She wanted to rail at him, but she'd done enough of that and it hadn't changed his mind. It hurt her that in spite of all they'd been through together and the many ways she'd tried to help him, he hadn't changed his mind about telling her father. So she sat there in silence, wondering what she must do to change his mind.

The reverend broke the silence, attempting to soothe Esme's taut nerves. "No one has asked, child, but how do you feel?"

Esme observed her newfound friend for the first time since she'd abandoned her disguise and was relieved to discover his eyes still looked kindly upon her.

"I feel fairly well," she answered him, giving him a shy smile to show that she appreciated his concern. "I'm still a bit shaken, but that will go away in time."

She thought she saw something like wistfulness pass over Ian's face at her friendliness toward the older man, but she was certain she was mistaken. Ian didn't care about her. He saw her as a nuisance as long as she refused him her favors.

Deborah Martin

"If you feel the need to talk about what happened this morning," Reverend Taylor said, "I should be happy to listen."

His words brought her up with a jolt. In her concern about what might happen to her, she'd pushed the events of that morning to the back of her mind. But a sick feeling engulfed her as she realized the reverend referred to Henley's rape attempt. My God, she thought, by now, they all knew what had happened. She felt filthy, as if the sailor had somehow come from the grave to defile her again with his touch. How could she face these men when they knew the degradation she'd been subjected to?

Reverend Taylor watched in alarm as her face mirrored her horrifying thoughts.

Ian too noticed how quiet she'd become. "Perhaps it would be better if Miss Montrose not think about this morning at all, Reverend." He rose from the table. "May I escort you to your cabin, Miss Montrose?" he asked in a voice filled with concern.

Hearing her name, she started. As she glanced around the table, she realized that the men watched her closely. She was humiliated to think that they had guessed her thoughts. Their pity for her was all too clear on their faces. Oh God, she thought, if they continued to look at her like that the rest of the trip, she'd never blot out the memory of what had happened that morning.

The minister seemed belatedly to recognize that Esme needed something to take her mind off what had happened, not to remind her of it. He gave her his usual friendly smile and then leaned forward, ignoring Ian who stood awaiting Esme's answer. "Are we still having our Christmas celebration,

Miss Montrose? If so, we'd best get to work on that tree."

She nearly said no. She didn't know if she could stand to pretend to be cheerful after all that had occurred. But she realized what the minister was trying to do and knew he was right. She had to put the morning's events behind her if she were to survive the whole experience.

"Of course we're having our celebration," she said, flashing her friend a grateful smile. Then she noticed Ian standing across from her. "I—I'm sorry, Lord Winthrop, what did you ask me?"

"Nothing of any importance," he assured her. "By all means, trim the tree. I wouldn't want to stand in the way of Father Christmas."

Esme stood shakily to her feet, leaning on Harold for support when he leapt to her aid. Then she, Reverend Taylor, and Harold made their way back to her cabin, the two men making wry quips in a deliberate attempt to lighten her mood. Briefly, she wished it was Ian supporting her as she hobbled down the deck, but at least she could feel his eyes follow her every movement. The thought comforted her more than she dared admit.

As Esme opened her eyes, she remembered it was Christmas. Despite all that had happened the day before and although she was miles away from civilization, Esme was happy Christmas had come and they'd taken the trouble to celebrate it. She sorely needed to be reminded that men could be something other than violent beasts. So far Harold and Reverend Taylor had done their best to use the Christmas holiday to show her that. She knew she'd be grateful to them both for a long time.

Esme slipped her legs over the side of the bunk

and wriggled out from underneath the mosquito net. She touched her ankle to make certain that the bandage Harold had wrapped it with the day before was intact. It was. Gingerly, she put her weight on her foot, pleased when she only felt a slight pain. Her ankle must not have been twisted as badly as she'd at first thought, for although it hurt to stand, by placing most of her weight on her other foot, she could walk without even having to hold onto anything.

In spite of her ankle, it didn't take her long to slip into her corset and petticoat, although she cursed the day her aunt had bought her the gray gown as she struggled with the tiny buttons down its back. Somehow she managed to fasten them all. Then she ran a brush quickly through her long hair. She hesitated in front of the mirror as she glanced at the silken tresses that fell to her shoulders. She knew she should tie them back or put them up, but without hair pins or even a ribbon—for she'd left by the stream the one holding her braid—she couldn't do anything except let it float freely.

As quietly as she could, she opened her cabin door, peeking out to see if anyone was awake yet. Then she hobbled along the deck to the back of the boat. There stood the tree where they'd left it the night before. She, Harold, and the reverend had stayed up late trimming it. First they'd cut the branches to give it a softer shape. Then she'd strung the red berries as Reverend Taylor and Harold had gone off to hunt in their cabins for other items to use as decorations.

She'd laughed when they'd returned with a garish red handkerchief of Harold's and several white ones of the reverend's. But best of all had been the ten ascot pins Godfrey had contributed, stating that he'd better get them back as soon as Christmas was over or someone would have to answer to him.

In all the noise and fun, Esme hadn't had time to think about the sailor or what he'd tried to do to her. And even when Ian had appeared, stern and disapproving, to tell them Esme ought to be in bed after her day's ordeal, she'd been too tired to protest or to think about the ordeal he'd referred to.

Now she was glad they'd put so much effort into decorating the tree. In the early morning sunlight, Godfrey's ascot pins glittered and twinkled. The handkerchiefs, which they'd tied together to form another garland, seemed to dance on the limbs of the tree as a gentle breeze wafted over the deck. Esme stood admiring their handiwork for a moment.

But she didn't linger, for she knew there'd be no Christmas dinner without her. With Henley's death, the entourage had lost their cook. Ian hoped to hire one in the next village, but she was determined they not suffer in the meantime. She intended for them to have a decent Christmas dinner.

At least she need not worry about cooking the ham, she thought as she bustled around the pots and pans that Harold had transferred from the cook's boat for her. Henley had brought two salted, smoked hams with them. All she had to do was rinse and slice them, which she did.

In no time, she'd found Henley's store of biscuits and fresh fruit. She pushed up her sleeves and began to peel and slice two ripe mangoes she'd been lucky to find since it was still early for them. So intent was she on her work that she didn't notice Ian had come up behind her until he spoke.

"Good morning," he said.

Deborah Martin

She whirled to face him. He must have bathed in the same stream she had, she thought. He wore only his trousers and a thin damp shirt that clung to the firm muscles of his chest. The first few buttons were undone, revealing a few crisp sprigs of chestnut hair. She could see wisps of that same hair on his forearms, for he'd rolled up his sleeves, revealing finely corded arms that he now held crossed over his chest.

She swallowed hard as she looked up into the gray-blue eyes that were noting the way her own eyes lingered over his body. He seemed pleased, although he didn't smile.

"I brought your clothes," he said, dropping a bundle at her feet. Her jacket, her trousers, even her ribbon were all there, a bit grimy, but at least usable.

"Thank you," she replied, and turned back to slicing the mango, trying to hide the way the sight of him unnerved her.

"Just what do you think you're doing, dear girl?"

As she swung around to face him yet again, she noticed that despite the solemn expression on his face, his smoky eyes twinkled mischievously.

"I'm preparing dinner, my lord," she said tartly, "and I'd thank you to leave me to it or I'll never finish on time."

Reaching over her shoulder, Ian clasped the plate of fruit and set it at a spot distant from her. Then he removed the knife from her hands and set it by the mango. His hands lifted her chair from behind, turning it halfway around so she faced him.

She fixed him with a regal stare, but he only seemed amused by her attempts to maintain her dignity.

"We don't need you to slave away at dinner for

264

us, Esme," he said, leaning down to place his hands on the chair arms at her sides. "I'm certain we've enough tinned goods for a meal."

"I can do better than tinned goods, and I don't mind cooking," she retorted. "Unless you're worried I might poison you?"

"After I saved your life? Surely you're not that angry with me," he answered as he took her hand in his.

Her fingers were sticky with mango juice, but he didn't seem to care. His eyes never left hers as he brought her hand to his lips. But he didn't kiss her hand as she'd expected. Instead he sucked the sweet juice off the end of first one and then another finger. Unable to move away, her gaze fixed on his sensual lips. But when he moved to take the last finger in his mouth, she recoiled, snatching her hand away in anger at both him and herself. He gave a low sarcastic laugh.

"So I see you *are* still angry with me. It won't do you any good. I'm not changing my mind about leaving you at the consulate and telling your father," he stated as he straightened to his full height. Then he twisted one arm behind him to clasp something he'd placed on the table. With a flourish and a mocking bow, he presented her with a bouquet of wild orchids.

She stared in amazement at the tiny amethyst blossoms that cascaded over his hand in streams.

"I regret this is the only Christmas gift I could find at such short notice and under such circumstances." His voice was almost tender as he spoke.

Her hands trembling, she took the flowers from him. She knew that orchids had little fragrance, but she buried her face in the blooms anyway, pleased when she caught a faint scent. She beamed up at

Ian as she placed the flowers on the table beside her, happy that the sardonic expression on his face had given way to one of pleasure.

"Thank you, Ian," she said softly. "It's the loveliest Christmas present I've ever received."

To her dismay, he bent down again to place his hands on either side of her.

"Then perhaps," he whispered as his eyes searched hers, "you might show me your thanks in a different way."

The pleased expression she'd worn moments before faded from her face. "Is that why you brought me flowers?" she asked with downcast eyes. "So you might claim some reward?"

"No, damn you!" he exploded as he seized her chin with his hand, holding it as if to command her to listen. "But I don't understand why you deny me what I know you've given another. I'm not ugly nor old. And despite what you claim, I know you feel something for me. Yet you act as if my touch would defile you as much as Michaels's would."

She tried to wrench away from his grasp, but his hand held her as his lips swooped down to her cheek and burned a path to her mouth. She willed herself not to respond. She resisted the urge to open her lips, holding herself as rigidly as she could against the insistent urgency of his mouth on hers.

As he jerked back angrily, she held in check the tears that threatened to spill down her cheeks. "You've offered me far less than Michaels," she said in a voice as calm as she could manage. "Yet you expect as much or more from me. Even he planned to marry me before he ravaged my body. But you wish only to take what is not yours—what is mine to give. You expect me to do as you ask simply because you wish me to and because you think I—

I am more experienced than I am. I can't dissuade you if you persist in that notion. But it makes no difference if what they say of me is true or not. It's still my choice to decide whom I will kiss and whom I will not."

She continued, no longer able to stop the tears that streamed down her face, "I thank you for the flowers, and I thank you for saving my life but . . ." This last she could hardly choke out. "But I hadn't realized that the price of your affection and protection was my honor. Now that I know it, I will try not to place myself any more in your debt than is absolutely necessary."

"Esme, I—" he began, his fingers brushing the tears from her cheek, but she pushed his hand away, refusing to look at him.

"Don't touch me, Ian," she said in a voice that was barely a whisper. "We only have a few days left before we reach Chiengmai and you hand me over to my jailors there. In the meantime, I wish you'd just leave me alone. You want to see me married to a man I detest, yet you expect me to fall willingly into your arms. I can't give you what you want, so I think it best we be together as little as possible in the future."

"You really don't understand, do you?" He gripped her chin yet again, trying to force her to look at him. "Once you boarded this boat, you made me responsible for you. I can't just let you disappear into the crowds in Chiengmai where you might be abused by other men like Henley. Surely you can understand that!"

She raised her eyes to his, surprised to see the lines of pain creasing the corners of his glittering gray eyes. Then she reminded herself that Ian's interest in her was purely physical.

"I understand only that I'm to be forced into marrying William Michaels. It doesn't matter if you personally hand me over to him. If you leave me at the consulate in Chiengmai and tell Father where I am, you'll have placed me in Mr. Michaels's care as surely as if you gave me to him yourself. For that, my lord, I can't forgive you."

His mouth tightened ominously as his fingers released her chin. He drew himself up to his full height, towering over her like the stone statues of Buddha she'd glimpsed in Bangkok that held their hands out as if to say, "Stay away." His eyes were the cold gray of granite, and his hands at his sides could just as easily have been pushing her away. His lips parted and she waited for the barbs she knew he would throw at her, but a sound behind him kept him from speaking.

She looked beyond Ian's rigid form to find Reverend Taylor observing them. "Hello, Reverend," she said quietly.

Ian remained standing tensely before her.

The older man took in her damp flushed cheeks and the frozen stiffness of Ian's back. "Would you like some help with dinner, child?" he asked, his kind brown eyes radiating an inner warmth.

"I think I would, sir," she responded, rising from the chair. As she passed Ian, he lifted his hand to clasp her arm, but she continued walking, forcing him to either relinquish his hold or restrain her further. She knew he wouldn't do such a thing in front of Reverend Taylor.

"I need to retrieve more items from the other boat," she told the minister, "but I need some help walking."

"Sit down, Esme," Ian growled as he whirled

around. "I'll get what you need and Reverend Taylor can help you here."

"Thank you," she murmured, struggling to keep her voice from quavering. Then she rattled off a list of items she wanted, not daring to look at him.

As soon as he'd left the boat, Reverend Taylor took her arm and led her to a chair. "Tell me what's wrong. Perhaps I've misjudged the situation, but it seems Lord Winthrop's interest in you is greater than he led us to believe."

She smiled bitterly. "Greater and lesser," she replied, allowing him to hold her hand between his two bony ones. "I see now that he's like most men. No better and no worse."

"And you thought he was better than most?" he asked, his face mirroring his concern.

"I thought—" she began. What had she thought? That Ian would relent? Yes, she'd thought that. That his rescue of her from Henley proved he cared more about her than she'd realized? Yes, she'd thought that, too.

She sighed. "It doesn't matter what I thought."

"There you're wrong, child," the reverend said, patting her hand. "It seems to matter a great deal—to both of you. But you must be patient. Lord Winthrop is unaccustomed to feeling responsible for a woman, I suspect. He's been responsible for men, families, even countries perhaps but not young women. I don't believe he likes it very much, especially when the woman is as pretty as you are."

When Esme glanced at him in surprise, he laughed. "Just because I'm a man of the cloth doesn't mean I don't notice such things. I even had a wife once." His face clouded for a moment. "She was beautiful and strong but she had a terrible accident one day and...Well, I never remarried. No one could take her place in my heart."

"I'm sorry," Esme said softly.

"It was long ago," he responded. "But I remember what it was like to love a beautiful woman and to fear that love just as Lord Winthrop does."

Her face fell as she toyed with a napkin on the table. "But Ian...I mean, Lord Winthrop... doesn't love me. He thinks terrible things of me."

"Yes, Harold told me what made you flee Bangkok."

She looked at him in alarm. "The stories about me and Mr. Rushton and Lord Winthrop aren't true!"

"I didn't think so and Harold doesn't seem to believe them either. My instinct tells me you're as innocent as you claim or you wouldn't be resisting Lord Winthrop."

"I wish he could see it. But he—he just wants—" How could she tell a minister that Ian only desired her?

"Sometimes it's difficult for a man to distinguish between love and desire," he said, startling her with how much he understood. "But given time, he may discover for himself that the two are the same for him."

"I don't have time. He's leaving me in Chiengmai in a few days. Then I'll have to marry a man my father has chosen for me—a man I detest."

The reverend's face showed his sympathy for her, but his smile seemed to reassure her everything would be for the best.

"Don't be so certain Lord Winthrop will be able to do what he says when the time comes. He may surprise you."

Moonlight Enchantment

Thinking of Ian's words about his responsibility toward her, Esme despaired in spite of Reverend Taylor's kind words.

"Perhaps," she said. "But I think he won't."

To her despondent certainty, the reverend could answer nothing.

Chapter Fourteen

Christmas dinner turned out better than Esme expected. The ham, which she fried on the boat's charcoal stove, was succulent and delicious. She prepared a platter of tropical fruit and boiled the last of their fresh vegetables. When she added fried potatoes and the ship biscuits, the entire dinner proved more than adequate and even moderately festive.

She worried that Ian might be morose during the meal, but whatever emotions he felt he masked well. All in all, dinner was delightful, notwithstanding that they had no plum pudding for dessert and that the weather wasn't snowy but balmy, as the temperatures during the day rose until the men sweated under the frock coats they donned for the occasion.

After the dishes were washed, she found a spot on the deck where she could be alone, thankful that the men, with nothing better to do, had gone hunting in the forest. Drowsily, she watched a family of monkeys that had made their home in a bo tree not far from the boats. As they scampered from limb to limb, she giggled at their antics.

"Cute creatures but very pesky," a voice said beside her, startling her so she jumped.

She turned her head to find Chan watching her.

"You didn't want to go hunting with the others?" she asked, trying to keep the trepidation out of her voice. She steeled herself to show no reaction at his presence.

"No. I am not adept at hunting. I was reared in the city—in Hong Kong—so I came in contact with few wild animals."

She didn't know what to say, so she remained quiet, wondering why he sought her company.

After a long silence he spoke again. "You fooled me very well as Lek. I would not have guessed you were a woman."

"I'm sorry. I felt badly about deceiving everyone, but it seemed the only alternative at the time."

"You need not apologize," he hastened to say. Then he added lightly, "But I am curious. When did Lord Winthrop discover your identity?"

His expression held more than curiosity, but she was determined not to say anything that might give Chan the impression she knew about him.

"He found my dress when he searched the cabins looking for those stolen papers." Esme wasn't certain, but she thought Chan relaxed somewhat after she said this. "I assume you knew about those missing documents."

"Yes," he told her curtly. His face took on the bland expression of someone carefully schooling his features to betray nothing. "I still wonder if Henley

273

might have taken them. Has his lordship mentioned anything more about them to you?"

"No," she said, resisting the urge to turn away from his inquisitive stare. "Not really. He hasn't seemed too concerned with the matter." She gave a shaky laugh, and Chan joined her.

Then they sat in silence for a moment.

"You know," he said at last in a sympathetic voice that didn't ring true, "I don't blame you for not wanting to marry William Michaels."

"You know him?" she asked in surprise.

For a moment, Chan's guard seemed to slip, and he frowned. Then his face became expressionless again. "No. But I know of him. I suppose an attractive young girl like you wouldn't wish to marry an old man like him."

"It wasn't that."

"Oh?" he asked, and the way he observed her made her nervous.

"He—he repulses me. I don't know why. And I don't love him. I know you probably think that strange, since most Oriental marriages are arranged, but my parents' marriage had always seemed so happy that I wanted one like it."

"I see," he responded, once again seeming to relax. "No one has mentioned your mother in these discussions. Only your father."

She thought it odd he should be so curious. "My mother is dead," she said in a tone that warned him not to pry.

He looked as if he were about to say something else, but seemed to think better of it.

It was a measure of her uneasiness around him that when Ian approached them a few moments later, coming up behind Chan as silently as a ghost, she jumped.

"You gave me such a scare, Ian!" she told him, not noticing she'd used his first name in front of Chan. "Why must you always sneak up on people? And why aren't you out hunting?"

"I should ask Chan the same thing," Ian said, the steel hardness of his eyes betraying his casual tone.

"I don't hunt, Lord Winthrop," Chan replied, "so I came in search of company."

"I'm afraid I'm going to disappoint you then," Ian said as he strode across the deck to stand beside Esme's chair. "I'm taking Esme into the woods for a much-needed lesson in knife play."

"What!" Esme exclaimed.

"I thought you might want to learn how to defend yourself against men like Henley. Are you interested?"

She wanted to tell him she wouldn't go anywhere alone with him. But she wasn't about to stay and withstand Chan's interrogation. Besides, the idea of learning how to use a knife intrigued her. She'd like to be able to fight her own battles for a change and she knew Ian could teach her if anyone could.

"Certainly," she replied as she stood to her feet and smoothed her skirt. "But only if you promise not to laugh at my first fumbling attempts to aim."

"I promise," Ian said, a wry smile spreading across his face as he placed her hand in the crook of his arm. "Not a chuckle."

Leaning on his arm heavily, she walked with him down the deck until they were out of Chan's hearing.

Then she paused. "You must also promise not to kiss me."

With only a hint of a smile in his eyes, he promised solemnly he wouldn't kiss her. Wary of him, she nonetheless accompanied him off the boat, allowing him to support her with his arm around her waist to avoid her putting weight on her still sore ankle.

When they were out of sight of the boat, Ian's pace quickened slightly. "What did Chan say to you?"

"He asked me who you suspected took the papers."

Ian's face darkened. "What did you tell him?"

"That I didn't know."

"That's all he wanted to discuss?" he asked, his eyes watching her with keen interest.

She frowned, remembering the strangeness of the conversation. "No. He also seemed interested in my parents, for some reason."

Ian contemplated that bit of information for a moment. "Have you any idea why he'd be interested in them?"

"None." Then she added as a thought flitted through her mind, "Although ever since you told me about those fake suicides Chan created to get rid of the men he set up, I've been thinking about my mother."

Ian glanced sharply at her. "Why?"

"I found out recently that Mother committed suicide. Father showed me the note she left and everything, but, still, I can't accept she did such a thing. She had no reason to."

"Are you sure?" he asked, his voice suddenly gentle. His arm tightened protectively about her waist. "Sometimes parents hide things from their children very well."

"That's what Father said. But I don't care. The note she left said she was in love with another man." She shook her head violently. "I don't believe it. She loved only Father. She would never have betrayed him. I'm sure of it!"

Ian's eyes narrowed for a moment, then he shook his head as if dismissing the thought. "Does your father believe she betrayed him?"

"Yes," she said, her anger rising. "But he's wrong to believe so."

"Don't you think your father would know more about what your mother would or wouldn't do?"

That bit of logic stopped her for a moment. Her mind said Ian was right, but her heart knew her mother could never have betrayed her father, regardless of what he believed. "Oh, I don't know, Ian. But you didn't know her. She wasn't like that at all."

"People can surprise us sometimes," he said wryly.

That was certainly true, she thought with bitterness. If her father could prove so different from her image of him, what about her mother?

She fell into a pensive silence as they wound their way through the forest. But her thoughts shifted when they reached a clearing similar to the one where Henley had attacked her. For a moment, the events of the morning before flashed through her mind, making her struggle to forget them.

She glanced at Ian, who was observing her closely as if he knew what she was thinking. It always unnerved her, this ability of his to discern her every thought from the expression on her face.

"Next time," he said with resolution, "you'll know what to do."

Determined, she nodded.

Then he placed in her hand the carved ivory handle of the knife she'd seen him use. She nearly dropped it as an image of the blade protruding from

277

Deborah Martin

the sailor's back assailed her, but he folded her fingers around it, refusing to let her release it.

"I'm sorry I can't give you a different knife," he murmured, "but I couldn't find one of the right weight and size for a woman. This one will fit easily in a sheath strapped to your leg."

"You—you're not giving it to me, are you?" she asked, surprised.

"I can buy another one. But I want you to have this now. It's important to me. I'd feel better knowing you could protect yourself if need be."

"That sense of responsibility preying on you again?" she couldn't resist saying with a lift of one delicate eyebrow.

His eyes were smoldering gray coals as he studied her face. "If you wish."

Under that burning look, the blood drained from her face. Why did he always make her feel this shuddering of life whenever he looked at her?

She strove for control. "Shall we commence with the lesson then?" she asked lightly.

He smiled as if he knew the affect he had on her. But he merely answered, "By all means."

Then he moved behind her, reaching around to grasp her right wrist with his right hand as he slid up against her back. She stiffened as he placed his other hand casually on her waist.

"Relax!" he commanded. "You can't throw a knife with any accuracy if your wrist is as rigid as a board."

She willed her wrist to go limp, although the touch of his fingers was almost more than she could bear.

But her awareness of his body soon abated as the lesson began in earnest, for Ian was a relentless teacher. He barked commands as if she were one of

278

his men, twisting her wrist left and right and up and down until it ached. He was unstinting with praise when she threw well, but harsh with criticism when she faltered in her execution.

She threw the knife again and again into logs, at branches, even into the ground. After what seemed like hours of practice, hours of listening to Ian's instructions, she began to hit what she aimed at with reasonable accuracy.

"You'll have to practice a great deal more," he said when she finally tossed the knife down and sank onto the ground, weary and ready to rest.

"I will, Ian, I promise," she gasped out. "But my entire arm aches and it's beginning to get too dark to see. Can't we continue this tomorrow?"

Ian's face registered his surprise as he looked around him for the first time since they'd entered the clearing. "You're right. We've been here far longer than I realized."

He sat down beside her in the grass. "I'm sorry I let you practice so long. We can only rest here a moment if we're to find our way back to the boats before nightfall."

"Of course," she said, massaging her aching wrist.

"This was only the beginning, you realize. Throwing a knife is fairly simple but you must learn how to thrust with it if someone is close to your body—like Henley was. You must be able to slide it into a man's ribs if need be."

She shuddered. "I don't know if I could ever do that." She picked up the knife beside her and fingered the tiny carvings on its handle.

"If you'd had it yesterday," he asked harshly, "would you have used it?"

She thought for a moment, remembering the sick

feeling that had enveloped her when Henley had pinned her down. "I suppose I would have."

He released his breath in a rush. "Good."

Reaching inside his waistcoat, he unstrapped the leather band circling his waist, which held the knife's sheath securely against him. He slipped the band off. Taking the knife from her, he replaced it in the sheath. Then he adjusted the band so it was shorter. She noticed the band was designed to be worn around the waist or shortened so it could be strapped to a leg.

His hand gripped her right ankle, which lay on the grass as she rested on her hips with her legs stretched out.

"I can do it," she murmured, placing her hand on his, but he ignored her, lifting her skirts so her leg was bare to midcalf where her drawers began. Then he strapped the sheath to her leg, drawing the band through the buckle until it fit snugly about her calf. His hand lingered a fraction of a second on the smooth skin of her leg before he withdrew the knife from the sheath.

"Don't!" she said as he started to cut off the extra leather extending beyond the buckle.

"Why not? It will only hamper you."

"But you might want the knife and the sheath back later."

"No," he said, cutting the leather off. "They're yours now."

His words struck her silent, for they felt somehow so final. He seemed to recognize it, too, for he didn't immediately pull her skirt back down, but skimmed his fingers over the taut skin of her calf, making her tingle wherever he touched her. She watched him, unable to do anything else. But when his eyes lifted to hers, alight with a raw desire she couldn't mistake, she covered his hand with hers.

"It's late," she murmured, the words almost a plea. "W—we should return."

He nodded, though his face hardened. He helped her to her feet, and they returned to the boats without exchanging a word. But Esme was painfully aware of his closeness as she clung to his muscled arm. Her blood raced, and her head pounded from a yearning she couldn't seem to escape.

She reminded herself that in a few days he'd abandon her to the whims of William Michaels. But a part of her didn't care, and she knew it. With a vehemence bordering on madness, she cursed herself for being so attracted to him.

With Esme's identity revealed, she couldn't ask the crew questions about the accident without raising their suspicions. They'd already lost face because they'd accepted her, never suspecting she was a woman. They didn't mind she was a *farang*. As Lek, she'd told them she was half-French, and that hadn't bothered them. But the fact that a woman had been giving them orders for weeks, even though the orders had originated with Ian, galled them. They continued to acknowledge her commands and grudgingly admitted she was competent, but she was well aware they weren't at ease with her.

That proved a boon to Ian's mission, because the fact that someone could work among them so easily in disguise made them fear other spies were in their midst. If indeed they'd been paid to manufacture the boat accident, they made up for it by taking only one day for repairs. The entourage was back on the river the day after Christmas. After that the days passed swiftly.

But as Ian had promised, the lessons in using a knife continued. He insisted that Esme know as much about protecting herself as possible, so he spent most of his mornings teaching her to manipulate the blade with stealth and cunning. The boat's rocking complicated matters, but Ian wouldn't relent, although he let her use a bone letter opener for the beginning lessons.

Ian worked with her tirelessly, until her wrists and arms ached from parrying and thrusting. She began to excel at removing the knife from the sheath unobtrusively. Several times she managed to get under Ian's guard. His praise at such times brought a glow of pleasure to her face.

One morning five days after they'd left the clearing, the crew captain announced to Esme that they should reach Chiengmai some time that evening. She went to find Ian to tell him and found him sitting on the deck.

"I think it might be best if you resume your disguise until after we dock," he told her upon hearing her news.

At her grimace, he smiled. "I've discussed it with the reverend and we agree it's the best way to keep your presence on the boats a secret. You need not be so elaborate about it, however. As long as you wear the clothes and glasses, walk with that dreadful stoop, and braid your hair, I don't think anyone will give you another glance. You can do without the makeup or the binding," he said, trying to be delicate.

"And what will you do with me once we arrive?" she asked to cover the blush that rose to her face.

"You and Godfrey will leave together. Then he'll escort you to the foreign hotel and secure you a room. There you can spend the night and make your transformation into a woman. Tomorrow morning I'll claim to have met you at dinner. Then I'll do what I can at the consulate to ensure their assistance in acquiring a position for you as a teacher and in watching out for you until a position is secured. Does that meet with your approval?"

Esme nodded. This was turning out better than she'd expected. With so much freedom, she could establish herself in Chiengmai. And perhaps Ian wouldn't feel the need to notify her father when he returned to Bangkok.

His next words shattered that hope. "When I reach Bangkok, I'll contact your father and assure him you're doing well."

When she didn't answer, realizing it was fruitless to argue with him, he rose from his chair and began to walk toward his cabin. Then he paused.

"I wish to see you in my cabin," he told her, "as soon as you've gathered your belongings and put on your disguise."

Then he left without another word.

It was midmorning before she finished her packing and approached his cabin. She knocked on the door hesitantly, wondering with trepidation why he wanted this final meeting. When his voice bade her enter, she opened the door slowly. He sat at his desk, his hands toying with the bone letter opener.

"You've learned to defend yourself well, Esme," he told her as he beckoned her to her usual seat opposite the rattan table. "But it's time for one final lesson."

He opened his waistcoat to reveal a new leather band with a new sheath. Nestled in the sheath was a larger knife than the one he'd given her.

"Until now we've assumed in our practices that your opponent was unarmed. But that won't always

be the case. It's time you learned how to fight someone who's also defending himself.''

He stood and withdrew his new knife from its
sheath. "Where's your weapon?"

She raised her trouser leg just enough to reveal
the sheath strapped to her lower calf. He nodded
his approval.

"Time for your final lesson," he said, gesturing
to her knife. "I want you to try and disarm me while
defending yourself from attack. If you can.''

She rose to her feet, watching him warily. Then
she gave him a sly smile as she stepped back from
the desk. "If I succeed, my lord, I ought to have
some reward after all the grueling training you've
put me through.''

He regarded her steadily. "What reward do you
think you deserve?"

She summoned up all her courage before speaking. "If I disarm you, you must agree to leave me
in Chiengmai without telling my father where I
am.''

Ian's mouth hardened as he considered her request. "You never quit, do you? Very well. I'll think
about it. But what will be my reward if I succeed
in disarming you first?"

She gave him a startled look. She hadn't thought
he would request anything in return. "You don't
deserve a reward. You've been fighting with a knife
for years. You know there's only a slim chance I
can best you.''

"But you haven't heard what reward I require."
His mouth curved in a slow grin.

She feared she knew exactly what he wanted. A
frown crossed her brow.

"Relax," he said lazily as he observed her distress. "I only want one kiss—nothing more.''

She swallowed as she thought about it. A kiss was little enough to give him if he won. He'd taken as much from her several times before. But if by some chance she could disarm him, she'd be free! The possibility was small but well worth the risk.

"I'll accept your terms, if you'll accept mine," she responded.

"Then it's a bargain. Prepare to defend yourself," he said as he clasped the knife in his hand.

In seconds, she'd pulled her knife from its sheath at her calf almost before he could circle the desk.

Her enthusiasm for the game made him smile sardonically. "I don't wish to die quite yet, so be careful," he muttered.

They circled each other warily as Ian searched for an opening. He'd taught her not to attack, since her lesser strength and prowess would make her tire more quickly than any male adversary. He'd instructed her instead to use the knife only in defense. He'd added that most men who attacked her wouldn't expect her to be able to defend herself, and thus she'd at least have the element of surprise on her side.

"That's it," he said now, his mouth a grim line as his eyes never left her blade. "Make me come to you. But be ready to anticipate my thrusts."

He lunged and she swerved aside, her knife skimming his sleeve as he passed her.

"Excellent!" he said as he pulled back.

Again they circled in the tiny cabin. She stumbled as her leg pressed up against Ian's bunk and he seized the moment to lunge again. She rolled away, but the tip of his blade caught on her jacket, ripping a hole in it as she moved.

"Concentrate on what you're doing," he said. "Use your other senses to be aware of obstacles

285

around you. Don't let anything distract you." He paused, then added with a devilish gleam in his eye, "Sorry about your jacket."

"I'm sure you are," she said as she raised one eyebrow. "I ought to make you repair it. I'll scarcely have time to do it before we reach Chiengmai."

Three or four times he lunged for her again, but each time she moved deftly aside, now aware of the placement of everything in the room. He smiled as she continued to elude him.

"You're doing very well," he said, only the slightest hint of mockery in his voice.

"Ah, yes," she replied triumphantly. "I can almost taste my freedom."

The next time he darted toward her, she slashed at his waistcoat, leaving a long tear in the tailored cloth.

"Sorry about your waistcoat," she said with a grin. But her smile turned to a shriek as he slipped under her guard, swinging past and behind her to encircle her waist with one steely arm. Instantly, she felt his blade at her neck.

"Never lose your concentration," he murmured against her ear. "Or you'll find yourself laughing on the other side of the grave."

She let out a long sigh.

"Drop your knife," he said, holding his own against her neck.

"You made your point," she said sullenly as she released the ivory handle of her weapon and the knife clattered on the floor. "Too bad I won't have any more chances to fight you. I might surprise you one day."

Her words reminded both of them that this was their last day together on the boat. She became aware of how tightly his arm clasped her waist. She felt his breath come more quickly on her cheek. He lowered his own blade and tossed the knife to the floor. She heard it strike the wooden deck, but she scarcely noticed, for his hand now caressed her cheek.

"Time to claim my reward," he said softly in her ear.

Her pulse quickened at the words, although she didn't move as he twisted her around to face him. As if to savor the moment, he let his eyes linger over her face, drinking in the sight of her wine-red lips parted slightly as her breath came in short gasps. He raised his fingers to touch the golden skin of her cheeks, which flushed delicately at his touch.

His fingers traveled to the ribbon that held her hair in its thick braid. He jerked the ribbon off; then he entwined his fingers in the glossy midnight strands, shaking them loose from the braid until they slid like silk over his rough hand. His fingers in her hair trapped her head, holding it for his kiss as at last he lowered his lips to hers.

She'd intended to be cold and unresponsive, for their bargain hadn't said she must kiss him in return. But at the touch of his lips on hers, she found she couldn't resist him and no longer even wished to. They'd worked together too many days in his tiny cabin for her not to want him at least a little.

His arm clasped her tighter to him so every curve of her body was molded against his. She felt the fingers of his hand stroke her back and then rest at the small of her back. She felt, too, the hardness of his thigh as it pressed against her own, for the thin material of her cotton trousers did little to shield her from his body.

As he sensed her lack of resistance, his lips moved

Deborah Martin

more demandingly over hers, imploring her to open her mouth to him. While his tongue ravaged her, she lifted her hands to the back of his head, her fingers immersing themselves in the crisp curls that covered his neck. Desire flooded over her, until she thought she'd drown in the waves of pleasure that rocked her body as his tongue played in the satin grottoes of her mouth.

He drew away from her for a moment, allowing her to glimpse the tumult in his eyes, before he buried his face in her hair and placed tiny kisses on her neck. His tongue darted into her ear and then stroked the delicate cave, making her hands clutch his head. Then his mouth captured hers again with a kiss so hard and searching she didn't realize his hands were moving over the buttons of her jacket, deftly unfastening them one by one, until his hands had traveled nearly to her waist. Then they crept inside to unbutton her batiste camisole.

"I couldn't ask for a sweeter reward," he murmured as his lips hovered close to her ear. "Except more of the same."

She gasped as he lifted her in his arms. But he silenced her feeble protests with his lips, and she was so caught in his rush of passion that she scarcely noticed when he moved to his bunk. Her arms clung to his neck as he lay her gently on the bed, never relinquishing her lips.

She knew what he was doing, knew if she let him continue she wouldn't be able to control his passion, but she didn't want to stop him. The tender kisses he planted on her neck and shoulders as he drew aside the lapels of her jacket, then the edges of her camisole, sent shivering ripples of longing through her.

He sucked in his breath as he saw her well-rounded breasts, their small ruby nipples trembling under his gaze. Then he lowered his head to taste first one and then the other, swirling his lips delicately over their tips until Esme thought she'd cry out, so delirious was she from the sensations coursing through her body.

He lifted his head, his eyes dark with triumph as he saw the naked desire on her face. She closed her eyes, wanting to escape his knowing stare, but as his hand kneaded the soft flesh of one breast while his mouth played with the other, her eyes flew open again. At the sight of his brown hair against the polished ivory of her naked skin, she recoiled in shock, lifting her hands to his head in an attempt to pull it away.

"Please stop," she said in a ragged whisper. "Oh, please stop!"

"Why should I stop something that gives us both so much pleasure?" he said hoarsely as he raised his head to gaze into the frightened darkness of her eyes.

"You said...nothing more than a kiss," she choked out as he let his lips trail lightly over the tender curves of her collarbone.

He lifted himself on one elbow. His lips curved in the hint of a smile but his eyes warmed her with their intense glow.

"That was before I realized a taste of you could never be enough to satisfy my hunger after weeks of only crumbs. How can I resist when I know your hunger is as great as mine?"

She shook her head in denial, but her body betrayed her by arching against him as he renewed his assault. His lips kissed a path down her belly to her navel, pausing there to tease it with his tongue. She closed her eyes in mute surprise and murmured a low protest, for the caress sent shock waves through her. Then his mouth continued down to the coarse broadcloth of her trousers. Her eyes flew open as his hands fumbled with the knotted cloth for a moment before freeing it. He drew the cloth down and began to unbutton her lacy drawers, pressing his lips against the skin each time another inch was bared.

She watched him, dazed and bewildered by her inability to resist. His breath warmed her skin everywhere his mouth caressed it. He seemed to soften her resistance with every touch of his lips. He'd uncovered the first tufts of the springy hair that covered her most intimate parts when they both heard the sound of footsteps outside his cabin door.

Instantly, a harsh rapping followed.

"What is it?" Ian growled as his hands tightened on her hips, holding her beneath him. Flashing her a warning glance, he rose to sit on the edge of the bunk.

The interruption was all it took to bring Esme to her senses. Hastily, she began to fasten her drawers, ignoring the pressure of Ian's hands on her hips.

The anger in Ian's voice was evident even to whomever stood on the other side of the door, for the man hesitated before answering. "I wish speak you," a Siamese voice finally replied. When no answer came, a stream of rapid Siamese followed his first pronouncement.

Ian looked as if he wanted to hurl something at the door.

"He says we will be at the dock in twenty minutes," she told Ian with a breathless catch in her throat.

Ian frowned as a muscle twitched in his jaw. Then he sighed. "Tell him I'll be with him shortly."

She translated the words for the captain, no longer caring if the man knew she was alone with Ian in his cabin.

During the conversation, she'd managed to refasten everything Ian had unbuttoned. She sat up, swinging her legs over the side of the bunk. Then she started to stand, but he put his hand on her knee to restrain her.

"We're not through," he murmured in a determined voice. "I can promise you that."

Tenderly, she lifted his hand from her knee and placed it on the bunk beside her. She rose shakily to her feet. "I'm afraid, my lord, that we're very much through. Here in Chiengmai we go our separate ways."

He leapt from the bunk and turned her around to face him.

"Is that what you really want?" he demanded, lifting a hand to caress her cheek. "Do you believe what lies between us can be so easily dismissed?"

She swallowed as his fingers moved to stroke her wild, disarrayed hair, which tumbled over her shoulders.

"I don't know," she answered truthfully. "But I certainly hope it can, for to continue as we have is to court disaster."

"Would it be a disaster to let me make love to you?"

"Yes. Because that's all you wish to do."

His face darkened as he realized what she meant, and his hands fell to his sides.

"I warn you now," he said as she walked away

from him toward the door. "I won't leave Siam without making you mine."

She paused. "Then you'd best plan to stay in Chiengmai a very long time," she said softly before leaving his cabin.

Chapter Fifteen

Ian listened as the consul's assistant, Joseph Langland, a wiry little man, explained the current state of affairs in Chiengmai. Relations between the Siamese and the French had remained much the same since he'd left Bangkok. The French continued to make short expeditions into Siamese territory in an attempt to goad the Siamese into declaring war, and the British were still insisting Siam had no cause to be alarmed.

"Prince Mataya is becoming increasingly upset over the French presence here," Langland said. "Last week he threatened to send his guard north to confront the French expeditionary force in Mong Sai. It took all my powers of persuasion to keep him from doing so." Langland fingered his mustache nervously. "He wouldn't listen to me, because he said I was of no importance. I tried to explain the consul was ill, but he remained agitated until I insisted you'd be here shortly."

"When do I meet with him?" Ian asked.

"Tonight. His men have been watching for you at the docks. As soon as you arrived, he sent someone over with an invitation to dinner."

Ian groaned inwardly. He'd hoped to spend the evening with Esme. After what they'd started that morning, he needed to see her again, to talk to her and work out some arrangement. He couldn't stand leaving her in Chiengmai, and he was no longer certain he wanted her at the consulate, where he wouldn't be able to see her whenever he wanted. Their encounter in the cabin had convinced him he could make her see reason and accept him as her lover. Perhaps he could even persuade her to lodge with him, at least for the duration of his stay in Chiengmai.

Suddenly he realized that Langland was no longer talking about the prince, but had asked him a question. "I beg your pardon?"

"I said," Langland repeated irritably, "is the native boy who arrived with you downstairs or did you already send him to lodgings?"

"What native boy?" A dreadful premonition gripped him.

"His name's Lek something or other. He was supposed to be your interpreter. Is he here?"

How did Langland know of Esme? Ian kept his face blank. "Why do you ask?"

Langland twisted his mustache with shaky fingers. Then he hesitated and stared at Ian as if trying to assess something before turning toward his desk and picking up a piece of paper. He handed it to Ian.

Ian noticed it was a telegram dated only a few days after he'd left Bangkok. Addressed to the consul, the short message read, "Please hold Lord Winthrop's interpreter at consulate until Montrose arrives. Boy named Lek Khantachanaboon. Montrose will explain." It was signed by Henry Rushton.

Ian struggled to maintain his composure in front of Langland, but it was difficult. He couldn't believe Esme's father was on his way to Chiengmai. What did the man plan to do? Drag her back to Bangkok to marry Michaels? And how had he discovered where she'd gone?

He grimaced. That was all too easy to guess. Esme's "dear friends" must have told her father of her plans. But what was Ian to do now? He couldn't simply hand her over to Langland, not without talking to her first.

"Well?" Langland asked impatiently.

"The boy's safe and will remain with me," Ian said firmly as he made his decision. "I'll make certain he's sent to Montrose when the man arrives."

"This is so irregular," Langland muttered. "I don't know quite what to do. I mean, Rushton says—"

"He says to hold Lek until Montrose arrives. I plan to do just that," Ian said, his eyes daring Langland to defy him.

"But I'm responsible—" Langland persisted.

"I take all the responsibility for my actions. Don't worry, Langland. They won't care who holds him as long as he's kept here."

Ian knew that wasn't entirely true. Obviously, Esme's father was hoping she'd managed to keep her identity a secret or he would have used Esme's real name. Montrose wouldn't be pleased at all to know that Ian not only knew Esme's true identity, but was rapidly becoming quite intimate with her.

Deborah Martin

Ian smiled grimly. Rushton had signed the telegram. Perhaps he'd worried about Esme's welfare. Perhaps he was more enamored of his little mistress than anyone realized and had promised Montrose he would leave his wife and marry her if Montrose brought her back. Ian shook his head. No, he couldn't believe Esme's father would go along with such a scheme.

Ian crumpled the telegram in his hand at the thought that Esme's father might be planning to carry Esme back to marry Michaels. Ian had never quite believed it would happen. But he had to admit Esme had always been convinced her father would never end her betrothal to the merchant.

Ian suddenly knew he couldn't allow her to be given away to a man like Michaels. He wasn't certain he ever could have, but he definitely couldn't now. The very thought of it chilled his blood. There was only one course of action he could take if Esme's father persisted in wanting her married, and that was somehow to force the man to refuse Michaels's suit.

Ian almost pitied Langland who stood pacing before him. He could tell the assistant was overwrought by the responsibilities heaped on him during the consul's illness. But Ian refused to release Esme to anyone until he knew what her father wished to do with her.

"Do you have any ideas about why this Mr. Montrose wishes to speak to the boy?" Langland finally asked, obviously not eager to antagonize his superior, but worried nonetheless.

"A few," Ian stated, but didn't elaborate.

Langland's face fell as he seemed to realize Ian wasn't going to enlighten him or relent in his decision.

"I suppose that's all right then," Langland murmured uneasily. "As long as the boy is under your control."

"Don't worry," Ian said coldly as he rose from his chair, thrusting the telegram in his waistcoat pocket. "I'll attend to him right now."

"What about tonight?" Langland asked in alarm as Ian strode purposefully toward the door.

"I'll be back in plenty of time to dine with the prince," Ian stated as he paused with his hand on the doorknob. "Is there someone who can take me to my lodgings?"

Langland moved past Ian to the door. He pushed it open and walked into the hallway.

"Prasert!" he shouted, and a young Siamese boy who looked no more than thirteen emerged from behind a pillar. He was clad in an ill-fitting Siamese army uniform, complete with carved sword. Ian nearly laughed at the sight.

"I am here, *Khun* Langland," the boy said, drawing his chest up bravely. "Prasert is ready for duty."

Langland glanced at the boy in annoyance before turning to Ian. "This, I'm afraid, is your houseboy. He'll show you where you're to live, and he'll be in charge of the servants."

Ian raised one eyebrow skeptically.

"I'm sorry we couldn't find anyone older," Langland hastened to explain. "But so few lower-class natives speak English in Chiengmai. He studied at one of the schools here, and his English is quite good. Don't worry. He's competent for his age. But I'd be careful if I were you. These Siamese will steal you blind if you don't watch them."

Ian studied the sturdy boy who tried hard to stare straight ahead and maintain his stance of brave readiness in spite of his obvious humiliation at

Langland's words. "Has this particular Siamese ever stolen anything?" Ian asked Langland coldly.

"Well, no, but—"

"Then I'm sure he'll do quite nicely," Ian replied. Relief flooded the boy's face.

"Remember what I told you," Langland said in warning to the boy.

Prasert's back stiffened. "Yes, *Khun* Langland," he replied proudly.

Langland would have said something else, but Ian cut him off. "Shall we go then?" Ian asked, his tone showing that he trusted the boy to be as competent as Langland said he was.

"Yes, sir!" Prasert responded, pivoting smartly around and marching for the door.

Ian followed, an amused grin spreading over his face. Once they were outside, the boy relaxed somewhat and turned to eye his employer curiously.

"You are a very big man," he said admiringly, his eyes traveling the length of Ian's tall frame. "Not like *Khun* Langland."

Ian's lips turned up slightly as he struggled to keep from showing his amusement, for he knew the boy would be insulted if he thought he was being laughed at.

"I need to go to the hotel where foreigners stay," Ian told him. "Then you can take me to my lodgings. After that, you'll need to fetch my bags from the docks."

The boy's eyes widened. "You wish me to go with you to get the bags?" he asked uncertainly.

"No, of course not," Ian replied with a frown. "I'm sure you can handle them yourself."

Prasert positively beamed at those words. "Yes, sir! I will take excellent care of your bags."

He seemed so different from the boy who'd

flinched at Langland's reminders that Ian wondered what Langland had said to him in private.

"What did *Khun* Langland want you to remember?" Ian asked.

Prasert frowned but didn't speak.

"Tell me," Ian said. "You work for me now."

The boy drew himself up proudly. "He said you are a very important man, almost as important as His Highness. He said I must take very good care of you and not make you angry or I would be in great trouble." His voice grew bitter. "He is worried. He wanted a *farang* to work for you, but no *farang* here speaks Siamese and also performs servant work. He thinks all Siamese are untrustworthy."

Ian was glad he'd told the boy to fetch his bags alone. "Don't worry, Prasert. If you behave as if you can be trusted, then I most certainly will trust you."

"I have never stolen," Prasert said as he thrust his small shoulders back. "You can trust me. I will work very hard for you, do anything you say."

Ian smiled. "Good. Because I already need a great favor from you."

Prasert eyed him cautiously. "What favor?"

"There's a girl with me. A young girl. She pretended to be a Siamese boy and sneaked aboard my boat, but I found her out."

The boy snorted. "She must be very stupid."

Ian flashed him a wry smile. "No. Just foolish. But *Khun* Langland thinks she's a boy. I don't want him to know she's not. In fact, I'd prefer he not know anything about her. Do you think you can keep my secret?"

"This girl," Prasert asked shrewdly, "is she beautiful?"

"Yes," Ian said, his expression softening as he

299

remembered how Esme had looked lying beneath him on the bunk.

Prasert gave him a knowing grin. "I will keep your secret. *Khun* Langland will not hear anything from me."

"Good," Ian replied.

Then they set off in the direction of the only hotel in town, Prasert leading the way proudly as he answered the questions about Chiengmai that Ian threw at him.

They entered the hotel to find Esme with her back to the door, sitting stiffly in a chair in the lobby while Godfrey paced near the door.

"Thank God you're here!" Godfrey said in an undertone as Ian approached him. "I'm afraid you'll have to change your plans and bring her to the consulate now. The hotel is completely filled for the evening."

Ian glanced around at the small room that served as a lobby. "It's no wonder."

"She's upset, too, I don't mind telling you. She asked someone about teaching positions, and they told her there are none. I tried to get her to go to the consulate, but she refused to move until you got here. She's going to resist you on this, I can assure you."

Ian studied the dark bent head several feet away from him and sighed. Esme was going to do far more than resist him when she found out what he planned. He squared his shoulders and moved to stand behind her.

"Esme," he said softly.

She turned her head, her eyes mutinously confronting him. She rose and came around the chair to face him. "I don't suppose you've changed your

mind about dragging me to the consulate," she said
acidly.

His gaze took in the lines of weariness in her face
and lingered lovingly on her stubborn chin. Again
he wished he'd met her under different circumstances.

"As a matter of fact, my plans have changed. If
you'll follow me and my young guide, I'll accompany you to your quarters."

Godfrey glanced at Ian in surprise. Then a slow
grin spread over his face that Esme fortunately
didn't see. Ian stared at Godfrey with such venom
that Godfrey hastened to wipe the smile off his face,
but his eyes held a knowing expression that made
Ian angry.

"Have you changed your mind about telling my
father where I am?" she asked softly, a smile beginning to cross her face.

"Not exactly. But I've changed my plans. You
can't stay here and you can't stay at the consulate
just yet."

"Why not?" she asked, her eyes narrowing in suspicion as she realized only her lodgings were to
change, not her situation.

"I'll explain when we reach your quarters," he
told her. *Our quarters*, he added to himself.

"I'm not moving an inch until you tell me what's
going on," she said, crossing her arms over her chest
in open defiance.

"Then I suppose I'll have to carry you kicking and
screaming," he said flatly as he started toward her.

"You wouldn't!"

"I certainly would. And no one in this town would
stop me either, not when they think you're Siamese.
All I have to say is you're my slave, and no one will
question anything I do."

Deborah Martin

Esme's face acknowledged her defeat. She knew as well as he did that, while slavery was officially outlawed in Siam, it was sometimes still practiced, especially outside of Bangkok. Esme's shoulders slumped, but her eyes gazed accusingly at him.

"Get her things," Ian said to Prasert, gesturing to Esme's bag on the floor in front of her chair. When the boy didn't move, Ian turned to him, intending to repeat his order, but was stopped by the look of incredulity on his face.

"This is the girl?" he asked in amazement. "She looks so . . . so . . ."

"Siamese?" Ian asked with a grin, for Esme was still maintaining her disguise as much as possible.

"No," Prasert said stiffly. "I knew she was not Siamese."

Then he realized what Ian had just ordered him to do and moved quickly toward her bag. But Esme reached it before he could and swung it up over her shoulder, speaking to him in rapid Siamese.

The boy started to take the bag from her, but when she jerked it back from him, he looked helplessly at Ian.

"What's the problem?" Ian asked Prasert.

"She says she will carry her own bag. She says she will not look like a Siamese boy if she does not carry her own bag," Prasert said, so overwhelmed by Esme's command of Siamese that he immediately translated her words, forgetting she spoke English better than he did.

"As you wish," Ian told her, shrugging his shoulders. "Let's go," he said to Prasert. Then he stepped forward and took Esme's arm, but she wrenched it away from him.

"Don't worry," she said icily. "I won't try to run away just yet."

He watched her stalk off in front of him, her back straight and almost regal as she shed the bearing her disguise had required and reverted to being herself. He followed her and Prasert, who had to run to catch up with her so he could show the way.

What a mess! he thought to himself as he walked behind them, unable to avoid noticing the sensuous swing of her hips and the proud tilt of her head. He absolutely refused to let her father take her back to marry Michaels. But what if her father agreed to end the betrothal? What then? Could he still watch her leave, knowing he might never have another chance to be close to her? He didn't think he could, but he had only a few days to convince her to stay with him.

She'd already insisted she'd never be his. He knew she was holding out for marriage. He wanted her so badly even that alternative tempted him. And it wasn't just her body he desired, it was her mind, her soul, her love. Yes, he wanted her love most of all, curse it! He wanted her to feel for him the way she must have felt for Rushton, for he now felt certain she didn't give herself freely to just anyone.

His hands clenched and unclenched as he walked behind her. God, it was hard to believe she'd loved Rushton. And the man didn't even deserve it! Rushton was aiding Montrose in bringing her back to marry a man she detested! Either the bastard was incredibly callous or—or she was telling the truth. The story really was a rumor and she was pure as the freshly driven snow.

He considered that possibility for a moment. His caresses had always embarrassed her, but she'd certainly understood what they meant. She'd never recoiled from them as women who have never felt a man's touch do. He discounted that first kiss, for he knew that night she was trying to get something from him. No, she was about as innocent as Delilah. His mouth hardened. God, he really was letting her get to him. He was almost ready to believe the denials of a girl who'd already proven she could play a role to perfection. Obviously, his experiences with Caroline hadn't taught him a thing.

At that moment, she glanced back to make certain he was behind them. That fleeting glimpse of her face stiffened his resolve. He would have her. Why should he torture himself like this? He would make her his mistress and make her love him. But he had to guard against feeling too much for her, or he'd find himself being foolish and making the same mistake twice by offering to marry a woman who would only make his life hell.

By the time they'd stopped outside a high fence, Esme was so furious she could barely contain her anger. Her temper had been rising ever since Ian had announced he planned to have her before he left Siam. His words had infuriated her. She'd begun to like him a great deal, and when he kissed her the way he did, she could almost forget he believed she was Rushton's mistress. But his words had reminded her painfully that nothing had changed. He still thought he had the right to take her without benefit of clergy.

As she'd sat in the hotel lobby, growing more incensed by the hour over the way he was cavalierly running her life, she'd made a decision. He could take her to the consulate, but he'd have to drag her there, for she wasn't about to aid him in destroying her hopes.

Then when he'd said things had changed, she'd believed he was going to allow her to live as she wished in Chiengmai. Not that it would have helped, since according to the hotel manager, the English schools were losing students rapidly. The Siamese were so afraid of the French they'd begun to suspect all foreigners.

But she could do something, she felt certain. Surely someone would give her a position. She could sew and cook or watch children—anything to keep from returning to Bangkok.

She glanced around as they entered through an unobtrusive gate in the stone fence. She gasped in surprise as she saw well-kept gardens surrounding a larger house than she'd expected. Unlike most houses in Siam, this one wasn't on stilts. Instead it sat at the top of a small artificial hill created to keep it from flooding during the rainy season. The fence surrounding it had pieces of glass embedded in the top to keep thieves from climbing into the yard, a security measure used only in houses belonging to the very wealthy.

She watched Ian suspiciously. He spoke not a word to her as Prasert opened the door and ushered them both in the house and through the hallway into a drawing room. What did Ian plan to do with her? Who was paying for these "lodgings?" Did he think to set her up in this lovely house as his mistress? Was that why he hadn't taken her to the consulate?

He was staying at the consulate, of course, which she had no doubt was as large and elaborate as the one in Bangkok. Did he plan to keep her presence a secret so he could convince her to "reward" him for taking care of her as he'd expected her to reward him that morning?

If those were his plans, he was in for a surprise, she thought as her eyes scanned the room, noting the expensive teakwood furniture and lush Oriental rugs. The moment he left, she'd lock the doors and never let him in again.

She dropped her bag gratefully on the floor. The walk had been longer than she'd anticipated and her bag had grown very heavy. But she'd refused to give Ian the satisfaction of seeing her accept his or Prasert's help. Still, she'd taken an instant liking to the Siamese boy, who'd regaled her in Siamese with wild stories about Chiengmai.

"I will get your bags now," Prasert told Ian. "I will return in a few minutes."

"All right," Ian said curtly as Esme looked at them both in bewilderment.

"Why are you bringing his bags here?" Esme asked Prasert in Siamese, ignoring the anger that flooded Ian's face. "Lord Winthrop isn't staying here."

Prasert looked at Ian, confused. "She says you will not reside here."

Ian gazed steadily at Esme. "She's mistaken," he told Prasert, his face expressionless.

Esme stared at Ian in open dismay as she realized what he was saying. "Prasert," she said in Siamese, lifting her bag, "if Lord Winthrop is lodging here, then I'm not. Bring me to some other house or to a temple. I'll pay you, don't worry about that." She hadn't spent a penny of her money yet and Ian had perversely insisted on paying her a salary through-out the trip. She thought she had enough to live on for a few weeks anyway.

Ian's face hardened as Prasert began to answer her in Siamese.

"You will not speak Siamese to her in my pres-ence," Ian interrupted the boy. "Is that under-stood?"

Prasert nodded quickly, his eyes wide.

"What did she tell you?" Ian asked him.

Prasert swallowed. "She said—"

"I'm perfectly capable of speaking, thank you," Esme replied. "I told him to take me to other lodgings because, if you're staying here, I'm not."

Ian's eyes narrowed, but he didn't answer her. Instead he nodded Prasert toward the door. The boy slipped out, eager to avoid the confrontation.

"You can't make me stay here!" she insisted as Ian came toward her. "I'd rather stay at the consulate than with you!"

"Your father's on his way to Chiengmai." His eyes seemed to soften as he said it.

The color drained slowly from her face. "You telegraphed him," she accused.

"No," Ian hastened to tell her. "This arrived at the consulate weeks ago."

Reaching into his waistcoat pocket, he pulled out a crumpled piece of paper and handed it to her. With trembling hands, she smoothed it out, her dazed eyes finally taking in the words of a telegram sent from Bangkok and signed by Henry Rushton. She couldn't believe what she read. Her father had asked for Lek. But the very fact he knew the name she traveled under made it clear he knew everything. Her heart sank as she realized her trusted friends must have told him where she'd gone.

"Notice the date," Ian said gently. "Your father should arrive within a few days, at most a week."

"A week," she said in a voice barely more than a whisper. Oh no, she thought in despair. It had all been for nothing. She'd be marrying Michaels after all! Tears welled up in her eyes, and she fought to keep them back. Then she imagined Michaels's lips on hers as Ian's had been, only she knew the mer-

307

chant's kisses would repulse rather than move her. Suddenly everything seemed so fruitless—her battle to save herself from a wretched marriage, her attempts to protect her virtue. Why had she struggled so hard? The bitter tears began to slip down her cheeks.

She didn't resist as Ian's arms slid around her, pulling her close against his hard body.

"Hush, love, it will be all right," he whispered in her ear as he stroked her back soothingly. "Please don't cry."

"I'm sorry, Ian," she sobbed out. "I just can't believe that after all this I will have to marry Michaels."

"You won't have to marry him, I promise," he said hoarsely.

She lifted her head to gaze in his eyes. Like a potent charm, they sent shivers of anticipation through her, but when he lowered his lips as if to kiss her, she strained away from him. He wouldn't release her, but he allowed her to place her arms between them, her palms flat against his chest. She ignored the desire flaming in his eyes, ignored the answering fire it ignited within her. She couldn't lose herself in his kiss, not until she knew what he meant.

"You'll not tell my father where I am?"

"You won't have to marry Michaels," he stubbornly repeated, not answering her question.

"Why won't I have to marry him?" she whispered, almost afraid to hear his reply.

"Because I won't allow it." His hands gripped her waist as if he never intended to let her go. "If your father has come to take you back to Michaels, he'll have to contend with me first. I won't let anyone else have you, I swear it."

"Are you . . . are you saying you'll marry me?" she asked with downcast eyes as she toyed with the buttons of his shirt. At his answering silence, her chin trembled.

"I see," she said unsteadily, lifting embittered dark eyes to accuse him. "No, the son of an earl wouldn't wish to marry someone like me, would he? So I suppose you plan to make me your mistress. What's the phrase they use in England? You'll 'take me under your protection?'"

"Would that be so terrible?" Ian asked gently, lifting one hand to brush a stray tendril of hair from her face. His hand remained to caress her cheek, and then slid down to her slender throat where his fingers stroked the soft skin.

Would it? she thought. She wasn't sure anymore. When Ian touched her, she found it hard to withstand his assaults, not just because he was so handsome but because she'd grown to know him. She admired his quick wit, his intelligence, and the gentleness that was as much a part of his nature as was his temper. Ian knew how to make her laugh and how to comfort her. He would be good to her, of that she was certain.

But she realized with a start that being his mistress would never be enough for her. She wanted more. She wanted his name, the symbol that he desired her above all others. Most of all, she wanted his love.

The knowledge hit her with such force she shook in Ian's arms.

"What is it?" he asked with sudden concern. "I didn't mean to upset you. You know I've wanted you ever since we first met."

Yes, she thought. *That's just it. You want me. But you don't love me.* And she wanted his love more

309

Deborah Martin

than anything, she thought suddenly. Why was that?

Finally she admitted to herself the awful truth. In spite of how she'd fought him, in spite of the things he believed her capable of, she loved him. She stared up into the face of the man who held her, seeing him as if for the first time. Oh, yes, she did love him. But she couldn't tell him that, knowing he would reject her. She couldn't bear to have him think she only said the words to manipulate him. Nor could she stay with him in this house now that she'd acknowledged her feelings for him.

"Let me go, Ian," she said, trying to wrest herself from his arms. "Please let me go. I can't be your mistress. And I can't stay here with you. Let me go to the consulate and await Father's arrival."

"I can't let you leave," he said roughly, his eyes tormenting her as they searched her face. She twisted her head away to escape his gaze. "Why do you fight me so hard, love?" His arms entrapped her as she struggled to pull away from him. "Do you still hate me so much?"

"No!" she exclaimed. Then more softly, she added, "No, I don't hate you at all."

"Then how do you feel about me?" he asked in a tortured voice.

When she didn't answer, he gripped her chin, trying to force her head around. "Damn it, Esme, look at me!" he commanded, but she wouldn't.

"Then listen to me," he told her. "Just listen." She stilled her movements for a moment. "The telegram asked that Lek be detained. *Lek*, not Esme. Your father probably hopes no one yet knows who you are. Don't you want to spare his feelings? Do you really want to flaunt the fact that you've spent the last few weeks on a boat with six men?"

"I could remain in my disguise," she answered. "I could stay at the consulate as Lek and no one would be the wiser."

"No. I won't allow it. They'd probably confine you, and I don't think you'd want that. You have to stay here. I told them I had Lek in my custody, and they agreed to let me be responsible for you until your father comes."

She wanted to stay with him, too. But she was afraid if she did she'd not be able to resist him. No, her only choice was to leave. But not to go to the consulate. She knew she couldn't go there and give up so easily. Not now that she knew what love was like. Once she was out of Ian's lodgings, she'd find some place to stay and think of a way to keep from marrying Michaels.

"I can't live in this house with you, Ian," she said softly.

"You must! At least until your father comes."

She tried another tack. "What happens then?"

"I'll hide you and refuse to tell him where you are until he agrees to release you from marrying Michaels."

"And if he agrees?" she asked tremulously, her black eyes lifting to meet the tempest in his gray-blue gaze.

"That's up to you," he told her, but his arms tightened around her waist and the stiffness of his face softened as he stared at her. "You could stay with me."

"And be your mistress," she said flatly.

"It won't be like what you think—"

"No?" she said, hurt filling her voice. "You'll always be faithful to me? Always stay with me? Take me with you wherever you go? *Always love me?* she thought.

He was silent and **she knew** she'd pushed him too far. He didn't trust her entirely, so how could he pledge his life to her? He wouldn't, not for the sake of one night's passion.

"Is that the real reason you won't let me go to the consulate?" she asked, her voice unsteady as she tried to keep him from seeing how deeply he'd hurt her. "Do you still hope I'll come to your bed, even knowing my father will arrive any day? Do you believe I'll give myself to you in exchange for your help in convincing my father to set me free from Michaels?"

He flinched as her accusations struck him. His mouth went rigid. "I hoped...I still hope...that you'll bow to what is between us. That you'll stop this silly resistance. But that isn't the only reason I want you here."

"Yes?" she asked hesitantly.

"Damn it, Esme, I need you!" His hand slid up to grasp her braid at her nape, forcing her head up to within inches of his mouth. "I can't bear to have you at the consulate where I'd never see you. If you discard your disguise, you'll be chaperoned to the teeth until your father comes. If you remain Lek, you'll be locked up. Either way, I won't be able to see you, to talk to you. God help me, but I'm a selfish bastard, and I want you here in this house!"

Looking into the feverish blaze of his eyes, she knew how much his admission had cost him. Her gaze fell to his lips, so close to hers, so capable of kissing her into submission. Even the blood pounding through her seemed to say, "Yes, yes, do as he says! Relent, relent!" But she couldn't. Deep within her, she knew if she did, she'd never be satisfied. She wanted more than he would give her, and to accept only part of it would be torture.

She dropped her eyes beneath his stare. "I—I can't, Ian," she whispered. "I just can't stay here with you."

His hands released her abruptly. When she glanced at him, his face was stony, implacable, with no hint of tenderness.

"You'd rather marry Michaels than stay with me?" he asked, both hurt and anger evident in his voice.

"Must it be such a choice?" she blurted out.

His eyes narrowed. Then he gripped her arms. "You plan another escapade, is that it? Some other way to escape your father? What will you do? Roam the streets of Chiengmai alone? Continue to fend for yourself as Lek?"

"I—I don't know," she murmured, hardly able to think as he held her. "You needn't worry about me, though. I'll be all right."

"You certainly will," he told her emphatically, thrusting her away from him. "I've no intention of throwing you to the wolves. Whether you choose to or not, you'll stay here until your father comes."

"You wouldn't keep me here against my will!" she cried.

"I intend just that," he said, turning toward the door.

"I'll never forgive you for this, Ian," she said in a hoarse whisper. "You'll regret holding me here."

He paused, his back rigid. "Perhaps," he responded. "But I'll regret it more if I let you leave. So you must stay."

Then he stalked from the room, slamming the door behind him. With a sinking heart, she heard the key turn in the lock and knew she was trapped.

Chapter Sixteen

When Esme realized Ian had locked her in, she beat her fists against the door in fury. How dare he do such a thing? He had no right! She cursed herself for having implied she might not go to the consulate. It might not have made any difference, though. He seemed determined to keep her at his lodgings.

In angry defiance, she planted her hands on her hips and surveyed the room. Unfortunately, it had no windows and no other doors. Did he plan to keep her there the entire time? If so, he was in for a real fight. She would make so much noise that eventually he'd have to release her, if only to get some peace.

She put her ear to the door and strained to listen, trying to determine if he'd left the house. She heard only silence. Restlessly, she paced the room, wondering what to do. In a few moments, she heard the gate door open and then the door into the house.

Prasert must have returned with Ian's bags, she thought.

After several minutes, the door to the drawing room swung open. Ian stood there with Prasert at his side.

"I want you to remove those clothes," Ian said curtly. "You may wear this." He thrust her silk sarong at her. "You have five minutes of privacy to change. If you haven't changed clothes by then, I'll be forced to undress you myself."

He turned on his heels, but Esme darted toward him in fury. "Wait!" she said, grasping his arm. "What do you hope to accomplish by this?"

He glanced down at her, a grim smile crossing his face. "I hope to ensure you don't do anything foolish. Chiengmai's a dangerous place for a young girl to be alone. And while I doubt you'll be able to leave with Prasert watching you and the gate locked, I'm not taking any chances. Without your boy's clothes or your gray dress, I doubt you'll venture far. Be glad I'm leaving you something to wear."

Her fingernails dug into his arm. "You despicable cad! I can't go around dressed in this. It wouldn't be proper!"

He laughed mirthlessly. "It didn't seem to stop you before." Then his steel-hard eyes softened a bit as he took in her obvious discomfort. "It's only until your father comes, love. You give me no choice. I can't let you wander the streets of Chiengmai in a boy's costume that wouldn't protect you for long. I know you won't leave wearing that sarong, not after what happened in Bangkok. And the sarong will make it difficult for you to scale the walls."

Ignoring the anger on her face, Ian turned to Prasert. "When *Mem* Esme hands her clothing out to

you, take it and her other belongings and store them
for her. But she's not to have them until I say so,
do you understand?''

"Yes, *Than*," Prasert replied.

"Do you intend to keep me locked up in this room,
too?" Esme asked bitterly.

"No. Once you've dressed, you're free to roam the
house. You won't even have to endure my presence.
I'm going out now to arrange for someone to keep
an eye on our friend Chan. And when I return, I'll
only have time to dress before I go to dinner this
evening with Prince Mataya. I should be out until
very late."

Then he closed the door again and locked it. At
first she stared incredulously at the door. She
couldn't believe he was going to such extremes! Yet,
knowing the sense of responsibility he felt for her,
she acknowledged it was typical of him to believe
he had no other choice.

Still, to lock her up in such a high-handed manner
and demand she give all her clothes to him! No, she
thought as she looked at the sarong in her hand,
not all. Only the respectable ones. For a moment
she hesitated. Suppose she did defy him and refuse
to change clothes? Unwillingly, she remembered
how effortlessly he'd removed her clothing earlier
that day, and she knew he'd make good his threat
to undress her if she resisted.

She threw the sarong down in frustration. For
now, he'd won. But she'd think of a way to best him
and escape, even if it took all her energy to do so!

When the five minutes were up and Ian entered
the room without so much as a knock, Esme was
sitting casually in one of the chairs, dressed in the
native costume. She'd had to pin the garment dif-
ferently, because of the rip in it when Henley had

316

torn it, but it was wearable. Yet she felt uncomfortably naked underneath the silk cloth, even
though she wore her drawers. In acute embarrassment, she avoided his eyes. She'd sink through the
ground in mortification if he made any reference at
all to the dress's provocativeness.

But he only flashed her a cursory glance before he
nodded his approval. Then he whisked her other
clothes up and stalked through the door without a
word, leaving the door open.

She followed him into the hall, watching as he
gave her clothes to Prasert and issued a few instructions in a voice too low for her to hear. Then he left,
just as he'd said he would, leaving her relieved he
wouldn't be around to gloat over her defeat.

As soon as Ian was gone, Prasert looked at her,
then gazed at his feet in embarrassment. "*Than* said
you might like a bath. Do you wish?"

She smiled grimly to herself. For a jailor, Ian
certainly was being thoughtful. She wanted to refuse anything he offered, but she knew she'd regret
it in this case. A real bath in a tub sounded too
delightful to resist. She'd bathed daily in the river
once her disguise had been revealed. But she'd
never been able to get as clean as she'd have liked,
for she'd always feared being seen by one of the
men.

"That would be lovely," she told Prasert.

He nodded his head and departed. For the first
time since she'd arrived, Esme surveyed her surroundings. The teakwood walls were highly polished so the rich dark wood shone. But in spite of
the dark walls, the house felt light and airy, for
every room but the drawing room had several windows facing out on the gardens. Plush Oriental rugs
in fanciful designs partially covered the shiny hard-

Deborah Martin

wood floors. Esme inspected the furniture, noting that most of it was intricately carved teakwood or expensive black lacquerware inlaid with mother-of-pearl. She wondered if the prince himself had provided the house for Ian, because it certainly was elaborate for rented lodgings.

Only a short time passed before Prasert reappeared. "Your bath is ready, *Mem*," he said softly.

She followed him through the house and into the back pantry. There she was surprised to find a huge copper tub filled with hot water. At home the only tub available had been a wooden one scarcely large enough to fit her torso, much less her legs and arms. Compared to that, this tub was sheer luxury. She noted that Prasert had put out towels and soap for her.

"I will be outside in the servant quarters," he said, holding his body erect. "You call, *Mem*, if you want me."

As soon as he left, she peeled off the silk sarong and stepped eagerly into the tub. Reveling in the warm water, she covered herself in a thick lather before lying back to relax.

Her mind played over the events of the day, focusing on her last few moments with Ian. He was determined to put her in a position where she'd have to acquiesce to his desires. Well, she was just as determined not to allow him to make her his mistress. Unfortunately, whenever he held her, she seemed to lose her reason and with it the power to withstand his caresses. But no matter what she felt for him, no matter how much he made her quiver with restless anticipation, she mustn't give in. She must make him see she couldn't remain in the house with him.

Her father would reach Chiengmai soon. If Ian

did as he said, she'd be free of Michaels, but at what price? Once Ian championed her, the situation would only worsen. Though her father might not have believed her aunt's charge of Esme's indiscretion with Ian, now he would either be convinced she was Ian's mistress or believe she'd been unwillingly compromised by Ian. She knew how he'd react in either case. First he'd try to make Ian marry her, which would be a nightmare. She didn't think she could bear the humiliation she'd feel when Ian rejected her father's demands.

And once her father had exhausted that possibility, he'd take revenge and try to destroy Ian. Worse yet, he could succeed, despite Ian's position. Her father might be angry at Henry Rushton's supposed involvement with his daughter, but he'd not hesitate to use the influence Rushton could provide. The telegram proved that. With Rushton on his side, he could easily have Ian barred from diplomatic circles.

It would serve Ian right, she thought but only for a moment. Despite the terrible things he believed about her, she couldn't stand the thought of his losing everything because he chose to protect her. She wouldn't let him take that risk. She'd remove the possibility entirely, even if it meant going to the consulate and marrying Michaels.

Then her throat constricted at the thought of having Michaels's clammy hands on her body. How on earth, she thought, could she be happy with such a man? The realization that she'd be giving him her virginity, that only he would know her intimately, filled her with horror.

But what alternative had she? Ian had made it clear he wouldn't set her loose in the city. Her only chance to leave the house was to convince Ian to

Deborah Martin

let her go to the consulate and wait for her father.
He'd said he didn't want her to go there, but perhaps he'd change his mind if she pointed out what
her father could do to his career. Yes, she thought
with a trace of bitterness, that might do it. He'd
always been concerned about her affect on his career. When she showed him what might happen, he
was certain to send her away.

She stifled a sob. Why had she fallen in love with
such a man, one determined to possess and protect
her but not make her his legally? She thrust that
thought from her mind. Longing for Ian to be different wouldn't change anything nor make her feel
any better. The only solution to her dilemma was
to forget about him until she could confront him
with her new argument.

Sinking further into the tub, she allowed the delights of the bath to influence her mood. As the
warmth of the water seeped into her skin, she relaxed. Somehow it would all turn out, she tried to
convince herself. Sleepily, she rested her head on
the edge of the tub. Perhaps Mr. Michaels would
change his mind about marrying her. Perhaps her
father would be so happy to find her that he'd listen
to reason this time. "Perhaps..." she murmured
aloud as she drifted off to sleep.

The sound of a door shutting upstairs woke her.
She shivered. The water was cold. How long had
she been asleep? Hurriedly, she stepped from the
tub. She rubbed herself roughly in her haste to
dress. Nimbly, she tied the sarong around her waist
and the scarf around her breasts. She spent only a
few seconds trying to rub her hair dry before she
gave up and threw her head back.

Barefoot and slightly damp, she walked through
the house in search of Ian. She didn't have to go

320

far to find him, however, since he stood in the hallway, his silk top hat in his hand. As he set the hat back on the stand and turned toward her, she thought to herself that he looked splendid. His black frock coat set off his deep tan. The waves of crisp chestnut hair framing his face beckoned to her fingers to lose themselves in that shining glory. His eyes shone like drops of molten silver as they watched her. With a rush, she was reminded of that night in the jungle and how much she'd been attracted to him even then.

Nor was there any mistaking the glint of desire in his gaze when it fell on her. Both of them stood mesmerized. His eyes raked her, making her conscious that her hair fell in an unruly wet tangle about her shoulders and that the silk clung to her damp body.

"Long bath?" he asked with wry tenderness.

"I fell asleep," she murmured, longing to turn from the room and run. She felt exposed in front of him.

"You've had a long day," he said sympathetically, taking a step toward her.

Her mind shouted a warning and she backed away, resolved to keep him at a distance. Trying to remain aloof, she reminded herself of her plans to change his mind.

"We have to talk, Ian," she said with as much firmness as she could muster, struggling to ignore the conflicting emotions his presence elicited within her.

"I have no time to talk now, love. I'm expected at the consulate in half an hour." His hand snaked forward to grab her waist, throwing her momentarily off guard.

"Oh, I see," she said, unnerved by the intimate

way he held her. Summoning a small amount of strength, she said in a voice that wavered, "Then I suppose you should go. Our discussion may take some time. We can talk when you return." Gently, she pushed against him, but he didn't release her.

"I do have a few minutes," he murmured, lowering his lips to brush her bare shoulder. His nearness made it hard for her to think, and she struggled feebly to escape his arms.

"You must go, Ian. I wouldn't wish to make you late."

His grip on her waist tightened. "I don't know if I would mind that so much," he whispered, then nibbled her ear.

She tried to summon the anger she'd felt toward him earlier, tried to ignore the warmth stealing over her body. But she couldn't seem to muster any righteous indignation.

"I'm sorry I must be out tonight," he said in a husky voice, lifting his head to stare at her with a blatant longing on his face that he took no pains to hide.

Seized with a sudden inspiration, she said brightly, "You could take me with you. I could go as Lek and be your interpreter! Oh, please, let me go, Ian! I've never seen a prince's palace before." If he would take her, perhaps she could find a way to slip off!

But her seemingly innocent pleas didn't fool Ian. "You'd like that, wouldn't you, love?" he said, one eyebrow quirking upward. "The moment my back was turned, you'd be off. No, I don't think I'll take such a chance."

When she flashed him a murderous glance, he grinned.

"Not that I wouldn't love to have you with me,"

he said, lifting a hand to touch her cheek.

She swung her face away to avoid his caress, but he moved his hand to clasp her neck, holding her to receive his kiss. Stubbornly, she kept her mouth closed, fighting the impulse to respond. But when his tongue continued to tease her lips and his fingers slipped down to stroke her bare shoulder, her resistance began to melt. As his firm mouth played gently over hers, she at last admitted him. His tongue probed every part of her mouth, tempting her to lose control over the emotions he stirred in her. With a low moan, she opened herself to him like a tiny bud unfurling its petals to the sun. His hand moved from her waist to cup her bottom, pressing her hard against him. She didn't even recoil when she felt, through the thin material of her clothes, the rigid proof of his desire against her softness.

"Oh, God," he groaned as his lips left hers. "I would give the world to stay here with you tonight."

She raised her eyes to his, mindless of anything but an aching need to have him hold her forever. "I would, too," she murmured, then cursed herself when the words were out of her mouth. "So—so we could talk," she added quickly.

He gave a warm rich chuckle as he pulled her up against him again, making her aware of his longing for her.

"I don't think we'd do much talking if I stayed."

His air of easy confidence in his ability to seduce her brought her up abruptly, reminding her she must be on her guard against the insidious desire he sparked to life in her. She pushed frantically against his chest, surprising him by the strength of her resistance so that he released her.

"You must go," she said urgently.

He sighed. "Will you wait up for me? So we can have the discussion you want so badly," he added sarcastically.

"Yes," she replied, unable to meet his eyes and aware that he stood unbearably close. "But you must promise not to touch me so ... so intimately. It isn't right."

"Don't worry. We'll sit on opposite sides of the room, and you can speak your mind without fear of my ... ah ... tempting you to do things you shouldn't. But bear in mind that you won't change my mind about your leaving here. So if that's what you plan to discuss, you might as well not wait for me."

"I'll wait," she said, lifting her eyes in challenge.

His gaze held a glint of suspicion but he shrugged. "As you wish." He reached for his hat once again and settled it on his head. "I don't know how late I'll be, but I'll return as soon as possible."

With those oddly husbandlike words, he walked out, leaving Esme to wonder if perhaps he felt more for her than he'd admitted.

After he left, Esme wandered upstairs to explore the house more thoroughly. She discovered only four huge rooms, all bedrooms. After determining which room was Ian's by the bags and trunk in it, she surveyed the other rooms, wondering which she should choose to sleep in. Each was elaborately furnished with canopy beds crafted of finely carved teak, the coverings made of sumptuous brocades, with matching teak dressers and full-length mirrors.

It took her only minutes to decide on taking the bedroom that was as far away from Ian's as possible, a beautiful room done entirely in shades of burgundy and white. While surveying the room, she caught sight of her image in the full-length mirror that stood at one end. Instantly, the blood flooded her face as she noted how sensual the Siamese native dress really was.

The shimmering silk skimmed lightly over her hips, encasing them just snugly enough to outline the curves of her body when she walked. With the scarf leaving one shoulder and her midriff bare, the entire ensemble was incredibly provocative. She tried to adjust the scarf more modestly, but no matter how carefully she repinned it, a thin line of skin showed above the sarong's edge. And above that enticing hint of skin, the tightly wrapped silk fully accentuated the soft swells of her breasts.

She swallowed nervously. Damn Ian and his plans! How would she be able to escape his attentions when all he'd left her to wear was this? She had to find some way out!

A cough in the doorway made her aware she was no longer alone. She turned to find Prasert timidly holding out her comb.

"I know *Than* said you were not to have your belongings, but I thought you might want this," he said nervously.

Prasert! He could help her. He seemed willing to a certain extent. She must try to remain on his good side, and if Ian didn't listen to reason, then perhaps Prasert would.

"Thank you," she said, flashing him an appreciative grin. "I'm very grateful for your kindness."

He flushed furiously. "Do you wish to eat, *Mem?*" When she nodded, he added, "Dinner will be ready in a few minutes."

He left and she worked a few minutes on her tangled hair until at last each strand shone as it fell over her shoulders. Peering closely at her eyes, she was delighted to find Lamoon hadn't been wrong and her lashes had indeed grown back. Then she took one last look at herself and sighed. Wouldn't her aunt be horrified if she could see her niece now? she thought. With a swift dart of anger at the man who'd put her in this predicament, she went downstairs in search of Prasert.

She strode through the rooms to the pantry. Through the back door, she caught sight of him talking animatedly to a small boy. She started toward them and then paused as she realized he'd gestured toward the house. Pressing a few coins in the boy's hand, Prasert sent him off in the direction of the street. She decided Prasert was sending the boy to get food from the market, although she thought it odd that Prasert had made it sound as if dinner were being cooked on the premises.

Shaking her head, she walked to the dining room she'd noticed earlier. She knew Ian probably wouldn't return for a few hours, and she didn't know how she could stand it. On the other hand, perhaps it would be wiser not to wait up, dressed as she was. She could confront Ian with her arguments in the morning.

Further thoughts on that matter were forestalled by Prasert's entry into the dining room with a tray of food that smelled wonderful. He placed a plate full of steaming curry and rice on the table in front of her. A platter piled with pieces of pineapple and papaya followed that. Finally he set down a carafe of red wine and a glass.

She gestured to the wine. "Why do you bring me wine and not tea?"

"All *farangs* drink wine," Prasert said firmly. "This is very good. His Royal Highness sent it especially for Lord Winthrop."

She knew he'd be offended if she refused it, so she claimed to be inordinately fond of red wine and poured herself a glass. When he saw her seated at the table, he turned to go. She was suddenly unwilling to eat alone in the big empty house.

"Prasert?" she asked hesitantly. "Would you mind very much joining me for dinner?"

"Yes, *Mem*," he said and sat down stiffly across from her.

"It's not a duty," she said softly in Siamese. "It's just a request—from a friend."

His face broke into a grin as he lowered his gaze shyly. Then he nodded in quick acceptance. "I would be honored."

"Then find yourself a glass and have some of this wine. And stop calling me *Mem*. My name is Esme."

"Essmay," he said, trying the sound out. "A very beautiful name."

"Thank you."

Quickly, he left the room and returned moments later with a glass. After pouring him some wine, she tackled the delicious food before her, savoring the spicy curry that she'd only eaten occasionally in Bangkok when visiting her two friends.

The evening passed slowly, but Prasert's presence helped calm her nerves. Once he was certain she didn't think him presumptuous, he bombarded her with questions about why she masqueraded as a Siamese boy and why she'd run away. She saw no reason to hide the truth. In fact, it was a relief to concentrate on something besides Ian's impending return.

In her anxiousness, she didn't notice that she drank more wine than she ever had at home. When at last Prasert rose from his chair and said he regretfully had to leave, she discovered she felt drowsy.

"You wish to retire now?" he asked politely.

"No, no. I wish to wait for Ian—I mean, Lord Winthrop. Go on. I'll just read a book in the library." She was certain she'd seen a library adjoining the dining room. Or had it been somewhere else?

Prasert looked at her doubtfully. "I think you should go to bed. You look very tired."

"No, no," she said crossly. "I'm fine."

But when she stood up from the table, her body felt so heavy she could hardly lift her feet.

"I will help you," he said and hastily moved to her side to support her.

"I want to go to the library, but I feel so very heavy." She giggled. "Stop trying to hold me up, Prasert. You're much too small!"

But he ignored her protests and placed her arm around his shoulder. He braced her and led her toward the library, which did indeed adjoin the dining room. When at last she'd reached the cushioned settee, she plopped down on it in relief. Her body seemed to stretch out of its own accord as she tilted sideways and rested her head on her hands.

Prasert glanced at her nervously. "*Mem* should go to bed."

"Prasert should go 'way!" she said, with a titter at her own humor. "I'll just rest here a minute. Now go 'way!"

Prasert shrugged before lighting the lantern that stood on the library desk. Then mumbling to himself, he left the room.

"So soft," she murmured into the cushion before her eyes closed. "Very soft . . ."

The only sound remaining in the library was the sound of gentle, even breathing.

Ian's impatience had almost reached its limit. They were already on the tenth course with no end in sight. Prince Mataya had announced his desire to save the political discussion for the next day, so even the conversation had been less than stimulating. Godfrey and Harold attempted to hide their boredom, while Langland and his wife had been unusually quiet for some time.

Mechanically, Ian sipped at the excellent wine provided by the prince. Dinners with Oriental rulers were always long and arduous. Usually, he enjoyed what was essentially an obstacle course of words. But tonight he wasn't in the mood to endure the beginning formalities, the tedious conversations in which each person tried to keep the other from losing face, and the endless polite civilities necessary to smooth the process.

Tonight he wanted to be with Esme. This desire to be with one woman every possible hour of the day was new to him. How had he let her slip under his guard so easily? He was accustomed to being a solitary man and not really needing anyone else. Suddenly he found himself constantly wondering what it would be like to spend every evening with Esme, to have her fussing over him as she must have done with her father. How would it be to have her waiting for him at the end of every day?

She was one of the few women he knew who could understand the difficulties he faced. She'd grown up in two cultures. She knew how easily words and gestures could be misinterpreted. As it was, he couldn't wait to get back and tell her about Prince Mataya. He knew she could explain for him some of the peculiarities he'd noticed in the way conversation was handled. He wondered if she'd waited for him.

With relief, Ian noticed that the dishes were being removed and trays with bottles of port and glasses were brought. A hint of a smile touched his lips as he realized Prince Mataya had chosen to end the meal as he knew a European would. In a short while they'd be able to leave.

Langland nudged him. "Thank God it's nearly over."

Prince Mataya, a slender man with coffee-colored skin and delicate gestures, was speaking to the consulate interpreter. Ian hoped the prince was dismissing them. The consulate interpreter said something in reply, but evidently the prince insisted that he translate his words.

"Lord Winthrop," the interpreter said haughtily. "His Highness wishes to know why your wife didn't accompany you tonight. I explained you have no wife, but he insists you have a foreign woman lodging with you. He asks if she is your wife or your concubine."

Ian was aware that the eyes of Harold, Godfrey, and Langland had turned to him—Harold's face showing alarm, Godfrey's amusement, and Langland's surprise.

As he met the prince's steady gaze, he recognized this was a test. Since the prince had provided the house, he obviously had his spies among the staff. Perhaps even Prasert worked for him. The prince probably knew everything: what the sleeping arrangements were; that Esme had arrived disguised; perhaps even that Langland believed her to be a boy. Esme had told Ian that the Siamese avoided confrontation at all costs. If the prince knew as much as he had implied, then he realized that the situation was delicate. So the only reason he could have for asking such a question was to test Ian's honesty.

Ian could answer in two ways. He could evade the question, which the prince would accept as Ian's attempt to save face. But he suspected that choice would lower the prince's opinion of him. Or he could tell the truth. Lying was not an option. Not only was it repugnant to him, but it would be unwise as well, since he'd no idea how much more the prince knew or could find out. He had no choice but to be as truthful as possible.

"Your Highness," Ian said slowly, addressing his words to the prince, although he knew the man spoke no English. "The woman you speak of is not my wife or my concubine. She is, shall we say, my servant."

As the interpreter translated Ian's words, the prince's face betrayed his skepticism. Suddenly Prince Mataya surprised everyone by addressing Ian directly in heavily accented French, ignoring the others present.

"I have been informed that your servant is a beautiful *farang*, yet she dresses and speaks as my people do. I want to meet this servant who behaves so oddly. Will you bring her with you two nights hence for some theatrical entertainment?"

"If you so wish," Ian replied, stiffening as he wondered why no one had told him of the prince's ability to speak French.

"It is my desire," Prince Mataya answered.

Ian wanted to know more. He wanted to know why the prince wanted to meet Esme and how the man knew French. But His Highness had already turned to the interpreter who was announcing that the prince now wished to retire. The guests rose to their feet and bowed as he left the room. Then one of the prince's attendants led them out of the palace and to the street.

As soon as they'd left the palace behind, Langland pulled Ian aside. "Pardon me, sir, but I must know what that French business was about. My French is rusty, I'm afraid. Couldn't catch a word. Who's this woman or servant or whatever she is?"

"Don't worry yourself about it, Langland," Ian said coldly. "She's just someone I hired. Prince Mataya wishes to meet her."

"Why?" Langland asked, surprised.

"Who knows? One of those whims of royalty perhaps," Ian said casually. "But it's an easy enough thing to give him."

"Of course. Well, if that's all, I won't mention it in my report." He released Ian's arm. "The wife and I must be off. We've brought the carriage. Shall we drop you at your lodgings?"

"I'd rather walk. His Highness made certain he had me within arm's reach. It's only a short distance."

"Fine. Then I'll see you tomorrow at 10:00 sharp."

"Certainly," Ian said absently.

But he wasn't to be allowed to walk in peace, for as soon as Langland and his wife left, Harold strode up.

"I wish to talk to you, Lord Winthrop," he said, emphasizing Ian's title.

"I'm in a hurry. Can't it wait until tomorrow?"

"No. I gathered from the conversation in there that you've not put Miss Montrose in a hotel at all. Godfrey wouldn't tell me where she was when I asked this afternoon. Now I discover she's at your lodgings! I hardly believe she chose to be there. She clearly dislikes you."

Ian stopped dead and turned to confront the man stalking him. "Stay out of this. It's none of your concern. Why don't you just return to your own lodgings and forget about Miss Montrose? I promise you she's well taken care of."

Harold wasn't the kind of man to cause trouble. But Ian could tell his intentions at the moment were deadly serious.

"None of my concern! Someone must look after Esme! No matter what the gossips say, Lord Winthrop, no matter what foolish ideas you harbor about her, she's not the kind of woman you think. She's too innocent for the sort of thing you intend."

These last words were said with such disgust that Ian's anger flared, as well as something else he'd never expected to feel—acute jealousy.

"So now she's 'Esme' to you? I'm afraid, Harold, you're heading in the wrong direction if you intend to court her. In spite of your naive assessment of her, she's not the lily-white virgin you'd like her to be. She's a warm-blooded, passionate woman, one who would never be satisfied with a man like you, and at present she's waiting for me to return. So if you'll excuse me, I'd like to do just that!"

He strode on, but Harold didn't leave his side. In a few minutes, they had reached the gate of Ian's lodgings. Ian pounded on the wooden door set within the gate, then turned to Harold with an expression of challenge.

"This is where we part," he said fiercely.

"I want to see her," Harold replied with a stubborn tilt to his chin. "I want to be certain she's here by choice."

The door opened behind Ian, and Prasert peeped around the corner.

"You can see her tomorrow!" Ian snapped.

"I want to—"

"Tomorrow!" Ian pivoted and strode through the door, slamming it shut behind him.

Prasert cringed as he saw his new master's anger.

"I've a bone to pick with you, my boy," Ian said harshly as he stood inside the gate, looking up at the house.

"A bone? I do not understand."

"You promised not to reveal Esme's presence in this house."

Prasert concentrated his gaze on his toes for a long moment. "I didn't tell *Khun* Langland," he said at last, lifting his eyes to stare at his master.

"But you told the prince, didn't you? You gave him a full account." Ian's gaze bore into him, but Prasert didn't flinch.

"Yes. He is my first master. You are a very important man, *Than*, but he is the most important man in the city. His Highness asked to know everything about you. Whatever he asks of me, I must give him."

Ian relaxed as he surveyed the boy in front of him. Prasert was right, of course. A man's first loyalty was to his regent, and if anyone could understand that, Ian could.

"Would your loyalty to your prince allow you to give me some information about him?"

"Perhaps . . ." Prasert said with fearful hesitation.

"Why, when, and how did he learn French?"

Prasert smiled. "My master is very wise. He does not know who will win—the French or the Siamese. He does not wish to gamble with his provinces. So he has been studying French with a tutor for two years now. Very wise, yes?"

"Very wise indeed," Ian responded thoughtfully. Then he added, "That's all for tonight. You may retire."

Ian's blood began to race with anticipation as he turned toward the house. Was Esme waiting for him?

"Sir?" Prasert ventured.

"Yes, what is it?" he asked impatiently.

"*Mem* waits for you in the library."

Ian smiled. "Thank you."

As Prasert strolled back to the servants' quarters, Ian entered the house quietly. With an enthusiasm he couldn't quench, he headed for the library. A moment's glance revealed her curled up on the settee with her eyes closed.

"Esme," he said softly.

No answer. He knelt on one knee and shook her. Her eyes fluttered open for a moment.

"So tired," she murmured, the words slightly slurred.

Ian smiled bitterly as he caught a whiff of the liquor on her breath. No wonder she slept so soundly, he thought.

"Must wait for Ian," she muttered. "Make him release me."

Sleepily, she turned on her other side and nearly fell off the settee in the process. Ian caught her. He stood to his feet with her in his arms and looked down at the woman he held. The dark lashes feathering her cheeks lent her a look of innocence he found difficult to ignore. Again he wondered how she could have been Rushton's mistress. His arms tightened around her as he strode to the stairs. She wanted to convince him to release her, did she?

Well, tomorrow he'd let her have her say. Then he'd have his. He wanted to know just what Rushton had meant to her. He deserved to know that much.

As he climbed the stairs, she snuggled against his chest. In the process, her scarf shifted, nearly revealing one breast. He swallowed convulsively as he felt an instant response in his loins. Perhaps it hadn't been wise after all to make her wear that sarong. He'd never been so hungry for any one woman in his entire life. It was going to take all of his restraint to keep from waking her, from making love to her tonight.

When he reached the top of the stairs, he carried her into the bedroom nearest his. As he lay her gently on the bed, he realized he'd never be able to undress her without doing something he'd regret. So he left her clothed. She made little protest when he pulled the coverlet from underneath her and covered her with it. Instantly, she curled into a ball and settled her head against the pillow with a murmur.

He stood and watched her a moment, his eyes drinking in the sight of her silky hair tumbling over the pillow then disappearing under the coverlet. Her wine-hued lips parted slightly as if in invitation. He bent down and planted a soft kiss on them. Her eyelids flew open, and a glimmer of recognition briefly shone in her dark eyes.

A solemn expression crossed her face as her eyelids drooped. "I waited for you, Ian," she whispered against the pillow so softly that he had to bend down to hear her words.

Then her breathing became steady and even again, and he knew she was asleep.

Chapter Seventeen

Esme was awakened by the sound of a loud groan—hers. She opened her eyes a crack, but the sunlight streaming into them made her close them again.

Where am I? she thought as she forced her eyes open and painfully maneuvered her body into a sitting position. One look at the lavish furniture and the brocade coverlet reminded her she was in Chiengmai with Ian, staying in his lodgings.

Then she realized she wasn't in the room she'd chosen.

How did I get in here? she wondered. She remembered eating dinner and drinking far too much wine. And vaguely she remembered going with Prasert into the library. After that, her mind was completely blank. Except for the lovely dream she'd had of Ian carrying her up the stairs and placing her on the bed, she thought with a smile. The smile faded from her lips as she realized it hadn't been a dream. Someone must have carried her upstairs, since she certainly hadn't climbed the stairs herself. And that someone must have been....

Oh no, she thought in horror. *What did I do last night? Could we possibly have—have....*

She glanced down quickly and relief flooded through her as she realized her sarong and scarf were intact. No, she hadn't done anything to be ashamed of, aside from drinking too much.

Willing her head to stop pounding, she swung her legs over the edge of the bed and stood up. She didn't know how she could spar with Ian in her condition, but somehow she'd have to. Many more evenings with him, and she might find herself waking up one morning in an entirely different situation.

As she straightened her clothing, she wondered if he'd left the house yet. She desperately wanted to get their discussion out of the way before he left. Her head reeling from the effort, she stumbled into the hall where she discovered, to her chagrin, that the clock said noon. Moving as quickly as she could, she entered the room she'd chosen and found the comb. She gave her hair a few quick strokes. Then she descended the stairs as gracefully as possible, gripping the banister as if her life depended on it.

When she entered the dining room, she was pleased to find Ian there, standing by the table and chatting with Prasert. She could tell Ian was preparing to go, for his satchel was on the table in front of him and his hat rested on a chair. When the two men turned to look at her, she managed a smile. Prasert returned it, but Ian did not, although his slate eyes seemed to warm a bit.

Languidly, his gaze traveled over her. "I trust you're feeling rather wretched this morning," he said smoothly. "Sit down. Prasert will bring you a concoction I drink when I overindulge. I was just describing it for him."

Curtly, he nodded to the boy, who hastened out of the room. She colored at his reference to her inebriated state the night before. With as much dignity as she could muster, she seated herself in the chair across the table from where he stood.

"I'm sorry, Ian," she said softly, unable to meet his eyes. "I really didn't mean to imbibe quite so much—"

"No need to apologize," he said tersely.

A long silence ensued while she gathered her courage to broach the subject she wished to discuss with him.

"I still need to talk to you," she said at last, leaning forward as she lifted her face to eyes the color of gun metal.

"What about?" he asked in a deceptively casual voice.

"I know you said you won't let me leave," she said, going right to the point, "but I don't think you've completely considered what your determination to keep me from marrying Michaels might mean."

"Oh?"

"If my father arrives and discovers I've been with you all this time, he'll be furious and assume the worst, no matter what has passed between us. And when you admit you won't marry me, he'll try to destroy your career, Ian. He could do it, too, with Mr. Rushton helping him."

She wished she hadn't had to state her case so baldly, but she was afraid if she didn't, he wouldn't hear her out. Satisfied that she'd presented a convincing argument, she glanced up at Ian expectantly. She wasn't prepared for the look of cold rage that hardened his face to stone.

"Is this some sort of thinly veiled threat, Esme?" His knuckles whitened as he gripped the edge of the table. "If I don't marry you, then you'll bid your lover to attack?"

The expression of shocked disbelief that crossed her face seemed to check any further accusations he'd planned to make. But as her disbelief turned to anger, she rose from the table in a blind fury, oblivious to the nausea that swept over her at her sudden movement.

"How dare you!" she said as she leaned forward. "You keep me prisoner in your lodgings, but you twist it to make it appear as if I were trapping *you*, forcing *you* to act against your will!"

He flinched visibly.

"I thought you'd be concerned your actions might harm you," she continued mercilessly. "What a fool I was! Marry you? You must be mad! Why would I choose to marry a man who distorts my every word, who believes I'm capable of the most wretched, awful things imaginable—"

"Oh, God, Esme, I didn't mean it!" he choked out, remorse flooding his face as he came around the table toward her.

But she was so lost in her own bitter pain that she paid his apology scant attention. How could she have been so blind? He didn't care for her. Even now he believed she was a scheming harridan.

He tried to gather her into his arms, but she pushed him away. "If you hate me so much," she whispered, "if you think such awful things of me, why keep me here? Why not send me out into the streets? That's all I asked of you in the first place."

"If I hated you," he said in fierce desperation, "I

would. But God curse me to hell, I don't hate you. And I won't let you leave, especially with so many matters unsettled between us."

"There's nothing to settle," she said coldly.

"Oh, but there is," he insisted, his hand moving to brush her hair. "I shouldn't have said what I did, love, but the fact remains that Henry Rushton seems always to come between us. You have never really told me the truth about him."

"I *have* told you the truth!" she exclaimed, pushing his hand away.

"I doubt that very much." His gaze seemed frozen with pain. "His name was on that telegram—not your father's—and I want to know why."

"But I don't know why!" she protested, her hands clenching into fists in her frustration.

He stood there looking down at her, his face implacable. "Then you'd better start working on your imagination, my dear, because one way or the other, I plan to get some answers!"

Her black eyes flashed mutinously at him. "You are the most reprehensible, horrible—"

"I'm sorry I can't stay to hear the entire recitation," he broke in, "but I've an audience with the prince in less than an hour. I was expected at the consulate two hours ago, but you said you wished to speak with me and I didn't wish to wake you. I can't tarry any longer. But we're not finished yet," he assured her as he picked up his coat and began to pull it on. "I don't know how long I'll be, but when I return, I want the truth—all of it. Every last sordid detail. I want to know once and for all about Rushton and what he meant to you."

With that, he grabbed his satchel and stormed from the dining room and out of the house.

She shook with fury as he left. The nerve of him,

to accuse her and then demand explanations she couldn't give him! What was she to do? She'd told him the truth about Rushton, but he'd stubbornly refused to believe it. Well, she wasn't going to sit there and wait for him to bombard her with questions that she couldn't answer. She had to escape this madhouse!

"*Mem?*" Prasert said from the doorway, coming slowly forward to bring her a concoction that wrinkled her nose. "*Than* said you should drink this. To make your head feel better."

"The only thing that will make my head feel better is getting away from him!" she shouted furiously in Siamese. When he cringed, she softened her tone. "Prasert, I want my clothes. What have you done with them?"

"I'm sorry. I can't give them to you," he answered, backing away from her as he saw the determined glint in her eye. "Lord Winthrop said not to, so I can't."

"All right then. Give me some of yours."

He looked at her in surprise.

"He didn't say I couldn't wear another boy's clothes," she insisted.

"I will not aid you to run away," Prasert said firmly. "The master trusts me. I will not betray him."

"But surely you don't think he's right to keep me here against my will!"

He became very uneasy. "I'm sorry, *Mem* Esme, I really am. I like you. But I cannot disappoint my master or my prince. They wish you to stay so you must stay."

She looked at him in surprise. "Your prince? What does your prince know of me?"

But Prasert wouldn't answer, nor would he

change his mind and help her. She gave him no peace for the next few hours. While he served her the lunch she felt too ill to eat, she pleaded with him. When lunch was over and he requested permission to retire, she refused to give it to him. She argued with him, she harangued him in vivid Siamese, and at last she begged him. But he stubbornly refused to relent, although she knew that her pleas upset him a great deal.

They were both in the drawing room when one of the other servants entered and whispered something in his ear. He nodded and then turned to Esme.

"There is a visitor here to see you," he said blandly.

She paled. Surely her father hadn't reached Chiengmai yet, had he?

"A—a visitor?"

"Yes. He said his name is Thurwood."

Her eyes lit up. Harold! He could help her! After all, he'd always been quick to defend her.

"Send him in," she told Prasert who hesitated. "Go on! *Than* didn't tell you I couldn't have visitors, did he?"

While Prasert hurried to the front door, Esme went to the mirror, trying to smooth her hair into some semblance of order. She groaned as she realized what Harold would think when he found her living in Ian's lodgings, receiving visitors in Siamese native dress. But she had no choice. It was either receive him in the sarong or not see him at all, and she must see him.

When Prasert returned with Harold, she cringed as she saw a look of disapproval cross her friend's face for the merest instant. She sat down self-

Deborah Martin

consciously in the nearest chair, and he took the one next to hers.

"I'm sorry it took me so long to come. I wanted to see you last night, but Lord Winthrop wouldn't let me. And today I couldn't get away from the consulate until a few minutes ago. Are you all right?" he asked with concern, his eyes traveling over her strange garb.

"I'm as well as can be expected under the circumstances," she replied honestly, flashing him a hesitant smile.

"He hasn't . . . I mean, you're not—"

"I'm not his mistress if that's what you're trying to ask," she hastened to assure him. She couldn't stop a blush from spreading over her face. "But I can't stay here, as you can well imagine."

"No, of course not," Harold replied matter of factly. "I'll take you to the consulate."

"I'd rather not go there, either." Briefly, she explained her dilemma, emphasizing that her father would arrive any day and she didn't want him to be shamed or to assume she'd been Ian's mistress.

"You mean that—that rakehell took your clothes away? What made him think he could do such a thing?" Harold asked, his face incredulous.

"Don't blame him. He had his reasons," she said hesitantly, wondering if she should tell him of Ian's fear that she might strike out alone in Chiengmai. No, she couldn't tell Harold that. If he knew she had considered it, he might not help her.

"Now you're defending the cad," he said in disgust. "If you ask me, Esme, you don't owe Lord Winthrop anything. While you're excusing his actions, he's announcing to everyone that you're here in his house."

"What?" She stared at Harold in confusion, but

she could find no sign in his face that he lied.

"How do you think I learned of your presence here? Prince Mataya asked about you last night and Ian informed him you were his servant. His Royal Highness had apparently heard all about you, presumably from his spies. He even wants to meet you, and Ian agreed to arrange it."

So that was what Prasert had meant!

"No," she whispered, "How could Ian acknowledge that I was staying here? Now everyone must know! It's bad enough those other lies were spread about me. Did Ian have to add fuel to the fire? I'll never convince my father to end my betrothal now. Never!"

Her loathing for Michaels washed over her again, and she stifled the sob that rose to her lips.

"There's another way to prevent the marriage," Harold said, taking her hand in his. "You could marry someone else."

"If you mean to convince Ian to marry me," she said harshly, "you're wasting your time. He's already said he wouldn't."

Harold looked offended, but he continued to hold her hand. "Actually, I didn't mean his lordship. I meant myself."

When she raised startled eyes to look at him, she noticed that he gazed at her affectionately, almost reverently.

"But—but why would you wish to marry me?" she stammered. "Everyone supposes me to be a terribly wanton woman."

"Those awful lies! I don't believe a word of them!" Harold protested, gripping her hand when she tried to remove it from his. "I know you for the innocent, kind woman you are."

The smile she gave him was bittersweet. She

could have kissed him for believing in her. He was such a dear man that she was tempted to accept his offer. And it would solve all her problems. She wouldn't have to marry Michaels, and Ian would be forced to relinquish his plans to have her without marrying her. But she couldn't play such a rotten trick on Harold, marrying him when she loved someone else. He deserved to marry someone who returned his love.

"Thank you, Harold, for such a kind offer. I'm sorry," she said with real regret. "But I can't marry you for the sake of convenience. You ought to have a wife who loves you, and I'm terribly afraid I don't."

She withdrew her hand from his, and her throat constricted with pity as a flash of pain crossed his face.

"But I love you," he persisted. "And I know you care for me, at least a little. We could have a comfortable marriage, much better than any marriage you'd have with Michaels."

He was right, she knew. Theirs would be a marriage of mutual consideration and kindness. But that wasn't enough for her and she was certain that eventually it wouldn't be enough for him either.

"If I marry Michaels," she said gently, "it will be because I'm forced to. And I'll fight it with every inch of my being. But any husband I choose for myself will be one I care for."

"And have you yet found a man you could care for?" he asked, his eyes searching her face.

When she wouldn't look at him, his eyes widened and he grasped her hand tightly again. "Oh, dear Lord, Esme, you can't be in love with *him*, can you? How could you be so foolish? Everyone says he's a rake who casts women aside when he's through with them. He'd give you nothing but heartache. How can you think of loving such a man?"

"Don't you think I've told myself the same things over and over for the last few weeks? But it's no use at all. Try as I might to believe them of him, I can't."

"He doesn't deserve you. I could give you a pure love. I would treat you like a queen. He wants only to...to..."

"I know what he wants," she said sharply. Then her face softened. "I'm sorry, Harold, but I can't help what I feel. Much as I'd like to take the escape you offer, I can't. It wouldn't be fair to either of us."

He pleaded with her a few moments more, but she wouldn't give him the answer he wanted. And the more he argued, the worse she felt. Here was a wonderful man willing to care for her, and all she wanted was one who was unwilling even to trust her. As Harold said, Ian was not a good choice for any woman.

But in her heart, she didn't believe that. While he'd often been unfair in his estimation of her, he'd never forced her to do anything immoral. Even the night before, when he could have taken advantage of her, he'd left her alone. She knew how much that had cost him, because she'd felt his desire before he left. No, Ian might not love her, but he'd also never pretend to in order to bed her. He'd always play fair and treat her honestly. It wasn't his fault she'd been unwise enough to lose her heart to him.

"All right then," Harold said, at last admitting defeat as she stared at him in silence. "At least leave with me, and I'll find some place for you to stay. You said you wanted to get away from here. Now's your chance, while Ian is in that audience with the prince."

A noise in the doorway to the drawing room startled them both, causing them to look in that direction. And there, his face implacably cool, but his eyes the steely gray that Esme knew was a sign of his anger, stood Ian.

"I hate to disappoint you, Harold, but the audience is over. And now that you've satisfied yourself I haven't tortured her or locked her in some dungeon, kindly leave." Ian's voice was full of such cold scorn that Esme shuddered. He removed his frock coat and tossed it over a chair as if to demonstrate more forcefully that Harold and not he was the intruder.

"Just do as he says, Harold," she said softly.

"Not without you," Harold responded with bravado, although he too seemed to fear Ian's wrath.

"She's staying," Ian said, striding over to stand behind her chair. His hands gripped her shoulders as if to keep her in the chair by sheer force.

"Please, Harold," she begged as Ian's fingers bit into her.

"You heard her," Ian stated coldly.

Harold looked at Esme's face, which rapidly drained of all color. Then he stiffened and lifted embittered eyes to Ian.

"You're a fool, Lord Winthrop," he said in a caustic voice. "You have a perfect jewel right in the palm of your hand but you don't even appreciate it. You wish only to wear it for a time and then toss it away. I'm not such a fool. I offered her what you wouldn't—marriage."

"Don't, Harold!" Esme pleaded, attempting to rise.

"Is this true?" Ian asked behind her as his hands tightened painfully on her shoulders.

She nodded, her voice too choked with emotion to speak.

"And I suppose you accepted," Ian said bitingly. "Anything to get out of your marriage to Michaels and away from me."

Esme knew he spoke in jealous anger, but his words wounded her. Harold's face turned red as he saw the pain in her face.

"Actually, your lordship," he spat out, "she rejected my suit. She seems to care a great deal for someone else, so she won't marry me. But I still cling to the hope that she'll change her mind when she discovers he's unworthy of her."

Ian's hold on her shoulders loosened somewhat.

"Go, Harold," she said, her eyes pleading with him. "You've said enough."

Flashing Ian a look of utter contempt, Harold turned on his heels and left the room. But Ian remained behind her chair, his hands resting on her shoulders, even after the outside gate door slammed shut behind Harold.

After what seemed an infinite amount of time, Ian spoke, "Why didn't you accept his offer?"

"It doesn't matter," she replied, her hands twisting nervously in her lap.

He circled the chair to face her, standing with his arms crossed and his legs spread wide. She refused to look at him.

"It matters to me," he said in a tone so bittersweet it made her want to cry.

When she didn't respond, he leaned down to brace his hands at her sides, trapping her in the chair. "Is it Rushton? Do you still love him?" he asked her, his voice tortured.

Deborah Martin

She paled. Then taking him by surprise, she pushed him in the chest so he stumbled back a step. Rising to her feet with rage and pride warring in the haughty tilt of her chin and the flashing of her eyes, she slapped him as hard as she could manage.

"Harold was right," she whispered. "You *are* a fool."

Then she fled the room, but her sarong hampered her movements. Even though she flew up the steps to her room as quickly as possible, she didn't have time to make it inside before Ian was behind her, grasping her around the waist to keep her from getting in the room and shutting the door.

Her hair swinging wildly about her shoulders, she beat at the unyielding band that held her.

"Put me down!" she shouted. "I want to go to my room!"

"Not until we discuss some things," he hissed, the muscles of his arms straining against the thin linen of his shirt as he struggled to subdue her.

"We have nothing to discuss. I'm not staying here! If I have to roam the streets of Chiengmai like this, I will!"

She kicked backward against his legs with her heels, but with only her bare feet, she couldn't hurt him enough to make him release her.

"You might as well give up," he muttered in her ear. "I'm not about to let you go just yet. So the only thing your squirming is doing is provoking my desire."

Her body went rigid in mortification as she realized he wasn't lying. Abruptly, she went limp in his arms, and he let her slide down the length of him to the ground, though he maintained his hold on her waist.

"You know I won't force you into anything while

you're here. I would have done so long before now if I were going to," he said, echoing her earlier thoughts. "I only want to protect you. Why won't you let me?"

"Because I don't trust you," she said, hardly knowing what she was saying as her body began to respond to his nearness.

"It's not me you don't trust," he said softly. "It's yourself."

Then he swept the curtain of her hair aside to press his lips against a sensitive spot on her neck, branding her with his mark in the only way he knew how.

"Please don't," she whispered as her skin tingled under his touch.

He twisted her around to face him, his hands like vises on her shoulders.

"Who is the someone else you care for too much to marry Harold? I have to know!"

In that instant when their eyes locked and silver lightning met dark earth, she knew she couldn't fight her feelings for him any longer, no matter what happened.

"You already know," she told him.

As understanding dawned, a look of triumph replaced the tormented expression on his face. He caught her up fiercely against his chest. Then his mouth crashed down on hers. She wrapped her arms around his waist, all reservations dissolving in the warmth of his kiss. His passion consumed her as liquid fire coursed through her body, devouring her. He drew back from her lips for a moment.

"I've waited so long for you to want me," he murmured, his breath hot against her ear. "And you do want me, don't you?"

Deborah Martin

She did, so much she couldn't think, couldn't begin to object. "Yes," she answered, her hands stroking his back.

"And I want you, love," he whispered.

Then his hands were tangled in her hair and he was kissing her with a searing intensity she'd never dreamed possible, his hands roaming over her body like flames licking greedily at a wax figure as she melted at every sensuous touch of his fingers.

"You won't deny me this time, will you?" he asked, and the warmth of his gaze upon her was an exquisite torture she could hardly endure.

"No. No, dear heart, I won't. I can't anymore."

At her use of the endearment, he groaned, burying his face in the graceful curves of her neck to plant a kiss. Within his arms, she felt she'd found her place. Her body fit so well against his she wondered why she'd resisted so long. She knew she was mad to be doing this, knew that later she'd regret such a foolhardy decision. But her desire to demonstrate how much she loved him, to erase from his face the pain that Harold's words had etched there, forced her to thrust her misgivings aside.

As his lips moved over her cheeks, her eyes, her brow, she felt an elation that inflamed her senses, making her aware of every tensed muscle, every slight touch of his body against hers. But mingled with that was a growing fear. Ian didn't believe she was a virgin; he would assume she knew what to expect and what to do. While Lamoon and Mai had told her some things about what went on between a man and a woman, they'd spoken only in euphemisms she didn't always understand. And they'd said that the first time there was pain, sometimes a great deal of pain.

Ian sensed her sudden reluctance, for he stopped

352

kissing her to gaze in her eyes. Then with a growl, he decided to take no chances and swept her up in his arms, seizing her lips again as he carried her down the hall and into his room.

The sun was setting, flooding the room with an unearthly fire that danced off the golden silk coverlet and gold-threaded rug. A shimmering haze of light surrounded them, making them both feel a part of the burning orb. Amidst the brilliant glow, Ian gently lowered Esme to the bed, his gray eyes smoldering coals that promised flames to come. Then he sank onto the coverlet beside her, and his hands stroked the soft lines of her face as if to be assured she was really there.

"Kiss me," he said softly as he lay on his side next to her, propped up by one arm while the rough fingers of his other hand encircled and caressed her slender neck.

Her eyes lifted to his in surprise. The sweetness she saw there decided her. She couldn't ruin the moment by speaking of her love and risking his rejection. But she could show him how she felt. She leaned up to press her trembling mouth against his. Then her unconscious seductive instincts took over, and she darted her tongue timidly out to lick the crevice made by his slightly parted lips. His hand tightened on her neck as he opened his mouth hungrily over hers and sucked her tongue into it, teasing and playing with it until she gave a soft moan of delight. Her hands clasped his neck, feeling the bristly short hairs bend under her fingers.

As he prolonged the kiss, his fingers trailed down the slope of her neck to where the gold pin held her scarf in place. In seconds he'd removed it and pulled the scarf loose and down to bare her breasts. As she felt his hand cup one firm mound, she tore her lips from his, drawing back slightly at the shock.

"Don't shy away from me, love. Your body doesn't," he murmured as he lifted smoky eyes to watch her face, the pad of his thumb rubbing the sensitive center of her nipple.

It was true, she thought as he began to trace circles with his thumb around the breast he held captive, sending rays of warmth through her body. Then he lowered his mouth to the tip and she shivered with pleasure. She felt her nipple harden in response as his tongue flicked and sucked it. The heat of his mouth scorched her skin, arousing a blaze of need within her. She clutched his head, burying her fingers in the thick waves that glimmered with the light of the dying sun. His chin with its day's growth of beard rasped against her soft skin, but that only heightened the desire flaring within her.

The hand of the arm he rested on was cradled in the silky strands of her hair, but his other hand began to travel down, easily unknotting her sarong and jerking it over her hips until her drawers were exposed. Then his fingers began to work on the buttons of her drawers, while his warm mouth caressed her breasts until the tips were swollen with longing. Satisfied that she'd been caressed senseless, he sat up beside her and slipped his hands under the band of her drawers, lowering them until her body was bared before him.

Then his eyes traveled the length of her body as they gorged themselves on the feast he'd been so long denied. She swallowed, suddenly embarrassed to be lying naked underneath his gaze. Instinctively, she grasped at the sheet to cover herself, but his hand encircled her delicate wrist.

"Don't deny me the sight of you, love," he whispered hoarsely. She saw the exquisite torment in his face, and willed her hand to release the edge of the sheet.

He passed his palm over first one breast and then the other before gliding his fingers down the smooth expanse of her belly. They paused at her navel, and he lowered his head to plant a kiss in the tiny dip, his tongue darting teasingly. Then he lifted his head and her midnight eyes widened as his hand dropped lower, skirting the soft triangular patch between her legs to slip nearly to her knees. Slowly, he began to stroke the sensitive skin on the inside of her thighs.

"Your skin is so silky," he murmured, his burning gaze never leaving her face.

As his rough fingers began to trace curlicues tenderly up the smooth skin of her inner thighs, she felt the cleft between her legs dampen and ache with some unnamed desire. What kind of wanton was she to allow a man such intimacies without even resisting?

"Ian," she whispered and grasped his hand in an attempt to stop its steady motion. He responded by covering her hesitant body with his own, the force of his kiss pressing her back into the pillow. Her hand released his as desire flamed within her again. Then he plundered the cushiony softness of her mouth, his fingers again stroking up her leg until they reached the springy covering between her legs. Without warning, they dipped into the moist velvety warmth, and she froze at the intimate touch.

She wrenched her mouth away from his, her eyes like a frightened doe's. He looked at her questioningly as her fingers closed on his hand, trying to push it away.

"Did Rushton never do this to you?" he asked

Deborah Martin

harshly, his eyes fleetingly clouded with pain as he allowed her to draw his hand away.

His jealous words ignited a spark of anger within her. "No one has ever done any of this to me," she said, her eyes daring him to contradict her.

For a moment, his face lit up, but it faded quickly. "You can say that, knowing that in a moment I'll know the truth?"

His skepticism wounded her and she tried to thrust him off her, but his heavy weight didn't budge. Scowling, he gripped her arm pushing against him, forcing it down to the bed and pinning it there.

"Unless, that is, you didn't intend me to know the truth ever," he said as his face moved to within an inch of hers. "Unless you really are the tease I've always thought you to be. Did you lie, my dear, when you said you wanted me?" His voice was scathing as he resisted her feeble attempts to pull away.

"I want a man who trusts me, who believes I'm telling the truth!" she cried out, twisting her head to the side to avoid his searching eyes.

"I'm sorry, love," he muttered thickly, "you'll have to settle for me."

Then before she could argue, he began the battle for her desire by devouring her with his mouth. She tried not to yield, but he gave her no mercy, nuzzling her neck and kissing her resisting mouth with such ardor that at last her lips softened and he stormed the entrance. His mouth ravaged hers with a fierceness that made her tingle all over and forget the way he'd wounded her feelings. She reveled in his musky masculine smell. His mouth tasted of brandy and something else—perhaps coconut—a sweet, nutty flavor.

She was so wrapped up in his kisses she didn't even fight when his fingers slid back between her thighs. She shuddered violently as his fingers resumed their teasing motions. Her fingers crept around his waist, digging into his back through the thin material of his shirt.

As his tongue plunged deeper and deeper into the warm depths of her mouth, his fingers became bolder in their caresses until she felt as if they reached to her very heart. Like a candle burning at both ends, her body was being consumed in an uncontrollable passion.

The buttons of his waistcoat pressed hard against her skin, reminding her she hadn't yet seen him naked. Suddenly she wished more than anything to see him as bare as she was. With an eagerness that surprised even herself, she began fumbling with the buttons. He rose to kneel on the bed, his legs straddling her, and impatiently aided her in her attempts to rid him of his waistcoat and shirt.

When at last he tossed the unwanted clothing aside, she sucked in her breath. She'd seen men's chests before, because the Siamese often went shirtless. But their smoothly sculpted chests couldn't compare to Ian's muscular one, thickly spread with rich brown hair. She could hardly tear her gaze from the strong sinewy arms and flat firm waist. With sudden boldness, she flattened her palms against his chest, feeling the muscles tighten at her touch. His eyes locked with hers as he caught her hands and placed them lower, against the hard bulge straining against the confining cloth of his trousers.

Her face flushed with color as she jerked her hands away, lowering her eyes to stare at a spot somewhere to the left of him. He laughed softly, his lips curving in a wicked grin as he moved off her to stand beside the bed.

"Look at me, love," he commanded, and she forced her eyes to return to him. She watched entranced as he began to unbutton his trousers. But when he slipped them down in one quick motion, her eyes swung away, and he gave a throaty chuckle.

"You'd best become accustomed to the sight of me, my shy maiden," he told her as he lowered himself onto the bed until the entire length of his body was flush against hers. "Because I don't intend this to be our last night together."

Then his mouth was on one breast, his tongue laving every inch of flesh while his fingers moved lower to caress her intimately again. Her hands clutched the muscular sides of his arms as waves of radiating warmth pulsed through her lower belly. She arched upward, her hips lifting to receive his fingers more fully. Suddenly, his hand withdrew and he hovered over her, his arms braced on either side of her as his shaft pressed against the entrance to her soft satin-lined cave.

"Tell me now what man you desire," he whispered, his eyes like a sword probing her heart. "Tell me!"

Caught up in the lingering pleasure his fingers had given her and aching to feel something she couldn't explain, she gazed at him, her eyes alight with love, and said, "Only you, dear heart, only you."

His face glowed with victory as he entered her, filling her so completely, she tensed as she felt the intrusion, preparing herself for the pain she knew would come. He captured her mouth with his, stifling the protest that rose to her lips. Then he felt the obstruction that proved her innocence, and his body stiffened.

His eyes darkened in abject contrition. "Oh, my God," he moaned, his body poised within her. He closed his eyes and threw his head back, pain lining his face. "Oh, my God," he repeated as the full meaning of her innocence struck him.

The bitter thought that even until the moment of truth he hadn't really believed her was forced out of her mind by the urgent desire to comfort him. She stroked his face gently with her fingers. His eyes opened at her touch, and he brushed a kiss against her hand.

"You told me. Over and over you told me," he murmured in a voice heavy with self-recrimination, "but I didn't listen. How can you forgive me?"

Tenderly, she caressed his cheek as her eyes burned earnestly into his. "I have to forgive you. I can't help myself," she murmured truthfully.

He turned his head and kissed the tips of her fingers. Then he fixed her with an intense stare. "You're more than I deserve, love, so before I do any more damage..." He paused, his face tightening. "I suppose I'd best end this now."

He began to withdraw from her, but she clutched him closer. "No," she whispered as any reservations she'd had were consumed by her blinding need. "I want you, Ian. Don't leave me. Please don't leave me."

Her plea seemed to rip him apart. "Are you sure?"

She nodded. "Don't leave me," she repeated, her arms holding him tightly.

His gaze darkened. "I'll never leave you," he avowed. Then he moaned, and with one powerful plunge was completely and irrevocably within her.

A tearing pain gripped her momentarily. Her low cry seemed to torment him.

"I promise I won't ever hurt you again," he whispered fiercely before seizing her lips with his own as if to find forgiveness in the healing balm of her mouth.

For a moment, his body remained poised above and within her as his mouth tasted hers, while he allowed the pain to subside and her body to adjust to his fullness. Then he began to move with an aching slowness, coaxing from her body a spark of response that grew to a flame as his thrusts became stronger and deeper.

Hardly aware of what she did, Esme slid her hands down to clutch his taut hips as her body arched to meet each thrust. He quickened his pace with a groan, his mouth releasing hers then slipping to her ear where he sucked and nipped the lobe while uttering soft endearments.

The wet touch of his tongue flicking rhythmically in and around the delicate skin of her ear maddened her. His passion made her feel more alive than she ever had before, like a phoenix rising from the ashes to glow brightly with new life. In the room, the blazing glory of sunset had long since faded to the quiet light of dusk, but she felt as if the sun had been captured within them, imprisoned so it could continue to burn more and more fiercely until they were consumed by the blinding brilliance of its fire.

She began to tremble as the incredible heat of intense pleasure set her aflame. She heard him cry out her name, and then they were afire together, melting into one as they both reached complete fulfillment.

It was several moments before either of them could speak. He'd been only half lying on her, holding up most of his weight with his forearms and knees. Now he rolled to the side and lay next to her, resting his body on his elbow. He gazed down at her, a mixture of wonder and fear crossing his face.

"You certainly have an odd way of proving me wrong when I least expect it," he said grimly, his hand moving to stroke her cheek. Then his eyes wandered to her thighs, which were smeared with blood. His jaw stiffened and he paled. When he continued speaking, his voice sounded choked. "In my stupidity, I've wronged you terribly. You have every right to hate me now. I won't blame you if you do."

"Shh, shh," she said, taking his face in her hands. "I couldn't hate you if I tried." Then she lowered her eyes. "Besides, I'd be terribly hypocritical if I hated you for giving me such pleasure."

She stole a glance at him and found him staring at her with disbelief, his eyes a burning blue as he caught her hands and moved them up around his neck.

"Oh, God, don't ever hate me. I couldn't bear it."

"Nor could I," she responded. Then she gave him a long, deep kiss.

He drew back from her in surprise. "So I wasn't completely wrong about you, was I, you little flirt?" he said with a chuckle, drawing her into his arms as he lay back on the bed. "You *are* a wanton woman."

"I suppose I am, my love," she whispered sleepily against his stubbly cheek as she lay cradled in his arms. "But only with you."

Then the exhaustion of her long day swept over her and she fell asleep.

Chapter Eighteen

Ian stirred when he felt a heavy arm drop onto his belly. In seconds he came awake as he remembered who was in the bed beside him. He lay there half an hour before finally accepting that he'd get no more sleep. Moving so he wouldn't wake Esme, he slid from under the coverlet and swung his legs to the floor. He stood up and then pivoted to gaze a moment at her half-covered form. A smile played over her face in her sleep, and she curled up into a ball, clutching his pillow in her slender arms.

With a tenderness he never dreamed he could feel, he drew the coverlet over the rest of her, reluctantly hiding her naked body. This wasn't the first time that night he'd left the bed. Several hours before he'd slipped away to get some warm water and a cloth. Returning to the bedroom, he'd lit the lamp and then washed the blood from her as gently as he could to keep from waking her. But just as he'd finished, she'd roused enough to draw him back into her arms. They'd made love again, but he'd been more leisurely about it. He'd teased and caressed her all over until she'd begged him to take her.

The memory of her response made his loins throb again with desire. She'd given herself freely, as if her earlier reluctance had never happened. She'd thrown herself so passionately into their lovemaking that even now he marveled at it. He'd never seen a woman with such abandon, and he had certainly never expected such a thing from a virgin. But that was just like Esme. She always surprised him with a new side of her nature. He grinned wickedly. This side he definitely found appealing.

But now she looked completely innocent again. In repose, her face seemed almost childlike with her lips slightly curved in a smile and her hands folded beneath her cheek. If he hadn't known she was naked under the covers, if he hadn't just experienced her fire and passion, he would have thought her the most chaste woman imaginable.

He left the bedside at last and found his robe. After donning it and taking one last look at Esme, he walked downstairs to the library. He lit the lamp and then poured himself a generous amount of brandy before settling into a large overstuffed chair to think.

The knowledge that all his assumptions about Esme had been wrong had him reeling. If he hadn't felt the obstruction himself and seen her blood soaking the coverlet, he still wouldn't have believed it. How could he have been so mistaken about her? It hadn't just been the rumor that convinced him, for he had known the rumor about him and Esme was false—though it'd prejudiced him almost from the beginning. No, the deciding factor had been the ease with which she'd masqueraded first as a Siamese woman and then as his boyish interpreter. He'd never known such deviousness in any woman but Caroline.

Caroline. The thought of her made him groan. If he were honest with himself, he'd admit Esme's behavior had been mostly justified. But he'd blinded himself to her true nature because of some stupid woman who wasn't fit to associate with Esme, much less be compared to her. Others had known Esme for what she really was. Reverend Taylor had accepted her immediately, even after he'd heard all the gossip. Even Harold had tried to tell Ian what ought to have hit him in the face. But Ian hadn't listened, too caught up in his righteous anger over her supposed indiscretion to see the obvious truth.

He buried his face in his hands. He didn't deserve Esme, that was certain. She had courage far beyond that of any woman he'd ever known. She'd fought to keep from being married to a man she detested, while all Ian had done was make her life miserable. And despite all that, despite the way he'd treated her, she cared for him. Him! Perhaps she even loved him.

Well, he'd not give her the chance to regret it. And if she didn't yet love him, he'd somehow convince her to. He'd do the only thing he could do for a woman whose innocence he'd trampled. He'd marry her.

His blood quickened at the thought of Esme dressed in blue silk and dancing with him at those horrid embassy functions, Esme lying in bed with him, Esme with his child in her womb. He'd been a fool not to realize before that she was the only woman he could ever marry, the only one who'd share his life with the intensity and vivacity he craved. But he saw it now, thank God, and he intended to ensure she never wanted to leave him again.

If only he'd never heard Godfrey's vicious gossip, he might have seen it before. His eyes narrowed as he remembered Godfrey's story about Rushton and Esme. Someone would pay for starting that rumor. Ian would see to that. But it chilled him that someone should want to ruin an innocent girl's reputation for no apparent reason. He gazed intently into the flames of the lamp.

Or was there a reason? One no one had yet seen, one even Esme hadn't realized?

With determination, he stood to his feet, leaving the glass of brandy sitting on a small table. He strode to the stairs. It wasn't late, he noted as he stared at the clock in the hallway, only midnight. Godfrey was probably at the hotel bar where he'd said he'd gone the night before. Ian would get some answers from his gossiping friend if he had to tie Godfrey down to get them.

It took him only a few minutes to go to his room and dress. Then he hesitated by the bed, wondering if he should wake Esme to tell her where he was going. He decided not to. After all, he thought, he'd be back long before daybreak and the way she was sleeping now, she'd certainly sleep until morning without even noticing he was gone. Instead of waking her, he bent over to kiss her cheek lightly.

"Wait for me, love," he whispered in her ear. She gave an unknowing smile in her sleep that made him even more determined to make amends for his transgressions by determining why and by whom she'd been wronged.

Before he left the house, he found Prasert eating

in back with one of the servant girls and told him where he'd be. Then he strode out the gate in the direction of the foreign hotel.

It didn't take him long to find Godfrey, who, true to form, was in the hotel lounge, a drink in one hand and five cards in the other.

"Ian!" Godfrey shouted and set down his cards as he spotted his friend striding toward him. "Come join us. We can use another player."

"I'm not here to play cards, Godfrey," Ian said ominously, ignoring the other men at the table as he came up beside Godfrey's chair. "I want to talk to you."

"Not now, old boy," Godfrey replied, picking up his cards again. "I'm in the midst of a wonderful run of luck. Perhaps we can discuss the state of the world tomorrow."

"Tomorrow won't do, I'm afraid," Ian said, snatching Godfrey's cards out of his hand and throwing them face up on the table. "Someone I know has already suffered too long over this."

"Be a sport, Ian!" Godfrey cried as Ian took Godfrey's drink from his hand and set it down none too gently.

"If you don't come with me now, I'll have to tell your friends here all your tricks for winning card games."

"All right, then, you bloody bastard," Godfrey said coldly as he stood to his feet with irritation showing in his face. "But I hope it won't take all night."

"I hope so, too," Ian said as he steered Godfrey to a secluded corner of the room. "I've no desire to spend the evening with you—not when I left better company to be here."

Godfrey grinned as he realized what "company"

Ian referred to. "Is that what this is all about?" Godfrey asked as they both took seats at the tiny table. "You need help with your feisty 'servant?'"

Ian's face darkened, but he ignored Godfrey's barb. "I want to know again who started the rumor about Rushton and Esme. But this time I'd like to know why."

Godfrey looked suspiciously at him. Then he raised an eyebrow and let out a low chuckle. "Why are you suddenly so interested in old news?" he asked, smirking at his friend. "Could it be you've proven beyond a shadow of a doubt that the rumor was false?"

Ian's fists came down on the table, startling Godfrey with their force. "You may be an old friend, and you may not mean to be such a thorough ass, but if you *ever* again spread scandalous stories about my future wife, *whether they're true or not*, I'll make you regret you did."

Godfrey paled for a moment. Then as the full import of Ian's words struck him, his face broke into a slow grin. "Good God, Ian, your 'future wife?' Sounds like cause for a celebration to me." He waved his hand at a boy who served a table nearby. "You there! Bring us some wine!"

Ian forced Godfrey's hand back down to the table. "I don't have time to celebrate tonight, though you can be sure I'll wish to later. But right now I want to know about that bloody rumor!"

Godfrey shrugged as he tugged his hand from Ian's grasp. "I've already told you all there is to tell, old boy. There's nothing more. I suppose Lawrence did it for a lark."

"*You*, my friend, begin gossip as a lark. Most people don't, however. And even you wouldn't ruin a girl's reputation without having a very good reason.

Deborah Martin

You'd be afraid of her father's wrath, for one thing."

"True, true," Godfrey said thoughtfully. "And even her father seemed to believe the rumor or he wouldn't have set up that marriage to Michaels."

"Which means that someone was awfully determined to make it look like more than just idle gossip. Someone decided to make good use of Esme's reputation for being a bit unmanageable, shall we say, so that the rumor was believable. And I have trouble accepting that Rushton would have casually told Lawrence who his mistress was, without fearing it would get back to her father, his close friend. He certainly wouldn't have invented such a story under those circumstances."

Godfrey looked at him curiously. "Funny you didn't find the story's origins suspect before. When Esme proclaimed her innocence, you didn't even suspect she might be telling the truth?"

Ian's face was grim as he acknowledged Godfrey's hit. "I'm afraid I was blinded by a few inconsequential past events. And I was angry about the rumor about me. That's why it's so important I know the whole truth now."

"Well, the 'whole truth' seems to lie with Lawrence, if you don't believe Rushton was party to it. And Lawrence was very definite. He claimed quite plainly that Rushton and the girl were embroiled in a torrid love affair."

As Ian's mouth tightened angrily, Godfrey hastened to add, "Of course, Lawrence should be thrashed soundly for such a lie."

Ian's face softened as he watched Godfrey's nervousness with amusement. "As I recall, it wasn't Lawrence who told me in the first place, so I wouldn't plan on having people thrashed just yet."

Godfrey smiled uncertainly and shifted his gaze

from Ian's. "Returning to the subject of the purpose behind the story, I can't imagine why Lawrence would say such a thing about your Miss Montrose. He's never had anything against her or her father as far as I know."

"Perhaps someone else did and persuaded him to do their dirty work. Does anyone come to mind?" Ian asked, leaning forward eagerly.

"No...unless it were someone he owed money to. He's a wretched gambler and is always losing his pay at the tables. Perhaps someone he owed convinced him to do it."

"Whom did he owe? Do you know?"

"As it is, I do know. He told me one time in a fit of desperation while trying to persuade me to join him in some foolish moneymaking scheme. It's probably no secret anyway, since he owed half of Bangkok. He had promissory notes with me, Harold, Rushton, and a score of merchants, including the man Esme was supposed to marry."

"You mean Michaels?" Ian asked incredulously.

"Yes, yes, him. But it can't be him. He wouldn't want the woman he planned to marry to have her reputation besmirched. He'd already asked for her hand twice, so we know he'd intended to marry her."

Ian sat quietly in thought for a moment before his face went rigid. "Doesn't it seem convenient to you that Lawrence made his revelation right after Michaels's suit had been twice refused? Isn't it possible Michaels decided to ensure that the next time he proposed, he'd get an acceptance?"

Godfrey sat up straighter. "And all he had to do was threaten to call his notes in on Lawrence to get him to comply!" he said excitedly. "After all, Michaels's request must have seemed paltry in comparison to Lawrence's debts."

"I can understand Michaels's obsession with her," Ian said, thinking of all he'd come to admire in Esme. "But how could he want her at such a price? Her honor destroyed, her spirit broken, her love withheld from him? The man's a fool. But fool or not, he'll get the punishment he deserves, I promise you."

"I wish you luck on that," Godfrey said, leaning back in his chair. "The man is—"

But he didn't get to finish before a commotion at the door drew his attention.

"Lord Winthrop! Lord Winthrop!" Prasert was shouting.

Ian swiveled around in his chair as he heard his name.

"I see him," a short Chinese man was saying. "Thanks for the help, boy. You may return to the house now." But Prasert loyally followed the man into the room until both men stood by the table where Godfrey and Ian sat.

"Who is this?" asked Godfrey.

"Never mind," Ian responded, rising from the table as he recognized Wong, the man he'd paid to keep an eye on Chan. "Go back to your card game. We can finish our discussion tomorrow."

"All right," Godfrey said. Then with a wicked glint in his eye, he added, "And tomorrow you can give me the full details of how you managed to entice the wench into doing your bidding."

His comment barely registered with Ian who was intent on dealing with Wong. "Return to the house, Prasert," he said curtly. Then he led Wong out, hissing in Cantonese, "What are you doing! I told you to keep our relationship a secret."

"No time for that," Wong stated. "Your man Mr. Chan is presently with an individual of suspicious character. He may be the one you seek."

"Here in Chiengmai?" Ian asked as he followed Wong out of the hotel. "That's odd. Surely if this man is Chan's contact, he'd know that his arrival here would arouse suspicion."

"I cannot be sure this is the man. But he's European. He speaks English. If we hurry, you may be able to determine if he's the one."

"All right. I suppose it's a possibility. I can't think of any reason Chan would be meeting with a European otherwise."

In just minutes, they reached the docks where Chan had been staying on board one of the many houseboats crowded along the river. Wong led the way through the maze of boats. Then he paused on the rickety wooden decks of one with his finger to his lips, and motioned to the cabin door of a boat opposite the one on which they stood. They heard men shouting, and Ian could make out Chan's voice. Wong nodded his head toward the sound, then ushered Ian into a cabin facing Chan's that he'd used for surveillance.

"There are two men's voices, so I assume the European hasn't left yet. I suggest, sir, we stay here until the man leaves," Wong said.

"Yes," Ian responded. "I don't want to arrest Chan until I'm certain this man is his contact. For now, I just want to determine if the European is anyone I know."

"I've been watching Chan's door through this," Wong told him, gesturing to an unobtrusive crack between the door and its frame. "When the European comes out, let me know what you wish me to do. This will all happen very quickly, so you may

371

wish for me to follow him to his lodgings. But I'm certain I'll need no help apprehending him if that's what you want."

"You don't know the man's name, do you?"

"No. His boat arrived from Bangkok very late this evening. I heard him say so when Mr. Chan opened the door. Mr. Chan seemed surprised to see him. Also angry. After the European entered the cabin, I could no longer hear their conversation."

"I suppose I've no choice but to wait," Ian said with resignation.

Wong nodded and sat on the floor with his eye glued to the crack in the frame. Ian stood leaning against the wall above him. From his position, he could easily put his eye to the crack when Wong gave the word.

While he waited, his mind wandered to Esme. He hoped she still slept. More importantly, he hoped he'd be back before she awakened. He hated to think of her waking alone, wondering where he'd gone, especially when he hadn't yet told her he loved her.

With a shock, he admitted to himself he did indeed love her. Even while he'd thought of marrying her, he hadn't said he'd do it for love. Yet he knew now that was why he'd been willing, even from the very beginning, to risk reputation, career, and his own carefully constructed image of himself to make her his. If he'd been acting on his reason, he'd have left her alone after that night at the ball. But something had made him go to her house, something had made him keep her with him the last few weeks when he knew he should send her away.

His pride had pushed him to fight her. His stupid, willful pride had insisted he shouldn't allow himself to be fooled by a woman again. But his instincts had steered him right as usual, leading him to pursue her with a vengeance. Thank God he'd listened to them instead of his pride. She was his now, by God, and he'd make her see it as soon as he could get back to her!

"The door's opening!" Wong suddenly hissed.

Ian placed his eye against the crack just in time to see a body knocked to the deck of the adjacent boat.

"Don't come back here again!" Chan shouted at the man whom he'd thrown bodily out of his cabin. "I'm leaving this behind me, no matter what you say. You've got what you wanted from me and I tell you, I won't help you with the other! You'll have to get the girl yourself!"

As the European slowly came to a stand on the deck, facing Chan with his back to Ian, Ian thought to himself there was something vaguely familiar about the balding slope of his head and his portly frame.

"I'll get you for this, Chan!" the European threatened. "No one crosses me and lives to tell about it! No one!"

Chan slammed the door in answer.

It took Ian a few seconds to make his decision. He couldn't be absolutely certain that the man, whose speech clearly showed him to be an Englishman, was the one he sought. But either way, the Englishman didn't plan to deal with Chan anymore. And it was possible Chan was leaving town. This might be Ian's last chance to catch both men. He had to take it.

"I want him," Ian said to Wong in an undertone. "You take him and I'll take Chan."

"Yes, sir!" the Chinese man replied and was out the door in seconds, slipping along the deck and after the European.

Deborah Martin

Ian waited a moment before crossing to the opposite boat and knocking on Chan's cabin door with his left hand, while he kept the right lightly resting on the hilt of his knife.

"Go away, Michaels!" Chan shouted from inside. "I told you I want nothing more to do with you!"

Ian froze. Michaels! Chan's contact was Michaels! That made sense. As a merchant, Michaels could easily transport stolen documents to France while still appearing loyal to the British. But why did Michaels want "the girl?" And who was she? Esme?

Impatiently, he knocked again at the door. It swung open immediately.

"I told you—" Chan said, and then broke off as he saw Ian. "Lord Winthrop! I—I wasn't expecting you."

"No doubt," Ian said dryly as he pushed Chan back into the room and took in the pile of franc notes on a table in the corner.

Chan's face fell as he saw what Ian was looking at, but he tried to cover his confusion. "It's rather late, sir. Couldn't we talk in the morning?"

Ian smiled, but his eyes were cold glittering stones. "You'd like that, wouldn't you? Then you could slip out and no one would ever know you for the spy that you are."

Chan paled, but Ian saw him reach under his coat.

"An unwise decision," Ian remarked as he swiftly withdrew his knife and held it to Chan's throat. "I would have no compunction about killing you after you tried to frame Esme."

"I don't know what you're talking about," Chan pleaded as Ian clasped his arm, throwing the man off guard, then rotated Chan until Chan's back was to him. Ian continued to hold the blade to his throat as he searched Chan's coat and found the knife Chan

374

had been attempting to retrieve. When he was satisfied that Chan was disarmed, he gripped the man around the waist, yanked him up against him, and held the knife more firmly against Chan's throat.

"I already know about your spying activities. Those papers you stole were planted there by me. They're worthless. So there's no point in denying anything. I only waited this long to seize you because I wanted to know who you worked for. Now that I know it's Michaels, there's no reason for me to refrain from arresting you or for you to keep from telling me everything."

"I have nothing to say," Chan said, but the trembling in his body betrayed his growing fear.

Ian regarded the back of Chan's head coldly. "You've been with me for several weeks now, Chan," he hissed. "You know that while I abhor violence, I don't hesitate to use it in defense of the country and the people I love. Right now I'm not concerned about the details of your operation. I know a good many of them already. What I want to know is how Esme fits into all this. What does Michaels want with her?"

Chan was silent, but his neck tensed as if to remove itself further from the blade of Ian's knife.

"I don't think you understand me," Ian said, pressing the tip of the knife into Chan's flesh so hard it pierced the skin and a tiny spot of blood began to form against the frightened man's neck. "All I have to say is you resisted me and I was forced to kill you."

"They're going to hang me anyway," Chan choked out.

"Quite possibly," Ian said. "But until they do, you have a chance to escape. And there's always the possibility they'll be more lenient with you if you cooperate. None of that will happen if you don't tell me now what I want to know.''

"All right," Chan muttered as Ian pressed the tip of the knife again into his flesh. Ian withdrew the knife a fraction of an inch. "Michaels once desired the girl's mother for his lover. Now he desires the daughter because she resembles the mother."

Knowing there must be more to the story, Ian moved the tip of the knife closer again. Chan continued hastily, "Esme's mother didn't commit suicide. Michaels faked her suicide while her husband was away, because she saw him steal some papers from the consulate and then witnessed his giving them to another spy. Esme was with her mother the second time."

A cold chill gripped Ian. "But surely he realizes Esme couldn't have understood what was going on? If she had, she'd have done something before now."

Chan nodded. "He'd thought he was safe, even though Esme's mother had claimed, before he killed her, that she'd left a note revealing the whole story. Then recently, when Esme started asking Rushton and her family questions about her mother's death, Michaels feared someone would stumble upon the truth, but he didn't dare kill her for fear it would look too suspicious."

Ian frowned, angry with himself for not putting the pieces together long before. Esme had been convinced her mother's suicide was suspicious. Why hadn't he looked into it further? Because, he admitted, none of the connections had been plain. Until now.

"Go on," Ian said harshly.

"Michaels claimed that was why he wanted to marry her—to silence her. But he's also as obsessed with her as he was with her mother."

Ian's face stiffened. "I've already seen evidence of that," he said half to himself. "What does he plan for her now?"

Chan hesitated. "He wants to kidnap her. He says after Esme ran away, her father found out about his plans, about the rumor he began, and refused him again. I suppose Michaels plans to kill her."

That bit of information so stunned Ian he almost released Chan. Then his grip tightened ruthlessly. "What did he want from you?" Ian asked in fury.

"He said he'd pay me more money if I told him where she was."

Ian felt hollow. "Did you?"

"Of course not!" Chan insisted. "I knew that would be a foolish risk! If he killed her, no one would believe it was suicide this time. He'd be caught and he'd tell them about me. I would have been a fool to help him."

Ian breathed a sigh of relief. He hoped Chan told the truth. Fortunately, Wong was most likely capturing Michaels at this very moment. But Ian knew he wouldn't feel Esme was completely safe until she was in his arms once again.

Chapter Nineteen

Esme opened her eyes, wondering why she felt so warm and secure. She shifted under the coverlet and stretched out her legs. The soreness between them startled her. And then she remembered what had happened the night before, and her face was suffused with color. She rolled to her side, but no one lay beside her. Had she dreamed she and Ian had made love?

No, she thought as she realized she was in his room and not her own. She'd actually done it. In spite of her promises to herself, in spite of her determination to resist him, she'd willingly let him take her to his bed.

She knew she should feel ashamed. But how could she when her mind was filled with the memory of the incredible warmth of his caresses and the tender words he'd whispered? A smile brightened her face as she recalled how deliciously wonderful their lovemaking had been. If she'd ever dreamed it would be like that, she thought wickedly, she might have stopped resisting him long ago.

She sat up in bed, cringing as she saw the blood on the coverlet. That blood was hers, she realized with a start. Ruefully, she acknowledged the blood had its uses. At least now Ian couldn't accuse her of having been Rushton's mistress.

But did he think she'd be his mistress now? she wondered with sudden panic. Could she? Now that she knew fully the intimacies involved, could she go to him night after night, knowing he could discard her at any moment for some other woman? Worse yet, what if he married and still wished her to be his mistress? What if he wanted to do those wonderful things with his wife and with her at the same time? She couldn't believe he could be so callous. Yet she knew some men did that, perfectly nice men like Henry Rushton.

She frowned, disturbed by the pictures those thoughts evoked. She didn't want to think of all that...not yet. For all she knew, Ian intended to marry her and she had nothing to worry about.

Yet how likely was it that Ian would wish to marry a nobody who'd lived all her life in Siam when he could have any stunning beauty in England he wanted? He was the son of an earl; he had a position to uphold.

Firmly, she told herself to stop thinking the worst. Until she'd talked to Ian and discovered what he intended to do with her, she shouldn't assume anything. Based on what he told her, she'd make whatever decisions she must.

As she glanced around the room, she wondered where he was. She didn't see the clothes he'd removed the night before. A blush heated her face as

Deborah Martin

she remembered how magnificent he'd looked unclothed.

Abruptly, she threw the covers off and climbed out of bed. She couldn't lie abed all morning, worrying about what Ian planned for her. She'd have to find him so they could talk. Hurriedly, she gathered her scattered clothing and dressed. She was certain Ian would return her clothes to her now, but until she found him, she'd have to wear her sarong.

She glided down the stairs, hoping to find Ian in the dining room eating breakfast. But a quick perusal of that room showed he wasn't there. Nor was he in the library or in the drawing room. She began to worry when she couldn't find him anywhere. Could he have left for the consulate without saying a word to her? Had last night really meant nothing to him?

She forced such traitorous thoughts from her head. It was too early for him to leave for the consulate. Besides, she couldn't believe he'd leave her alone after last night without saying anything. No, he must have gone out only for a moment. Her face brightened. Maybe he was out in the gardens. And if not there, then Prasert would know where he was.

Eagerly, she walked to the back of the house and out to the servants' quarters. Prasert was already up and dressed, his sword strapped to his back. He squatted outside his tiny room, eating a bowl of rice soup.

"*Mem!*" he said, surprised, standing up so abruptly he upset his bowl. "You want breakfast. I shall get it."

"No, Prasert," she said as she placed her hand on his arm to restrain him. "I wish to know where Lord Winthrop is."

Prasert looked at her in astonishment. "He has not returned? But he has been gone for a long time!"

Esme's first impulse was to be hurt that Ian had left the house so long ago without telling her. Then she realized that if Prasert was worried about him, Ian could be in danger.

"Where did he go?" she asked anxiously.

Prasert noted her distress and hastened to assure her. "Not to worry, *Mem*. Last time I saw him he was at the foreign hotel. I am sure he came to no harm."

"Oh?"she asked, puzzled at why Ian would leave her to go to the foreign hotel. Had he news of her father?

"Before he left the house, he told me he would be going there. He said he would return soon. Then a Chinese man came in search of him and I took the man to the hotel. Lord Winthrop was there with another foreigner. I suppose they were drinking."

Relief flooded through Esme as she realized Ian was probably safe. But her relief turned to hurt confusion as she realized Ian had left their bed to go drinking.

"Who was he with?" she asked Prasert, telling herself that perhaps her father had arrived.

"I don't know, *Mem*. I only saw the man for a moment, but I know I have never seen him before."

"What did he look like?" she persisted.

"Oh, *Mem*," he said with sudden excitement as he remembered something. "He was the strangest-looking man. He had red hair! I have never seen such a thing! Do many foreigners have red hair?"

"Not many," she said absently as she remembered one foreigner who had red hair—Godfrey. Ian had left her to drink with Godfrey, the notorious gossip. Her first impulse was to be furious, but she quelled that impulse as she told herself Ian might have had a good reason for meeting Godfrey.

"You really must not be anxious," Prasert said as she stood frowning, deep in thought. "I believe he was there to do business with the foreigner."

"Business?" she asked with a puzzled expression.

"Oh, yes, *Mem*, I am certain that was it. I heard the red-haired man say to Lord Winthrop that he wanted 'full details tomorrow of' . . . Now how did he say it?" Prasert paused, his brow furrowed. "Ah, yes, of 'how you managed to entice the wench into doing your bidding.' I remembered what he said because I don't know those words, 'entice' and 'wench,' and I wanted to ask what they meant. I know 'bidding' means 'bargaining.' But what do the other words mean?"

Prasert's words gave her an unexpected jolt. When he continued to look at her expectantly, she realized he wanted a response. "You'd best ask Lord Winthrop what those words mean," she said coldly as she felt a peculiar tightness in her chest. "I'm sure he'd be more than happy to explain them."

Yes, she thought bitterly, *he'll probably give you the "full details," too*. She suddenly felt very ill, knowing that Godfrey knew everything.

"I'll go get your breakfast now," Prasert said, unperturbed by her peculiar manner, but she hadn't heard him or noticed when he strolled down the lawn to the outdoor kitchen.

Her stomach twisted into knots as she fought back the urge to cry. She'd been such a fool! While she'd been worrying about Ian's welfare, he'd been out boasting of his success with her to the very man who'd destroyed her reputation! How could he? How could he have casually shared something so intimate, especially with a man like Godfrey?

Her hands tightened into fists at the thought of the two of them laughing over her innocent trust. She'd given herself freely to Ian, believing he cared for her. She'd been so naive! He hadn't cared for her at all!

What could she have been thinking to make her behave so stupidly? She'd known from the beginning Ian was famous for his conquests; she'd heard the stories at the ball like everyone else. He'd never said he loved her, never made any promises. But she'd been foolish enough to think that despite all that, despite his station and position, he'd stoop to love her, even perhaps to marry her.

She groaned as she remembered the words she'd spoken to him and the wanton way she'd responded to his expert lovemaking. "Oh, God," she murmured aloud as vague images of her drawing him back into her arms a second time flitted through her mind. The second time...She'd been half-asleep, just groggy enough to be uninhibited. She had said and done things, unspeakable things, with him.

How could she face him now? She could just see him coming in the door half-drunk, arrogantly certain she would now do "his bidding" for as long as he found her amusing.

She shook off her self-pity as a slow-burning anger replaced it. How dare he? How dare he assume that just because she'd yielded to him, she could be treated like a—a prostitute!

With a bleak emptiness inside her, she considered her alternatives. She could stay and unleash her fury on him. But what good would that do? He would toss her some explanation and then kiss her in that way he had, and she'd find her body betraying her again. She could insist he marry her because he'd ruined her. Yet she had too much pride for that. She didn't think she could bear his rejecting her, telling her he'd never want someone like her for a wife.

No, she must leave. But she couldn't go to the consulate. She'd be too ashamed to face them, knowing the things Godfrey must already be saying about her. There was always Harold. But no, she couldn't ask him for help. He'd think she wished to accept his offer of marriage, and she hadn't sunk as low as marrying a man out of spite.

Paying no heed to the delicate silk fabric of her sarong, she plopped down on the wooden stoop of Prasert's room. Where else could she go? She only knew five people in Chiengmai—Ian, Godfrey, Harold, Chan, and . . . and Reverend Taylor! She leaped to her feet. He would help her! She couldn't believe she hadn't thought of him before. He'd always been so kind to her. Surely he wouldn't fail her now!

Then she turned crimson as she wondered if he'd heard she was living in Ian's house. He might turn her away if he knew. No, she decided, not Reverend Taylor. If anyone would understand her predicament, it would be he. In fact, perhaps he could help her avoid her father and escape her marriage to Michaels.

But how could she get away, with Prasert watching her every move and refusing to relinquish her belongings? A grin curved the edges of her mouth. She glanced down the lawn to the kitchen, but she could see no evidence of Prasert. Swiftly, she slipped into his room. Her clothes had to be there somewhere, since Ian had ordered Prasert to keep them.

She searched frantically through the tiny room, relieved that the Siamese, being Buddhist, lived sparsely with few possessions to clutter their lives.

In seconds, she'd found her bag stashed away in the corner of Prasert's room. At least she had clothes. But what about the keys to the gate? Was it possible Prasert kept them in his room, too?

A quick search of the room revealed she was in luck. Hanging on a nail in the corner was a ring of keys she assumed belonged to the house. She clasped the bag and the keys against her chest and darted out of his room and into the house, depositing her belongings in a dark corner of the pantry. As she went back out to seek Prasert, she cursed herself for not having tried to escape before. But she knew if she were honest with herself, she'd admit that until now, she had wanted to stay with Ian. She chided herself for that and then sighed at the fruitlessness of having such regrets. At least she'd come to her senses before her father had arrived.

When she found Prasert, he was gaily talking to the Siamese cook who was frying meat in a pan.

"Prasert," she told him plaintively. "I don't wish to have any breakfast. I feel a little ill. I think I'll lie down until Lord Winthrop returns."

Prasert's eyes widened in alarm. "Is there something I can do for *Mem*?" he asked, concerned.

"No, no!" she hastened to tell him, feeling wretched for deceiving him. "I'll be fine after I rest. I just need some time alone."

"Certainly!" he murmured. "But if *Mem* should wish anything, just call to me and I will get it for you."

"Thank you," she said softly, managing a weak smile. "But you needn't worry about me for the next few hours."

Then she strolled back to the house, trying to appear nonchalant. But when she entered the pantry, she moved quickly, changing into her Siamese boy's clothing and braiding her hair. She decided to strap her knife to her calf underneath her trousers. She wished she could leave Ian's gift behind, but after what had happened with Henley, she knew she dared not. Then she strode to the front of the house, bag in hand.

Once outside, she gave one cursory glance back to the place where she'd given her virtue away to a man who scorned her love. Then determinedly she turned away. Her hands shaking, she tried several keys until she found one that unlocked the gate door. As quietly as she could, she opened the door. Leaving the ring of keys hanging on an inside nail, she darted into the street. She held her breath in fear that Prasert would hear the gate door as she pulled it closed. But evidently he was too engrossed in his conversation with the cook to notice she was leaving. In moments, she was down the street and gone.

Ian was exhausted as he knocked at the gate door to his lodgings. He'd spent four grueling hours on the boat with Chan. He could have brought Chan to the consulate, but until he was certain Chan and Michaels were the only ones involved in the spying, he had to keep his mission secret. So he'd questioned Chan at the boat and waited for Wong to return with Michaels. But when Wong had finally appeared, it was to tell Ian that Michaels had eluded him. At that news, Ian had left Chan in Wong's hands and had hurried back to his lodgings. He didn't think Michaels had had time to discover where Esme was staying and kidnap her, but he was taking no chances.

Now all he wanted was to determine she was safe.

Then he planned to take a hot bath and drop into bed. Preferably with Esme by his side, he thought with a weary smile.

Impatiently he pounded on the door again. When no one came, he tried the handle and the door opened. A sudden chill gripped him. Prasert never left the gate door unlocked. Drawing his knife, he approached the house stealthily. When he entered, he heard nothing. With a sickening lurch, Ian realized that if Michaels were in the house with Esme, the pounding on the gate door would have warned him of Ian's approach.

He carefully ascended the stairs to his bedroom, hoping against hope Esme would be in bed, still asleep. But she wasn't. Ian crept from room to room, terrified of what he might find. He'd just finished with the last bedroom when he heard someone on the stairs. He crouched immobile, ready to attack.

But the person who emerged at the top was Prasert.

"Lord Winthrop!" he cried in surprise, his expression changing to one of fear as he saw Ian with knife in hand, ready to pounce on him.

Ian straightened and sheathed his knife. "Where's *Mem* Esme?"

Prasert looked at him with an irritation that lingered from the fright Ian had given him. "Very funny, *Than*. She asks where you are, you ask where she is . . . You are both making me into a crazy person!"

"You saw Esme this morning?"

"Of course," Prasert answered with greater respect as he remembered his place. "She came outside and asked where you went. She was very worried, *Than*, when I said you left many hours ago.

387

She told me she felt ill and would be asleep for many hours. I did not wish to disturb her, so I left her alone. Have you checked the bedrooms?''

"All of them," Ian said, groaning inwardly. He wished he'd told his faithful servant what to do if Esme woke up looking for him. But Ian simply hadn't expected to be gone so long.

"That is very odd," Prasert said. "I told her you were at the hotel, because she seemed so anxious about you. I told her you were drinking with a foreigner with red hair and not to worry, but that only upset her more."

Ian's blood ran cold. The only foreigner she knew with red hair was Godfrey. Prasert had, understandably, led her to believe Ian was out on the town with Godfrey. He could only imagine what she'd made of that, and whatever it was, it wasn't good. He'd have some explaining to do when he found her. But first, he had to find her.

"Tell me exactly what you said to her," Ian demanded.

Prasert related the entire conversation. When he came to the part about Godfrey's comment, Ian's face twisted in anguish as he silently cursed his friend's glib tongue.

"We've got to find her," Ian stated. "I've already checked up here. You search the grounds while I search downstairs."

Without even pausing to explain further, Ian dashed downstairs. With grim determination, he combed the rooms of the first floor while Prasert searched the grounds and the servants' quarters, but neither of them found anything.

"What was she wearing when you saw her last?" Ian asked Prasert, who had come up behind him.

"What she has been wearing—the dress of my people."

Ian didn't think she'd leave the house in that. Not after what had happened at the docks when she'd worn it before. "You didn't return her clothes to her, did you?"

"No, sir! You gave me an order. I do as you command."

A terrible thought struck Ian. Prasert had said she was outside when they had talked. Outside by the servants' quarters.

"Fetch me her bag!" Ian ordered. "I want it now!"

Prasert scurried out of the house to do his master's bidding. But when he didn't return immediately, Ian followed him. He found Prasert in his small room, tossing his belongings about frantically.

"She took it, didn't she?" Ian said in a voice that scarcely hid his growing dread.

"I—I do not know who took it," Prasert stammered, trying bravely to hide his consternation. "But it's gone!"

In a daze, Ian walked back to the house. She was gone. Somewhere out there a man wanted to kill her and she was unprotected. She was alone, hurting, convinced he didn't care for her, and it was all his fault.

With leaden feet, he entered the house. He didn't blame himself for leaving her so long alone. That was the result of circumstances beyond his control. What he blamed himself for was never showing her just how much she meant to him. Over and over he'd told her he wanted only to bed her. True, he'd shown commendable restraint until last night. Nonetheless, he'd made certain she came to him despite her fears and reservations. And when at last

389

she'd willingly succumbed to her desires, he'd still questioned her motives, accusing her of teasing him. Even after he'd discovered the truth, he'd made love to her twice and never once said he loved her or wanted to marry her. He couldn't blame her for thinking he didn't care. What else was she to think?

He trudged into the library. He was paying now for all those weeks of mistrust, for refusing to see what she really was. But he wouldn't let it end there. He'd find her before Michaels did, if it meant searching the entire town inch by inch!

"Please, sir, I did not know she wished to leave or I would never have left her alone by my room," Prasert said with remorse as he entered the library. "She seemed so concerned for you when I told her how long you had been gone. I—I never thought—"

"It's all right, Prasert," Ian said absently. "I don't blame you. I just want to find her now. She...she could be in danger."

Prasert straightened, his hand moving to his sword. "I will help you, sir! We will find her. Everyone must have noticed a *farang* girl walking through the city alone. She will be easy to find!" he said confidently.

Ian's voice was tinged with bitterness. "Unfortunately, she's probably not dressed as a *farang*. I have no doubt she's wearing her disguise."

Prasert's face fell. Then he brightened. "Ah, but, still, she is unusual. She looks Eurasian and wears her hair as Chinese do, not as Siamese. I tell you, sir, we will find her."

"I hope so," Ian said softly. "I hope so."

But several hours later when a search of the consulate, the foreign hotel, and all local places of refuge had turned up nothing, Ian wasn't so certain. Ian had posted a hired guard on Chan and sent Wong out to track Michaels, but Wong had had little luck in finding the merchant. Esme and Michaels were both somewhere in the city. Ian could only pray they weren't together. Fortunately, Michaels had never seen Esme in her disguise, so he wouldn't recognize her dressed as she was. But the disguise made it so much harder for Ian to find her that he almost wished she weren't wearing it.

When he found her, Ian thought, he'd make sure she never left him again if he had to tie her to him with a rope. But first he'd tell her he loved her as many times as it took to convince her he did.

"Where do we go now, *Than*?" Prasert asked, bringing him out of his reverie.

"Back to the house, I think. I know of nowhere else to look and in a few hours I'm expected at the palace. Your prince has a great many spies in Chiengmai. Maybe one of them can tell us where to search. If not—"

"He will help you," Prasert assured him. "He likes you because you know the Siamese ways and you treat him with courtesy. You are not like those other men who come with their big words but think Siam is a backward nation."

Ian smiled and thought how ironic it was that the woman who'd taught him so much about Siam had made it possible for him to ask a favor of a monarch, a favor that involved finding her when she didn't want to be found. His face softened as he looked at Prasert. Perhaps the boy was right. Perhaps they would find Esme after all. He certainly hoped so.

* * *

Deborah Martin

Esme lay on the bed, staring at the spartan furnishings of her room. Reverend Taylor had been kind to her, even though most of his fellow missionaries had been disapproving when she'd come to the door dressed in Siamese boy's clothes. The women in particular had eyed her suspiciously. But she'd been fortunate that Mrs. Calvert, the widow she'd known in Bangkok, still taught at the mission school. She'd taken Reverend Taylor's side and offered Esme a room in her small house. It was nothing more than a servant's room, but Esme didn't care. She was just glad she'd managed to get away before Ian had returned.

She rolled over and pressed her face in the pillow that was already wet with her tears. How was she to endure the terrible ache that spread through her every time she even thought of Ian? Try as she might, she couldn't get him out of her blood. She kept hearing him say, "I promise I won't ever hurt you again." Was it possible he'd meant it? Had she been too hasty?

No, she told herself firmly. She was just thinking wishfully as she always had. She was trusting him to keep his word when he'd shown her time and again he didn't deserve her trust. She was attributing to him the emotions she wanted him to feel. If he'd loved her, he'd have told her so. If he'd cared at all, he wouldn't have told the prince about her or revealed their intimacy to Godfrey. No, he wanted her only because he was interested in conquests.

She kept reminding herself of his perfidy as she tried to thrust out of her mind the image of him taking her with tender sweetness. But she couldn't shake the feeling that she'd made a mistake she might regret for the rest of her life.

Someone knocked at the door, giving her a welcome respite from her mournful thoughts.

"Come in!" she called out as she sat up on the edge of the bed and was pleased when Reverend Taylor entered the room with Mrs. Calvert on his heels.

"How are you feeling, child?" he asked, his brown eyes warming as he observed that she'd changed into her English clothes.

"Better," she said. "I can't thank you both enough for taking me in. Ian . . . I mean, Lord Winthrop intended to protect me from my father's ire and convince him to end my betrothal, but I—I couldn't let his lordship do that."

When she'd come to the mission, she'd stuck to her original reason for wanting to leave Ian because she couldn't bear to voice her real reasons. But she knew the reverend realized the story was more complicated than she claimed. He'd been aware on the boat of the way things stood between her and Ian.

"Horace and I understand completely," Mrs. Calvert said with a shy smile in Reverend Taylor's direction. "Some men are just too gallant for their own good. But you did the right thing, dear, by coming here."

Even in her depressed state, Esme couldn't help but notice that Mrs. Calvert's eyes lit up when she spoke to "Horace." And he didn't seem immune to her charms, either. At least someone had found happiness, she thought, resolving not to ruin their enjoyment with her own problems.

"There is something we have to talk about," Reverend Taylor said hesitantly, his eyes lowering to the floor.

"Yes?" she asked, puzzled by his sudden refusal to look at her.

"I'm afraid, child, that Lord Winthrop knows you're here."

"What!" she exclaimed, starting up from the bed. "But how could he know so soon?"

"I don't know," Reverend Taylor said. "But a messenger from Prince Mataya arrived a few minutes ago, who is asking specifically to speak to you. Obviously the prince knows you're here. And how else would he know your whereabouts unless Lord Winthrop told him?"

Esme's heart sank. *How else indeed?* she thought. Then she remembered what Lamoon and Mai had told her about the network of loyal servants men in power often had in foreign households. It was quite likely the prince had spies in the mission community.

"There's a possibility Lord Winthrop doesn't know. Prince Mataya might be aware of my presence here because of...of...well, other things." She didn't want to alarm Reverend Taylor needlessly by telling him that someone who worked for the prince might be a member of his small community. "But I suppose we should determine what he wants."

"I think that would be best," the reverend said with a note of relief in his voice. "Come this way," he told her, leading her to the tiny room of the house that served both as dining room and parlor.

With trembling, hands, Esme introduced herself in Siamese to the messenger and invited him to be seated. He didn't seem at all surprised by her knowledge of the language. He spoke the usual opening pleasantries to her and she responded in kind, wondering all the while what the purpose of his visit was. At last, he withdrew a scroll from his pocket and unrolled it.

"His Royal Highness Prince Mataya," he read aloud with great formality, "commands the presence of Miss Esme at a theatrical entertainment to be held at the palace this evening."

Esme sat there in stunned silence. Reverend Taylor and Mrs. Calvert both understood the message and stared at the messenger in disbelief.

"Why me?" Esme asked the messenger without thinking.

He seemed annoyed she should even appear to question a direct command of his prince, but he shrugged his shoulders and replied anyway. "His Royal Highness wishes to meet you," he said, as if that answered the question.

Esme's mind reeled in confusion as she wondered what the invitation meant. Had Ian convinced the prince to intercede on his behalf? She couldn't believe he'd involve a royal personage in his personal life, especially a foreign one. Yet, if he was willing to gossip about her with Godfrey, it was quite possible he'd have no compunction about asking the prince for a favor. She tensed as she remembered what Harold had said—that Ian had already told the prince about her and had even agreed to arrange a meeting.

She stiffened angrily. Yes, Ian must be behind all this. But if he meant to humble her by making their relationship public, she wouldn't give him that satisfaction. She couldn't refuse the prince's command, thus causing His Royal Highness to lose face. To do so would jeopardize the work of the missionaries who'd been kind enough to take her in. But an idea occurred to her, causing her face to crease

Deborah Martin

in a grin. Perhaps there was another way to get out of going.

She rose unsteadily to her feet and faced the messenger who seemed to be waiting for her acceptance of the invitation. She *waied* very prettily before giving her answer.

"Sir," she said with as much politeness as she could muster. "I am very honored by His Royal Highness's desire to have me as a guest. And I would be extremely pleased to attend. Unfortunately, I don't own the attire appropriate for such a splendid affair. This dress and some more humble clothes are all I have. I wouldn't wish to offend the prince by arriving in such clothing. Perhaps you should explain this to His Highness. He may wish to postpone my appearance until a time when I can dress in clothing more suitable to his exalted eyes."

The messenger smiled. "His Royal Highness informed me you might voice such an objection. He is aware of the problem and thus has sent a gift that he is certain will remove any impediment to your attendance."

Swiftly, the messenger clapped his hands and two Siamese men entered with a small trunk. The messenger opened the trunk, revealing rich burgundy satin that Esme realized with a sinking heart was clothing. Her conclusion was confirmed when the messenger lifted the cloth out of the trunk, revealing it to be a simple, but elegant, evening gown that looked as if it would fit her perfectly.

The messenger's face was inscrutable as he watched Esme's reaction. "His Royal Highness had it made for you," he said, "after Lord Winthrop agreed two nights ago to escort you to the theatrical entertainment. The prince seemed to believe you would be inadequately equipped for such an occasion."

Esme colored as she realized how the prince would know she didn't have a gown. She hesitated to believe Ian had told him, for Ian wouldn't want another man giving her dresses. No, Ian's lodgings were, as she'd suspected, provided by the prince. And Prasert was probably one of the prince's servants. Since Prasert had been holding her clothes, it would have been an easy matter for him to take her measurements from her clothes and send them to a seamstress so a dress could be made for her.

She tensed with anger. How easily all her plans were destroyed whenever it suited someone to do so. It was all she could do to keep from throwing the gown in the messenger's face. She'd had enough of people controlling the events of her life without even consulting her!

But as Reverend Taylor looked at her questioningly, Esme acknowledged that again she had no choice. She had to obey the prince's command or risk destroying the work of good people like Horace Taylor.

"You accept the gift?" the messenger asked, although it was more of a statement than a question.

"Yes," she replied, trying to force a smile to her lips.

"A carriage will be here for you at eight o'clock. You will be ready then," he stated with more assurance.

"As His Royal Highness wishes," she said dully.

"Very good." Then he spoke the usual closing amenities, to which she responded with an ill-concealed lack of enthusiasm. Finally he left.

"Why have you been issued such an invitation,

child?" Reverend Taylor asked anxiously as she sank into a chair.

"I really don't know."

"But I don't understand—" he began.

"Nor do I. Either Ian wants me there for some reason of his own or His Royal Highness really does wish to meet me. I can't imagine why a prince would want to meet *me*. But I don't think Ian would risk his reputation just to see me. I suppose it's possible Ian won't even be there. I certainly hope that's the case."

"Do you really wish to be parted from him, Esme?" Reverend Taylor asked as he sat in the chair beside her and patted her hand.

Mrs. Calvert watched in silence, but Esme sensed she knew more about the situation than Esme had at first realized.

"If I thought he really cared for me, I'd return," she said, leaving unspoken the fact that she'd be his mistress if that was what it took. "But I can't bear to be with him, knowing the kind of man he is and the way he feels about me."

Reverend Taylor glanced at Mrs. Calvert before he took both of Esme's hands in his. "I think you've misjudged him," he said kindly as she looked at him in expectation, knowing that he would give her sound advice. "Lord Winthrop isn't the kind of man to misuse a woman—not purposely. He's probably much like most men, unaccustomed to telling a woman how he feels. But he'll learn if you give him time. Don't close your mind to him yet, child. Not until you're certain you're right."

Esme's eyes fell to her hands, which tightly squeezed the reverend's. She wanted to believe him but she was afraid to. If he were right, she'd have to accept that she'd refused the only man she could ever love. And that possibility was so hard to face that she told herself Reverend Taylor was wrong. He didn't know Ian like she knew him.

"I already know I'm right," she told Reverend Taylor passionately.

But her heart didn't agree and she knew it.

Chapter Twenty

As the royal carriage bumped through the dirt roads of Chiengmai, Esme's hand slid down her leg to touch the knife strapped securely to her calf. It seemed so incongruous wearing it while she was dressed in such finery. But she didn't know how the evening might end. She might find she had to return to the mission alone or on foot, and she had no desire to run unprotected through the streets of Chiengmai.

She hoped, however, she wouldn't be forced to return to the mission on her own. Her flight from Ian's lodgings that morning had taught her Chiengmai was no place for her to be alone. The town wasn't really dangerous, particularly since it wasn't a port city; so no foreign sailors and pirates milled about to cause trouble. But Chiengmai's oddly mixed population of Lao, Chinese, hill tribesmen, Burmese, and Siamese spoke a variety of distinct languages. It hadn't been easy that morning to find someone she could talk to. And if she'd found it difficult getting responses to her questions as Lek, she'd certainly have trouble doing so dressed in a ball gown.

When the carriage entered the palace gates, she stared about her. Until that moment, she'd dreaded the coming evening. But the sight of the immaculately groomed grounds, with their bushes trimmed in the shapes of animals and birds, cheered her as she realized she'd never before seen a palace. She'd always wanted to see the great king's palace in Bangkok, but she was certain the prince's in Chiengmai would be nearly as fascinating.

Eagerly she craned her head forward in an effort to glimpse the palace through the carriage window. In moments her attempts were rewarded as the carriage neared a building standing at the front of a large group of opulent structures. It reminded her of temples in Bangkok. The high marble walls were surrounded by galleries fronted with pillars that stretched to the red tile roof. The roof sloped downward on both sides to curve upward at the ends. She knew the gabled roof was intended to prevent evil spirits from entering the house. The Siamese wanted to ensure that, when spirits dropped from the sky and slid down the roof, they'd reach the curved ends and be tossed back up into the sky.

But the roof wasn't the only concession the Siamese had made to "the spirits." There was also a miniature house in front of the first palace building that was meant for the spirits of one's ancestors. She knew it was probably even now equipped with food and drink for those spirits.

As the carriage drew up in front of the first palace building, she could see lights glowing through the tall windows cut every few feet in the walls. The music of a Siamese orchestra tinkled and twanged in the darkness.

She suddenly felt very self-conscious. She was about to meet a Siamese prince! That thought made her extremely nervous. But at least she was dressed appropriately. In addition to the gown, the prince had sent a pair of satin slippers and two lace-edged taffeta petticoats. Mrs. Calvert had arranged Esme's hair for her and loaned her some gloves. Esme glanced down at the rich gown she wore and smiled with satisfaction.

Then her eyes fell on the dress's low cleavage, and her satisfaction vanished. This gown was nothing like the one she'd worn to Blythe Rushton's ball. With its sensuous lines and deep neckline, it was clearly meant for a woman, not a virginal girl. But, in spite of herself, some feminine instinct deep within her reveled at the chance to look beautiful to Ian. Why did she feel this way even after all that had happened between them?

A dark frown passed over her brow as the carriage drew up to the palace. She might feel this way inside, but at least she could mask her feelings in public. She'd show him he meant nothing to her, that she shared his nonchalant attitude toward their joining. She would push him away verbally, if not physically, so he wouldn't ever hurt her again.

As the palace servants stepped forward to assist her from the carriage, she wiped the frown from her face and climbed down, her head held high. He wouldn't make a fool of her again, she resolved. And when the evening was over and she returned at last to the mission, she'd put Ian firmly out of her mind once and for all! Having made that resolution, she fixed a smile on her face and followed the servant who led her through the tiled corridors of the palace.

They stopped before a doorway while her name was announced. Idly, she wondered why the prince's servants continued to call her Miss Esme. Surely if Ian had asked the prince to invite her, he'd also have told the prince her full name? In the split second before she entered the room where the prince received guests, she realized her first assumption might have been correct. Prince Mataya might have discovered her presence at the mission through his spies. After all, Ian had never used her last name in front of any of the servants. There was a very real possibility he might not even know she was coming.

She had no time to think about that, for she was entering the room full of more than a dozen foreigners, most of whom she didn't know. Yet their eyes were all on her, filled with curiosity, with the exception of Harold and Godfrey, who both seemed surprised to see her.

She noticed the others only briefly, however, because standing almost directly in front of her with a stunned look on his face was Ian. His silvery eyes traveled over her with ill-concealed astonishment at her attire. Then they glittered with fury. She barely had time to note that he too looked absolutely stunning in his black frock coat and claret silk ascot, because oblivious to everyone's eyes on them, he strode toward her. She braced herself to meet him with a bland expression.

"Where the hell have you been?" he hissed. His hand closed on her arm with painful insistence as he reached her.

"Lord Winthrop!" she exclaimed loudly with a

coy smile, as if he were a casual acquaintance. "So good to see you again."

He ignored her attempt at nonchalance. "Do you have any idea how worried I've been?" he asked, his gray eyes darkening like clouds before a storm.

The smile faded slightly from her face. "I'm surprised to see you show such concern for a lowly *servant* like me."

The taut lines around his mouth softened as it registered that she'd spoken the same term he'd used to describe her to the prince. But the firmness of his grip didn't lessen as he tried steering her toward a doorway leading out onto one of the galleries. She refused to move, holding herself as rigidly remote from him as possible even while her heart thundered in her ears.

"I know you're angry," he muttered under his breath. "And you've every right to be, but I can explain. We need to talk, but not here with all these people. Come outside with me."

She knew she dared not. He'd just kiss her and then she'd accept whatever he said. But later, when she had time to remember, she'd hate herself for having allowed him to manipulate her.

"I can't imagine what we could possibly have to talk about," she said, trying bravely to sound aloof.

Did she imagine it or did a flash of pain cross his face? She couldn't believe it. She didn't think anything she said could hurt *him* as much as he'd hurt her. Still, she was convinced as she stared up into his bleak eyes that he wasn't entirely immune to the despair she attempted to mask.

"Please come outside with me," he whispered fervently, his hand tightening on her arm. "I've been like a madman searching for you ever since I returned to find you gone. You at least owe me the chance to explain why I left last night."

She felt trapped by the palpable pleading in his eyes. *I will not listen to him. I will not!* she thought, but she feared if he held her there much longer she would. She tried to wrest her arm unobtrusively out of his grasp, but he wouldn't release her and she didn't want to make a commotion in front of so many people. Glancing desperately around the room, she looked for someone to help her. Her eyes fell on Godfrey. With a smile, he lifted his glass to her and she froze as the blood rushed to her face.

Ian followed her gaze in time to catch Godfrey's gesture.

"You told him about what we . . . You told him, didn't you?" she said in a small voice, her entire body quieting for a moment in tortured shame.

Ian hesitated long enough to convince her that he had.

"Let go of me! I don't want you touching me!" she cried, no longer caring who noticed as she tried to jerk her arm free.

"It's not what you think!" he told her, refusing to relinquish her arm.

"You don't know what I think!" she cried. "And don't pretend you care!"

He clenched his teeth and began to push her toward the gallery doors. "We're going outside, if I have to drag you there."

But before he could make good his threat, a Siamese servant stepped into the room and announced the arrival of His Royal Highness, Prince Mataya. Esme sighed with relief at the timely reprieve, only to realize that Ian refused to release her arm, although he'd halted his move toward the gallery. She stood in numbed silence beside him.

She scarcely noticed when the prince entered the

room, she was so aware of Ian's body next to hers, the sleeve of his coat barely brushing her arm. Only when the prince came to stand at the center of the room did she really look at him. He wore a long robe of golden thread over an ivory silk European-style shirt with an embroidered *panung*, a long piece of cloth Siamese men wrapped around their waists and between their legs, leaving the calves bare. His jeweled slippers glittered in the light.

As she gazed at him, she noticed he was the kind of man one would consider handsome, with his light brown skin and almond-shaped eyes. But she was too conscious of the affect Ian was having on her, as he stood beside her in his immaculate evening dress, for her to think any man handsome at that moment except Ian. The thought upset her. Why did it have to be Ian, she wondered, who captured her heart? Why couldn't it have been someone else, someone like Harold?

She sensed that Ian's eyes were on her, but she refused to look at him, her eyes riveted on the prince. She tried to ignore the sensations flooding through her at the touch of Ian's hand on her arm, but it was difficult. Her body trembled so much at the heightened awareness his nearness created in her that she had to force herself to take note of the prince. Belatedly, she realized he was moving toward them with a stiff air of regal superiority. But once he reached Ian, he relaxed, a warm grin crossing his face.

Ian released her arm, giving a deep bow. Instantly, she realized a curtsy would be expected of her and she gave it, hoping she hadn't hesitated too long. But the Siamese prince seemed unaware of her error, including her in the broad smile he flashed Ian.

"So very good to see you again, Lord Winthrop," the prince said in heavily accented French.

"I am honored by your notice, Your Royal Highness," Ian responded with a slight bow of his head.

The prince's grin widened as he turned to Esme. "And I suppose this lovely lady is Miss Esme, the ...ah... servant that you've kept so well hidden," he said, his eyes approving as he took in her appearance.

Before she could set him straight about who she was, Ian's voice stopped her. "I'm afraid," Ian said, "that things have changed, Your Royal Highness, since I told you Miss Montrose was my servant."

Esme stared down at the floor in horror, aware that everyone in the room listened to their conversation. She was mortified that Ian would do this to her, that he would announce her status as his mistress to the whole world!

"You see," he continued, "Miss Montrose is my fiancée. We were keeping it secret until her father arrived and I could ask him formally for her hand. But I believe it would be better to announce it now, don't you, dear?"

His words so stunned her she couldn't speak, but only nodded her head slightly as her eyes met the prince's. His Highness seemed to be laughing as he took in her discomfiture, although his expression didn't alter from the one he'd assumed of polite interest.

"Then I must apologize," Prince Mataya said cordially. "I suppose you British would consider the gift I sent your fiancée most inappropriate."

"Gift?" Ian said in confusion, taken completely off guard.

"Oh, no, Your Royal Highness," Esme interjected in flawless French. This time it was her turn to sur-

407

Deborah Martin

prise Ian. "The gown didn't offend me. It's truly
lovely, and I thank you for it. I'm certain his lordship agrees."

"Yes," Ian said stiffly, but Esme knew he wasn't
happy about the prince's having given her a gown.

Stubbornly, she told herself she didn't care. But
she knew she did, especially since he'd attempted
to save her reputation by announcing he planned
to marry her. She didn't believe he really intended
to, but she welcomed his gesture.

"Lord Winthrop didn't tell me how lovely you
are," Prince Mataya said, suddenly switching to Siamese. "I can understand why he would wish to
keep you at his side."

"Your Highness is too kind," she said in Siamese,
bringing a smile of pleasure to the prince's lips.

Ian stiffened beside her, but dared not question
why they spoke in a language he didn't understand.

"I hope you did not mind my inviting you here
with so little time for preparation," Prince Mataya
said, his eyes twinkling mischievously. "My servant, Prasert, seemed to feel intervention was necessary. He knows I admire Lord Winthrop and wish
to show my gratitude for his efforts in keeping the
peace. My servant thought this would be the best
way to do so."

Esme weighed her words carefully. She dared not
let her feelings for Ian jeopardize the future tone of
the negotiations. "Your Royal Highness is a most
generous man. I'm certain Lord Winthrop will appreciate your show of gratitude." Even if she didn't,
she thought.

Prince Mataya smiled slightly. "His lordship is
indeed blessed. Not only will he have a wife of sur-
passing beauty, he will also have one who is as
adept at diplomacy as he is."

Then the prince moved on to greet each of the other guests in Siamese as the interpreter translated his words into English as necessary.

"What did he say?" Ian murmured, his hand clasping her arm again.

"I don't think I'll tell you," she whispered. "At least, not until you release me."

"Don't tell me then," he replied without loosening his grip. "It makes no difference."

She turned her eyes to him pleadingly, but he met her gaze with steady assurance. His face held no hint of a smile as his eyes stared at her. He lifted his eyebrows in a silent question.

She didn't know what question he wanted answered, so she turned her head away from him. Then his thumb stroked her arm. She stiffened, yet he continued to rub the tender soft skin on the underside of her arm until she felt herself relaxing. That one touch was enough to fire her memories of the night before. Without thinking, she lifted her free hand to her throat as if to pull a collar tighter around her neck but there was nothing there to draw together. She felt uncomfortably exposed, but a glance around the room showed her that the other women were dressed no less immodestly than she.

The prince had finished his formal greetings and was now talking casually with one of the men from the consulate, the signal to everyone else that they could begin again to converse among themselves. Esme tried again to remove her arm from Ian's grasp, but he refused to free it.

"Please let me go," she spoke in an undertone, her voice trembling with the emotions she sought to control.

"Not until you agree to speak with me alone later," he replied in a low voice.

"Why? It was kind of you to tell the prince I was your fiancée, but I won't hold you to it. I know you didn't mean it."

"And what if I did? Would you have me?"

His words, spoken in a husky voice of passion, thrilled her with their obvious sincerity. Did he really mean it? Did he intend to marry her? Then she sobered. Perhaps he did. But if so, it was because of his sense of honor. It would be just like him to feel he must marry her because he'd taken her virginity. Yes, that must be it.

She was tempted to say yes, to accept his offer. But she couldn't, not when she loved him so much. In time, his lack of love for her, his cavalier attitude toward their relationship, would torment her. She couldn't accept anything less than his love or she'd be unhappy her entire life.

"Would you?" he repeated softly.

"No," she said in a voice that was barely a whisper.

His reaction to her answer surprised her. She'd expected to see relief on his face. Instead he seemed wounded for a moment, but she was convinced she'd only imagined it, since his face then became a complete blank.

"Why not? You said last night you cared for me. Has that changed?" he asked, his thumb tracing circles on her smooth skin. He stood so close to her she could smell his musky scent. It unnerved her, making it hard to concentrate on why she was so angry with him. She stood immobile, trying to resist his spell.

"Has it?" he whispered again.

"No," she whispered back, unable to say anything else.

"Then what would it take to make you say yes?"

She ached to tell him the truth, that she wanted his love, nothing else. She could even face being his mistress if she knew he loved her.

"Something you don't have it in you to give," she said raggedly.

At that, he was quiet so long that she glanced up at his face. What she saw there surprised her. His normally self-assured expression was gone. In its place was a look of complete bewilderment. His eyes fixed on her and a glimmer of what seemed to be hope in them stunned her into silence.

"Say you'll talk to me alone later tonight!" he said with sudden fierceness, his hand nearly crushing her arm. "What I have to say deserves a fair hearing. Promise you'll talk to me!"

Only a woman completely immune to Ian's charm could have resisted such a plea. And Esme knew she was certainly not that woman. Flashes of him carrying her through the jungle, teaching her to fight with a knife, and vowing to shield her from her father passed through her mind in an instant. He was right. He did deserve a chance to explain.

"I will," she murmured. But she added, determined he wouldn't think he would easily convince her, "You're not going to change my mind, though, Ian. Nothing you can say would make me go back to that house."

He dropped her arm then, but his voice was determined as he told her with confidence, "There is one thing I could say."

Yes, she thought. *There is one thing*. But she didn't think he'd say it. That thought hurt her more than anything. She had promised, though, to hear him out, and she'd keep her promise. Then she'd put him out of her mind. Forever.

In the meantime, she wanted to be as far away

from him as possible for the rest of the evening. It wouldn't do to sit beside him and have his body close to hers. She'd be incapable of rational thought later if she did.

So when Harold walked toward them, she rejoiced inwardly.

"You look stunning, Miss Montrose," he said as he came up in to her. "She outshines them all, doesn't she, Lord Winthrop?"

"Yes," he agreed, his voice holding an undeniable note of possessiveness.

"Thank you both," she murmured. Then, not wishing to witness another confrontation between the two men, she changed the subject. "I wonder what this play will be about. I've seen a few Siamese theatrical performances, but never one in a prince's palace."

"They're always amusing," Harold replied, following her lead, although his eyes seemed to challenge Ian. "I believe we're about to enter the prince's private theater. Would you accompany me, Miss Montrose?"

"Esme's company has already been spoken for, I'm afraid," Ian cut in harshly, his hand ready to take her elbow.

Esme shrugged off his hand and took the arm Harold offered. "Lord Winthrop," she said with a gay coyness she didn't feel, "you know quite well I made only one promise to you. It didn't include sitting with you during the play. If you wish me to keep the promise I did make, then you must be fair about these things and allow me to choose my own companions."

Ian's lips tightened, his steely eyes impaling her, but he remained silent as she flashed him a bright smile.

"Later then," he said at last, the words bitten out.

"Yes," she replied, the smile fading from her face as she watched him leave her side to stalk to the other end of the room.

"My word, Esme!" Harold said in a rush after Ian was out of hearing. "I've never seen him so angry. Is he still furious with you over what happened yesterday?"

"No. Though I don't think he likes you much right now."

Harold smiled. "You're probably right about that. But I don't care about him. I want to know if *you* like me."

She scarcely heard him, she was so busy staring after Ian, whose jealousy pleased her in spite of herself. When Harold's words did register, she was unaccountably annoyed.

"Yes, yes, of course I like you," she responded after tearing her eyes away from Ian and forcing herself to bestow a smile upon Harold.

"But not as much as you like him," he said wryly as he began to lead her in the direction everyone else moved in.

"Harold, please don't—"

"Certainly," he clipped out. "We won't talk about Lord Winthrop. But I do wish to know one thing. I noticed you didn't arrive with him. Does that mean your father found you?"

"My father?" she asked, confused.

"You didn't know?"

"No," she said, her voice turning bitter. "I suppose Ian thought it best to keep that bit of information from me."

"He might not know. Lord Winthrop came by the consulate for only a few minutes this morning and then left. Your father arrived later. Langland told your poor father that only Lord Winthrop knew where 'Lek' was. So your father went to Ian's lodgings, but no one was there. Finally, he checked into the hotel late this evening."

"I should go back to the hotel and talk to him after the play is over," she said gloomily as the thought of the impending struggle with her father over her marriage to Michaels beset her. "I can at least tell him I'm staying at Reverend Taylor's so he won't worry about me."

"You mean to say you left Ian's after all?"

"Yes. In fact, I'm only here because the prince commanded me to come. I went to Reverend Taylor's mission this morning."

"I take it Ian didn't know you were leaving," Harold said with just the faintest hint of triumph on his face.

"No, he didn't," she said stiffly.

"Why did you leave? Yesterday you seemed quite taken with him."

She glanced at him, surprised. "You—you mean Godfrey hasn't said anything to you?" she asked, lowering her voice to a whisper as they entered the theater and took seats in the chairs provided in the back of the room for the foreigners.

"What has Godfrey got to do with all this?" Harold asked, his eyes narrowing in suspicion.

"Nothing," she murmured. "Nothing."

"Have Godfrey and Ian done something to you? What's happened?" he persisted, leaning closer to place his hand on hers.

"Please, let's not talk about Ian anymore," she said as she withdrew her hand from his grasp. "Let's just enjoy the play, shall we?"

Harold sighed. "Whatever you wish," he said, but

she could tell her steady refusal to consider him as a suitor rankled.

They both remained silent while the room filled with foreigners. Then the prince's wives and children crawled in, their heads touching the floor in obeisance to the prince as they entered the room. They sat on cushions on the floor. Prince Mataya had an alcove of his own, where he sat serenely at a small table and called comments to his guests. A woman, whom Esme assumed was his favorite wife, was at his side. And close enough that he was almost in the alcove with the prince sat Ian. As Esme watched, the prince bent over to say something to Ian, gesturing in the direction where she and Harold were. Ian stared straight at her, his eyes narrowing as he responded to the prince's remarks. She turned her head quickly back to the stage, but not quick enough to miss seeing the prince give a hearty laugh.

Inwardly, she cringed as she realized that by sitting with Harold instead of her supposed fiancée, she'd made Ian lose face. But it was too late to change her decision, even if she wished to. Nonetheless, when the lights dimmed and the elaborately garbed Siamese dancers moved onto the stage, she felt an immense relief.

In certain ways, the play differed little from other Siamese performances she'd witnessed. Music provided by a small Siamese orchestra accompanied a chorus that sang the story while the dancers acted it. All of the dancers were women. They moved in slow, measured steps, occasionally prompted by a wizened old Siamese woman who sat below the stage with a sheaf of paper. The costumes were what made the play different. They were sumptuous and gorgeous. Silks and golden-threaded cloth abounded as did jeweled silver-and-gold head-dresses. The actresses all wore long, curved gold fingernails.

At first Esme was able to forget herself, enraptured as she was by the poetic, delicate movements of the dancers. But in a short time, Esme began to find she couldn't even escape thoughts of Ian during the performance. The play was a love story about a prince and his concubine. The seductive dances of courtship between the prince and his love made her mind turn to thoughts of Ian with his lips against hers and Ian's hands sweetly fondling her most secret places. Her eyes kept darting to Ian of their own accord. And every time she glanced his way, he seemed to know it and to return the look, his lips curving in a faint smile. She wasn't certain that sitting away from him had helped at all. Just knowing he was in the room made it difficult for her to concentrate. She tried to harden her heart against him and prepare herself to resist any explanations he would give her, but all she could do was replay over and over in her mind their last night together.

Suddenly she felt a hand touch her arm, making her start.

"Excuse me," a voice whispered in Siamese. "You are *Mem* Montrose?"

As she turned her eyes from the stage, she focused on a young manservant squatting down behind her.

"Yes."

"A gentleman is outside who wishes to speak with you. He says he is your father."

Esme sighed in resignation. Somehow her father had heard where she was and had come to fetch her. After telling Harold in whispers that her father was waiting and she must go talk to him, she rose.

Then she hesitated as she wondered if her exit would be taken as an insult by the prince.

"Will I offend His Royal Highness if I leave the room?" she whispered to the servant.

"No, no," he replied. "I have already told him of the man, and he has given his permission."

"Thank you," she said, and then followed him out of the room as unobtrusively as possible.

The servant preceded her down a long corridor until they reached the front anteroom that led to the steps of the palace. The servant bowed and left her, but she didn't see anyone.

"Father?" she called.

Before she could react, someone moved up swiftly behind her and clamped a hand over her mouth.

"Don't say a word unless you wish to die young!" commanded a voice that wasn't her father's. Then she felt something cold and hard pressed against the side of her ribs.

At first she stood motionless in fear, stunned by the feel of the weapon against her side. Then her mind raced as several questions flashed through it at once. Who held a weapon on her? Why? And what was the weapon? It wasn't a knife or she would have felt the tip of the blade. No, she thought, it was probably a pistol.

"Walk!" he hissed in her ear and shoved her ahead of him, releasing her mouth but keeping the gun against her side.

She obeyed, although she stumbled as she tried to walk while being propelled forward by him. Not being able to see the man's face made her terror even greater. But as he continued to push her forward, she realized his voice sounded vaguely familiar. Desperately, she searched her mind, trying to think where she'd heard the voice before. Despite

Deborah Martin

the forceful words, it sounded like an older man's voice. She only knew a few older men—Henry Rushton, Reverend Taylor, and—and William Michaels.

"Oh no," she whispered.

"I said to keep quiet and I meant it," he muttered in her ear as they neared the door.

Her mind began to work frantically. Was it possible Mr. Michaels had arrived with her father? If so, why was he holding a gun on her? Did he plan to punish her for running away?

She tried to walk slowly, hoping someone would see them and stop Michaels, but he pushed her relentlessly on until they were outside. Her heart sank as she noticed the carriage waiting at the bottom of the stairs. But out of the corner of her eye she saw Prasert lounging against the steps as he talked to one of the servants. As if he heard her silent pleas, he glanced at her. He started forward but stopped as Michaels's hand moved for a second, revealing the pistol he held against her.

Then Michaels was thrusting her forward into the carriage and shouting directions to the driver in Siamese. In the seconds it took him to follow behind her, she reached down for her knife, but before she could even lift her skirts to grasp it, his fist crashed down on her head. Mercifully, she descended into blackness.

Chapter Twenty-One

Ian had just noticed Esme was absent from her spot next to Harold when Prasert slipped into the room and crawled to where Ian sat.

"*Than!*" Prasert whispered. "*Mem* Esme has been taken away by a man in a carriage."

Prince Mataya, close enough to hear Prasert, leaned forward with great curiosity. "It is her father. I gave her permission to leave the room to meet him." Then he frowned. "But I didn't permit her to leave the palace."

"Your Royal Highness," Prasert said in Siamese, his head touching the floor. "I don't believe she meant to insult you. I'm not even certain she intended to leave."

As he repeated those words in English, Ian leaned forward in his seat.

"I cannot be sure," Prasert said in English to Ian, "but I think this man had a gun in his hand."

Deborah Martin

"Describe him!" Ian commanded.

"He was bald, not very young, and fleshy, although he seemed very strong from the way he held her."

Slowly, he repeated his words for the sovereign in Siamese while Ian's whole body went rigid as he realized who'd taken Esme. It wasn't her father, that he knew. Her father wasn't bald. But someone knew to use her father to lure her. Only a few people in Chiengmai would have known. And only one person wanted her dead.

"Your Royal Highness—" he began urgently in French.

"You have my permission to depart," Prince Mataya said curtly as he saw the grim expression on Ian's face. "Go find your woman. And may the Lord Buddha bless your endeavors."

"Thank you," Ian replied. Then he stalked from the room and waited impatiently outside as Prasert crawled out.

Prasert sprang to his feet as he cleared the door. "I heard the man tell the driver to take them to the docks by the Meping river," Prasert told Ian, trying to keep up with his long strides.

"How long ago did they leave?" Ian asked.

"Only a few moments ago."

"Still," Ian said with a frown, "they'll reach the docks before us. It might take hours to determine which boat they're on. And there's always the possibility he could be on the river with her before we get there."

"I wanted to stop him," Prasert said earnestly, his young brow creased with worry. "But I feared for her life. He had a gun. She looked at me, *Than*, with such pleading I could scarcely endure it. If we don't find her—"

"You've not failed her," Ian broke in, although

his fear that they'd be too late gripped him. "We'll find her."

Silently, he blamed himself for the fact she'd been taken. He should never have let her leave his side in the first place. He should have told Harold to mind his own business, should have told her of the danger she was in. But he'd thought there would be plenty of time for that, after he'd told her of his love for her and convinced her to marry him. Stupidly, he'd assumed she'd be safe at the palace.

But it did no good to torment himself with such recriminations, he thought. It would only slow him down, and at the moment, speed was most important to him. Because he had to reach her in time, before... He refused to consider what might happen if he didn't.

Esme's mind gradually cleared, although the pounding in her head confused her for several minutes. When at last she opened her eyes, the first thing she noticed was that the room swayed unsteadily beneath her. It took her a few minutes to realize she was on a boat. She lay in a corner, her wrists and ankles bound and a piece of cloth tied securely over her mouth. With a groan, she remembered who'd taken her. But where were they going? What did Michaels plan to do with her?

After a moment of frantic worrying, she forced herself to calm down. Dimly, the sounds of dock activity assailed her ears, and she realized that the boat was still docked. She had that to be grateful for at least. And Prasert had seen her leave, possibly even heard the directions Michaels had shouted. She had nothing to worry about. Prasert would fetch Ian, and she'd be rescued. It was just a matter of time.

All too soon the door opened and Michaels stepped into the room. He cast a cursory glance her way before he sat down on the bare floor a foot away from her and began to remove his boots.

"Now we wait," he said with smug satisfaction as he dropped the second boot on the floor. "Your Lord Winthrop is certain to make his appearance any minute. He shouldn't have trouble finding us. Everyone heard what I told the driver, and I made certain to fix a piece of that lovely dress of yours on one of the nails of this boat. He should be able to see it once the moon is out, and it will be out very soon."

An uneasiness stole over her when she glanced at her dress and found it had indeed been torn. She groaned involuntarily as she realized Michaels *wanted* Ian to follow them.

"Ah, yes, my foolish little girl," Michaels said with delight as he noted her chagrin. "I'm not so stupid as to leave a trail behind me, unless I wanted to be found. Would you like to know why I wish your lover to find us?"

She didn't respond to his taunts, despite her wish to know his plans.

"I'll tell you," he continued, turning his eyes to the door and laying the gun across his lap so he could lift it at a moment's notice. "I want you here when I kill him. And, of course, I need you to ensure he writes the note exonerating me. Otherwise, I won't have time to flee, and I need that, especially if I take you with me."

Her blood froze at the thought of Michael's killing Ian. She had to stop him, but she didn't know what to do. She wasn't certain she could talk him into changing his mind, even if he did remove the gag. With his talk of being exonerated and fleeing, he seemed to have his mind set. But she still had her knife, she realized. And if she moved her hands slowly and he continued to keep his eyes fixed on the door, she might be able to pull up her skirts and remove her weapon without his noticing it. To that end, she shifted into a sitting position, as if trying to get more comfortable.

He glanced at her, but his gaze returned quickly to the door. "I regret you must sit there trussed like a goose," he stated flatly, "but I'll make it up to you later. We're going to have many pleasant years together, I promise, after I get us out of the country. You'll have to remain locked in this cabin, of course, until we reach Bangkok. But once we've booked passage to France, you'll find I can be quite generous with my women. And we'll be miles away before the British government determines I'm really the spy Lord Winthrop claims I am. When he signs that note saying he masterminded the entire thing and forced Chan to name me as his cohort, those idiot British will believe it. By the time they know the truth, it will be too late."

While he talked, she inched her hands toward her feet. She heard every word and what he said made some sense, although she didn't completely understand what he was talking about. He glanced at her again, to see what reaction his words had on her. She ceased her movements but he didn't seem to have noticed what she was doing.

"Well?" he said. "What do you think of my plan?"

She stared at him coldly in answer.

"Here, girl," he said with a sneer as he reached behind her head and worked loose the knot holding the gag. "There's no need for this anymore, now that we're away from anyone who could help you. Except Lord Winthrop, of course. Your cries will only bring him sooner and that's all I wish—to have in my grasp the man who took my betrothed from me."

The gag dropped away, but he didn't remove his hand. Instead he roughly tugged at her hair until the pins that held it gave way and her hair tumbled down around her shoulders. She cringed as he caressed her cheek.

"That's much better," he told her. "We want him ready to do anything when he comes through that door. And when he sees you with your hair down, looking like a little innocent, he'll want to slit his own throat before he lets you die. You see, my dear, that's the bargain I'll make with him. In exchange for letting you live, he must write that note."

"He won't do it," she said contemptuously to hide the desperation she felt. "He doesn't care about me at all. Only last night he left my bed to go drink with one of his buddies."

It pained her to say such things, but she had to make Michaels believe her. Her words got a strange reaction, however.

Michaels stared at her in confusion before his eyes narrowed cruelly. "You think to hoodwink me into believing you don't know about Chan and me. But I'm not so easily fooled. If you were at Lord Winthrop's house last night, then you know your lover spent the night capturing Chan and sending his men after me."

Esme sat motionless, his words wreaking havoc with her emotions. If Michaels was telling the truth, then while she'd been sleeping the night before, Ian had left her, not to gloat over his triumph over her, but to capture Chan. And she'd been so cruel to him! Her hands tensed into small fists as she thought of the way she'd tormented him. She'd never given him a chance to explain. Remorse overwhelmed her. Why had she been so quick to assume the worst?

Michaels continued, oblivious to her distress. "Oh, yes, Lord Winthrop thought to catch us both. He should have realized I've escaped detection all these years because I'm too clever for the British. Chan was an imbecile and got himself caught, but I'm not so stupid. It was a pity for him, though, because I couldn't let him live after that. He should have learned by now that anyone in the Orient can be poisoned."

He fell silent at last, his eyes moving once again to the door. But Esme was filled with horror. Michaels and Chan! Michaels was Chan's contact, the one Ian had been searching for. Now Michaels had killed Chan. And he planned to kill Ian!

A bitter tear escaped one eye, sliding down her cheek as the painful truth hit her. If she'd listened, instead of fleeing from Ian, she might not be in this position waiting for a spy to kill the only man she could ever love.

Well, she wasn't going to let it happen, she decided. She'd find a way to prevent it. Pleading with Michaels would be useless. He knew he was cornered, and desperate men did anything to save themselves. She doubted he'd listen to reason. His plan would never work. She knew the British weren't that stupid. But she didn't think he even cared. His desire to kill Ian seemed to override his intelligence. Her only chance was to get her knife.

Furtively, she began to move her hands downward again. When her fingers reached her feet, she decided she'd better make Michaels talk some more, so she could lift her skirts while he was engrossed with watching the door and speaking to her.

"How did you find me?" she asked, saying the first thing that came to her mind while she grasped the hem of her skirt and petticoat.

"Tonight? I searched Lord Winthrop's lodgings while he was gone today. You weren't there, but I didn't think you would be. After hearing Chan's story, Lord Winthrop was bound to have you hidden. So I followed him, certain he'd lead me to you eventually. And my persistence was rewarded."

"You took a big chance by asking for me as my father. Lord Winthrop might have followed me out," she said as she deftly slid her petticoats up, her hands searching for the hilt of her knife.

"True," he replied. "But if he had, I would have simply waited for another opportunity."

"I see," she said absently.

Her heart pounded as her fingers felt the stiff leather that sheathed her blade. Wildly, she cast about for something else to say.

"How did you determine I was in Chiengmai?" she persisted, her hand closing around the handle of her knife.

He laughed, his eyes still fixed on the door. In that moment, she pulled the knife from its sheath and buried it quickly in her skirts.

"Your father should receive the credit for that," he boasted. "After you left, he was furious, mostly with himself. He collared Rushton's poor secretary again and managed to get the truth out of him. You should have seen your father. When he found out I had started the rumor—"

"You!" she said, her body stiffening in anger.

"Yes, of course. How else could I have gained your hand in marriage? When he found out, he wanted to kill me. He actually threatened to if I didn't discover where you'd gone. That didn't prove too difficult. You didn't cover your tracks very well, girl. The priest whose glasses you stole made quite a fuss about it. And reports at the dock of an orphan wearing those glasses and seeking work as an interpreter with Lord Winthrop's entourage confirmed your destination. Armed with what knowledge he'd gleaned, your father convinced your little Siamese friends to divulge your plans. Then he left for Chiengmai and I followed two days later.''

"Later?" she asked, the knife forgotten for a moment. "But my father just arrived."

Clearly, she'd said something Michaels hadn't expected. He cursed vilely. "He shouldn't be here at all! Imbeciles! I'm surrounded by imbeciles! Couldn't those fools do something so simple as to sabotage a man's boat? He should have been delayed for weeks, not a few days!"

She couldn't stop the expression of relief that rose to her face. At least Michaels hadn't harmed her father.

He grimaced as he saw her expression. "It doesn't matter. He'll not find you in time, and if he does, I'll find some way to take care of him."

Her relief turned to fear. *Please don't let Father fall into his trap, too*, she prayed silently. But his words goaded her on. She gripped the knife more tightly, wondering what to do. She wanted to cut through the ropes that bound her feet, but she was certain he'd detect any such movement. And he was too far away for her to use the blade against him. With her hands bound so tightly, she couldn't even throw the knife. All she could do was wait and hope for fate to give her the chance to defend herself.

But she could keep him distracted, perhaps enough to give Ian the upper hand when he did

427

come. If he came. She tried not to think about that.

Instead she asked Michaels another question. "Why did you wish to marry me so badly you'd tell that horrible story about me?"

That question made him turn his eyes from the door and stare at her with an unnatural gleam. His gaze made her flush uncomfortably as she felt his eyes trail down to where the deep cut of her dress revealed the top of her breasts.

"I wanted you," he whispered feverishly. "I still want you, even though that English aristocrat has defiled your body."

"He hasn't—" she began.

"Silence!" he ordered. "We've talked enough. There will be time for that later—after your lover is dead."

His eyes stared at the door again. He wouldn't allow her to distract him with conversation, so she resorted to the only other distraction he might accept. She began to cry. It was easy to continue once she'd started. She thought of all she'd lost because of Michaels and the tears flowed freely.

"Cease that stupid noise!" Michaels spat out.

"I c—can't," she stammered truthfully as she noticed through bleary eyes that her crying was beginning to irritate Michaels. Was that good or bad? She could only hope his irritation would keep him preoccupied enough for her to aid Ian.

But Michaels was too single-minded for her to be successful. "Shh, shh," he said suddenly. "Someone has stepped on board." His eyes shone with a sinister gleam. "The guard I stationed should have him in a few minutes."

She hushed her crying, her ears straining to hear what he'd heard. Her heart pounded as sounds of a scuffle on deck seeped into the cabin. At first Michaels smiled smugly, but as all became silent and no one came to the door, he cursed viciously under his breath.

"It seems your lover is more adept at fending off attackers than one would expect of a diplomat."

Roughly, he pulled her onto his lap and rested the cold nuzzle of his gun against her temple. She buried her hands in her skirts to hide the knife clenched between her fists.

"Lord Winthrop!" he shouted. "You might as well come in, unless you really don't wish to see Miss Montrose alive again!"

There was nothing but a cautious silence outside the door. Michaels cursed under his breath.

"Call to him," he whispered harshly in her ear.

"No!"

"Call to him or I'll shoot him right now through the door."

She swallowed convulsively, trying to decide what to do. Surely Ian was intelligent enough to stand away from the door. But there was a slim chance he might not.

"Ian!" she said in a voice that was barely a croak. "Ian!" she called more loudly. "Move away from the door! Run!"

"You little bitch!" Michaels hissed, lifting his gun to shoot. But the door crashed open before he could pull the trigger.

Ian's face was a tortured mask of fury as he came through the doorway, his blade drawn and ready. As his eyes took in the scene, he impaled Michaels with a cruel stare.

Esme gazed at Ian fiercely, putting all the love she could into her eyes. "Get away while you can!" she cried. "He won't shoot me. He's already said so! It's you he wants!"

"Shut up!" Michaels bit out, continuing to aim the gun at Ian. "Lord Winthrop knows quite well what I'm capable of. Don't you, my lord?"

"If you so much as scratch her, Michaels, I'll make sure you die a far more painful death than the one you administered to Chan."

Michaels spat on the floor at his side. "Chan! That worm didn't deserve to live. I hope he realized that as he writhed in agony."

Esme's hands tightened on the hilt of her knife. She couldn't use it, not while Michaels held his gun on Ian. She couldn't take the chance he'd have time to fire a shot before she could reach him.

"Drop your weapon!" Michaels yelled, but Ian kept it firmly in his hand.

"What do you hope to accomplish by killing me?" Ian asked coldly, stepping toward the gun with confidence.

"Stay there!" Michaels shouted as he lifted his free hand to Esme's neck, stroking it downward then squeezing her breast painfully. "The girl doesn't lie. I don't intend to kill her. But I have no qualms about torturing her for the hell she's put me through. How I treat her is up to you. If you agree to my proposal and die like a gentleman, I'll see she lives a pleasant life. If you don't, I'll shoot her right here and now—in the leg, the arm, it doesn't matter where."

Esme shuddered, but her eyes begged Ian to ignore Michaels's threats.

"Now drop the knife!" Michaels ordered.

"What do you want?" Ian asked, his mouth a grim line as his knife clattered to the floor.

"I want a note from you stating that you masterminded the entire spying scheme, that Chan worked for you and not for me."

Ian surprised them both by smiling in cold amusement. "You've really miscalculated, Michaels, if you think one note written by me could convince the British government not to hound you to the ends of the earth. Particularly when my dead body is found."

"Ah, but that's the beauty of it," Michaels said with a wicked chuckle. "You'll have killed yourself. I'll put the gun in your own hand."

Another cold smile crossed Ian's face. "I see. More fake suicides. Don't you think that ploy's getting a little stale? The British government knows about the men you and Chan framed. They'll find it odd that yet another spy has taken his own life."

"It won't matter," Michaels said stubbornly, though he unconsciously lowered the gun a bit. "I'll still have the girl. No one's going to come near me as long as I have her."

"And how will you control Esme once you've gotten her away?" Ian persisted, inching even closer. "When she finds out you killed her mother, she won't rest until she sees you dead."

"Shut up!" Michaels screamed, moving the gun against Esme's head. "Don't move any closer or I really will kill her!"

"You killed my mother?" Esme whispered incredulously. "But why?"

"She knew I was a spy. She saw me taking papers from Henry Rushton's desk. Then that day in the market, the day she died, she saw me give them to a man from the French consulate. You saw me, too."

Esme strained to remember her mother's last day. They'd gone to the market, that was true. In a flash of memory she recalled her mother's odd behavior, the way she'd abruptly left the market and hurried them both home.

431

"Oh, my poor mother," she whispered aloud.

Michaels's hands tightened on her. "I desired her as I desire you, but she hated me. She would have told someone about me. Before she died, she claimed she already had. Then after you started asking Rushton questions..."

Esme shivered with fear as she remembered telling the minister resident that she couldn't believe her mother had committed suicide. Had that triggered all of this?

"I knew she couldn't have written that note herself," she whispered. "I knew she'd never loved anyone but Father."

Her words seemed to anger him a great deal and he said cruelly, "Oh, she wrote it all right. But only because I said I'd kill you too if she didn't."

Esme let out a strangled sob. "You didn't have to kill her," she said hoarsely. "You didn't—"

"You don't understand," Michaels growled, his hold on her waist slackening a fraction. "I loved her and she rejected me. Given the chance, she would have betrayed me."

"Michaels!" Ian said sharply, taking advantage of the man's temporary weakness. "You might as well give it up. As soon as I reached this boat, I sent my servant to summon the prince's palace guard. They'll arrive in moments. It's all over now. Give me the gun."

The second she felt Michaels clutch her again and saw him swing his pistol back toward Ian, she knew he'd rather die than be taken.

"I'll not go alone!" he cried.

Without even pausing to think, she brought her knife up into his arm and felt it bury itself in his flesh. He screamed as his arm flew up and his other arm released her, but the pistol was still in his hand.

She heard a shot and saw Ian fall to the floor, but she wasn't certain which had come first. She didn't take any chances. Squirming around, she slashed at Michaels's chest. He dropped the pistol, which went skittering across the floor toward Ian, but the fist of his uninjured arm crashed into her belly and she crumpled, the knife dropping from her fingers.

Doubled over in pain, she saw Michaels's hand reach for her knife. Then she heard another shot and he fell backward, a bullet wound in his heart. She spared him only a glance before turning her head toward the door. Her heart raced in giddy relief as she saw Ian, kneeling on one knee, his hand still holding the smoking pistol.

"It's all over, love," he said, his warm gray eyes softening as he met her frightened gaze. "I think it's finally all over."

Chapter Twenty-Two

Ian and Esme stood alone in the cabin where Michaels's dead body had so recently lain. Only moments after Ian had shot him, the palace guard had arrived. They'd taken Michaels away and Prasert accompanied them as they carried the body to the consulate as Ian requested. The Siamese had asked that Ian submit to an official inquiry into the entire incident, particularly since the Siamese guard Michaels had on board had been wounded. Their willingness to accept Ian's assurances that he'd be at the consulate in the morning relieved both Ian and Esme, for neither felt able to handle such an inquiry right away.

But while Ian had been stating his case through the palace interpreter, Esme had been reliving the whole nightmare. And the more she thought about it, the more she blamed herself for nearly getting

Ian killed. If only she'd waited to hear his explanations. If only. . . .

"I think we should return to the house and get some rest," Ian said, interrupting her self-recriminations.

She gazed at his wounded arm, now bandaged, and felt a quick stab of guilt. "Oh, Ian, I'm so sorry, so very sorry," she said in a strangled voice.

"What have you to feel sorry about, love?" he asked, pulling her close to him. "You didn't shoot me. Michaels did. In fact, you probably saved my life."

She lowered her eyes. "But if I hadn't left you in the first place, you wouldn't have been put in danger. I'll never forgive myself for that."

"Esme," he said softly. "If anyone needs forgiveness, it's I. Aside from the fact that I allowed you to become embroiled with Chan and his plans, I also refused to face the truth about your character, even when it was so obvious everyone else saw it. And when at last I was forced to face it, I foolishly neglected to tell you until it was too late."

"Shh, shh," she whispered as remorse flooded his face. She lifted her hands to stroke his hair.

"And then," he continued, his eyes staring blindly ahead of him, "because I wanted to wait until we were alone to tell you how I felt, I let you out of my sight when I knew Michaels was planning to kidnap you. No," he finished bleakly, "It's not you who needs forgiveness."

Feeling relieved, she realized he'd felt just as much guilt as she had. She thought for a moment, choosing her words carefully. "You're right, of course," she said at last with light sarcasm as she moved her fingers from his hair to caress his cheek.

"I should be furious with you. You've come to my rescue three times now. And it was you, after all, who taught me to use the knife in the first place." Subtly, her tone changed. "But I think I can find it in my heart to forgive you."

Then she leaned up to press her lips to his in the most delicate of kisses. His hands flew to cup her face. He drew back from her, his eyes the fathomless gray blue of a storm-tossed lake as he stared intently into her eyes.

"I don't deserve you, love," he murmured.

She gave him a timid half-smile. "I don't deserve you, either, so we're even."

Then he smiled, the incredible warmth of it flooding her with joy. His arm snaked around to hook her at the waist. Bending her back over his arm, he took her lips hungrily, his mouth tasting the sweet richness and wanting more. She clung to his neck with fierce abandon, determined to make him see how much she needed him.

When they were both weak with longing, he dragged his mouth away from hers with great reluctance. His eyes were a smiling smoky gray as he gazed down at her lips, deeply reddened from his kisses.

"You never gave me the chance to explain what happened the night we made love," he said softly, pulling her against his chest and lifting his hand to stroke her satiny hair.

"I already know," she whispered. "Michaels told me you were capturing Chan."

"And about Godfrey?"

Her face darkened a bit. She'd forgotten Prasert had seen him with Godfrey. "I—I suppose you have a good reason for that, too."

His arm tightened around her waist possessively.

"As I said before, it isn't what you think. I went to find Godfrey, hoping to discover who'd begun the rumor about you. Because of that foolish story, I'd kept you away from me. I had to know who was responsible for putting me through such hell. Anyway, Godfrey reached his own conclusions when he saw how certain I was that the rumor was false. He made that blasted comment about 'the wench' just to irritate me, and certainly not because of anything I revealed during our conversation together."

"Thank you for telling me," she said quietly as she turned to look at him.

"There's more." His eyes took on a somberness that worried her.

"Yes?"

"It wasn't just that rumor that made me wary of you. It was also that I believed you were a different kind of woman—a faithless flirt like the woman I was once engaged to—"

Her eyes widened in genuine surprise.

"Oh, yes," he said with a half-smile. "Not all women consider me a monster. I almost married a woman who resembled you in a few superficial ways. Like you, she was unpredictable and refreshingly daring. But, unlike you, she was unprincipled."

"And unfaithful?" she asked.

"And unfaithful."

"But surely you could tell I differed from her when you came to know me better."

"Yes," he replied harshly. "I could. I knew what you were, but I refused to acknowledge it out of pride and stubbornness and just plain stupidity. And that, my dear, is what I deserve your forgiveness for."

Her eyes swept over his ravaged face with a look

of pure love. "I'll give it to you gladly," she said with a saucy grin, running her finger down the firm tendons of his neck to his muscular chest. "But only if you tell me one thing." Her finger hesitated in its sensuous journey, trembling slightly.

"Anything, love."

Shyly, she refused to meet his probing gaze, her eyes on his shirt. "This evening you said you had something to say that would change my mind about everything. What . . . what was it?"

A mischievous grin crossed his face. "You should know the answer to that by now," he murmured, his lips pressing a kiss to her brow.

"Still, I want to hear you say the words," she whispered anxiously.

His eyes were solemn as he clasped her hand against his chest. "I love you," he said with the fervency of a priest taking a vow. "I love you more than you'll ever know."

A dazzling smile lit her face. "And I love you," she said with midnight eyes glowing. "So very much."

With a fierce growl, he buried his face in her neck, planting kisses on the smooth ivory skin. His hand crept up to caress her breast. She heard the soaring music of desire swell in her ears. They were both so lost in their own world that they didn't feel the boat move as someone stepped on board.

Suddenly the door slammed open.

"Unhand my daughter, you—you unprincipled rogue!" a man's voice shouted, startling them both.

"Father!"Esme cried as James Montrose strode into the room, his face livid.

"You, sir, ought to be horsewhipped and—"

"I want to marry your daughter, Mr. Montrose," Ian responded levelly.

That made James hesitate for a moment and gaze suspiciously at Ian. Then he noticed a pool of blood on the floor and recoiled visibly. "What is going on here?" he demanded, lifting his eyes to Ian and his daughter.

Prudently, Esme pulled away from Ian and hastened to explain about Michaels, Chan, and Ian, judiciously leaving out the fact that she'd spent two nights alone in Ian's house. Although her father looked skeptical, he had to admit most of her story fit with what he'd discovered about Michaels. But when Esme reached the part about her mother's death, his body went limp. Esme rushed to him in alarm and held him close as he wept.

"Oh, child," he finally said in a voice that was strained and weak. "And to think I almost married you to that man!"

"Only Aunt Miriam made you consider doing it," she said staunchly.

Her father's face became grim. "You needn't worry about her anymore. The moment I discovered the truth, I packed your aunt off to London. I couldn't bear the sight of her or to hear any more of her lies. Then I came here."

"It's all right now, Father," she whispered.

"I went to your house, Lord Winthrop, in search of my daughter, but no one would tell me where either of you were," he said accusingly, still somewhat suspicious of Ian's part in the entire drama.

"I told them not to say anything to anyone because I knew Michaels was looking for her," Ian explained.

Her father gave Ian an assessing stare. Then his face softened as he smiled wryly. "I finally found someone at the consulate who knew you were at the palace. But when I got there, you were both gone and they told me the palace guard had left you here. They gave me a garbled story about the kidnapping that I couldn't begin to understand. I rushed here right away." He hugged his daughter tightly. "Thank God you're safe, child." Then he added slowly, "And Lord Winthrop, too, of course."

"Does your concern for my safety mean you'll consent to our marriage?" Ian asked, wanting his answer before James had a chance to learn he'd kept Esme a prisoner in his lodgings.

Esme's father stared at Ian as if trying to decide whether to trust him or not. Then his face relaxed as he glanced at his daughter and saw the pleading in her eyes.

"Only if she wants to," James replied gruffly. "I won't be responsible again for sending her off on a wild escapade."

Ian's eyes turned to Esme. "Will you marry me, love?" he asked her tenderly, his face showing his fear she might refuse him again. In entreaty, he held out his hands to her.

With a mischievous twinkle in her eye, she glanced up at her father and then back to Ian.

"You should know the answer to that by now," she said softly in deliberate imitation of his earlier words.

Ian smiled then, a deep knowing smile. "Still, I'd like to hear you say the words."

She took the few steps needed to reach him. Grasping his hands, she pulled them around her waist and leaned up to kiss him lightly on the forehead.

"Yes, sweet love," she told him. "Yes."

Epilogue

A brilliantly white full moon shone in a clear night sky, illuminating the two solitary forms standing with arms entwined in the doorway of a house that overlooked the Chao Phya River. Esme drank in the scene, happy to be back in Siam after her four years spent traveling the Orient and England with Ian and, later, with their two-year-old son.

"Did you have any trouble getting Richard to sleep?" Ian asked.

"No. You know how he is when we first arrive in a new city. He gets so excited that he falls into bed exhausted when bedtime arrives."

Ian smiled. "At least this time he has a comfortable bed."

She nodded. "It was gracious of His Majesty to give you such a lovely house by the river for the

Deborah Martin

duration of our stay," she said as she laid her head wearily on Ian's shoulder.

"I'm sure he was only being politic. The entire legation has been treated with the utmost courtesy. He's eager to have this treaty signed with Britain and France so that the trouble between the French and the Siamese will come to an end."

"I'm happy they chose you to accompany the legation. Being back in Bangkok with Father again has been wonderful."

Ian smiled wryly. "Your father seems delighted at the thought of becoming a grandfather again."

Esme giggled as she snuggled closer to her husband. "Father's already driving me mad with suggestions for names, and the child's not due for four months."

Ian's hand moved instinctively to her belly, sliding underneath the open folds of the batiste wrapper to caress his wife's smooth roundness.

"How do you feel?" he asked with an aching tenderness in his voice.

"Wonderful." She lifted her lips to touch his cheek. Then she saw something out of the corner of her eye that made her turn her head. "Ian, look!" she exclaimed, her eyes widening with pleasure.

He followed her gaze to the river where it seemed ablaze with a hundred flickering joyous lights.

"Loy Krathong," Ian murmured.

They stared in awed silence as the candle-lit boats bobbed and rocked in the rapid current of the swollen river. Like tiny pilgrims rushing to a holy place, the *krathongs* swept past the couple. Ian and Esme could hear the noises of people up the river, laughing and singing the lilting tune that always accompanied the festival.

"Would you like to hear the legend of Loy Krathong?" she asked in a hushed whisper.

"Nothing would please me more," he replied, the brilliant display making him want to linger a while longer with his wife in the night air.

"Supposedly, the custom began seven hundred years ago," she related softly, "when a beautiful Hindu maiden became the favorite consort of a Siamese king. The king was Buddhist, but the maiden continued to practice her Hindu religion in private. When the time for a particular Hindu festival arrived, she did as she'd been taught and secretly made a *krathong*, a boat containing offerings for the genii of the river, to obtain pardon and absolution for her sins. The king saw it when he and his court were climbing into his barge. He was so delighted by its beauty and fine workmanship that she presented it to him as a gift.

"As a devout Buddhist, he couldn't rightfully light it and place it on the river when it was intended as a tribute to a Hindu spirit. But he so longed to see the affect it made when it was lit, that he hit upon the idea of dedicating it to Buddha before allowing it to be launched. Once it was afloat, the king effusively complimented his consort for her talented creation. This prompted those who watched to make their own *krathongs*, light them, and set them on the river. The king found the custom so delightful he ordered it to be done annually in honor of his beautiful and talented consort. Thus the festival was born."

Ian drew her closer as she finished. "An interesting story, my dear," he said, brushing the silken strands of his wife's hair with his lips. "It just proves that some men will do anything for the women they love." His hand slid up from her belly to fondle one full breast. "I'd be curious to know if the king's consort thanked him for his efforts later in private."

"If I were a king's consort," she replied, raising her face so that the moonlight fell full upon it, "I would certainly think of an appropriate way to show my thanks."

"Oh, would you now?" he whispered, his mouth lowering to within inches of hers. "And what way might that be?"

"Shall I show you, Your Majesty?" she teased. She reached up to grasp his neck and close the space between their lips.

"Please do, my lovely consort," he murmured before taking her lips with his in a drugging kiss. Then he drew her back with him into the room, leaving behind the silent river with its dancing *krathongs* that passed on, until the only light remaining was the light of the enchanted moon.